Edrad _____ s his chest. "We have to _____ he Galactic Environmental Protection Association. You can't let this project run out of control. People will die if you do."

Missa Volk narrowed her green eyes at him. "You'll do what I tell you. I am in charge of this project!"

"Then do something!" Dennison exclaimed. "You've seen for yourself what's happening. Don't pretend you haven't. If you're not going to do something, I will! _I'll blow the whistle!_"

"How dare you?" Morganstern demanded. Volk grabbed her assistant's arm.

"No," she said to Dennison. "You do what you have to do. If you feel that you'd rather jeopardize the grant for fifteen of your fellow scientists, destroy our project, our careers and standing in the research community—our _dreams_—you go right ahead."

"You're damned right I am going ahead," Dennison said, and strode with much dignity out of the hut.

"What are you doing?" Morganstern asked Volk in a harsh whisper. "We can't afford exposure."

"Don't worry," Volk said grimly, her lips pressed together. "Dennison won't be in any shape to send a message. . . ."

"EXCITING AND TOUCHING . . . BELIEVABLE AND GRIPPING. I LOOK FORWARD TO READING MORE ABOUT THE TAYLOR TRAVELING MEDICINE SHOW."

—Christopher Stasheff, author of the _Warlock_ series

DEADLY EXPERIMENT
OUT OF CONTROL

Ace Books by Jody Lynn Nye

TAYLOR'S ARK
MEDICINE SHOW

Books by Anne McCaffrey and Jody Lynn Nye

THE DEATH OF SLEEP
CRISIS ON DOONA
TREATY AT DOONA

MEDICINE SHOW

JODY LYNN NYE

ACE BOOKS, NEW YORK

If you purchased this book without a cover, you should be aware that this book is stolen property. It was reported as "unsold and destroyed" to the publisher, and neither the author nor the publisher has received any payment for this "stripped book."

This book is an Ace original edition,
and has never been previously published.

MEDICINE SHOW

An Ace Book / published by arrangement with
the author

PRINTING HISTORY
Ace edition / August 1994

All rights reserved.
Copyright © 1994 by Jody Lynn Nye.
Cover art by Peter Peebles.
This book may not be reproduced in whole or in part,
by mimeograph or any other means, without permission.
For information address: The Berkley Publishing Group,
200 Madison Avenue, New York, NY 10016.

ISBN: 0-441-00085-1

ACE®
Ace Books are published by The Berkley Publishing Group,
200 Madison Avenue, New York, NY 10016.
ACE and the "A" design are trademarks
belonging to Charter Communications, Inc.

PRINTED IN THE UNITED STATES OF AMERICA

10 9 8 7 6 5 4 3 2 1

To the Friends of the Rain Forest

You know who you are!

PROLOGUE

Field Director Missa Volk stared over her lab table at Edrad Dennison when he burst into her hut, waving a sheaf of documents. The quondam main office of the LabCor field research unit was strewn with datacubes and tapes, amidst imperfectly squared pillars of plastic printout sheets. Moving with remarkable grace for such a big man, Dennison threaded his way hastily through them to thrust a handful of documents at her, narrowly avoiding upsetting one of those pillars. Uneasily, she took the papers.

"Here!" Dennison exclaimed. "You wanted proof. Here it is. Our marvelous experiment to benefit humanity—all warm-blooded creatures—has all gone horribly wrong. I told you so, dammit, and you've paid no attention. But now I have evidence. You must pay attention to that." He smacked the top of the sheaf with a huge hand.

Volk eyed him warily, then glanced over the top sheet of the report. In a very patient voice, she said, "You've made a mistake, Dennison. There's nothing wrong here."

"Nothing wrong?" Dennison asked, disbelievingly, his wiry eyebrows nearly touching in the center of his face. "Look at that." Leaning forward, he flipped the first page out of her fingers and pointed to the second. Volk recoiled from his thrust, then read the paragraphs he indicated. "I've supplied full calculations. I've given you charts, figures, again and again. There are significant discrepancies between our projections and the actual results. It is no mistake. The nanomites have approximately double the effectiveness we estimated, and are running completely out of control. We've got to stop everything to search out and destroy the ones that have gotten away. What happens when they reproduce?"

"Nonsense," Volk said lightly. She handed back the sheets, waving away the suggestion of discrepancy with her long, slim hand. "Everything is perfectly under control, Ed. In fact, I'm pleased with the progress we've been making."

"What?" Dennison stared at her.

"You heard the director," said Morganstern, a man of medium height with a powerful stocky build and deep tan skin that made him look as if he were made of polished teak. He leaned forward over the table. "There's nothing to clean up or fix."

"No," Dennison insisted. "We have to . . ." His booming voice trailed away and he stared. "You're stonewalling me, Missa. This is a dangerous matter. You can't just let this go. We have to get help from somebody, now!"

Volk stood up. Dennison, towering above her, seemed somehow less substantial a being. "Ed," she said, long suffering evident in her voice, "do you want to jeopardize our grant? We'll never reach the next contract stage with LabCor if we start making waves about something that just isn't that important."

Dennison gaped. "Is that all you can think about, money? In that case, I'll have to go to the Inspectors General myself."

"You can't," Morganstern protested, shocked.

"I will." The scientists glared at one another across the table. Volk was the only one who looked calm.

"Ed, Lionel, please. Don't you believe in our project? When we started out, you were one of the most energetic supporters we had. Don't deprive us of your help."

"I don't care what else you say," Dennison said, crossing his arms across his chest. "It isn't going the way we planned. Things have changed. We have to report this situation to the Galactic Environmental Protection Association and LabCor and ask for help. You can't let this project run out of control. People will die if you do."

"People will die if we don't continue with our work," Missa Volk said. "They die every day. You know that. Isn't it part of the problem?"

"Yes, but this time it's going to be us! And what about the

rest of the colony? And the ottle population? We're visitors on their planet."

Missa Volk narrowed her green eyes at him. "You'll do what I tell you, Ed. Everything is fine, under control. You step outside this group with classified information and I'll see to it that you never create a more significant chemical reaction than mixing baking soda with vinegar. I am in charge of this project!"

"Then do something!" Dennison exclaimed. He pounded the table with a fist. Volk stared at his hand. "Dammit, people will die if you let it run unchecked. Here, I've documented all the instances where human subjects have been exposed to over-doses of the nanomites. You've seen for yourself what's happening to them. Don't pretend you haven't."

Volk eyed him coolly. "And just what is it you want me to do?"

"Stop the project," Dennison said flatly. "Withdraw the remaining doses, isolate the ones we know about, and start policing the area for any leaks where the natives might have been exposed."

"Out of the question," Morganstern spoke up. "LabCor will be sending an inspection squad out here within the month. We can't risk any appearance of impropriety."

"Impropriety?" Dennison exploded. "Look, if you're not going to do something, I will. I'll blow the whistle."

"How dare you?" Morganstern demanded. Volk grabbed her assistant's arm.

"No," she said to Dennison. "You do what you have to do. If you feel that you'd rather jeopardize the grant for fifteen of your fellow scientists, destroy our project, our careers and standing in the research community—our *dreams*—you go right ahead."

"You're damned right I am going ahead," Dennison said, and strode with much dignity out of the hut.

"What are you doing?" Morganstern asked Volk in a harsh whisper. "He'll be on the net in two minutes, pulling down a medical inspector. We can't afford exposure. Our contract calls for absolute confidentiality. . . ."

"Don't worry," Volk said. "I saw this coming. Hampton tipped me off days ago that Ed was getting edgy. I have already anticipated his attempts to send a message to the Galactic

Government. The lines are cut off and they'll remain off until I'm good and ready to restore them."

"And after that? We need those comm lines, too. He can wait a day or two before bringing chaos down on our heads."

"After that?" Volk said grimly, her lips pressed together. "Dennison won't be in any shape to send a message." She raised her eyes to meet Morganstern's and nodded significantly. He looked surprised, then after a moment's consideration he nodded back slowly, as if entranced. "See to it," she said.

•1•

"Stand to quarters!" Gershom Taylor barked, leaning forward in the pilot's seat of the scout-trader *Sibyl* and taking firmer hold of the controls in his long hands. "That ship's coming about again. Dammit, who are they?"

Dr. Shona Taylor, his wife and partner, sprang up from the crash chair next to his to make room at the console for Eblich, the co-pilot, then ran aft along the narrow corridor of the *Sibyl* toward her laboratory. A sudden lurching turn made the metal panels screech against one another, and threw her into the bulkhead. Handing her way along carefully, she dragged herself toward the lab module.

The growing feeling of uneasiness she had been nursing since the shipyard two days before had blossomed into certainty. After months of careful maneuvering, redirecting their subspace calls and messages through two or perhaps three dummy numbers, paying their bills through an anonymous credit line for supplies, they had made a single mistake which pinpointed them in space for anybody trying to find Shona Taylor. Evidently, somebody was still looking.

It had been a mistake to stay so long in the shipyard at the edge of the Venturi system, but the necessary refit of the *Sibyl* had taken that much time.

The Taylor Traveling Medicine Show and Trading Company had originally consisted of four people. Gershom, as captain, also acted as the outside man, negotiating trades. Ivo, the shuttle pilot, was Gershom's second in making deals and getting the cargo from warehouse to ship and out again. Eblich, the co-pilot, also acted as bookkeeper, calculating the value

5

against gross profit of the stores maintained on board by Kai. They were a tightly knit functional team. All at once, three years past, two more humans had been added, with a third one present but not yet accounted for, plus all of Shona's animal team and the impedimenta of a working physician who was also an environmental illness specialist.

Shona always felt apologetic for the hardships caused by her signing on permanently aboard the *Sibyl*. The crew, whom she loved like family, had pushed away her apologies, but she knew that having her there all the time had changed their gestalt, taking up room they were accustomed to using. Not that they ever acted like it, but she was an intruder. She brought with her a big lab, which could not be reduced in size, a child, and then an infant, and a vaccine dog, a chemical-sniffing cat, two rabbit food-tasters, several mice, and an ottle. Though the additions were anticipated and welcomed by the extant crew, the inevitable growing pains could not be ignored. Gershom couldn't yet afford to move up to a larger ship. Renting a ship for such a high-risk occupation as trading was out of the question. Expansion had been the answer. A new addition would give Shona space of her own and enable the men to realign their own living quarters and personal space with her as an integral part of the whole. The Venturi yard had been approached in the greatest of secrecy to undertake the refitting.

For a small additional fee, Venturi was persuaded to stretch the rules just a little bit to enlarge the ship without registering her engine numbers in the galactic database, as required, until the job was done and the *Sibyl* was safely on her way to another system.

With the help of Shona's uncle Harry Elliott, a loan officer at a major bank on Mars, the Taylors negotiated a renovation loan which was simply added without fanfare to the balance of their mortgage, paid by monthly debit from their credit account.

The *Sibyl*, always over-engined for her configuration, had had her nose sliced off and the body behind it divided in two to add a third cargo hold between the others for Shona's laboratory module. The space forward of the hold gave the Taylors the additional room they needed for living quarters and more storage, reached by a hatch between the starboard hold and Shona's complex. An atmosphered corridor fitted with airlocks divided the port hold from the lab. With the new generator installed at the head of the addition, both storage bays could circulate full life-support systems when what they were carrying required it. Before, the holds had been a cold, uncomfortable place to sleep, as Shona herself could testify.

Shona saw to it that Gershom was kept busy during the major work on his ship, to keep him from whimpering over its well-being. He loved the *Sibyl* like a friend, a close cousin, another woman. Shona, indulgent rather than jealous, had to find ways to distract him from hanging around the shipyard. Even her natural cheerfulness had been strained by the time the work was finished. Venturi was a main stop for colonists and traders outbound to unexplored quadrants of the galaxy beyond. The people looking for the Taylors could have chanced upon them at any moment. With great care, they had avoided any references to their pasts, use of last names that were familiar or traceable, and paid cash or bartered for supplies. The data leak had to have occurred in the shipyard itself.

And I know just when it happened, too, Shona grumbled to herself. I *knew* it when they entered our number on-line with the alterations for the GG registrar. Everyone was shaking hands and beaming at each other over finishing the job at last. We were so thrilled about the beautiful refit, I didn't think to delay them. For two days it's been irking me what was wrong with what should have been a lovely moment. Someone was watching the communications net, waiting for a clue to where we were. And they got it. And here they are.

Shona could see the moment replayed in her mind over and over again like a looped piece of data. It was her own fault. All she'd had to do was reach out and stop the master of the shipyard from entering that last keystroke, ask him to wait until they'd lifted ship, and darn it, she hadn't.

She was flung against the bulkhead as Gershom negotiated a braking turn, putting on the port aft thrusters and firing the starboard rockets forward. The much bulkier ship responded ever so slightly more slowly than she had before. Even Shona could sense it. She knew the other crew members were hanging on in agony, urging the ship forward with their very wills. Too late, lines of warning lights illumined down the corridor, stepping in series toward emergency stations. Howls, both mechanical and animal, resounded off the metal-and-plastic walls. She handed herself the rest of the way into her lab as a crash shook the ship. They'd taken a hit, but no sirens wailed.

"Thank goodness, not a hull breach," Shona thought, then realized she'd spoken aloud. She swung in the door of the laboratory module. With its hull made of space-grade ceramic and its reinforced metal skeleton, it was the safest place on the ship.

Her foster daughter, Leilani, looked up with huge dark eyes. The girl had been trying to urge Shona's shaggy black dog, Saffie, into her crash cage set against the bulkhead underneath the worktable. The big dog didn't want to go, and was scrabbling at the padding with desperate feet. She whined at her mistress through the thick mesh as Lani latched the door behind her.

"Who is it?" Lani asked, hurrying to catch Shona's Abyssinian cat, Harry, who saw involuntary imprisonment ahead of him and was obstinately staying out of reach. The howls of distress were coming from him.

"Mama!"

Shona grabbed up her two-year-old son, Alexander, who was toddling unsteadily along the perimeter of the room, handing himself along the cabinets in true spacer fashion. With deft fingers, she slipped him into a papoose-style carrier attached to the wall and strapped him in.

"There you go, sweetie," Shona said, pecking him swiftly on the cheek. He reached for her, but she turned away to help gather up the other animals. The rabbits and mice were in their boxes. Only the cat remained free.

"Mama, down!"

"There he goes, Lani." Shona dropped to her knees and crawled toward the corner where Harry had spotted an open cabinet door to hide behind. Together they lunged. Shona snapped the door shut, and Lani tackled Harry. As the cat protested shrilly, they locked him up in the crash cage next to Saffie. There was one more warm body to be accounted for. "Where's Chirwl?"

The ship changed direction again, and mother and daughter slewed across the floor. Shona helped Lani crawl on all fours to the crash seats on the opposite side of the room and buckled the restraints around her.

"Is it *him?*" Lani asked in a whisper, looking around.

"How could it be?" Shona said, without having to ask which "him." "He's in prison." Lani shivered, and Shona put a gentle hand on the girl's arm. A normally cheerful woman of thirty, Shona glanced about her with worried brown eyes. Two smile lines, like single quotation marks at the corners of her generously made mouth, indented sharply in concern. The fact that he was in prison billions of klicks away didn't mean they were out of the reach of Jachin Verdadero, and they both knew it.

Verdadero had once been the chief operating officer of the Galactic Laboratory Corporation, the largest, most diversified company in the galaxy. Up until the time he attempted to use Shona as a dupe to cover his conspiracy to commit mass murder, he had been coldly killing off entire populations of outdated planetary colony settlements for the billions of credits that the contracts were worth. He had considered the personnel to be unnecessary and costly liabilities, and had treated them accordingly.

Lani's natural family, and the whole population of her native planet, Karela, had fallen victim to an engineered virus let loose in its midst by a hireling of Verdadero's. The perpetrator had also died in the plague, leaving no way to trace the connection to the top office at GLC, or so Verdadero had hoped. Only Shona's tireless care saved the child from sharing her people's fate. In the process, she had also inadvertently foiled Verdadero's purpose in slaughtering the colony. Instead of devolving to the Corporation, the wealth of Karela fell to Lani, leaving her an heiress, but orphaned. It took months of negotiation with the Galactic Government, but the Taylors had obtained permanent custody of Lani and were in the process of adopting her. A stable and loving family had done much to erase the trauma the child had suffered, even though Shona had to admit that the *Sibyl*'s crew was hardly what one would call a *traditional* family environment.

The increasing number of fatal coincidences in her wake had alerted Shona to the fact that there was more going on in the targeted colonies than environmental breakdown. Verdadero's final crime was engineered so that Shona would fall victim as well, posthumously taking the blame for the rash of plagues that had seemed to follow her across the galaxy from Corporation colony to colony. She survived to expose Verdadero's plot to the authorities.

For dethroning him just before he was about to accomplish a spectacular feat of embezzlement, Verdadero harbored a deadly grudge against the Taylor family, Shona in particular. Though forbidden outside contact while in prison, he had managed to put out a "dead or alive" contract on her through the great communications net that tied the settled systems and spaceways together. The file containing the contract was periodically wiped from the net by the system operators, but it seemed always to reappear. Investigators couldn't tell how it was reentered, or who was responsible, since the source code was different every time. Assassins greedy for the spectacularly large award turned up now and again to try their luck. Shona had to admit that only purest good fortune had kept her family and the *Sybil*'s crew from falling victim to one of them. She prayed that their luck would hold once more.

The intercom line from the bridge opened. "Are you all right back there?" Gershom asked.

"We're fine," Shona assured him. She tightened her grip on Lani, who huddled down tightly under her arm.

"Daddy! Gemme down!" Alex shouted. Concerned, Shona glanced up at her son. In his cocoon the baby was safer than they were.

"Getting a look at them now," Gershom said. From where she was crouched, Shona craned her neck to see the video link. The scout ship displayed on the screen didn't look that much different from their own. Shona could see the streamlined forms of sophisticated engines, probably capable of executing long jumps without juddering like the poor *Sibyl* did. And also, Shona noted with a wince as a brilliant white tracer beam shot out of her bows, the *Sibyl* wasn't armed with anything more deadly than a sonic probe to burst small asteroids heading for the hull.

"Lasers! Damn them," Ivo's voice rumbled through the intercom. He was at the third command position, monitoring telemetry.

Gershom must have been anticipating such an attack, because the ship slewed sideways beneath them. Lani grabbed Shona's shoulders as her foster mother slipped and landed on her rump.

"Ow!" Shona clutched the restraining straps of the empty chair as she clambered to her knees. "That hurt."

"One must making it stop!"

The cry came from underneath Shona's examination table in the center of the room. She let go of the straps and wriggled forward on her belly. Bracing herself with one arm on the table leg, she fished underneath with the other hand. It emerged grasping a fistful of black-brown ottle fur. The ottle, protesting, came with it.

The humans who discovered their first sentient alien neighbors described the creatures as possessing a muscular, oval, almost disklike body that was flexible to an extreme, quadrupedal with the pair of extremities nearest the small, round-eared head having opposable digits capable of sophisticated manipulation. The tail, though of no great length, was strong, and used by the littoral creature to aid in water propulsion. In fact, it looked rather like an Earth turtle crossed with an otter, hence the term "ottle." In an effort to promote understanding of them among humankind and learn more about their new friends, several ottles had volunteered to leave their homeworld of Poxt and live among humanity. These volunteers were to be returned upon demand to their home planet, but in the meantime would be free to observe humanity and teach their hosts about their species and culture. Shona had submitted an application to have one of the ottle ambassadors come to stay with her. To her delight, she'd been approved. Chirwl had been with her now for over seven years, but had lately decided that he wanted to return to his homeworld. Shona greatly regretted that their long and warm association was shortly coming to an end.

The small alien permitted himself to be hauled by his scruff over to the impact seats. He turned his bright black eyes longingly toward the limp leather pouch that was his sleeping bag, hung high on the wall next to the baby carrier. Shona clutched him tightly to her middle and pulled the shock webbing around them both.

"I am being after not trusting the other machine—urk!" Chirwl squeaked as the belts and webbing tightened. Harry the cat wailed in sympathy.

"Neither are we," Shona said. "It's the laser. I never trust anyone who shoots at me."

"Why does not the *Sibyl* it tell to go away? They are of the same species."

"Stop talking," Shona said, angling her head away from his. "Your whiskers tickle. Anyhow, ships can't talk to each other. They're non-sentient."

"Mama!" Alex called, stretching out his arms to her over the lip of protective padding. "Mama, down!"

"No, sweetie," Shona said in as calm a voice as she could muster. "Not yet. You stay up there for a while where it's safe."

"Down, now!"

"No ID," Ivo's voice said over the intercom. "They disconnected the black box. We should've done that, too."

No black box. Shona fought the chill of fear that rolled down her spine. A spaceship engine could not legally be manufactured without the identifying chip that broadcast its identity to any receiver, and did not function without it, unless the chip was bypassed in an illicit shipyard. In some security-conscious parts of the galaxy, the lack of an answerback signal was grounds for a shoot-to-kill order. This ship wouldn't care that the *Sibyl* knew about the bypass, because it didn't intend that she should get away to tell anyone about it.

Shona glanced at Lani, whose eyes were saucer-wide. She tightened her arms around Chirwl and plumped him on her lap as if he were Alexander.

"Well, they can't get us this easily," she said cheerfully. "I don't believe luck has run out yet for the Taylor Traveling Medicine Show and Trading Company."

"No," Lani agreed nervously. She stared up at the screen. The other ship was wheeling, attempting to get below them. Gershom was following their every move, tilting the *Sibyl*'s axis to fall alongside their attacker. The lights in the lab dimmed slightly, and Shona braced herself. On the screen one of the enemy's hull plates shifted by itself, and the ship veered away from the point of impact. Gershom must be using the sonic probe as a cannon, hoping to dislodge something vital in the other ship's defenses.

"Our business name has a little joke to it. Do you know what a medicine show is?" Shona asked, drawing the girl's attention back to her with a little nudge at the shoulder. Lani shook her head.

"Well," Shona said, using her best storytelling voice, "back in the pre-electronic age on Earth, salesmen who traveled between primitive, isolated towns offered potions with miraculous properties for sale. They promised these potions would wipe out pneumonia, make you taller and sexier, fix your rheumatism, fill dental cavities, and grow back hair!" Lani giggled. Alexander, hearing someone laugh, put in a stentorian burst of merriment. Shona smiled. "Sometimes they'd have entertainers traveling with them, who put on a performance to attract the attention of the folks living around there. There might be other useful goods for sale. Then, once the pretend doctor—they were called quacks—had the audience's attention, he'd start his sales pitch. 'Step right up, folks,'" Shona said, waving one arm in the air. "'Try our am-aaaaz-ing tonic, guaranteed to cure what ails you—and only one credit—I mean, one dollar—a bottle!' In those days, a dollar was a lot of money, but such a fantastic elixir was worth it."

Lani listened seriously, not cracking a smile.

"What happened? Have the formulas been lost since then?"

"No, they were fraudulent," Shona said, her eyes twinkling. Lani's face fell. "The most genuine thing about the potions were the corks in the tops of the bottles. Sometimes the bottles themselves contained nothing more than water. The quacks hoped to be well out of town before the townsfolk caught on to the charade. It was the presentation that was the important thing, the illusion that their particular preparation could cure all ills. Once away from the town, the fake doctors were safe from all retribution by those people who thought they were going to grow hair or get younger by drinking the phony medicine."

Lani's eyes went wide. "But no town told the others?"

"They couldn't. In those days people could only travel from place to place with great difficulty," Shona explained. "Distances between towns were very short by our way of thinking, but people had to go on foot or use horses or ride in oxen-powered carriages. They had no energy tracers, no computers, no mass communication nets they could use to spread the word—only simple linear systems from one specific place to another."

Lani sneaked a glance at the screen. "Wish there weren't any nets now. They *know*."

"Oh, honey, this won't go on forever," Shona said, forcing optimism into her voice.

"These mechanical nets are too efficient, as well you realize," Chirwl said, following Lani's thoughts. "How is it our assassin-payer is not supposed to be communicating and he is, always? To tell him no communication he makes, yet to stop him talking not to those who still may use those services— Urk!" he croaked, as Shona squeezed him.

"Chirwl, you're no help," she said crossly. "I would like to converse on a topic other than our possible demise at the hands or devices of our determined pursuers. Do you mind?"

"Ah!" Chirwl said, with an apologetic twitch of his whiskers. "I am following. Perhaps to speak on the beauties of my homeworld which I to look forward am?"

"That would be nice." The small alien settled himself more comfortably amidst the restraining straps on Shona's lap.

"Of trees and rivers I dream," said the ottle, his soft voice whistling. "One infinitely tall and the other infinitely long. There do I go between always. Those my friends and I to rest on the bank under sunlight and speak long about theories and speculations of why that have been passed down through many generations and never solved. The rain that falls with a tip-tap-tap on the back of my sleeping pouch soothes, and the wind sings songs in the branches." The picture he painted was so vivid and beautiful, Shona was transported away for a moment. She let out a wistful sigh.

"That sounds wonderful."

"I miss weather," Lani said in her small voice. "Even storms."

Suddenly, the ship jumped and juddered, and a vibrating hum ran through the hull plates at their backs.

"Me, too," Shona said, bravely keeping her voice level. "I want to get into the outdoors and breathe non-recirculated air. It's been more than four months since we were on a planet with atmosphere. I'd like to walk a mile in one direction without running into walls. Not on a treadmill!"

"There is plenty of long direction," Chirwl said eagerly. "I shall show you the best way to walk, near my home-place and heart-tree."

"I want to meet your family, Chirwl. Are your parents alive?"

"The generative ones who raised me, yes."

"Generative ones? That doesn't sound . . . loving, if you know what I mean. Don't you have names for them like Mama and Dada or something like that?"

Chirwl chittered in his own language. "The deficiencies language of Standard to blame for that. I am thinking to name otherwise but it does not translate as I would wish. In my tongue one calls *these* names to the raising ones." Here Chirwl cooed and whistled a series of distinct, different, and liquid phrases in his own tongue. "And here are what they are called by loving offspring." He emitted some softer phrases.

Shona attempted to repeat the first series. "I can't say that without whiskers and an overbite," she admitted. "Weren't there three sounds? Do you have *three* parents?"

Her voice was swallowed up in a hurricane of noise from the engines and thrusters. The first hard jerk in the ship's momentum threw her head backward against the padding in the jump seat. Alex's cry of surprise when he too bumped his head added to the cacophony of Saffie's barking and Harry's yowling. Shona, Chirwl, and Lani huddled together in their midst, silent, listening. The video screen recovered from the white afterimage of an explosive blast thrown at them by the other ship, and they heard the orders barked out by the crew on the bridge. Shona gave up all hope of maintaining a cheery conversation, and clutched her loved ones to her. She wondered what orders the attackers had been given. Did they have to bring back the Taylors alive, or just proof of the kills?

The strain of living under constant threat had begun to tell upon Shona. Never knowing whether something as simple as giving her comm number to a new friend might result in another attempt upon their lives constricted her. She was used to being open and friendly with everyone she met, and wanted her son and daughter, and any future children she might have, to grow up the same way. Her deepest fears were not for herself, but for them.

"How are you doing back there?" Gershom's voice asked over the intercom.

"I take this as a personal insult," Shona shouted over the whining of hull plates. "I was just about to download my mail for the first time since we went incommunicado! More than four months' worth!"

At her bravado Gershom let out a bark of laughter that ended in a whoop. The ship lurched to one side, and Shona watched bolts of light shoot past their port hull.

He thought it was funny, but it was true. Shona felt

personally frustrated, since she was normally a voluble correspondent. She'd pleaded with her many friends not to send
news too frequently and only at random intervals, to throw off
anyone who might be monitoring her comm number while they
were stuck in one place. They knew she wouldn't be messaging
back until she was safely back in clear space. There might be
fifty communications from her friends and relatives stacked up
and waiting, out of reach. She'd been planning to wallow in the
news, enjoy a good natter by proxy with people she hadn't
heard from in ages, tell them at glorious leisure what had been
going on with her, what Lani had said, how Alex had grown,
and then this anonymous *brute* of a scout ship had appeared out
of nowhere to delay the pleasure she'd been denying herself for
security's sake. For four months they'd been completely
circumspect. One careless moment, and here they were running
for their lives again. She willed all her strength to Gershom,
hoping that they could outrun the assassins one more time.

The other scout had a canny helmsman. Gershom managed
to stay level with the stranger, but could never maneuver to a
vantage point that would let him go on the offensive. That first
defensive shot with the asteroid sonic probe had alerted the
other ship that the *Sibyl* was not completely helpless, so it
paced him carefully. Still, Gershom had the advantage of
experience. Guiding a scout ship might be less hazardous now,
but Shona could still remember some of the tales he'd told her
while she was still in med school. One was about a pack of rival
traders making orbit all at the same time over newly established
colonies. The *survivor* got the trading contract. Probably the
settlers were afraid to say no to a bully who could drive away
or kill all the competition. Gershom had managed to live
through that time; he could make it through this.

She knew what kind of weapons rough traders tended to
pack aboard their ships: crude mining lasers, sonar probes like
their own, frictionless magnetic charges loaded with explosives
that were as much a danger to the attacker as the one attacked.
Their pursuer's armament was sophisticated, and probably
new. She guessed he must be a professional, like a bounty
hunter.

Her head spun as the ship twisted under her. The hull plates
groaned and shrieked with the strain. On the screen, the
would-be assassin spiraled away. Gershom had pulled the *Sibyl*

into a controlled maneuver that threatened to pull them apart, but it got them down and away from the other ship's guns. They slowed, hang-gliding on a simple vector, waiting. The enemy craft, after a momentary pause for surprise, followed the same looping, graceful whirl, aiming to come level, but it had fallen into Gershom's trap. As soon as the ship's belly turned toward their viewscreens, its plates started shuddering. Even a thousand klicks away, Shona could tell they were in trouble. With a brilliant shot, Gershom had hit them in the sensitive joins between the engine housing and the scout's main body. The *Sibyl* kicked into motion again, turning and twisting to follow the attacker, now turned prey, pummeling it with the crude sonic beam. Laser shots from the other ship went wide, lancing away into space.

Suddenly the enemy ship seemed to remember it should be the dominant player in the confrontation, and thrust over its central axis to face the *Sibyl* directly, training its lasers to burn and destroy. But by the time it did, the Taylors' scout ship was a small, bright dot, shrinking toward singularity.

When the *Sibyl* went into warp Shona and the others were once again pitched hard into the bulkhead. She'd recognized the singing of power growing in the engines just moments before it happened. There hadn't been time to cry out anything more than "Brace yourselves!" and then the air was squeezed out of her lungs. The *Sibyl* vibrated, while the images on the screen whirled into an impossible moire of streaks and colors, then went abruptly black. In faster-than-light warp, exterior visual pickups were useless. Once they passed over the threshold of light speed, the harsh vibrations died away, and the ship's ride was as smooth as if she were not moving at all. In the sudden silence Alex took a few experimental gulps of breath and burst into furious tears. From where she sat, Shona cooed at him.

"Come on, sweetheart, it wasn't that bad, was it?"

"Yaaaaahh!" the baby wailed, nodding his head. Harry, always company whenever he heard misery, burst out in empathetic cries. Lani gazed from one to the other, her eyes worried.

"It's just warping, honey," Shona said smoothly to Alex. "You've been in warp lots of times, right? This time I didn't have a chance to warn you. You're always brave the other times. You want to be a big, brave boy for Mama and Daddy, don't you?"

He gave forth a hiccuping sob, but reined in the quivering lip that thrust up toward a tear-reddened nose. "Uh . . . uh-huh?" he managed uncertainly.

"Good, sweetie. I love you. You're my hero, do you know that?"

"Uh-huh. Mama?" He fastened his brown eyes on her.

"Yes, Alex?"

"Down?"

"Soon. I promise." Alex wasn't happy, but the stormy tears abated.

Gershom's solemn dark-eyed face appeared on the screen. "Are you all right back there? How are the kids? How are you?"

"Happy to be alive, thank you," Shona said. "Good maneuvering."

"Don't thank me yet. We'll be lucky if we don't hit anything when we come out of warp," Gershom said, shaking his head. "Because of our visitor, I had to bounce without finishing the calculations. We may have a surprise at the other end."

"Well, we made it *into* warp," Shona said firmly. "We will be all right. We always are." Gershom smiled at her determined optimism, and Shona wished for his sake that she meant it. "How long will the jump last?"

"About an hour. That should confuse our pursuers, who probably think we're going to take a long leap—that would be logical, to put as much distance between us as possible. After we clear, we have to figure out where we are, so it'll take me a while to coordinate the next jump. Why don't you plan to find the nearest beacon and listen to your messages?"

"That's a *wonderful* idea," Shona said. She smiled, feeling a little of her usual good cheer come trickling back. She unstrapped herself and set Chirwl down on the floor. The ottle shook himself, then described a forward roll with his flat body tucked into a hollow tube. Shona stood up with her hands over her head, stretching until every muscle in her back had unkinked.

The ottle shook himself all over, settling his short, plush fur. "How soon to Poxt?" he asked Gershom.

"I won't know how far off course we went until we come

out," Gershom said apologetically. "I hope you're not going to be jumping up and down with impatience."

"I will not jump, if you ask not," Chirwl replied, turning another somersault. "Though I will wishing to be at home more than soon."

"I'll do what I can," Gershom said. "This shouldn't lengthen our trip more than a few days. Is that all right?"

"All right is yes. I shall be swim," he said, coming out of the somersault on all fours. "Thinking of Poxt makes me wish for water." He trotted toward the bathroom.

"Fine and dandy," Shona said. "I'm just happy to be alive." She stretched again.

"Mama, down!" Alex said, holding out his arms to her.

"One second, sweetie."

Before turning the baby loose, she freed the cat and dog, who hurried to their feeding station. Harry dashed ahead, spun, and held up a paw full of hooks toward Saffie, halting the dog in her tracks, then took a long drink. Shona guessed he was parched from yowling. The black dog waited her turn patiently, then slurped her noisy way to the bottom of the little reservoir. With a tiny whine, she looked up at her mistress.

"Nose it on, Saffie," Shona said, pointing to the low-set lever. "Come on, girl. You know how." The dog still hesitated. Shaking her head, Shona knelt and ruffled the dog's fluffy ears, then kicked on the faucet with the heel of her hand. "I think she just wants me to do it to reassure her," she told Lani. The girl knelt on the dog's other side and put an arm over her shaggy back.

"She was scared."

"So was I." Shona stood up and went to take Alex down from the impact cocoon. She undid the fastenings around the papoose roll. "Here we go, sweetie."

"No," the toddler said, clenching his hands on the straps and fixing his mother with an obstinate gaze. He put out his lower lip. "Don't want down now."

With a sigh, Shona hefted the carrier onto her back. "I don't know where you got that stubborn streak. Come on. You can help me listen to the mail. Here goes the horsey! Ready?" She galloped toward her cabin with the baby on her back shrieking his delight.

"Alone?" Lani said, from the floor.

"No, of course not," Shona replied, turning around at the door. "There might be news for you from Aunt Lal or Susan, since you so seldom send any messages yourself." Lal was Shona's pet name for her aunt Laurel Elliott who had raised her and embraced Lani as a new great-niece. Lani blushed. She was shy about sending messages, but she loved getting them. "Come on," Shona urged cordially. Lani unfolded her long legs and hurried after them.

·2·

The second room of the lab module functioned as Shona's bedroom while she was on a planetside assignment. She left her private comm unit hooked up in there most of the time, partly to keep it out of the way of the ship's day-to-day operations.

Long ago, someone had discovered that if a lab was always set up inside its own unit, it didn't have to be set up again in haste, and it could be isolated and sterilized in cases of quarantine. Laboratory modules belonged either to the Galactic Government or to the Corporation for temporary use on exploration or colony missions, but Shona's was a new one, on permanent loan to her. Manfred Mitchell, the new CEO of the Corporation, had sent her a series of temporary short-term assignments to give medical care to various Corporation dependents. Under the circumstances, she couldn't risk taking another available module from a dock for every assignment. Thanks to Verdadero, she had to worry that a strange lab might be booby-trapped or damaged. Also, having her module permanently assigned was useful in avoiding delays in the case of emergency missions. *Locum tenens* work paid well, too, and had helped the Taylors pay for part of the refit.

The one bed and the communications console took up most of the space in the smaller chamber. Cleverly designed drawers fit underneath the bed. The closet, set into the narrow space between two of the module's bearing beams, was large enough for her uniforms, clean suits, and sweat clothes. In the three years that had passed, there had been neither time nor money to replenish Shona's wardrobe. Now that the *Sibyl* was spaceborne again, perhaps they would find opportunities to trade with weavers and couturiers in various colonies. Lani, who settled with liquid grace on the bed beside her, had the slender legginess of a tri-dee model, and looked good in whatever she put on, be it rags or high fashion. Shona, with her shorter legs and more everyday hips, went for classic style and jewel-like colors. Still, she knew material pleasures had limited value to her. She would rather go naked than be without her friends and children, and felt lucky to be surrounded by them all the time. If Verdadero's assassins ever got a chance to harm them—but no, she would fight and die to defend them from him.

Shona waited impatiently for the *Sibyl* to finish its jump. The promised hour crept by as slowly as the night before a birthday party, and Alex fidgeted on her lap. She played hand games with him, and sang little songs which he occasionally joined in with a tuneless crowing. Lani left her place for a while, returning with a covered bowl filled with colorful beads, and a skein of thick thread. Silently she offered the bowl to Shona.

The beads had come from an arts and crafts outlet in the Venturi shipyard mall. Shona and the others had spent a long time walking around there. Window shopping was one of the few forms of cheap entertainment they had. She and Chirwl had stood sadly outside the confectionery shop, looking in at a display of Crunchynut bars, a candy from Earth that they both loved. They were priced right out of the galaxy, since they had been imported all the way from Terra. Shona sighed, but there was still no money to buy anything but essentials. Not even her nimble brain could work out how luxury candy could be considered a staple.

In the craft store, a man with a torch and a minute pair of clippers was chopping tiny beads from glowing rods of glass. Lani, growing desperate for something to do while the refit slogged interminably on, found the demonstration going on in the little store, and excitedly hurried Shona over. In some of the longest sentences Shona ever heard her say, Lani explained a fortune-telling game played by her people on Karela in which colored beads were strung into a necklace. Though liquid credits were scarce at the time, they scraped up enough to buy a quantity of the beads. Shona didn't dare let Lani pull an electronic transfer of funds from her trust account at Mars-Bank. Luckily, the beads were inexpensive. The material was glass waste from slagged scientific equipment and the portholes of derelict ships. Trace minerals dyed the rods into every color. Charmed by the girl's quiet, wide-eyed admiration, the craftsman indulgently fumed some of the clear beads with platinum and gold coatings out of circuit-board connections for her. She took her newfound purchases, and insisted that each of the *Sibyl*'s crewmen, and some of her new friends in the yardmaster's office, pick handfuls that she strung for them.

"Each color has its own meaning," Lani had explained to the crewmen, placing the chosen beads in a small bowl. She picked them out one by one with her needle. "I don't look how they fall. That's fate." The order in which they were added was supposed to tell a person's fortune for the rest of his or her life. The number of beads was a multiple of the years in one's life span.

In the strain of holding her family together during the refit, Shona hadn't wanted to look farther into her future, even in play, than to know that she would leave the shipyard safely. Now, with their journey begun again, she had no reason to let her worries interfere with a simple game that gave Lani pleasure. At the girl's instruction, she dipped her hand into the bowl, mixing the smooth beads with her fingers, then pulled up a handful. Lani quickly held out a smaller, high-sided bowl into which Shona carefully dribbled her catch. She looked into the big bowl, and then at her choices. Curiously, she hadn't picked out more than a single orange, yellow, or white bead in the whole, random handful, and only six golds.

"Red, black, silver, purple, green, blue. Pretty, huh?" Shona asked Alex, who kept reaching for the covered bowl, placed carefully out of reach. "Oh, no, sunshine. You can't eat these."

"Love, adventures—many, Mama—friends, wisdom, life, peace," Lani said. Shona watched as she brought up a bead on the tip of the needle, not looking as she chose, then knotted each into place on the thread. The girl's fingers were deft with the small bits of glass and even-sized knots. Alex watched spellbound, his eyes huge over the thumb in his mouth.

"You'd make a good surgeon, sweetie," Shona noted. Lani dimpled, and ducked her head over her work.

In light of Lani's extraordinary wealth, it was surprising how much pleasure she took in simple things. Lani kept little in her tiny personal cabin except for gifts she had received from the Taylors and from Shona's family on Mars, books, and her doll,

the single relic she retained from her life on Karela. The crew
had agreed to let her have the minute cubicle—a more than
generous gift considering how much precious cargo could be
stored in an eight-foot cube, but everyone thought it was a
worthy sacrifice for the girl they had adopted as an honorary
daughter. Eblich, a kindly man with five children of his own,
planetside, was the particular person to whom Lani turned for
paternal comfort and advice. Neither of them spoke much or
often. Shona supposed that was part of the bond. Perhaps
Lani's own father had been a laconic man. In a nod to the
mission of the trading ship, Lani was made to understand that
she'd have to bunk in with Shona or the animals if they took
aboard a load that was sensitive to temperature or needed more
than the available cargo space if the price was right. Knowing
Kai's skill at shoe-horning an elephant into a cookie jar, Shona
thought it was unlikely the girl would ever lose her room. Still,
the theory was important for the girl to learn. Living in space
had its rules, and chief among them was that you didn't crimp
your own air hose. If something paid the bills, it got priority.

Paying the bills had continued to haunt Shona's sleep.
Because of the expensive refit and the long time away from the
trading lane, the Taylors were in actual danger of running out
of money before they could recoup the cost of the construction.
Sometimes she lay awake, seeing huge numbers play before
her eyes like afterimages: mortgage, upkeep, taxes, fuel, the
cost of carrying loads of cargo that hadn't been paid for, losses,
and constant repairs because of attacks. Shortly before the refit
they'd lost a premium load of fresh candy because a would-be
assassin's mining laser had breached their container hull.
They'd had to go back and replace the candy at their own
expense. Cargo insurance paid off late, if at all. Acts of God or
Nature might have been covered, but armed insurrection was
not. Shona watched Lani knot one more gold bead onto the
long string, and shook her head.

Lani had been awarded most of the assets that had devolved
to her after the destruction of her colony, making her a very
wealthy young woman. Brought up in a virtual barter economy,
she had no idea of the power her money commanded, except
that her adoptive parents never seemed to have quite enough of
it. Nor did she understand the delicacy of the situation into
which her wealth put the Taylors. She kept trying to give them

money, but Shona had been firm about refusing it, insisting that the money belonged only to her, and it wasn't as important to them as Lani was. It was difficult for a generous child, scarcely into her teens, to understand the complexities of legal battles, and how rumors could so easily ruin a reputation.

The finished span showed the red of love and the green of life plentifully interspersed with blacks, silvers, and purples, ending with red for love and blue for peace. Lani tied off the circle and offered it to her mother.

"The story of my life," Shona said, slipping it over her head, "*literally* from beginning to end. Looks like I'll die in bed. Now, if you could only assure me I'd die solvent. Which color is for money?"

Alex seized the hanging end and yanked it closer to his face to investigate, pulling Shona's head down with it.

A hollow groaning rose through the bulkheads around them. At last they felt the disorienting drag of the ship slowing down into clear space. In the next room Chirwl finished his swim. Shona could hear him splash out of the tub, shaking the water out of his fur so that it struck the walls in a noisy shower. The adjoining door slid open, and the ottle lolloped across the floor to clamber up beside the crowd on the bed. The cat rubbed against him cozily, then turned his head to pretend they didn't know one another. Saffie slurped her big pink tongue over the ottle's head. Shona smiled. One big happy family. Any bigger, and the small bed wouldn't hold them. From the intercom in the next room, they could hear the crew's voices as Gershom gave orders, and echoed the engine noise inside the walls.

"All clear," Shona heard Gershom say. At once, she kicked on the comm unit and booted up. The software program searched out the nearest line-of-sight beacon to the *Sibyl*'s location. They must have come out of warp almost on top of one, for there was an instantaneous response.

"Hurray!" she cheered. "Civilization at last."

The small screen filled with the Galactic logo, then swirled into blackness, waiting for her to enter an access code. Shona hit the Answerback button on the top left of the keyboard. A new logo spun forward.

"One Moment Please."

Alex bounced up and down happily.

"Look, Mama!"

"Yup, I see it." With her baby cuddled on her lap, and Lani's head on her shoulder, Shona felt absolute contentment as she watched her new number scroll up the screen. For security's sake the code had been changed again, so she had written it into her communication program instead of memorizing it.

"This may take a while," she said, stroking the girl's silky black hair. Lani had grown so much. In no time she would be taller than Shona, who wasn't very tall. Funny how it had worked out that though she was their foster child, Lani looked enough like Gershom with her dark, solemn eyes and small, folded mouth that people automatically thought she'd been born into the family. Alexander had Shona's fairer coloring, with light brown eyes and hair, and a plump, pink mouth. If the poor child ever encountered real sunlight under atmosphere, he'd probably freckle like she did. He was a cheerful, loving baby who seemed to have inherited his mother's native optimism.

Chirwl, on the other side of the bed, perused the menu that appeared next on the screen. The comm unit was the only piece of mechanical or electronic equipment, besides the food preparation devices, that he really liked. Ottles were anti-machinery, or rather non-machinery-oriented. Their culture was based on barter and philosophy, and there was nothing they needed that they couldn't make. As one of the students sent out from his world to study humanity, Chirwl acknowledged machinery as part of the curiosities of the new race but regarded all those unnatural things with deep suspicion.

"What to do first?" he wondered. "Shall one hear the news from other places or see mail?"

"Oh, Chirwl, how can you ask?" Shona chided him playfully, reaching for the icon for personal mail. "It's been months!"

She suffered through a long, long pause while the net found the data posted to the new number. Shona's copious correspondence had been the source of much pain for the Galactic Bureau of Investigation agents trying to shield her. Anyone could trace her location from the beacons to which certain numbers were delivered. In the end, the GBI set up several accommodation accounts that collected her mail, splitting her trail into five to seven branches. These branches sent her messages on to other branches that eventually dumped them into the main number she used now. Shona was never certain that some of her messages weren't lost along the way.

The diversity of letters on the list, a veritable feast after social starvation, delighted her into a wordless exclamation. Her best friend, Susan MacRoy, had sent every week. Aunt Laurel and Uncle Harry Elliott popped up once in a while on the list. Shona was pleased to see her forgetful scientist friends on Erebus had managed to hold onto the comm program she'd set up for them. Even though it was a weak link in the security chain, she'd requested that the GBI not change their access number to her during their periodic sweeps. Though each had multiple academic degrees, none of her dear friends on Erebus was capable of probing the niceties of a simple Execute file. Create artificial life, perhaps; program a video unit, no. Shona held her hands over the keyboard, enjoying herself for one moment more.

"What are you doing?" Lani asked. "Why not play them?"

"I'm just anticipating, honey," Shona said with a grin. "—That's long enough." Her fingers dove toward the keys.

Susan's face appeared on the screen. "Hi, twin! You couldn't have picked a worse time to go incommunicado. I would give *anything* to be able to talk with you right now. The tri-video is in the middle of production, and everybody's driving me crazy asking for details of events that happened when I wasn't there!" Susan rolled her large blue eyes skyward. "Wish you could be here to help me record your life story. We've got the most gorgeous guy to play Gershom. I thought they were going to computer-enhance his image to make him look more like the real thing, then the Legal Department said that would be bad—make him a target for casual busybodies, you know. I mean, your pictures are in the news-files. Anyone can look them up if they want, but who says that the whole galaxy needs to know?"

"That's for certain," Shona agreed. On the screen, Susan's image nodded violently as if she could hear her friend's comment. Her long lashes dipped wickedly, inadequately disguising a twinkle. Shona recognized it was a sign Susan was about to drop a bombshell. She waited.

"Anyhow, the big headline for the day is that Dree Solana is playing you! She merely signed today, twin, so this is fresh-out-of-the-mold *news.*"

Shona gasped with delight. Dree enjoyed a reputation as a serious character actress who won drama award after drama award and could pick her parts as she chose. Anything starring Dree had automatic viewership in the billions. Susan's career had "arrived" as the entertainment folk would say, if her first mass production could attract a lead player of that magnitude.

"I am so thrilled, every time I think about it I hyperventilate!" Susan continued. "I love working on a project with actual funding. It means I don't have to subsist on nutri, which I hate, but not as much as you do, I know."

"Oh, that's for certain," Shona said. She had a long-standing, if cordial, dislike of the food substitute. The bland substance satisfied all nutritional requirements except for taste and texture.

"Nooo-treee," Alex echoed, making a face. Shona looked apologetic.

"Well, it is convenient for making baby food," she said. "No doubt about that. Sorry, honey."

"Then there's the cutest little muffin playing Lani. Doesn't really look much like her, but she's a good actress. If you're still hide-and-seeking when it airs, I'll upload the video to you. *Everyone's* going to be glued to their screens. I think you're going to be famous. I think we're all going to be famous. I wish I could see your face. More to come. Watch this space! I bet Alex is getting big. Send me pictures! Over and out, kiddo."

Eagerly Shona reached for the control to record a reply, then checked herself. "What am I doing?" she asked the others with a shake of her head. Saffie raised her head and cocked intelligent eyebrows at her mistress's self-deprecating tone. "This message is almost five months old. I'd better see everything else first." And yet she itched to start recording. She missed Susan, who had shared part of their adventures in exile before she went back to try and interest an independent tri-video producer in the story.

Shona read the next line item in the list, a title and address on Mars, then hastily skipped the cursor over it. "I'll listen to that later," she told Lani. "More official notices! Boring. Oh, look at this!"

The next message was from her uncle Harry. He stared straight ahead of him into the video pickup, his plump, freckled face looking uncomfortable above the tight collar of his business tunic. Suddenly aware of the Record light before him, he cleared his throat.

"Honey, this is a quick note. I secured the addition to your loan. It's okay. Uh, send soon. Your aunt says, give you her love. So do the kids."

Shona whistled as she punched the Delete command. "This sure is an old message. I heard from the bank while we were at the shipyard, and we've been paying through our assorted noses ever since. What's next?"

Her many correspondents had sent various parcels of news, mostly asking when she would be back on beam. Shona happily recorded quick notes to them all, letting them know that the *Sibyl* was flying again. Chirwl put in a few words to the scientists on Erebus, whom he considered fellow philosophers.

The bulk of the transmissions were more updates from Susan. Occasionally they were sent from the cabin in her ancient runabout, but more often from a public box in the middle of a busy space station, with men in uniform, family groups, and coveralled workers burdened with video equipment crossing in the background. The production was going well. Progress was made from one message to another regarding Susan's attempts to charm, then persuade, then bully the producers into telling the Taylors' story the way that she wanted. Shona approved of the way Susan seemed to grow in confidence from one note to the next. Before, pure charm and talent had been her chief means of negotiation; she had since added savvy.

"They cottoned on to the facts about Lani but couldn't understand the human angle of the whole thing," Susan lamented. "And all they could think of was the money—which I suppose in their cases would have been the primary reason to adopt her—but they had no business suggesting that was why *you* did." Shona made a face, but didn't comment. "I'm making friends with the video editor, in hopes that she'll let me soften the part up, change the dialogue in the audio comp before it goes back to the director. She understood the difference, and I think she's sympathetic. We both figure it'll be easier to get forgiveness than permission for altering the script." Susan sighed. "Here I am going on as if having my dream job is nothing but a nightmare. It's not true, twin. I'm having a great time. I just hope I think the efforts are worth it in the end. And

I hope you like the show. I can't believe it airs in two weeks. Over and out."

"Exciting," Lani said, her face aglow.

"You said a mouthful, sweetie," Shona agreed.

"Can one word fill a mouth?" Chirwl asked.

At last, the message following in the scroll contained the promised video. Shona let the titles run long enough to see Susan's name in the credits as the producer, then shut it off. "There it is," she told Alex, her eyes shining. "Your Auntie Susan. We'll screen this later when we can all watch it. All right?"

She recorded a message of congratulations to Susan. "I am so proud of you, twin," she said. "While I'm not sure I want to relive that part of my life, I'm looking forward to seeing it because *you* did it. I hope this is the first of a thousand successful projects. Much love, and out!"

In a hopeful mood, Shona pulled up the next message, which was from her uncle Harry's bank on Mars. Instead of the plump, mustachioed face of her late father's brother, she was confronted by a narrow-eyed man with black, gimlet eyes. He held up a datacube.

"Doctor Taylor, I am Chang-an Zeles, the chief loan officer of MarsBank One. I have here before me your file, and specifically the record of your last payment. The release of funds was significantly after the due date. I have been made to understand by your uncle, a man for whom I have the greatest esteem, the personal difficulties under which you are working, but those do not free you from the basic responsibilities of meeting your obligations on time, especially since they are such substantial obligations. I have no choice but to assess late fees and interest." He touched a button on the console in front of him. A flat graphic replaced his uncomfortably sharp features.

Numbers dropped one by one into a stark white column in the center of the screen. As the figures appeared, Zeles explained them in an emotionless voice. At the conclusion, the total bobbed up from the bottom of the frame, knocking the other numbers upward in a surprised flutter as if they hadn't expected the kick in the backside. Shona winced at the amount even as she bristled at the implication that she was using her uncle's position to avoid paying her debts on time. Then she looked at the date.

"Wait a minute!" she exclaimed. Freezing the message in place, she brought up her account record. "I got an ack notice back from the central database when I released the money— yes, here it is. I did pay on time."

"You have paid but he thinks you have not?" Chirwl asked. "Who is right?"

"I am," Shona said, with grim satisfaction. "And he recorded this in advance of the overdue date. Look at the time code."

Chirwl curled into a ball and put his paws over his eyes. "The numbers do a dance I do not like. I think I see the very soul of the machine, and it is cold."

Lani leaned closer. "He was early," she said.

"Uh-huh," Shona said. "I bet he had a lot of debtors to dun, and this went out with the queue without anyone checking. Yes, there we go," she said, pointing to the remaining communiqués in her file.

After a short note from her aunt Laurel, she had another message from the same loan officer, looking rather more harried.

"Had to record one out of turn, did you?" Shona said to the screen, with satisfaction.

"Zeles here," the dour man said peevishly. "I wish to acknowledge the receipt of the payment on your ship mortgage."

"Good," Shona said.

"We are rescinding the interest, and leaving only the late charge. It will be added to the principal. Please make note of that when remitting your next payment."

"What?" Shona exploded. "But we weren't late! We don't *owe* anything."

She recorded a terse message saying that since the credits had been in place before the galactic due date, ". . . I would appreciate it if you would rescind the late charge, too, since as you can see by the acknowledgment enclosed that the payment was not late. Thank you. *Aarrgh*!" she growled as she shut off the Record function. "Sometimes the personal touch is more repellent than just getting a quick notice from a computer."

"Will you be to send it now?" Chirwl asked.

"No," Shona said. "I've got a lot of gossip for Susan, I have to send to my aunt and everyone to let them know we're up again, and Lani might have a few words to say?" The girl reddened and shook her head. "No? Surely later, sweetheart— One connect is all I dare risk, and I want to save that until we're ready to warp again. We could be pinpointed if there's a lot of unexpected activity from a remote beacon like this one." Shona sighed. "I'll be a lot happier when we don't have to run anymore. I thought when they put you-know-who away that it would be the end of our troubles." Lani silently looked at her hands folded in her lap. Shona reached over and squeezed the girl's fingers. "Well, it wouldn't do if things got boring, would it?" she asked. "One day he'll run out of money, or influence, or he'll just get tired of chasing us. You'll see."

"I hope so, Mama," Lani said solemnly.

"I promise— Oh, no, not again!"

Following in the queue were three similar sets of messages from Zeles. Each time, to Shona's extreme irritation, he assessed interest charges and late fees, then rescinded the interest, but not the penalty for being late, until the fourth payment due had accumulated a rider of several hundred credits in penalties.

Columns of figures swirled onto the screen and arrayed themselves in neat rows. Shona followed each calculation with a sinking heart. The very rise in the amount of debt dismayed her.

"If you persist in maintaining such a poor record of payment," Zeles warned, "the bank may have no choice but to call in the loan."

Shona felt the blood drain out of her face. Standing up, she handed Alex to Lani, and went looking for Gershom.

"Do you have a few minutes?" she asked him.

Gershom viewed the dunning notices without comment. Shona watched the muscle at the corner of his jaw twitch at the veiled insults directed at them by the loan officer. The muscle sagged entirely when Zeles mentioned foreclosure. Gershom glanced at his wife, who gave him a helpless shrug.

"It'll take us forever to get that straightened out," she said. "It's been months since this started to happen, and we've sent them no explanation because of where we've been. They'll keep on adding penalty fees until we're paying as much on them as on the principal."

He gave her a wry smile and shook his head.

"We'll have to pay for now," he said quietly. "Send to your uncle to get the records straight after the fact. We can't afford to have the bank pull the mortgage over a mistake, so we have to eat humble pie for a while."

Her hands shaking, Shona tapped on the command for a release of credits. She went back to wipe out her tart rejoinder to the bank's first transmission, and recorded in its place a new message pleading for someone to straighten out their accounts and read their "deposited-by" dates, since her records showed that she was on time. Thinking of their swiftly sinking bank balance made her heart follow suit. The refit had been very, very expensive, eating up all of the bonus given to her by Manfred Mitchell of the GLC, plus what she'd earned in her missions before and after Verdadero's crime came to light. They needed to find a way to raise capital, or there was a real danger the bank would end up owning a newly, beautifully refitted trader scout-ship.

"That cuts us very close to our panic balance," Shona said. "Next to nothing at all."

"I will give you some money," Lani said at once. "Pay off the ship."

Shona hugged her distractedly.

"No. That wouldn't be right. Thank you, honey, but we'll make it."

The girl looked bewildered. "Why can't I give money to you? Why won't you accept? I saw the bank balance."

"We're not hiding it. But your money's yours, not ours, sweetie. You'll want it when you grow up."

"Not all of it," Lani protested. "There's so much. I couldn't spend it all in my life."

"We won't take anything from you, and that's the end," Gershom said, perhaps a little more sharply than he intended. Shona, her nerves taut from the almost-fatal encounter with the killer scout, and then this financial onslaught which threatened them almost more than physical peril, jumped to her feet.

"Just a moment," she said. "There's no need to snap at Lani! I know how much you value our independence. That means we have to find a means of earning our way out of debt. It's that simple."

"Oh, it's simple, is it?" Gershom demanded. "Suppose you tell me——"

"Just a moment," Shona said again. She turned to Lani, who was pale with fear. "Honey, will you excuse us?" The girl fled to the laboratory, taking Alex and Chirwl with her. The animals, sensing tension, vacated the room at once. Shona closed the door, then returned to her perch on the edge of the bed. Gershom leaned over her and repeated his last question in a taut, furious voice, pitched so it wasn't audible in the lab.

"Suppose you tell me how I can keep in touch with suppliers when the GBI keeps changing my communication code? If they can't find me, they'll use another carrier. They don't care about our problems. They only care if their goods get out intact and on time. And as for buyers, there's a thousand ships just like ours in the spaceways. Most of them don't have families to support."

Shona felt the blood leave her cheeks. That was an unexpectedly low blow. Gershom realized it as soon as the words were out of his mouth. She'd lost her first baby under tragic circumstances, and he hadn't been able to be with her at the time to help her through it. They'd been hoping to raise a larger family with some measure of security while they were both young enough to have the energy to do so.

"I'm sorry, sweetheart," he said, sitting down beside her and putting an arm over her shoulders. She didn't feel much like being touched, but she let him lean against her. A moment later, she'd regained her equilibrium and hugged his ribs hard. He relaxed with a sigh, and moved his hand up to cup her cheek in his hand. Shona, her fingers in a tense knot, managed a tiny, hopeful smile.

"Maybe it's just too soon to think about another baby," she said, with difficulty, picking her words with care. She'd started this discussion when she should have known he was vulnerable. She had wanted to share her frustrations and tensions, and by the Blue Star, she'd succeeded. "Too impractical to start another. Alex is just toddling. It would be difficult for me to handle two in diapers at once as well as a career and managing our finances."

"You don't have to be *that* brave about it," Gershom chided her gently, blowing a teasing breath down into her bangs. She turned her face up to his, thinking again that she had married the handsomest man she had ever met, with his long dark hair, long dark lashes, and beautiful, strong cheekbones. "We ought to have another before our space moose gets too attached to being the youngest child."

"It'll work out," Shona said firmly. "We managed to get through refit. We got away from that contract killer. We can manage without taking money from Lani."

"We'll have to," Gershom said meaningfully. "I don't want to risk having the authorities remove her at the last minute on a technicality."

"I'll ask Mr. Mitchell for a loan. Perhaps the Corporation could advance me some money."

"They owe you a great deal for saving their necks," Gershom agreed. "And for hurrying to do their assignments no matter where for three years, without complaint. A small loan shouldn't be out of line." He threw a glance at the closed door. "Was there anything in the messages from the Child Welfare Bureau?"

Shona scrolled upward through the menu of her messages. "Yes. I wouldn't let Lani see it, but since you're here we'd better know the worst."

The female caseworker's face was familiar. Shona and Gershom had dealt with her almost exclusively for the past three years. She was remarkable chiefly in that she never showed any signs of emotion whatsoever. "Captain and Dr. Taylor, I must inform you that the final hearing on your adoption of the child Leilani has been postponed once again . . ."

"What?" Gershom exploded. "Why?"

". . . friend-of-the-court brief filed by Mr. Brogau Din van Keyn. On behalf of the Anti-Exploitation Watch. Mr. Din van Keyn points out that it might be harmful to the child's psyche to be adopted by a couple with no permanent home . . ."

It was Shona's turn to protest. "In this century? There are millions of people living on spaceships. There are people who've never been in planetary atmosphere!"

"Shh," Gershom said, rewinding the frames. "I thought I heard a buzzword. Yes."

". . . whose financial obligations are too great to properly support a child, and may thereby subject her to unnecessary emotional strains."

"There it is," Gershom said. "They still think we intend to use her as a cash cow. Until they can prove otherwise, they'll delay the final paperwork."

"Damn them," Shona said. "The GBI promised they'd expedite the adoption three years ago. See here, we can prove we haven't taken a millicredit from her. We love *her,* not her money."

"Yes, but to other people it's an obvious attraction. Probably the way they'd treat her in our place. I admit it's a great temptation, *especially* when she keeps pitching her fortune into our laps, *especially* now when we could use a friendly loan. But we don't dare. I didn't like the rumors I heard after that last hearing."

Shona nodded, rubbing her temples with her fingers. They had carefully kept any details of the case from Lani, except to let her know that it was still under consideration, but their lawyer had suggested that it would be wise to make certain their actions reflected their intention to give the girl a good and stable home, regardless of her financial expectations. In light of the extraordinary amount of money Lani was heir to, some members of the panel viewed the Taylors with perhaps under-standable skepticism. They were cautioned that any irregulari-ties could result in having Lani immediately taken away from them. Lani was terrified at the prospect of losing her foster parents. Shona and Gershom vowed that they would not let that happen, no matter what it cost them. Shona regretted that in this case it might easily cost Gershom his precious ship. She bit her lip.

"Was there nothing but bad news in your mail?" Gershom asked lightly. "What does Susan say?"

"Oh!" Shona said, sitting upright under his arm. "There's one more message from her. Stay and see it." She read the Galactic time signature. "It's only two weeks old. I'm nearly up to date." She let it play.

The data transmission didn't open with Susan's face. Instead, it began with a clip from the *Galactic News.* Shona stopped it and ran it back to make sure the codes were correct. They were. She let the disk run.

A reviewer from the *Galactic News* appeared on-screen.

"Five stars for neophyte producer Susan MacRoy," the blue-haired woman gushed. "The story of the brave young woman who single-handedly defeated an ice-hearted murderer whose greed threatened to envelop the galaxy is a wow. This docudrama is based on news events of a few years ago involving the GLC that made the inhabitants of boardrooms tremble across the civilized universe. If bad guy Veringer is anything like the original he portrays, then the real number is a skunk who deserves to stay in deep-freeze for the rest of forever. Hot script, hot direction, and fabulous casting. Look for this one to pick up awards galore at the Stellars!"

Susan's face replaced that of the reviewer. "What do you think? Can you believe the great review? There are lots more! The disclaimer at the beginning of the video says 'Some of the facts in the following dramatization have been altered to protect the innocent,' and people have been all over me to know what's real and what isn't." She giggled. "I don't intend to tell. It's fun knowing something no one else does. We got great ratings, and I'm getting job offers from all over. I owe you and Gershom one fabulous dinner the next time I see you. Hope it's soon. Love."

Following the message were more of Susan's reviews, each as enthusiastic about the video as they were damning of the villain, a facet of the show that not one reviewer failed to mention.

"Evil personified!" one male dressed in silver lamé declared. "Absolutely wretched evil."

Shona and Gershom looked at each other.

"What did she put in that video?" Shona asked.

"We'd better see it," Gershom said. "Let the others back in, and we'll all watch it. I know that Ivo wanted to."

The picture ended with Dree Solana in her torn shipsuit, standing in the midst of her loved ones and embracing the dark-haired child, while the white-haired villain was haled off to justice. Triumphant music rose over the audio, blaring trumpets in their ears. The final credits flickered on the screen, all fading to a simple blue-black emblazoned with the logo of the video distributors. The *Sibyl*'s crew sat back and let out a collective breath. Lani scrubbed tears off her cheeks with her cuff, and glanced up at the adults. Shona shook her head solemnly.

"He's not going to like that," she said.

"Maybe he will not see it," Chirwl said.

Shona shook her head. "He'll see it."

The scene on the screentank held still on a single frame, that of a man with thick white hair, his mouth frozen in a scream as two other men in conservative dress dragged him from an opulently appointed office suite. Looking on at the white-haired man's humiliation were a tall man with long black hair; a skinny, elderly male with rheumy eyes; a burly stevedore, his light brown hair clipped almost to his skull; and a short light-skinned woman with a lush, bow-shaped mouth. Jachin Verdadero stared and stared at the screen, feeling the blood mounting up behind his eyes until the picture was blotted out in a haze of rage. The three-demensional quality of the holotank made it seem as if all he had to do was reach out to touch the characters. He wished he could. He would joyfully strangle the young woman who had put him here. He snatched up a handy datacube to smash through the plexiglass front, and then remembered what the prison guard had told him. The next time he destroyed anything in his cell, it would not be replaced.

Not that the suite of rooms to which Verdadero was confined bore any resemblance to a cell. As chambers of incarceration went, these were palatial. They were furnished expensively with every luxury, every comfort, every need a rich man might conceivably desire to hand, except a latch on his side of the door or a communications console that was connected to the outside world.

The elaborate combination unit that functioned as a video system, message player/recorder, music console, and personal computer was not hooked up to anything but a power cable. Verdadero played datacubes brought in that had been down-loaded for him, then carefully screened for content. Anything he brought out of the cell was screened, and wiped if found suspect by his so-far incorruptible guards. There was no appeal. His sentence was a long one, and his keepers often verbally wished he would become used to the idea of continued vigilance and settle in to model prison life.

Verdadero chafed at any bonds, no matter how slight. By whatever favor his attorneys had gleaned from the corrections system, his physical confinement was bearable. That he was unable to physically travel the galaxy mattered little, but the incarceration of his mind and will irked him. That was the single bond he endeavored to break. So far, he had been unable to circumvent the justice system's boundaries.

The video and its reviews, tendered to him after a gigantic bribe, hurt his massive ego.

"They will pay for this," he vowed. First the downfall itself: a financial setback he could handle; even a loss of time was acceptable. He was a businessman, he understood failure of ventures, and the stripping of planetary assets was risky at best—but the humiliation he suffered at the hands of that chit! That child! Verdadero ground his teeth, and stared at the video screen. The screaming male carried away to trial and imprisonment was him. No matter that they gave it another name, the soul was his. All his pride had been stripped away.

"They're gonna be laughin' at you from here to the frontier, Jaci," his guard said impertinently. The broad-faced redhead had entered silently behind him, had watched him clutch the datacube and release it.

Verdadero turned, and with incredible self-control, favored Duncan with a politely blank look. He refused to rise to the man's bait. The guard was an amateur at torment. "I made too good a target, a stereotype, Mr. Duncan. Even the mindless panderers of the entertainment industry couldn't resist that."

Duncan, deprived of his fun, made a sour face. "Yeah. You ready for your walkies, Jaci?"

Verdadero nodded. He glanced at the time displayed in the corner of his player screen. Just past the lunch hour. Domitio should be in the exercise yard. His contacts on the outside were happy to take Mr. Verdadero's money to keep sending messages around the net. It was time to increase the reward on the Taylors for subjecting him to such incredible humiliation. No, time to double it. With all the appearance of docility, he preceded Duncan out of the cell and waited while the guard locked the door.

·3·

Weeks after escaping from the would-be assassin, the *Sibyl*'s small shuttle floated lightly down through clouds on a course that spiraled toward the surface of Poxt. As the cottony white vapors parted, they got their first look at the main continent of the ottle planet.

"Blue Stars, look at all the trees!" Shona exclaimed, leaning forward against the impact straps. "I have never seen forests like that in my life." Gershom reached back through the division beside the co-pilot's couch for her hand, and squeezed it. Shona squeezed back appreciatively.

"It's beautiful," Lani breathed. Alexander was strapped in with her in the seat next to Shona. He crowed.

"I have never seen it from above," Chirwl said, clutching the top of Shona's chair with his sharp talons. "When I left home this many ago I was hidden in a place aft to shelter from the machine I was not familiar with riding in."

Ivo, in the shuttle's command seat, grunted. "You sure get a good view now."

The green canopy of the jungle below seemed to reach up toward them. By straining her eyes, Shona could see less distinct patches of other colors: brilliant scarlet, deep gold, and a stunning electric blue, plus strips of white along the natural gaps through which wide rivers ran. The white continued out over a wide delta, and spread along the shore of the landmass, flanked on one side by the jungle greens and on the other by aquamarine waters. Shona lost sight of the continent as the shuttle shot southward and dropped another ten thousand feet, covering ocean and islands and ice cap. By the time they looped

40

around again, the continent was much closer. The brightly colored patches became distinctive groves of trees, each with its own texture and height.

"Where do we land, Chirwl?" Shona asked. She had the ottle on her shoulders in his sleeping pouch, which doubled as a backpack so she could carry the short-legged alien.

"I would not know," Chirwl said, awed by the sight of his home planet. "I don't know have references from up here distance."

"I'm on beacon," Ivo said. "They got landing instructions on automatic. It's 'drive by automatic.' No real navigators gotta visit here."

"No one but ottles, scientists, and a diplomatic colony," Gershom noted. "Maybe they'll be eager to see a trader. I won't mind if we can't make any deals while we're here, but it would be nice."

"Huh," said Ivo, as the shuttle dropped beneath the canopy of leaves. "The day you don't look for business . . ." He glanced at the huge branches which were spread far enough apart to allow the shuttle to pass between them, but were so heavily overgrown with leaves and vines that sunlight was cut by more than half. He shrugged toward clusters of head-sized red globes hanging close to the enormous tree boles. "They're not going to want dried fruit, not with they own sources for fresh. What else we got? Electronic parts?"

"Everyone always needs replacement parts," Shona said optimistically.

They passed over a barrel-shaped object topped with a flashing yellow light, and twin rows of bright blue lights whose flashing chased toward the west.

"That's the beacon," Gershom said. Ivo nodded and flicked switches. The nose of the craft eased down until the landing wheels were bumping over the uneven surface of a narrow field. "Where to from here?"

The ottle was bouncing up and down in his pouch. "From here I know," he said, almost babbling with joy. "Do as this, please. See the black and red mark arrows upon the wall of the tree at the end of this path? Follow there, then turn."

Ivo grunted, pushing levers and solenoids. The shuttle rumbled and coughed when its jets shut off and the land engines came to life. Driving her like a truck, the pilot wheeled the

shuttle toward planetary north. The road, hewn out of raw
forest along a wide, slow-flowing river, led to an irregular-
shaped clearing where other small craft were tied down under
heavy tarpaulins and portable hangars.

"Stop here! Stop, stop," Chirwl chattered. The shuttle
lurched to a halt next to a narrow clearing large enough to
house it. Looming over them was a rough-barked tree taller and
deeper than the *Sibyl* herself.

Shona stared out the window at it.

"That's one mucking great tree," she said in admiration.
"Does your family live there, Chirwl?"

"Not there, but another close, near by one tree that is
missing, on the side of the river opposite from this one." A
small, sable-furred paw came over her shoulder and pointed a
sharp talon downward toward a gap in the dense canopy. "From
here we must walk to there."

"They're *all* mucking great trees," Gershom said, getting out
of the shuttle and stretching his legs. Shona handed him Alex
and followed down the steps, steadying herself on the ladder
with one hand on the rail and the other holding the strap of her
backpack containing the excited ottle. Lani scrambled down in
two long-legged jumps, and stood looking around her in sheer
delight.

"Ah, but not all alike," Chirwl said, inhaling and exhaling in
huge, happy gulps that blew gusts down Shona's neck. "Smell
the air, how delicious!"

Shona leaned back, drew in a deep breath, and expelled it in
a colossal sneeze. The cool, moist air was full of feathery green
scents that tickled her nose.

"Fresh," she said, laughing.

"I must touch the ground," Chirwl insisted. Shona pulled the
backpack off her shoulders. The ottle bounded out of the
leather sack and rolled head over tail into the wiry vegetation.
Lani giggled as the small alien cut capers, burrowing through
the undergrowth and scratching his back by rubbing up against
bushes and trees. He turned a half-somersault and lay on his
back ecstatically wriggling all four feet in the air.

"I've missed this," Shona said, holding out her arms and
spinning in a slow circle with her head thrown back. "Trees,

vines, air, clouds—am I turning into a groundbounder in my old age?"

"Not a chance," Gershom said, collecting her in a big three-way hug with Alexander, "because I feel the same way. And no one would ever accuse me of being a landlubber."

"It's the atmosphere," said Kai. "I feel a sensation of well-being in this heady atmosphere. Something around here must naturally generate a load of negative ions."

"Oh, no." Chirwl stopped in the middle of rolling over in the grass. "All is positive here, for life and joy and thought."

"It's all in the mental attitude," Shona said, grinning. "There's no sense in correcting him, Kai. He is right, thesaurusly speaking."

Sometimes it seemed to Shona that Chirwl didn't understand the human language at all, and sometimes he taught her something new about it that she had never considered. She sighed. She was going to miss him dreadfully, but she had to let him carry on with his life. They'd had seven years together. She could cherish the memories, although it wouldn't be the same. Chirwl must have shared her feelings. He'd said a woeful, lingering goodbye to all of Shona's animals. Harry pretended not to care when Chirwl came to pet him, turning an offended, fox-colored back on the ottle. Saffie, however, understood the seriousness of the occasion, and emitted sad little whines as Shona carried Chirwl and his pouch out of the lab module for the last time.

Ivo hauled Chirwl's heavy carryall to the door of the shuttle and tossed it to the ground, climbing down after it. With a grunt and one mighty effort he clasped the straps and shouldered the bag. The weight overbalanced to one side, sending him staggering.

"What's in here?" Ivo complained to the ottle. "You live in trees, so you don't need bricks."

"It's cat food," Shona said, with a grin. At Chirwl's request, Shona had gone on an eclectic shopping spree in the shipyard's satellite town and returned with some surprising choices. "Twenty-kilo bags. Foreign delicacies for the home folks. Chirwl likes the same flavor Harry eats, and figures his family will enjoy it, too. There's other presents, but mostly it's kitty kibble." Ivo shot the ottle a look of disgust.

"You eat good human-type food, too. Why didn't you bring some of that?"

"Ah, but it does not keep so well as my friend Harry's food, and nutri is not of interest."

"You can say that again," Shona remarked.

"Why?" Chirwl wanted to know.

"I hope there's nothing breakable in there," Gershom said, as Ivo dropped the bag heavily to the ground and hoisted it into a better position on his back.

"Small, soft things only, except for my thesis, which is in many parts that cannot be broken."

"If we're not as close as you say, I'm dropping it in the river," Ivo threatened, his black brows drawn into a V over a set face.

"Close! This way, this way," Chirwl said impatiently, scooting up the nearest tree bole and waving a paw toward a narrow path that led back into the forest and away from the reed bank. Reluctantly Shona broke free of her husband's embrace and picked the ottle up.

"We can go faster if I carry you." The ottle wiggled into the pouch, and Shona slung it on her back. "Where to?"

At Chirwl's direction, Shona squeezed in beside the gigantic bole of a tree whose striated bark was so thick she could have put her arm into it up to the shoulder. With difficulty, the men followed. Lani, bringing up the rear, slipped in after them as silently and effortlessly as a wood nymph.

"Remark your way well," Chirwl warned them as they set out into the thick undergrowth. "I shall teach you as young ones of my kind have always been taught. This ancient tree is the oldest heart-tree for this zone region. When Poxt cooled many eons back ago we left the original places where rivers began to be too icy. Now those lie under leagues of snow and no ottle goes there. It is too bad, for much philosophy was thought there, and many among us would be gratefully glad to read the musings of our ancestors."

"Does anyone live up there now?" Shona asked, peering up into the dense branches. "In the tree, not the arctic region."

"No. It is like a historical house residential shrine."

"Are all the heart-trees this big?" Gershom asked. "I've seen smaller space stations."

"No, most are younger," the ottle said, "so they do have not grown as tall."

Beyond the ancient treestead, the brush on the floor of the forest thinned and grew in scattered clumps no more than knee-high. Shona, with Chirwl still in her arms, was able to pick her way on the spongy jungle floor. Gershom and Lani trotted up swiftly to walk alongside them. The crew spread out behind, Ivo and Gershom with their hands on unbuckled hip holsters. Kai trotted along at the same gait as if he were still in the corridors of the *Sibyl*, his mind elsewhere. Eblich remained on the ship. He might have enjoyed the scenery more than Kai, but he had admitted in his taciturn fashion that he'd already said his farewells to Chirwl, and more would be painful. Besides, someone had to keep the *Sibyl* in orbit.

"Mama, whatzat?" Alex shouted, seeing an avian with scarlet plumage whiz by overhead.

"A bird, honey. I don't know what kind. See, there's a reptile," Shona said, pointing out a skinny, lizardlike form clinging to a branch. "Or should I say, a reptiloid?"

Clusters of colorful, long-tailed birds like bright flowers swirled around the heads of the hikers and flew away, calling out their surprise in hoarse, mocking voices. Alex reached up to grab for one and was disappointed when his hand came back empty.

"Pretty," he said.

Chirwl trilled excitedly. "Ah! Now, here is the tree in which I and my siblings played at racing with youngsters from many clans. And this is the one where several of us swore a pact never to tell falsehoods. The place of burning still shows." Shona noticed a blackened patch on the top of one thick, outspread branch.

"Burning?" she asked. "You have to take vows over fire?"

"Oh, no, for but a youthful childhood escapade," Chirwl said, a little sheepishly. "We took fire from one of the cookings, and over the flames one must hold one's paw while telling the words. If one is not quick, then fur will scorch. A test of memory it was as well as daring. And there is the heart-tree where the male-generative one who fostered me and my siblings lived in youth. The young tree that was growing up beside that place is gone. I thought it weak when I knew it."

"I don't see how you can tell all these trees apart," Gershom remarked.

"I have always thought that same confusion over buildings," Chirwl said. "Most because those smell so much the same as another. Trees do not smell alike. They have each their own perfume aroma."

"Really?" Shona asked, breathing deeply. To her, the trunks had a single, peaty, rich scent. Chirwl's keener senses could obviously detect something she couldn't.

"Your tree better not be far," Ivo said grouchily. He swung the heavy bag of cat food to the ground and stretched his back.

"It is not," Chirwl said, whistling happily. His whiskers tickled Shona's ear as he leaned closer to give directions. "Forward is the feed stream to the great river. Toward the purple flowering trees lies the bridge we are to be crossing."

A ribbon of deep blue sky opened up ahead. They felt a quickening and a warming of the light breeze. The fingers of the wind combed through Shona's short hair, and she smiled.

"See the river gap," Chirwl said excitedly. "We are on target for the bridge, since over your clothes you will not like to swim."

"I would," Lani said promptly.

"Maybe later, honey, after we've met Chirwl's folks," Shona said hastily. "I see it."

The inevitable thick brush that clusters along a river bank was interrupted very briefly by a Jacob's ladder of wire and planks anchored to the ground and to one of the larger trees nearby by means of knotted cable as thick as a man's wrist. The narrow span disappeared behind the undergrowth, but through small gaps they could glimpse sections of it suspended over the deep river cut. In the distance, the river's roar was audible, a soothing wash of white noise and chuckling gurgles.

As they drew closer to the river, its voice was overpowered by a loud buzzing. Ivo, stumping ahead, jumped in surprise when the clump of weeds he kicked emitted a cloud of black flies.

"Hey!" he yelled, backing off. He swatted at the droning mass with Chirwl's bag. "They sting! Get them off!"

"I did forget to tell," Chirwl called apologetically. "Seek the low-lying, lozenge-shaped leaf and rub it on your person. That will drive them away."

Shona scanned the ground for a plant with diamond-shaped leaves or petals. "There!" she said, stooping for a handful of white-furred green stems. "We'd better all use it." She put the ottle down and rubbed the weeds between her palms.

When crushed, the leaf emitted a lemony, spicy fragrance that was pleasant to human nostrils but drove the flies away at once. The spacers daubed themselves with liberal quantities of the natural insect-repellent, and stepped through the hovering mass of offended flies. Shona, carrying Chirwl, led the way onto the bridge, and halted in the center to look up and down the river.

The banks on both sides were unbroken expanses of dappled green down to the brown earth of the waterline. Even the break they'd spotted when parking the shuttle was invisible. Small eddies in the river's current showed where water creatures had dived for safety when the humans appeared. Avians swooped over the surface, snatching up insects and dipping for fish. The single, triumphant call of a bird echoed from far away. Shona sighed.

"It's so . . . untouched," she said. "On any planet where we've settled I'm used to seeing piers, water mills, or power plants sticking out into any body of water."

"This colonist group promised us to be very subtle," Chirwl said. "At first they cut many trees, but then found that we were here living above their heads. It was they stop, for now they knew this was not only their habitat, but ours, too."

Nothing disturbed the quiet except for the rushing water and their breathing. Lani rocked back and forth on the guy wires, her gaze drifting contentedly from one cluster of green to another.

"Like home," she said simply.

Shona searched her face for signs of sadness. Lani's last days on her native planet of Karela had not been happy ones. The girl, sensing her foster mother's eyes on her, turned and gave her a sweet, poignant smile with a little shrug of her shoulders to say she was all right. Shona moved close and gave her a quick hug.

"It's so peaceful here, isn't it?" Shona remarked, taking a deep breath of the fragrant air.

"Yes," Chirwl said. "It is conducive to long life. There is a philosophy that such an atmosphere in one might live forever.

An ottle who disagrees with that thought believes that there is no correlation, but refuses to live with great noises to test his theory. He wishes to live as long as any can.''

"Well, would you find it necessary to try a theory like that?" Kai said, shaking his head. "After all, a theory's not proof. Why risk your life on the chance that a notion's true?"

"Ah, but the true philosopher's thoughts is his try."

Though she was reluctant to stir, Shona thought she had better break up what might turn into a long session. "Chirwl, where does your mate live from here?"

"Shnomri lives in the tree under which we will be passing," Chirwl said, disappointed at having to stop such a stimulating discussion. "But I will not call upon that ottle until after I have said greetings to home. We shall go further on along this trail eight more trunks. In my heart-tree is where Wla lives. That ottle only is from my clan. As you do not, we do not mix close biology, too."

"You mean you avoid inbreeding," Shona said. She turned her head as far as she could to meet Chirwl's eyes. "You mean you have *two* mates?"

Chirwl, usually the most voluble of creatures, actually stopped talking, abashed. "It is not a discussion to be with others mostly. Of importance, but yes only to those involved in the trining."

"Trining—? Oh, like pairing." As long as he was discussing the topic, which she could never get him to do before, Shona intended to keep going until he clammed up. "Well, tell me about them."

"Wla, of my tree, is very young. Shnomri, of a-tree-much-nearer-the-river, is of my equal in philosophy, and it is for that ottle's sake which I take to space to meet you and other humans. My thesis is now at a point when I may set it before the seniors of thought, to have them discuss and judge if my think is good."

"Well, it's original, anyway," Shona commented. "That's got to count for something. I've got internal bioscans of you, and there's no place to put babies. Do both of your mates bear the young?"

"Not both. Only the receptive one, who is Wla. I am for biogenetic donation, so there is no need for the uterine sack inside myself. Shnomri is also for biogenetic donation, of ova, which is why Shnomri comes from elsewhere. To you, that one almost is male and female at once. Since Wla and I come from the same place, I am the least of importance in the trine, so it is not important that I am not there to discuss the upbringing of young until now. Wla will have been representing the clan."

"Do the others look differently from you? I mean other sexes, not other ottles. I've never met another ottle. Alien Relations brought *you* to *me*."

Chirwl twitched his whiskers. "Not on the outside are differences evident, except receptive ones, who are smaller for better hiding. Poxt can be not-welcoming to those with young to care for. The three leaders, each to represent one gender, make sure all know what protect needs to be taken."

"You have a triumvirate? Are they a mated trine?"

"Oh, no. Not necessarily, for governing changes as need does. Of ottles, some are with the same mates forever. Some change as they choose, or if peril or disease takes one from their three."

"I suppose all environments have their dangers. If something happened to one mate, would the remaining ones remarry—I mean, take a new mate?"

"Ah, in a faithful triangle the other two never breed again. It is most tragic."

"And which sort are you?"

"I like stability. It is what you do that I understand."

"I think that's a compliment," Gershom said.

Dennison heaved himself painfully up from his cot. He made it to a sitting position before he was quite out of breath. Where was he? He couldn't remember. He put a hand to his head, feeling for lumps, and felt skin. How odd. Where was his hair? He felt down the crown of his head to the cranium. Ah, there it was. He blinked blearily at the sun coming through the window of the hut. A man with brown hair stood next to the window. He recognized him as Hampton, one of Volk's most trusted assistants. Volk—! Yes, he remembered now. His notes, were they still hidden? He had to go tell somebody *what?* He rose and doddered toward the door.

"Oh, no, Ed." Hampton grabbed his arm and grinned down at him. Down? He was taller than Hampton. At least he had thought so. Dennison tried to straighten his back, but it wouldn't straighten any higher. He remained looking up sort of sideways, with his head tilted, because his neck hurt too much to turn it forward. "No," Hampton repeated. "You're staying right here."

"I have to go," Dennison insisted, pushing against the other man's superior strength. "I have to . . ." He forgot what it was he had to do. He slumped back onto the cot, and tried hard to think. Hampton went back to stand by the window.

While they were still hundreds of meters away from the clearing Chirwl had indicated, Shona and the others began to notice sleeping pouches suspended high against the trunks of the great trees. The papoose bags came in every color. Some were scarlet, mocking the huge red fruit they'd already seen, others a fresh and vivid green, some a blue-spruce color, a few a golden yellow-orange, and all the colors in between. Chirwl, who preferred a dark brown pouch, was apparently one of the more conservative ottles.

The walkers had been observed as well. Shona heard a shrill cry from high over their heads. More cries answered it, and the ottles began to emerge. From the first tree, dark, furry bodies came swarming down along channels in the deeply fissured bark to greet them. One or two, still high up, let out musical whistles and chitters to the next trunk along, to let others know that visitors were approaching. Shona saw the glints of sharp white teeth, pink tongues, and bright dark-brown eyes in the sable-furred faces. The ancient forest clearing was cut through at one corner by an old riverbed. The water was only inches deep, but it filled a pool. At the alarm, ottles clambered out of it, shook themselves dry, and hurried to join the throng.

By the time the visitors reached the clearing, they were surrounded by a knee-deep, chattering mob of sleek backs. To her delight, Shona found the ottles were not multiple replicas of Chirwl, but distinguishable by facial or vocal characteristics, like pudgy cheeks or big shoulders or a discernible soprano squeak; on the whole just the same kind of lovable, gregarious creature, but different, too. She'd wondered if when this moment came she would suddenly be disappointed that her friend was not unique in all the galaxy, but as soon as she met more of his kind the fear vanished. Each one had its own distinct personality. Chirwl remained one of a kind.

"Let down, let down!" Chirwl cried, all but clambering over her neck to get out of the pouch. Before he was even on the ground, he was engaged in a spirited conversation with a handful of others who clustered close to see him. Shona let him go, and made her way through the quarter-height throng to Gershom, who stood straight, like a human tree, looking on the scene with amusement. Alex sat in the crook of his arm like a statue, lips parted and eyes wide, staring.

"Sirenlike, aren't they?" Gershom said as Shona joined him and slipped an arm around her waist. He dropped his free arm over her shoulders. "Their voices go right through my head."

"A young one!" an ottle with a distinct whistle exclaimed from beside their heads. It was clinging to the bark sideways by its needle-sharp claws. It pointed at Alex. "Do let us meeting your young. So seldom meet do we."

Shona looked up at Gershom, who set the toddler down. A crowd of admiring ottles formed around him at once, poking inquisitive noses at him from a handspan away.

"Look at him." Gershom laughed. "His eyes are about to pop out of his head." Alex sat rapt, his back against his father's legs, reaching out to pat one ottle after another. He had always loved Chirwl, and seemed delighted to be surrounded by dozens and dozens just like his companion. Each ottle came up to speak with him and, recognizing the need of the young to explore, let him fondle its fur or touch its ears or tail. The joy bubbling inside his small body finally blurted out in one huge, explosive chuckle, and he started to babble at his new friends the few phrases Chirwl had taught him in the ottle tongue. Shona laughed. The whistling ottle leaped up to his post beside her head and stretched out a paw to touch her cheek for attention.

"How smart and how beautiful is your offspring," it said. "To our admiration he speaks to us, and yet he is very young?"

"He's known Chirwl since he was born," Shona explained. "Humans pick up languages very quickly when they are small."

"Is there documentation of phenomenon this one?" asked another ottle. "It could be yours individually is simply more intelligent and learnable than others."

"I would hope Alex is as bright as he seems," Gershom said, a little half grin quirking up the corner of his mouth. "But not only is there documentation, there are classes in many skills taught to very small children."

"Ahhhh. Most interesting." The two ottles scampered farther up the tree to discuss the matter.

"I think we might have started a new philosophical argument," Shona whispered, grinning.

Lani wandered here and there with wide eyes, caressing the trees and plants with familiar fingers. She looked at home at once, happy to be back in a deep-forest environment. Shona felt a twinge, thinking how much the girl must have missed her native planet after the Taylors swept her away to the sterile and cold habitat of a spaceship. At the time, there had been no choice, but now that the girl was growing up, she could soon make her own decision as to where she would live. Shona didn't want her to spread her wings too soon, but vowed she would be opened-minded and encouraging when the girl wanted to talk about her future.

Chirwl shouldered his way back to Shona through the milling throng of ottles. Behind him clustered a trio of creatures, one slightly smaller than the other two, all with visible rough, graying patches in the sable fur around their shoulders and tails. He chittered in his own tongue, then changed smoothly into Standard. "Be this is my very beloved Shona and her one-mate, Gershom. Know my generative ones," he said, twisting his flexible spine around almost his own length to introduce each. "Chlari, father of the cell, Thio, mother of the cell, and Tsanan, nurturer of myself and my siblings."

"Chlari, Tsanan." The name Thio sounded more like a descending whistle than a word. Shona did her best to imitate it. "I'm so very pleased to meet you. I've enjoyed traveling with your . . . offspring. All of us have. We'll miss him now that he's come home to stay. He's been a good companion."

"He looks well and happy," Chlari said approvingly. "He must also enjoy traveling with you."

Tsanan, hunkered next to Chirwl, rubbed cheeks with him, and whispered low in his ear. He replied in a childlike, cooing purr that Shona found endearing. It figured that Tsanan, as the one who cared for the young, would have been Chirwl's confidant and comforter while he was growing up. They were still close, and Tsanan seemed reluctant to be at any distance from her newly returned charge. Shona sympathized. She couldn't imagine the wrench she might feel if Alex went away for seven or eight years without ever being able to communicate directly with her, and she hadn't a clue what a typical ottle life span was. Had Chirwl been away half his natural life, or only a tenth? Less or more? Chlari grunted impatiently and twitched his whiskers. Chirwl and Tsanan reluctantly broke up their tête-à-tête.

"I have refutation for the theory of mine which you denied validity before going," the old one said. "You must come up to the sleeping place and peruse it."

"When I know where I shall be placing my bedpouch," Chirwl said, "we shall exchange notional documents."

"Eh, you can be taking it now." Chlari turned his back on his offspring and co-mates, and walked deliberately up the tree, disappearing into the crevices of the bark.

"That ottle is more than glad you are returned in safety," Tsanan said. "He had said of late that you were no more, that your travels had ended out there amidst in the stars."

"Didn't Alien Relations send back reports to you on how he was doing?" Shona asked, shocked.

"Oh, yes," Tsanan said, her black eyes gleaming mischievously. "Chlari is not believing them, for there is no logical proof other than their words, which are so limited in scope yet not narrow in meaning. Mere pictures. What are they but inventions of human machines of what may not exist? Thio assures him, but Chlari does not believe hir."

Tsanan pronounced the final word 'heer.' Because the ottle's pronunciation of Standard words was so flawless, Shona refused to believe it was a mistake of diction. She assumed instead that the term 'hir' was the pronoun assigned by the human colony's linguists to a concept with which they had been previously unacquainted: naming the two different biodonors of tri-gender extraterrestrials.

She was about to ask about possessive pronouns, when a shower of fingertip-sized rounds of wood rained down on them from above. Startled, Shona jumped out of the way and looked up. One pouch in a small cluster of three situated close to a thick main branch was squirming vigorously. More disks, assorted debris, and a fruit core plummeted down, bouncing off the heavy bark to fall amidst the other discards in the wiry grass and bushes at the tree's base.

"Chlari," Thio said, shaking hir head.

Chirwl and the other two elders carefully picked through the undergrowth for the fallen disks. Shona, Gershom, and Lani bent to help them. Ottles, with their small personal capsules and the wide world beyond them, kept very few possessions. That which they did not want they simply threw out of the pouches, never to be seen again in the thick undergrowth of the forest below. It was a trait Shona had had to deal with on shipboard, where everything Chirwl discarded ended up in very plain view on the floor.

"Not that one," Thio said, batting a disk out of Gershom's palm with a deft paw. "That is not Chlari's write. Let us."

Chirwl looked up at Shona with shining eyes as his small, deft paws sorted various oddities into piles. Thio took possession of one stack, and set them in order among the others before hir. "This is good typical of my home time. I am proud to be showing to you everyday life. It is not like yours, so I know you are interested."

"I am interested, Chirwl," she said, hunkered beside him with one hand lightly balanced on his sleek back. "You know I'm going to miss you."

"Perhaps in the future there can be more going," he said, nodding. "The pouch will not hold young ottles forever. More things to see I would like to know. Can you stay a while long for now?"

"Only a few days," Gershom said. "Now that the *Sibyl*'s in working order, I've got to get back to work. My clients are clamoring, and the bank is on our backs."

"Very alliterational," Chirwl said approvingly. "That is good backward poetry of the beginnings of words rhyming instead of the ends," he explained to Tsanan. The nurturer nodded, long front teeth clipped over her lower lip in concentration as she handed her last collection of disks to Thio.

"Now I have them all," Thio announced, and presented a double-pawful to Chirwl.

"Let me take those," Shona said, holding out her hands. She put them into Chirwl's pouch.

"Chirwl-lli?" a shy whistle inquired. The throng had receded to a distance to talk amongst themselves, leaving room for

another to come forward. Through the parted grasses slipped a
new ottle with fur that looked more fluffy than sleek. By her
size, Shona could tell she was a nurturer. Although mature, she
had a tentative, youthful gait. Her dark eyes were large in her
small, well-shaped head, and her sharp teeth very white.

"Wla!" Chirwl exclaimed. He tapped Shona's ankle with an
excited paw. "Encounter one of my proposed co-mates who is
Wla, also of my greatly extended family." Chirwl intertwined
his fingers with hers, touched noses and cheeks with her, and
they conversed together in their language of staccato whistles,
clicks, and chitters. She formed an interrogative sentence in her
own language, and he answered in Standard, to which she
replied. The two dropped in and out of their native tongue,
while exchanging cheek licks and ear rubs like a pair of cats.
Shona caught various phrases. "Place of gestation . . . choice
of beginning at once or waiting to see . . . thesis of
natural . . . Shnomri said, superior genes . . ." Shona
laughed. *So* typical of Chirwl. Wla glanced up at her in
surprise, as if aware of the humans for the first time.

"What is funny?" Chirwl wanted to know.

"You're both being so . . . so rational about what is for
humans the most emotional of relationships and responsibilities," she said. "I know we rarely go into marriage or
childrearing with such detailed plans worked out ahead of time.
We let love or parental instinct take its course most of the
time."

"We only work out the logistics of family life," Chirwl
chided her, "not the love and caring needed to go into between
we three for each other and our offspring. I have missed out on
many of the conversations, and must be brought up to knowledge on the decisions. It is important."

"I stand corrected," Shona said gravely. Gershom winked at
her. "Wla, I'm pleased to meet you. Chirwl hasn't told us much
about you, but I'm sure you're a deep-thinking philosopher,
just like him." Wla let out a shrill giggle and flirted her furry
eyelids. She looked up from Shona to Gershom.

"Only two generative ones are you. Was one lost?"

"No, we're a complete set. Humans have only two kinds of
generative ones," Shona told her. "We combine the functions of
ova-donor and nurturer into one like me. Both of us care for our

children, but only females are capable of carrying the young and producing milk to feed them."

Wla chittered with laughter. "Most strange! So much for one to do."

Abandoned by most of his admirers, Alex let out a squawk of protest and tottered toward his parents, almost falling over a bush. "Mama! Mama, pick me up!"

"I couldn't agree with you more sometimes," Shona said, gathering up her noisy offspring. She checked his diaper quickly, and gave him an approving pat on the seat when she discovered it was still clean.

Lani came to join them. Kneeling down silently next to Shona, she held out her arms to take Alex.

"No, thank you, sweetheart. I'll bear my own burdens for a while. Wla, this is our daughter, Lani," Shona said. "Also a good friend of Chirwl's. She comes from a forested planet like yours."

Ivo gave a bored sigh and let his burden slip noisily into the high grass.

"Ah!" Chirwl exclaimed, diverted. "And presents I have for family, indeed. Wla, where is Shnomri? That ottle must have in the sharing."

With a quick glance at Shona, Wla responded in a series of whistles and clicks.

Chirwl stopped her. "But to converse in Standard is more polite. Where is Shnomri?"

"Is not coming," Wla said, tucking her head almost underneath her body.

"What is wrong? Does Shnomri ail?"

Wla glanced up at Shona, blinked her eyes, and ducked swiftly into the nearest bush.

"Did I do something wrong?" Shona asked.

"I think Wla wishes private conversation," Chirwl replied.

"We like her very much, Chirwl," Shona said, nodding toward the hidden nurturer. "She's as cute as a button."

"Buttons make some sense," Chirwl said, and disappeared into the undergrowth after his co-mate. The humans heard urgent chittering, including a helpless wail from Wla.

". . . does not wish to come out of the pouch . . . for greet *anyone*, especially you . . . the co-mate."

Chirwl emerged a few moments later, shaking his head.

"This is unsuitable in behavior. There is some foolishness that Shnomri wishes not to appear in public. This I do not understand."

"It is outrageous," Thio agreed, siding with hir son. "I shall reason with Shnomri." The ova-donor headed back toward the trees near the river. Shortly, they heard loud remonstration from the pouches hanging over their heads. Thio, hanging from a handy branch two trees away, was arguing with a dark blue-green bag, which retorted in a mellow, determined voice. The bag emitted one final-sounding comment, and Thio, looking affronted, turned head-down into one of the bark channels.

"Disgrace, disgrace, disgrace," Thio said upon hir return, shaking hir head.

"I don't mind, Chirwl," Shona said, seeing that most of the clan was embarrassed by Shnomri's refusal to appear. "I'm looking forward to visiting the human settlement. Gershom and I should check in with them as soon as possible, to let them know we're here."

"The thicket and a wide dell and another narrow copse only divide us," Tsanan explained, pointing toward the east.

"Is not hard to find," Wla said, suddenly popping out of the undergrowth. "I will lead you."

The winsome young female lolloped to the edge of the clearing, bounding over the high grass, and paused coyly with her head bent to one shoulder, waiting. Kai was jostled out of a stimulating discussion with a pack of ottles to join the walk to the other side. Ivo seemed more than ready to get away from the multitude of chattering aliens, and stumped away from his well-wishers. Lani looked up at Shona, suddenly shy, no doubt, at the thought of meeting a crowd of strangers.

"Can I stay here?" she asked.

"Certainly," Shona said, "if that's all right?" She glanced at her hosts.

"Of course it is all right," Tsanan said, sidling up to the girl and patting her knee with a gentle paw. "A pleasure to have her stay."

"I will rousting out Shnomri in the midst of time," Thio said firmly.

·4·

"I'm excited we're going to see this settlement," Shona said. "It's probably the most important one in the galaxy. I remember when it was founded, do you? It must have been almost fifteen years ago because I was still in secondary school. It's been held up as proof that humans can coexist peacefully with another intelligent species."

"But of course," Chirwl said, diving in and out of the knee-high wiry grass. "Are we not proof an example our two selves? I will be curious to hear how good neighbors they are being."

"Oh, very so," Wla said. "Shnomri was ever visiting there, as were many others. Friends they we make good."

The ottles' path through the dense thicket was easily wide enough for human feet to pass. Wla dashed energetically a few meters ahead at a time, pausing every now and then for them to catch up. Shona, being small of stature, had less trouble following her than the men did. The low overhang of the trees suggested that humans seldom used the path; all of the men had to walk crouched over. Shona reached up to push the branches back, and came away with dozens of tiny thorns in her hands. No wonder no one had tried to clear the path. It would take a blowtorch.

To Ivo's audible relief, the ceiling opened up within a hundred yards. A gap in the forest canopy informed them that at some time in the past one of the ancient trees had fallen, leaving a broad, rolling glen open to the sun. Wla ran along a straight track through low, lush, fragrant plant life, then made a 90° turn at its end. She whisked up to a meter-high gap in a dense wall of green, then tittered self-consciously.

"Here is where we go, but you are too tall!"

"Where do we get in?" Shona asked, threshing up and back along the natural barrier, looking for an entrance. The bushes had dense, sturdy branches, and lobed, ovate leaves the size of her head, making them impossible to see through. There seemed to be no break in the hedge. She captured Alex's hand just in time before he grabbed a cluster of four-inch thorns. On the other side of the barrier she could hear voices and the hum of a generator. Gershom and the others spread out, looking for a way in.

"Not without a machete," Kai decided, planting his fists on his hips.

"Over here!" a voice called. Shona turned to see a tall man waving his arm above his head. "We thought we heard someone wandering around behind the garden. This way!"

"Garden?" Shona looked down, and, with a laugh, identified the spiky plants around her feet. "Artichokes!" Carefully, she picked her way out of the patch with her hand out. The man who'd hailed them beamed at her and clasped her fingers in a huge, flipperlike hand.

"Shona Taylor," she said, smiling up at him. "That's my husband, Gershom, captain of the *Sibyl*, and our son, Alex." Kai and Ivo stumped back between the cultivated rows, and introduced themselves. "We radioed you on the way in. I'm sorry about your crops."

"DeWitt Horne," said the man bowing over Shona's hand. His hair grew in a salt-and-pepper fringe around the bald crown of his head, and his beaky, high-bridged nose supported blue-green tinted sunshades. He grinned, showing white but irregular teeth. "Governor of this blessed plot, artichokes and all. No problem. I'm pleased to meet you, Doctor. Captain, men, a pleasure." He patted Alex on the shoulder, then shook hands with Gershom and the others. "Well, we don't get a lot of human company. Nice to have you here." He glanced down at the ottles, smiled at Wla, and raised his eyebrows at Chirwl. "I don't know this fellow. You must be the returnee. How do you do, friend?"

"I do delightfully, thank you, DeWitt Horne," Chirwl said,

glancing around at the clearing. "How this open place has expanded since I was departed from here."

Thumbs stuck in his belt, Horne rocked back on his heels and surveyed the open field with satisfaction. Six or seven now-distinct crops were flourishing in the acreage left open to the sky by the missing trees. All of them were healthy and bright green. He nodded several times.

"Yes, we're doing all right. All the clearing has been done with the permission of the ottle heart-trees. No one in my demesne trims a *bush* without asking. 'A course, we don't have anyone living here who isn't willing to coexist peacefully. Come and have a look around. You're welcome!"

Small domiciles, prefabricated rectangles with sloped roofs, were set with their doorways opening out into the common area. Each of the houses had bird-feeders, hanging plants, handmade ornaments, and other decorations hanging from the eaves, brightening up what would have been a tediously monotonous neighborhood on other planets. Container gardens and kitchen gardens were everywhere. Shona guessed all one had to do was throw seeds at the ground and then stand back to produce a goodly crop in this climate.

"Have you had any medical problems living on Poxt?" Shona asked, falling into step with the big man as he led them past the hedge and down one side of the irregularly shaped common area.

"The usual: exhaustion, allergies, insect stings, tail bites . . ."

"What?"

Horne grinned. "You haven't seen tails yet? They look like the south end of a northbound squirrel with no visible means of support. If you grab one by the plume, the animal, which is only about two, three centimeters long, detaches and runs for cover. If you catch it front-to-back, it can sink its choppers into you. They're tiny, but they're big-time sharp!" He showed Shona a small white scar on the pad of his forefinger. "I made that mistake myself. Our doctor inspected it, and put me under observation for infection. We're close enough in biostructure to ottles that we can catch some of the same things they do. Fortunately, there's nothing native here like rabies. No one will ever bring it here. I'll do my best to see to that."

Shona had no doubt he would. Though friendly and expansive, Horne's upright, military carriage suggested a natural knack for command which probably didn't brook defiance.

"How are you getting along with the ottles?" Gershom asked.

"Fabulously. There's nothing like an ottle for a good, reasoned argument," Horne said. "And they can be obtuse little buggers if they want to pretend they don't understand Standard, but I like 'em. In the beginning we shipped out some folks who were disappointed. They figured that any other intelligent life in the universe ought to be bilaterally symmetrical humanoids like us, except for having funny ears. Me, I'm just plain fascinated by the differences. Trisexual aliens! There's two kinds of bio-positors, you know: exterior plumbing, one donating sperm and one eggs, but you can't tell 'em apart unless they tell you. One of my favorites hasn't been coming around lately, a she-male called Shnomri."

Wla chittered unhappily.

"Anyhow, come on around. People will be glad to meet you. If you have a chance, I'd like a chat about what it was like to introduce our alien friend here"—he waved a big hand toward Chirwl—"into human society."

"I think I learned more from him than he did from us," Shona said as they walked. "Because he asked, I had to examine why I said or did some things, and occasionally I couldn't find a better answer than that's the way I'd always done it. I suppose I never thought about the reasons."

"Like?"

"Oh, why I wear socks," Shona said, laughing as she ran her fingers along a makeshift fence of loosely woven branches. Alex had captured a leafy twig and was busily tearing the leaves apart. "Or for that matter, why I wear shoes. Since we tend to build artificial environments all around us, he wanted to know, why not make one that is safe for bare feet. And then he watched me drop a lab beaker on my toe, and dance around trying to find the brush and dustpan without collecting more shards in my soles than I could help."

"*Quod erat demonstrandum.*" Grinning, Gershom spread his hands.

Horne was amused. "You had a microcosm of what we have here, Shona," he said. "We're always asking each other that kind of question. Ottles want to know everything. I think they'd make good researchers, if we could ever convince 'em that a human idea is worth investigating. The pressing need for practical exploration does not exist for them. Ottles have it relatively easy. They've licked their environment. Theoretical philosophy is about the only thing that keeps them falling back into non-sentient existence."

"I beg to differ," Chirwl interrupted, fixing the large human with a beady eye peeled for battle. "Would a species lapse into nonintelligence if well-fed and cared for? Then those humans who do not strive daily for their bread must also fall into non-mentality."

Horne shook his head. "See what I mean?"

Privately, Shona agreed with Chirwl, but she smiled at her host. The common green was nearly empty. A man or woman occasionally trotted from one of the houses along a path toward the big building at the foot of the gentle slope. One woman, working alone at a laptop unit, sat under a tree, only glancing up with a distracted nod as they passed. Between two of the huts Shona spotted a cluster of children involved in a game of blindfold tag, shrieking as they backed away from It. In a fenced field well-removed from the main living area were several head of brown-and-white cattle huddled in a group in the sun. Their eyes were closed. A couple of calves browsed on something yellow and green in the corner of the pen.

Uphill, there was a flurry of activity. An ancient man doddered out of a hut, heading toward the green. Behind him a couple of men in lab coats rushed out, retrieved him, and gently turned him back again. A dark-haired woman appeared at the door, and with an attitude of concern evident even at a distance, watched as the ancient hobbled back inside. Every house had a wealth of flowers and vines growing on or around it.

"This is a lovely place to have a home," Shona said to Horne. "You chose a nice site—or did the ottles suggest this place?"

"Well, kind of a meeting of minds. When we first came here, we were farther inland, along a tributary of the big river— turned out to be smack in the middle of one of their villages. Took us a while to figure out they were sentient—what the heck, I think the xenos were looking for television antennas and pressed concrete. The ottles had been watching us, waiting for signs of intelligence, maybe. To them, we never assembled for a village conference or wrote philosophical treatises. You must know what it's like founding a colony: everybody do their job, keep your jawing to a minimum. Not an ottle way at all.

"Well, after we figured each other out, we wanted a place that wasn't in the middle of their dwelling spaces and didn't have any historical significance to them. Out of the eight or so places they suggested, the biologists figured we'd do the least damage and could spread out the most here. It's also the closest of the eight to an existing ottle center-place, so go figure. I think it was a penetrating insight on their part; we've trained a lot of xeno exploration terms here since then."

"How do students react?" Kai asked.

"Thrilled!" Horne said, then qualified his exuberance. "Most of them, anyway. Some of the xenos have been openly disappointed, because I think they believed the tri-dee movies that say all sentient alien life is going to be bilaterally symmetrical humanoids with lobsters on their foreheads. It takes all kinds. Here's my house."

Horne's prefabricated hut looked like all the others, except for a flag with the symbol of the Galactic Government fluttering on a three-meter staff stuck in a bed of moss-covered pebbles.

"From here you can see everyone's front door. That's the only hard requirement I made when we laid out the settlement. I want everyone in line of sight until we're so big we've got to split in two like an amoeba. Otherwise, you can arrange your place anyway you like. We've got eighty people, adults and children, living in the main settlement right now, and twenty-two more in the annex." He pointed up a rising path toward a cluster of eight or nine huts arranged in an arc. "They're a bunch of researchers from LabCor. I don't know what they're doing, and so long as they don't pollute that site or this planet, I don't give a hoot. They don't mix with us *peasants* a lot." Horne lifted the corner of his lip in a sneer. Shona guessed that the LabCor workers had snubbed Horne's attempts to make them part of the big, happy family.

"Is the GG supporting you now?" Gershom asked.

"Oh, we get stipends," Horne said, with an expression that was a cross between a grin and a grimace, "but they expect us to get along on our own, pretty much. We might be their fair-haired baby right now, but they're looking forward to the day when having non-Terrans as your next-door neighbors is ordinary, so they want us to function like an ordinary colony. They'd love to turn off the subsidies, but I'll scream bloody blue murder to the media, and they know that."

"What do you do here?"

Horne let his big chest puff up with pride. "We're generalists. We're investigating the native chemical compounds and jungle foods, specializing in sustainable natural supply. Most of our colony's income comes from cataloguing the natural medicines that exist right here. We're moving slowly and carefully, not exploiting any source to destruction. We don't want what happened to Old Earth's Amazonian rain forests to happen here. Our researchers go mad with joy every time they make a new foray into the jungles. The ottles are happy to act as friendly native guides. They ask nothing better than to have people appreciate the wealth of natural treasures here on Poxt. They want us to see everything, and they'll tell you more than you ever wanted to know about a plant. You know, ottles talk a mile a minute."

"I know," Shona said, reaching a hand down to ruffle her friend's ears. "Chirwl lived with me for several years. Now that he's come home, I don't know how I'm going to stand all the quiet."

"I have been quiet, too, between saying," Chirwl said reproachfully. "But how can one communicate verbally if one does not speak?"

"Now, there's an ottle for you," Horne said with a laugh. "So we identify botanical samples and make analyses of their contents—natural stuff has trace elements that sometimes help the efficacy of a drug, and sometimes make a witches' brew of the whole thing. It helps that ottle biology is a lot like ours. They point out a plant that they use for a certain ailment, and if it's a problem we share, we research their folk cure, see if it's an improvement on ours. There's the same number of old wives' tales, too, though. I'm always hoping the oil for rheumatism that the ancients talk about turns up one day. We've had about three dozen near misses on that mix, but we don't know what went wrong. The ottles are always arguing we didn't boil it right, or we should have taken the root with the vine, or we *shouldn't* have."

"Are you in any discomfort?" Shona asked. "I can treat you if you want. The serum of the carti—"

Horne waved away her concern. "I've just got a few achy bones. Put it down to old age. In the beginning, there was too much to do to get the colony started. We wasted a ton of time arguing for continued funding, foisting off newshounds who wanted this whole thing to be a media extravaganza instead of an anthropological experiment, and just plain surviving from day to day. Now we're established, I guess I have time to sit back and enjoy my arthritis."

"But a calcite-dissolver for the residue . . ."

"Let be," Horne said, with finality. "I'm fifty-five. My dad made it to eighty-nine, and he was in the space service." Shona privately thought he looked much older. His forehead was deeply lined, and wrinkles rimmed his thin-lipped mouth. Hard work and responsibility had anticipated the calendar by some ten years or more. "Well, how about a tour? I can show you the test kitchens. You won't believe the terrific fruits and nuts abounding on this planet. Why, within an acre I can show you sixty species of luscious edibles that would make you swear off anything else you've ever eaten."

"Ching-ching," Gershom whispered to Shona as Horne stumbled downhill toward a corrugated-wall warehouse. "Governor," he said aloud, "I suppose you have a regular transport line shipping supplies of your produce off-planet."

"And you'd be right to so suppose," Horne said over his shoulder. "We use InterStar. Nice folks, supply all the main systems on their routes. Why—? Oh, that's right," he noted shrewdly, "you're a trader, too. Well, I always feel there's enough room in this galaxy for everybody, Gerald . . ."

"Gershom," Gershom corrected him.

". . . so maybe we can work something out. Say," Horne said, stopping in mid-path before a residential hut, "we're going to a working warehouse. Not too interesting, or too safe for the little one. Would you like to leave him with a minder for a minute? A nice, older couple. Mr. and Dr. Oktari. He's a nutritionist, a good one. She's a par-foo-mee-yer, and she's done us proud. Folks," he said, when a dark-skinned man and woman answered his knock, "this is Dr. Shona Taylor and her husband, Captain Gershom Taylor. I'm giving her a little tour of the place. Can you spare a few minutes to look after this young man— What's your name, son?"

"Ahesssh," the baby muttered into Shona's tunic front, suddenly shy.

"Alex," his mother corrected, over his head. "He's two years old."

"Well, he's a sweet thing," the woman said, holding out her arms for him. The baby looked up at her, eyes wide. Shona could tell at once he liked her kind face. Without any fuss, he put his arms around her neck and tilted his weight off Shona's hip. Hastily, the other woman gathered him up. "My, what a big boy you are." The woman glanced up at the man, and they shared a sweet, poignant look. Perhaps remembering their own first child, probably all grown up by now, Shona thought, noticing the copious scattering of white in the woman's dark cloud of hair and the man's bald pate.

"He'll be fine with us," Mr. Oktari said, patting his wife's shoulder. "You enjoy your tour. I have some toys to play with, Alex. Would you like to see them?"

"Yah." The boy, eyes shining, had already forgotten the existence of his parents. Grinning, Shona turned and followed Horne away from the hut.

"That's your mommy?" the man asked.

"Ya," Alex said, nodding. "Mommy."

"And you have a daddy, too?"

"Four." Alex helpfully displayed four fingers.

"You're not four years old," Dr. Oktari teased. "Your mommy said you're only two."

"Four. Four daddies."

When Shona returned from her tour of the inspection and refrigeration facility, the Oktaris eyed her with new respect.

"Has he been a handful?" she asked, retrieving the toddler, who was reaching for a length of corkscrewed plastic tubing that dangled from a hook in the ceiling.

The man hesitated. "Nothing I'm sure you couldn't manage," he finally said, exchanging an enigmatic look with his wife.

Horne led the way up the path. "What do you think of our wonderworks factory?" he asked.

"Very impressive," Shona said. "I liked the variety of storage facilities you have behind the test kitchens: ambient temperature, refrigerated, and frozen. Such a sophisticated setup."

"The flash freezer was an expensive investment, but it's paying off. We lose lots fewer marginal-life products when we can hand them off to the shipper in coldpacks."

Gershom and the others were nodding knowingly. "It'll be a pleasure to do business with you, sir," Kai said.

"I'll see what I've got, seeing as how you're right here, right now. How long are you planning to stay?"

"No more than a few days," Shona said, with open regret. "Time enough to meet people, take my dog and cat for a good walk, and say goodbye to Chirwl."

"Is it true what they said in that video: you're in environmental medicine?" Shona nodded. "Then you should drop in on Dr. Volk and tour her facilities. She might spare a fellow scientist more than just the time of day, which is all she gives me. I'll give her a call, if you want."

"What project are they working on?" Shona asked, remembering the old man and his keepers.

"I don't exactly know. My guess is that she and her people are working on a treatment for senile dementia. They've got a couple of sorry specimens living over there. I feel bad every time I see 'em, and hope what's wrong with them doesn't happen to me when I get old. I have to tell you, we don't mix much. Volk and her people aren't exactly unfriendly, more like standoffish."

"More your subject than mine," Gershom said, lifting his eyebrows toward his wife. "Mr. Horne, what about if you and I have a little chat about your export situation?"

"Fine, fine!" Horne said genially. "How'd you like to try some of our local brew? Non-export, strictly for internal use, if you'll pardon the bad joke. Come on, gentlemen. Just up there, Shona. I'll call and tell her you're coming."

Dr. Volk turned out to be the dark-haired woman Shona had seen from the governor's doorstep. She glanced at Shona and the ottles as they edged into the crowded hut at the top of the row.

"Yes?" She didn't stop to shake hands or make eye contact with them, but carried on hurrying around the lab unit, picking up one vial, then another, scrutinizing the labels, then discard-

ing each with a discontented expression. Shona thought she
didn't know exactly what she was looking for.

"Dr. Volk, my name is Shona Taylor. I'm a doctor, specializing in biomedical research in environmental illness. Governor Horne thought you might be willing to give me a short tour
of your research facilities."

"No tours," Volk said tightly, scattering disks with a distracted hand. "This isn't a tourist attraction. Our research is
confidential. I'm very busy, Dr. Taylor. If you don't mind? I've
got an emergency to deal with." She looked distractedly
through another rack, then pushed it away, all the time looking
up toward one wall of the hut as if she could see through it.

"Can I help?" Shona asked, immediately concerned. "Perhaps another pair of hands . . . ?"

"Environmental?" Volk appeared to be hearing Shona's
words at last. She looked up, green eyes flashing. "We have a
woman who is in deep anaphylactic shock. Do you know how
to treat that?"

"I can. It depends on what caused it," Shona said. Without
waiting, Volk scooped up an armful of vials and trotted toward
the door. Shooting an apologetic glance at the ottles, Shona
followed.

They passed the open doors of the other huts. Inside the first
few Shona glimpsed personal possessions and furniture. The
next ones contained lab equipment and numerous small computers, their drives chuckling away to themselves. She tried to
guess what the subject of their research was, but couldn't. One
lab setup looked much like another, from galaxy's start to
galaxy's end. Volk shouldered past the two tall men in lab coats
who were guarding the door of the last hut. With an apologetic
glance, Shona squeezed in behind her.

The small hut was divided by curtains into individual
dormitories leading off a narrow corridor of waving cloth. Volk
headed straight for the last room in line and swept the curtain
aside, revealing an elderly woman writhing on a camp bed. Her
skin was like wrinkled, yellowing tissue paper, and her teeth
were gritted. The teeth themselves were in surprisingly good
shape, but one was missing on the side, the gum puckering
around it like an empty wrapper. She was pale, and Shona
could see how shallowly she was breathing. Her lips puffed

painfully in and out. Shona hurried to kneel by her side, and picked up one of the bony wrists.

The pulse beat weakly. Shona pried up an eyelid to look at the pupil. "She's in shock. What bit her? How long ago did it happen?"

"About twenty minutes ago now," said a man with brown hair. He tossed back his long forelock in a gesture that reminded Shona of Gershom. "We were out in the forest. I didn't pay any special attention until Zeura collapsed; then I think I concentrated more on getting her back home. She's not heavy, but she was dead limp. I don't know what bug it was. Should I have chased it down instead?"

"No, you did the right thing." Shona reassured him. "Have you given her a stimulant?"

"We've given her epinephrine," said a small woman, whose short brown hair was mixed with gray strands.

"That usually does it in case of anaphylaxis, but you should have seen improvement already. Perhaps she's allergic to it," Shona said. "Can someone show me her records?"

"Records?" asked the small woman blankly.

"Yes! You know, you should have called for the nurses in the main complex. They're used to treating bites from the indigenous arthropodia." One of the men started to reply, then changed his mind. The woman on the bed groaned. Shona counted her pulse. It was thready. "Where are her records?"

Instead of dashing to the computer terminal attached to the wall, the scientists standing around behind her shifted uncomfortably and exchanged worried looks.

"I have to check it," Shona insisted. "If I give her something else, and she's allergic to that, it can kill her! Please! Time is limited."

Almost reluctantly, one of the men stepped to the terminal and entered a few words. He inserted the receiving end of a clipboard into the light-transfer port, then brought the unit to Shona. She read the details under "Larch, Zeura," and frowned. "This isn't very complete."

"It's all we have," said a dark man whose name tag said "Morganstern."

"Well, look here, there aren't any dates on it, let alone information on sensitivities or previous attacks. How old is she?" Shona shook the patient. "How old are you?" she shouted, trying to raise any kind of reaction.

The old woman focused wrinkle-ringed eyes on Shona, blank and glassy. Shona repeated her question, loudly and distinctly. Volk stepped up beside her. Larch's expression changed from blank and glassy to alarmed. She tilted her head back to Shona.

"None o' yer business how old I am." Her lip puffed out over the gap where the tooth was missing. "Askin' queschns like that!" Her eyes went blank again. Her pulse hadn't improved, but there were small spots of red in her cheeks.

"Poor thing," Volk said in a hoarse whisper. "It might be that at her age she can't remember how old she is. She was keeping her records herself. I didn't realize how spotty they were."

Shona gave her a curious look, then turned back to her patient. Such neglect of personal documents wasn't unheard of in the cases of elderly people, nor of members of a scientific colony, as witness her friends on Erebus, who had more important things to think about than noting down their last immunizations. She did think it was bad in a research project that subjects in the study were in charge of their own data, particularly in one that obviously studied the decline of the mental processes. It should have been the duty of one of the scientists to keep track. It *was* strange that the community didn't have more complete records on their master file.

"Is there an IV kit?" Shona asked.

"Saline? Glucose?" The woman with brown hair rummaged in a cupboard.

"Glucose is better," Shona said, uncoiling the tubing the woman handed her, and accepting a bottle. "I want to increase her blood volume. It should help." She hooked the bottle onto a metal hanger, and set the valve to a rapid drip. The old woman stopped struggling and lay still when Shona held her hand to keep her from pulling the needle out. In a very short time her skin became moister, and her breathing relaxed. Soon, she fell asleep, her lips parted. Shona counted her respiration, and was pleased to note that it was normal. She stayed by her patient's side until she was confident the woman was out of danger.

"Thank you," Volk said, letting out a long exhalation. "Sorry I was so snappish." The others murmured quiet thanks.

"I understand how emergencies affect people," Shona said kindly. Everyone seemed grateful for her forgiveness. "How long have you been here on Poxt?" she asked, just to pass the time while taking her patient's pulse again.

"Two years, seven months," Volk said, evidently deciding some facts about their study weren't classified.

"This is quite an installation. Yours must be an important project. Where are you getting funding?" Shona asked, with the air of someone who's shared the burden of applying for grants. Instead of being forthcoming in the way of one scientist to another, Volk stiffened.

"We're engaged in some work for an underwriting entity," she said obliquely. "I told you, our research is confidential. I'm sorry."

"I apologize," Shona said at once, rising to her feet. "I shouldn't be pressing you. I've done work under classified conditions. It's a strain, I know."

Volk unbent just a trifle. "I appreciate that. Come along. I can at least show you the facilities on your way out."

The array of equipment the LabCor team had at their disposal was impressive. Shona stopped for a moment to stare at the spectrographic computer, which was eight years newer and several grades of quality above the one she had in her own small lab. She made a mental note to price one when things started to pick up again. All the other appointments were similarly new and expensive. Volk was polite in letting her examine the workrooms, but Shona could tell she was impatient to have the unwelcome visitor on her way.

"Very nice," she said. "I'm envious. Well, thank you for showing me around."

"It's my pleasure," Volk said, sounding human for the first time. "Are you on Poxt for a while?"

"No, I wish we could stay. This is a wonderful place, isn't it? We're here to drop off the ottle I've been hosting for seven years. Chirwl is the larger of the two waiting in your office. I hope we'll be able to come back some day when we have more time to look around."

Volk nodded. "We've been so busy, I sometimes forget what the outside world looks like, and what manners used to be. Sorry about the bitchiness."

"I understand," Shona said. "I'm glad I could be of help."

"Another time, perhaps, I can be more obliging."

As they neared Volk's office, an old, old man staggered out of the jungle and bleated incoherently at Volk. His slack jaws were streaked with saliva, and his gummy eyes focused imperfectly on Shona. She felt a surge of pity, thinking he must be another one of the subjects, suffering from an advanced kind of senile dementia. He veered away from Volk, and babbled in a high-pitched voice at Shona.

"I'm Dennison," he said, urgently. "Get help, *please!*"

Volk shouldered him away, and grabbed Shona by the arm to hurry her off. The man shouted after them.

"Poor creature," Shona said.

"He's old," Volk said briefly. She showed no sympathy, so evident earlier with the old woman, but instead evinced a fierce satisfaction. Curious, but not atypical of the scientific mind that occasionally forgot it was dealing with human beings. Perhaps this man was the perfect specimen for their studies, and Volk took pride in finding a textbook example. Shona respected the mind's ability to focus, but shivered at the cold-bloodedness such concentration required. Or perhaps the old man had offended Volk in some way. The satisfaction seemed personal. Shona opened her mouth to ask, then closed it. Volk didn't strike her as the type to share confidences. Or maybe, Shona thought ruefully as she walked down the hill, Volk had seen Susan's video about their adventures, and wondered if she'd been having a cosy chat with a mass-murderer.

"Sure, we saw the show," Governor Horne said when Shona asked him about it. "Told you. A good yarn, but you can't tell a thing from those videos, they fictionalize so much. Whole thing could've been made up except for the names."

"Well, let me assure you we were the injured parties in that case," Gershom said. "Shona had nothing to do with those people dying."

"Sounded like the opposite to me," Horne said, waving away Gershom's concerns. "But don't ask me; could have been a good script. Still, I'm always inclined to think the best of people. You'd tell me if it was important. Well, if you folks aren't busy at suppertime, come on back. There's always room at the community table. We can talk about specifics of our deal then."

"What did you think?" Shona asked, as they made their way back through the forest toward the ottle center-place.

"He's liberal with his beer," Gershom said with a wry grin. "And his promises."

"It's good beer, too," Ivo said, patting his belly.

"I think we can do business. Horne's no fool. He knows to the last iota how much they can expand here without hurting the natural character of the planet, and they're at less than ten per cent capacity. He's right, too, in saying there's room for us." Gershom had a bounce in his step Shona hadn't seen since before the refit of the *Sibyl* began. "Every year they show a greater profit, get in a few more people. They're expanding slowly."

"What will we be carrying?"

"Perfumes, pharmaceuticals, raw materials for handcrafts, fish hides—the ottle bedpouches are made of cured fish-skin—tea, fruit, fresh and dried, natural dyes, seeds, maybe a few minerals." Kai ticked off the possibilities on his fingertips, his usual dourness gone. "Gershom gave him a diagram and particulars of the *Sibyl*'s holds, with special emphasis on climate control, and we all suggested we would be the best candidate for small, valuable cargoes. I think he was impressed."

"InterStar can't give them the kind of individual service we can," Gershom finished smugly. Shona could see his mind was already full of plans. She squeezed his arm.

"I'm so happy," she said.

"We can get back to normal pretty quickly, with a high-value customer like this," Gershom pointed out. "And it means that we won't lose touch with you, Chirwl."

"That also makes me happy," the ottle said, bounding forward swiftly to keep pace with the human's long stride. "For I have gone to much care to build our friendship. I do not wish it to end."

"Well, looks like it won't," Kai assured him. "You could see a lot of us every year."

At that thought, Shona felt a bound of good spirits. She squeezed Alex, who emitted a fat, happy chuckle.

"You need a change and a nap, young man," she told the toddler. "How is it you're staying awake so well?"

"Too much stimulation. Heads down," Gershom said, with resignation, as they approached the arcade of low-hanging trees. He stepped aside to let Shona and the ottles go first.

As they started down the trail, Chirwl and Wla suddenly bolted ahead of the group, disappearing under the overhang.

"What's wrong?" Ivo asked.

"No idea," Shona said.

Putting up a hand to shield Alex's face from twigs, she ducked her head to run after the ottles. Up ahead she heard their voices, then the rattling voice of an elder ottle. Thio had been waiting for them.

"You are seeming concerned," Chirwl said to hir, as Shona arrived.

"I have succeeded in making Shnomri emerge from the pouch," Thio said. "Come at immediate." The senior ottle turned in hir length and loped toward the end of the tunnel.

"What is the occurrence?" Chirwl asked, hurrying alongside. Shona trotted with them, leaving Gershom and the others behind.

"What's wrong?" she asked. Wla chittered in her own language at Thio, but the elder ottle paid no attention to questions.

"*Most* unprecedented," was all Thio would say.

In the clearing, hundreds of ottles were gathered, all talking at the tops of their lungs. Squeaking, chittering, and babbling burst upon Shona's ears like a peal of thunder. The milling crowd centered around the tree bole where Thio had been arguing. Lani stood with them, staring into their midst. When Chirwl appeared, the others made way for him, bounding up to continue their argument in the channeled bark of trees or under clumps of huge-leaf bushes.

The center of attention was an elderly ottle with a graying muzzle and gray streaks and patches throughout hir fur. As Chirwl caught sight of hir, he skidded to a halt and let out a shrill whistle. Shnomri met his gaze, then turned hir head away, trembling slightly with age. Wla hurried between Chirwl and Thio to nuzzle the newcomer frantically. Shona knelt down beside hir and smiled.

"How do you do? I'm Chirwl's friend, Shona. You didn't tell me Shnomri was so much older than you, Chirwl," she said, turning to him. He stared unblinkingly at his co-mate.

"This one is not," he said, in a shocked voice. "We are of the same birth year exactly!"

·5·

"I *know* who she is," Morganstern exploded, pacing up and down Volk's hut. "What I want to know is, what is she doing here?"

"Part of our funding comes from GLC," Volk said with a shrug. She sat in her canvas chair as if it were a throne, with her hands laid flat on the arms. "She works for them; you saw that tri-dee broadcast. Perhaps they sent her to look over the project."

"Then what about all those ingenuous questions about what we're doing?" Hampton asked. He was propped up against the door frame, staring at nothing with a speculative squint. "I don't think she had a clue."

"Testing us?" Volk suggested. "Making certain we're keeping the details classified as per our contract?"

"I don't think she knows about the contract," said Hampton. "She and her husband are here on their trading ship. She said they were returning an ottle to the homeworld. It's probably blind chance that she turned up here now."

"Blind chance?" Morganstern demanded, disbelievingly. He raked up his hair with both hands, leaving it in black and sliver spikes. His eyes were haunted. "The Angel of Death?"

"Come on, she wasn't the one who deserved the name; *he* was," Hampton said obliquely. "Remember?"

"But she was there when they all died!"

"Stop it," said Volk wearily. "She saved Larch's life. She's obviously not here to poison us. We're doing a fine job of that ourselves."

Morganstern continued to pace up and down the small hut.

Volk watched him for a while, then shaded her eyes to shut out the sight.

"Calm down," she said, massaging the bridge of her nose with thumb and forefinger, trying to rub out the knot of tension that was giving her a headache. "Your blood pressure will shoot up if you keep letting the stress build. That could be harmful. Sit down. Meditate. Keep your body rhythms slow and steady."

"I can't. And I don't see how you can be so calm."

Volk looked up at him. "Think of the eternal vision, Lionel," she said in a softer voice, willing him to calm down. "This is only a temporary setback. One day, one event out of the rest of your life." She tried to make it sound as if she believed it, too. Morganstern paused for a moment, shook his head to break the spell, and resumed pacing. Hampton shrugged.

"Dennison must have managed to get word out, that's all," he said.

"Impossible! The computer shows a log of every message transmitted. He hasn't touched it since . . . since . . ." Morganstern was unable to get the words out. Volk saw he was still haunted by what he had done at her command. They'd all had to watch Dennison's swift decline, and wondered if it would happen like that to them when the time came.

"Well, you can't have it both ways," Hampton said, unimpressed with Morganstern's remorse. "Either he did, and that's why she's here, or it's a coincidence."

Volk nodded sharply.

"Then it's blind chance—or so it seems. Perhaps she's working for one of the competition. The Corporation would love to scoop LabCor's research, and there go our grants. Any of the smaller concerns like Eternalife would love to pick up right where we've left off." She gave a short, bitter laugh. "I'd like to hand it to them, and see what they'd do when *this* happens to them." She held out her hands. Was the flesh thinner than the day before? Was the skin drier? She couldn't tell.

"What shall we do?" Hampton asked quietly. Volk was glad for the distraction. She dropped her hands to the chair arms and resolutely lifted her eyes to those of her associate.

"Keep a low profile, and don't answer any questions. I can check the ottle connection quite easily with the governor."

"You're going to go see him?" Morganstern asked. He spun on his heel and searched her face.

"Yes," said Volk, rising with a sigh. In the mirror that morning she had seen more gray roots in her black hair. A little dye, and no evidence that anything was wrong would remain. If Horne saw lines starting around her mouth and eyes, he'd put it down to the strain of her job. "Fortunately, the governor is not an observant man."

"He'd have to be stupid as well as blind," Hampton said. For the first time Volk noticed that gray was starting in the roots of his thick brown hair. "By the benchmarks, we're aging at more than five times normal. He was affected, too, you know."

"How ironic!" Volk said, her thoughts forcing a pained smile to her lips.

"What's so funny?" Morganstern asked.

"It's just ironic that this should happen to *us*."

Hampton smiled flatly. "Who else would be interested in this kind of research? Certainly not the ephemerals."

"Spoken like a true Foreverite," Volk said. "I'll see Horne now."

Three years before, representatives from LabCor had come to the enclave known as Forever to interview senior scientists, with an eye to giving one of them the position of chief researcher in a project they had in mind. Raden Miles, director of research at Forever, had declined to be interviewed, refusing to sign the confidentiality agreement LabCor insisted upon before they discussed specifics. Instead, he had listened to what they *would* say, then recommended that Dr. Missa Volk, his assistant director, speak with them. She had the requisite background, and the will to carry through difficult projects, but, Raden pointed out to her, she should not find this project onerous.

Details that LabCor's executives let slip during the very first conversation had Missa immediately reaching for the thumb-print platen. LabCor wanted her to develop a process, potion, or scientific system for keeping a human being young for as long as he or she lived. Extensive funding would be provided. She could pick her own staff. It was the dream offer for anyone involved in Forever. She was so excited she almost laughed out loud when they laid out the details of their proposal. Pay her? She'd pay *them* for the opportunity to create a genuine catholicon. It was what members of Forever had been striving toward for over two centuries. She firmly believed the goal was achievable, a belief she shared with her handpicked staff. They already held the deep commitment to finding the key to unlock the door of eternal life. But what was the use of living forever if one had to deal with perpetual old age?

The image in her mirror had shifted over the last weeks from hers to her mother's, and most recently was beginning to slide toward her grandmother's. Missa was frightened of old age and death, especially when eternal youth seemed so near to her grasp, but it looked as though that was her fate if they couldn't reverse the mistake they had made.

Dealing with Dennison had bought them time, but how much longer did they have until a representative or spy from LabCor came to look things over and discovered what was happening? They could solve the problem and get back on track, if this stupid, stupid mistake did not kill them first—or their funding wasn't cut off by the accidental interference of a well-known busybody and whistle-blower.

"Now, now, now, now!" DeWitt Horne shouted, gesturing with his hands to hold down the uproar. "Not everybody at once. Shona," he said, pointing at her. "You tell me what's wrong. Then everybody give me details"—he raised his voice over the ensuing babble—"one at a time!"

"What's going on here?" Dr. Volk demanded.

"Listen and you'll find out! Shona! Everyone, can it!"

The crowd that was gathered around the governor's hut quieted slightly.

"As you know, we arrived here only today, returning Chirwl to his homeworld. One of his co-mates, Shnomri, refused to come out of hir pouch to meet him." She saw recognition of the name on some of the faces. "We heard that Shnomri hadn't appeared in public in some time. In fact, Governor Horne commented on that himself, that he hadn't seen hir lately." She pulled her backpack around, and displayed the graying head of the ottle inside. "This is why!"

There was a collective gasp. Ashamed to be under the scrutiny of the crowd, the ottle bowed hir gray head and refused to look at anyone. Most of the faces were blank with shock.

"I'm not seeing that," one of the men said. "It's not possible."

"Shnomri has become old," Chirwl said emphatically. "This is not a logical growth."

"Are you sure that this isn't natural, that it isn't something that happens to ottles?" asked Dr. Oktari.

"Certainly not," Shona said. Gershom, standing beside her with his arms folded, shook his head emphatically from side to side. "Chirwl is precisely the same age as Shnomri, and look at him. His fur is still all dark, and his muscles are strong. In fact he was shocked flat to see hir. I've examined Shnomri, and found hir muscles are slightly atrophied."

"So this ottle has fallen ill?" Dr. Volk said, from outside the crush. "I'm sorry to hear that, but why is it a subject for discussion?"

"Because it has not happened before humans came to this planet," Chlari burst out sourly. "This is not an illness in nature. Others I see now with new eyes have grown old early, too. Varral, come forward."

"I stand here," a squeaky voice said resolutely. "My legs are stiffer than once were."

The crowed turned to look. The ottle had not advanced in age as much as Shnomri, but he had gray streaks in his fur, and the way he stood made him appear feeble.

"He's not the only one," Shona said. "Once Shnomri came out, several others said they've noticed signs of age, too."

Several ottles called out, describing their own symptoms. The humans, bewildered and concerned, looked from one to another, trying to understand the babble of ottle lingo and Standard. Shona's voice became lost in the din, and she shut her mouth to wait.

"All right, quiet!" Horne bellowed.

In the ensuing silence Chlari continued his tirade. "My think is that since Shnomri spent most time with humans, therefore that ottle is most strongly affected by contact. Others, who have less contact, are less older."

"That's a pretty quick decision," Horne said defensively, "based on one good look."

"I have not obstacles in my mind to block the truth," Chlari said forthrightly. "What I see, is. Humans have caused this."

"If humans hurt ottles, they must leave," one of the older ottles said at once.

Now the human settlers began to protest. Horne silenced them. "Come on, people, let's not be alarmists. We have to handle this like grownups."

"Well, the question is, if this is an illness the humans gave to the ottles, is there anyone in the human settlement who's started to age prematurely?" Shona asked. "With the similarities in biology, it would be logical to wonder if the phenomenon goes both ways."

"Well? Anybody?" Horne demanded.

"*I'm* graying," a woman said, coming forward. "I've been noticing it for months now. I . . . my reflection looks like my father's sister. It's too soon. I mean, I'm too young."

"Nobody thinks they're old enough to look middle-aged," one man said with a supercilious smirk, but Shona thought he must be in his early twenties. No sign of unnatural aging there.

"You're ridiculous," a short plump man snapped at the young man. "Look at the roots of my hair. It's almost all coming in gray. And I'm stiff in the mornings. How about that? Did the ottles cause it?"

"It's all in your minds," Volk said, her arms crossed, unconcerned. "You're creating a harmful mass fantasy that can threaten your own future well-being. Your mind can affect your body. You've all been under strain over the years. What surprise is there in seeing lines or gray hairs?"

At her calm voice some of the settlers looked at each other or stared at the ground sheepishly.

"Maybe you're right," said a blond woman. Shona guessed her to be about forty. "I . . . well, the body starts to change all by itself, doesn't it?"

"No! Come on, Marleen," a man said suddenly to the woman beside him. "Show them." The woman looked at the crowd, then dropped her eyes to avoid meeting any of theirs.

"This is very embarrassing, Steff," she said, her lower lip quivering. "All right." Abruptly making her decision, she grabbed Shona's hand and pulled her toward one of the huts. Shona opened the door. There was a small cry of surprise from within, and scrabbling noises. Shona peered into the dim interior. A figure, clutching sheets to its face, stood in the corner, frightened eyes fixed on Shona.

"I'm not going to hurt you," she said gently. She approached the figure, found it stood less than half her height, and put out a hand to lower the cloth. The face behind it was horrible. It was human, but so strange, like a mask. There were deep furrows in the ashy cheeks and forehead, and it bore a straggly beard. Shona noticed then that the fine hair was mostly gray and had receded above both temples nearly to the crown of the head. Between the cracked lips its teeth were small, and several were missing. Tears began to leak out of the matte-blue, marblelike eyes, and the being reached for the woman who knelt beside him. She settled the balding head on her shoulder and wrapped her arms around the shaking body, crooning softly.

"How old is he?" Shona asked, swallowing hard.

"Seven." Marleen burst into tears herself. "When he started to . . . to change, he didn't want to be seen by the other children. They can be so cruel, you know. He's been hiding in here, getting worse every day. I've been ashamed to ask for help. But now I know it isn't just him. Help us." She extended a hand to Shona. The ancient child let out a whimper of protest, and Marleen wrapped him up again.

"Poor one," Shnomri whispered from Shona's back.

Shona rocked back on her heels. "I've never seen anything like this in my life. Has he been tested for progeria?" Marleen shook her head.

"No, but I read up about it. That would have started when he was a baby, and he's been normal until, well, I don't know." Marleen glanced at the door. "Do I have to bring him out? He doesn't want to be seen."

"No," Shona said, rising. "Keep him here." She patted the boy-man tenderly on the back, and went out to rejoin the crowd. It was beginning to polarize into two groups, humans and ottles, and that worried her. She deliberately went to stand with the ottles, and described what she had just seen.

"Could it be some kind of culture shock?" a thin man asked. His face was lined and his temples white, but he must have considered them normal, because he hadn't complained. "We've passed germs back and forth through simple contact. Could something have mutated?"

"After so many years?" Dr. Oktari asked.

"That's not possible," Shona said at once. "The cause has to be something specifically here and now, on Poxt, and oh, six or eight months ago."

"Why then?" Horne asked.

"The length of everyone's white roots, for one thing," Shona said. "Hair grows approximately one centimeter every six months. It varies according to climate and personal biology, of course, but that's a guess. Friends, I've had Chirwl with me for several years. Neither he nor I, nor anyone in my family, have shown any signs of unusual aging, and yet this phenomenon is widespread in Chirwl's center-place. They've never had anything like this before, either. It worries me enough that I've sent my children into isolation in our shuttle and hope they weren't exposed to whatever's causing this. They'll stay there until we're ready to leave."

They hadn't gone without protest, Shona reflected. Lani had complained she didn't want to leave the beautiful forest, and Alex was upset that his mother was upset, and didn't want to be separated from her until she cheered up. It had been hard to pin on a smile when she left him in Lani's care, but she had done it.

"And this my co-mate has grown old, and we are of the same age," Chirwl said. "See me, see my fur. See Shnomri's."

"No doubt about it," Horne said. "Something's happened to hir."

"It is something of humans," Chlari insisted. "Your presence has caused this. It is the potential that to kill all of us."

Volk glared at him. "Don't be a fool," she said. "Mutations can come in any generation. In any species," she added, glaring at Marleen's husband, who stared at her, dumbfounded.

"If humans are harmful to ottles, they must go," Chlari said, warming to his topic. "That was the agreement of fifteen times back, and we will hold to that with all force." There was another general outcry.

"Now, now, friends, please!" Horne said, alarmed. "Let's not talk drastic measures here. Let's solve this problem."

"If there *is* a problem," Volk said. "I say it's spontaneous mutation in two cases, and nothing but genetics or stress in the others."

"I say it's a germ," the thin man said again.

"What, a shared virus mutation?" Shona asked, paths of

exploration beginning to take shape in her mind. "Pathogenic bacteria?" She turned to Volk.

"You're the environmentalist, you figure it out," Volk said, refusing to help her. "I am not concerned in this matter. None of my people have been affected. I think it's an isolated phenomenon, and you're all getting overexcited."

"This is terrible," said a big man with huge, restless hands and a red, bony face. Shona recognized him from the factory. "This means we can't export anything off-planet until we're sure it's not carrying the—whatever made this happen to us."

"That's less difficult," Shona said. "A disease or a syndrome has a cause. It leaves footprints, a protein or a toxin or a cause we can find. Analysis, chemical or spectro-comparisons of each product, should tell you if there's anything in there that shouldn't be."

The man looked grim. "Can we trust batch-testing?"

"We'll have to, or we're shut down," another worker, a woman, said.

"We have initial chemical analyses of everything, back from year one," Horne said. "They're all in the computer. If a good representative sample checks, then we're still in business."

Dr. Oktari shook her head. "But what about the spacers who carry our goods? We ought to hold back until we know we're not exporting the virus from person to person."

"Do you think the GG is going to let us ship to other destinations, in the condition we're in?" the stout man asked.

"Wait a moment," Volk said hastily. "We can't send the Galactic Government a message of panic based on assumptions. They'll shut down the colony at once."

"Well!" exclaimed Chlari. "If you have caused this, you must go away before all ottles age and die before their times."

"I tire," Shnomri said in Shona's ear. "Take me to my place." Shona nodded and turned to Horne.

"I'll be right back. Shnomri wants to go back to hir tree."

"Where that ottle goes, I come along," Chirwl said at once.

"And I as well," Wla chimed in.

Horne watched them go, still shaking his head. He glanced down at Volk, who had come up to stand beside him. "What do you know? Right under our noses and we've been going on like there's nothing wrong! Doctor, have you noticed anything like that up in your camp?"

"Certainly not. Governor, I wanted to warn you about that woman," Missa said. "You can't believe anything she tells you. She was involved in a series of heinous mass-murders."

Horne snorted in disbelief. "Then how do you explain Shnomri? I've known hir for twelve years!"

"It doesn't mean a thing," she said, shaking her head. Horne, as usual, was being obtuse. He'd gotten an idea into his thick head, and now wouldn't let go of it for anything. "And if you mean that poor freak in the hut, Bobby Orthon, there's evidence in human culture of unusually rapid aging. In the twentieth and twenty-first centuries *alone* several children died of old age before nine years."

"None of *us* are children, Doc, and some of us have mighty stiff bones, too."

"Her judgment is suspect. I simply wanted to warn you."

Shona returned along the path from the crop fields, and Volk watched her stump up the hill toward them. A tall man, her husband or mate by his protective attitude, strode down to join her, and escorted her the rest of the way up the slope. Volk was worried. Was that woman smart enough to figure out what had been going on in the colony? Could she foment an inquiry? Volk cringed at the thought of destroying the remaining nanomites. It might be another three years before they could create more with the same properties. While it might be a good idea to start over entirely on the minute engines, it was more likely they could come up with a stronger controller for their properties. There weren't many left to find; almost all had been used on Dennison. Concealing their research would be less difficult, since no one down here including Citizen Nosy Parker had the qualifications to understand it.

"I've been concentrating so hard on the people who've been affected by the phenomenon, I never asked how many haven't been," Shona said.

"Oh, lots," Horne said. "Me, for one." Volk almost laughed.

"Can you pin it down further than that?" Shona asked, looking around at the crowd of humans and ottles. "I think we've seen perhaps the two worst cases. Everyone else was more lightly affected. What do all the victims have in common, if anything? The same goes for the non-victims. What were

they exposed to? Is the parent virus or bacteria something a
settler brought with him or her from another planet? The vector
is important, too: how someone catches the aging virus, if it's
a virus." She turned to the thin man. "What was that you said
about culture shock? You could explore the possibilities of a
pathogenic organism that likes warm-blooded creatures. Have
any of your farm animals suffered? How about the local
wildlife?"

Volk snorted. Shona glanced around at the sound, but
ignored it. "And how would you handle it?" Missa asked.

"Well, I would start by inspecting the environment," Shona
said, facing her. "I'd investigate anything that's new since after
Chirwl left, and I'd want to go over the medical records of each
human in the colony, particularly those who've been affected,
to see if one of them brought it in from his or her point of
origin. That's where you should begin."

"Sounds like you're the very one for the job," Horne said,
looking pleased. "Dr. Taylor, will you undertake it?"

"Governor Horne, no!" Missa protested. Horne turned to
glare at her.

"Dr. Volk, put a sock in it. We have a problem here, and
you're pretending it doesn't exist. This little lady has got the
very background to put us right if anyone can, and it sounds
like she's got the smarts to go with it. How about it, Doctor?"

Shona looked up at Gershom, whose lips were set in a tight
line. He had wanted to go right off and start trading again. He
must understand that now she couldn't go off-planet with him.
Even if Chirwl wasn't involved, she could simply not walk
away from this situation. Her curiosity was aroused, but it was
also a concern of the heart. That little boy, so confused, so
unhappy, had touched her. She had to help solve this problem.

There was another concern: had the crew of the *Sibyl* already
been exposed to it? Shona considered the facts. If the syndrome
proceeded from casual contact no one was safe, not the
colonists, not the ottles, not the traders from InterStar nor the
visitors who came and went from this spotlit community, so it
must not be easily contagious.

Every day Gershom stayed here they lost money. The *Sibyl*
had to fly to earn, and it could mean the end of their traveling
days if Gershom didn't go. She'd understand if he felt he had

to leave her here. She had to stay. She tried to keep her thoughts out of her face, so as not to sway him unfairly.

At last Gershom opened his mouth. "What can I do to help?" Shona shot him a look of pure gratitude.

"This is *exactly* the reason why I married you," she said.

"I had wondered."

"You won't lose by it, folks," Horne said, watching the byplay between husband and wife. "Shona, all these people saw the video about your life. Fiction aside, we know your qualifications. I'm hiring you to look into this problem, and save our colony. This settlement is more than a place. It's a kind of dream humans have had. We don't want to lose it."

"We'll help in any way we can," said Marleen's husband.

Shona traded glances with Gershom. The prospect of a fee made him look a little more relieved.

"All right," she said. "I'll need my lab, and I'll want medical records from everyone in this colony."

"No problem," Horne said.

"I'm not participating any further in this hoax," Volk said. She turned away and marched up the hill to her hut. The door slid shut with a screech.

"Forget her," Horne said. "She's touchy. Come on in and use my console."

Several people followed Shona into the governor's hut, and crowded around in the large meeting room just outside his small office, offering suggestions through the open door. She tried to acknowledge everyone with a look or a nod, while at the same time going over the records. She set up search parameters, and got the program going. Eighty dossiers did not take that much time to process, and she began to run through the results. To her dismay, there were as many blank spots in the files as there had been on Larch's file in the LabCor compound. She called for the governor, who barged his way through the crowd to her side.

"They're kind of incomplete," Horne acknowledged when she pointed out the problems. "We've had computer crashes, and some of the data got dumped, back along. There's a few people, our tea detectives, who don't live year-round in the settlement. They're on the move out in the brush somewhere with a couple of ottles for company, looking for more medicinals, fruits, and teas. They keep track of themselves, and I guess they haven't downloaded in a couple of years. Also, you'll find the records for the babies are kinda empirical. We don't have a colony doctor, believe it or not. Have a couple of trained nurses and EMT's. We've had to ship maybe one serious case off-planet in the last fifteen years. That was about six months ago."

Shona nodded. "I don't see Dr. Volk's file here."

"I don't have her records," Horne said. "Like I said, they keep themselves to themselves."

"We need everyone's histories," Shona said, getting up from the console.

Volk wasn't alone when Shona confronted her in the cluttered lab. A dozen or so men and women stopped their animated discussion the moment Shona appeared in the doorway. At a signal from their boss, they filed silently out of the room. One man with brown hair, Hampton, stared at her as he left with an expression she could not comprehend.

"I've come for copies of your health records," Shona said.

"I told Horne I'm not participating in this shadow-chasing," Volk said, standing behind her desk with her fingertips braced on the top. The woman had regained her cool, impenetrable façade. "Now I am telling you. I am not sacrificing our privacy for your curiosity."

Shona didn't argue, but turned silently on her heel and went out the door. In a few moments she was back with the colony governor.

"I was afraid of this, Missa," Horne said, red-faced from having trotted up the hill. He strode right up to the desk and leveled a finger at the senior scientist's nose. "I order you to cooperate, or I'll send you and your whole bunch right off-planet."

"With a plague in the offing?" Volk said, smiling grimly, drawing her head away from his finger. "I think not, Governor. That's a threat you can't carry out."

Horne's ruddy face turned purple, but he controlled himself. "Then I'll get GG inspectors in here and shut you down," he said in flat tones. "Don't think I can't. Or won't."

Panic flared in Volk's eyes, and Shona felt sorry for her. "Our work is classified, confidential. My job depends on maintaining secrecy. If you bring in the inspectors, we'll lose our funding."

"Then cooperate." The easygoing mask of the governor dropped away like a discarded cloak to show a face of granite underneath. "It's easy. Just give me your datacubes, and we're in business."

Head high, Volk marched out of the office. In a few minutes, she was back.

"This is all I have," she said, handing him the datacubes.

"See how easy that was?" Horne asked cheerfully. Volk lowered herself into her chair with her eyes blazing. The governor put his arm around Shona and escorted her away.

Shona scanned the datacubes in the reader. "About what I suspected," she groaned, showing the screens to Horne. They're no better than yours."

"What's missing?"

"Oh, little things, but in this case important. Point of origin, planet of birth, birth date, and"—she scanned another—"this woman has no record of anywhere she's been, and her entire immunization record is missing. I can't track down anything without that information!"

Horne crossed his arms over his chest. "Where can we get this stuff?"

"The Central Records Office," Shona said at once. "Or any GG outpost. We can message them right away."

"No!" Horne exclaimed, as she started to bring up the communications program. "A message like that goes through too many hands. In one thing I agree with Dr. Volk. I don't want a lot of alarms going off until we have a handle on this thing ourselves. We report this at large, and we've got people coming out of our ears eighteen ways from Sunday. We'll get lost while a lot of bureaucrats decide on our fates. The ottles won't have to throw us off Poxt; our own people will do that to us. No, we need direct access to the files, tell as few people as possible."

"There's an outpost about fifteen days hard jumping from here," Gershom suggested. "Zedari Station. In fact we weren't all that far from it after our second jump coming to Poxt. They have a full library facility. I was through there about six years ago."

"Then you can find your way back?"

"Easily," Gershom said.

"This is a commission," Horne said, planting a forefinger on the desk. "As of this minute I'm hiring both of you to save my colony. I can't let what we've worked for slip away because of some elusive monster virus, or what-have-you." The finger rose and pointed at both of them in turn. "You, Gerald, go get the records. You, Shona, coordinate the investigation. My people will help you in any way they can. Stop this thing!"

·6·

By evening, Shona was exhausted. She had gone through every settler's dossier, and run a list of names and places of birth, where they were available. It was inconvenient that the system crashes had wiped out so much of the simple data she needed, but no one ever expected to have an epidemic.

Truthfully, there was little else she could do until Gershom could get files that were complete up until the date of arrival on Poxt. It was the previous residences and travel destinations she wanted to check. Also, she wanted comm numbers for the other ottle hosts, to see if any of them had experienced this strange, accelerated aging.

Gershom made calls while she was working on the files. He radioed the shuttle to explain the situation to Ivo and Kai. Shona glanced up from her console screen at the men's shocked exclamations. Ivo looked as if he were ready to throw up all the beer he'd consumed.

"It should be all right," Gershom said hastily. "I doubt we were exposed, but you can't be too careful. Where is Lani?"

"Putting Alex down for a nap," Kai said. "She was playing a game on the co-pilot's screen, but now she's inside sitting with him."

"She's bored," Ivo said. "Us, too. What do you want us to do?"

"Stay inside the shuttle. I'm calling Eblich to get Shona's lab ready to go down. As soon as he's finished, I'll call you back. Go get it, but limit contact. Don't let the kids into it. You all need to decontaminate before you go back into the ship."

"Right," Kai said. Shona ran another column of place names.

Three people had been on one vacation world all together. She checked the names: they were a family, and none of them had complained of aging. Absently she added Antari IV to her short list of "safe" planets.

Gershom broke the connection and called Eblich. The taciturn bookkeeper's facial expressions always told more than what he said. When Gershom mentioned the commission, a small gleam shone in Eblich's eyes. He promised to prep the lab and leave the way open for the other crewmen and the children to decontaminate before coming aboard. Then Gershom explained the rest of the story.

"Surely you weren't affected so soon," Eblich said, concerned. "Did you eat anything there?"

"No," Gershom said with regret, "and you can't believe the good smells coming out of everyone's kitchen. They asked us to dinner, you know. We don't dare touch it, and I'm starved."

"Bad luck," Eblich said laconically. "Can you eat nutri?" Shona heard that and shuddered.

"I suppose we'll have to," she said, stretching her fingers. "I'm hungry, too."

She begged Horne for the use of a lab burner and sterilized retorts. The governor was puzzled by the request until she explained quarantine and limit of contact, then gave her access to one of the small labs in the village. She and Gershom dined that evening reluctantly but resignedly on nutri chili. It wasn't bad, but the smells of fresh stew and hot fruit dessert from the community table upwind were devastating to their morale.

Chirwl brought his own meal and joined them while they ate their nutri chili on the doorstep of the lab hut. He came by himself, for which Shona was grateful. She liked Wla, but she wanted to talk to him alone.

"I'm sorry your homecoming had to be spoiled like this, Chirwl."

"Sorrow I also. Wla is as well as I remembered her, but Shnomri is bitter at seeing youth flee so unfairly. Hir temper has no padding around it at this time."

"That's a good description for what Shnomri must be going through," Shona said. "I hope that I can help."

"I to believe in you so others do also," Chirwl said confidently. "You will stay here, most welcome. I shall not miss you immediately this way."

"Me, too," Shona said, picking up the ottle and kissing the top of his head. "Saffie will be glad to see you."

"And I her," he said. "Cover yourself well tonight. Rain is expecting."

That night, the Taylors bedded down in the ottle centerplace, using a tent and other camping gear thrown out of the shuttle to them by Ivo. Shona used half a bottle of disinfectant on the interior and exterior of the tent, and held the panels up off the ground to dry. It was a shame to be so clinical about her preparations, but she knew she'd be a fool to ignore circumstances. She slid the flexible rods into their loops, and an oblong tent sprang into being.

Because of the ottle weather report, the Taylors went to some trouble to make certain the groundsheet and fly were thick enough to keep water from soaking through. While Gershom hammered in the corner stakes, Shona hung up the lamp and activated the gel heater in the floor of the tent against the night chill. A distant crash of thunder made her look up.

"Hurry up, woman!" Gershom said, dropping to his knees and squirming through the tent flap with the box of food and the bedrolls. "Here it comes." She wriggled in after him. He snaked out an arm and grabbed her, and she snuggled against him, listening to the wind in the woods.

The rain didn't begin immediately, but crept toward them through the jungle with a subtle whisper. Gradually, it hissed closer, and with a sizzle, began to patter on the roof of the tent. Gershom leaned forward, his eyes turned upward, and a smile broke over his face.

"It's restful," he said. "It's nice to listen to something without the constant hum of engine noise. Even with filtered earphones, you know it's always there."

"I like being planetside," Shona said. "Even under these circumstances. One day, wouldn't you like to have a little place dirtside, where we can stay once in a while? It doesn't have to be fancy—in fact, the less fussy it is the better."

"One day," Gershom promised. "When finances have eased up a little. Remember when we almost bought that country cottage on Alpha? I am so glad now that we didn't—it took every spare credit to fix up the ship, and we couldn't have gone another season without it."

"I know," Shona said, then fell silent to enjoy the sound of the rain. The single overhead light drew shadows under Gershom's eyebrow ridges, and threw his eyelashes into relief on his cheeks. She studied him for a moment, thinking that as well as she knew him, a change of light or mood could make him a stranger again. His eyes met hers and she realized he'd been studying her, too. He chuckled.

"Do you realize this is the first privacy, *real* privacy we've had in years?"

"Mmmm," Shona murmured, tilting her head back with her eyes closed, enjoying the sound of the rain and the sensation of being warmly enfolded. "I could get to like it, but I'm sure I'd miss the noise after a while."

"Oh, for the opportunity to find out!" Gershom said, with a little deprecating laugh. He was silent for a long time; then his arms tightened around her. "Shona, I want to apologize. I was an unbelievable bastard while the refit was under way. I'm sorry all of you had to put up with me, particularly you. I know you weren't to blame for our having to stay incommunicado all that time, but I was so miserable. My ship was down, my comm number had been changed a dozen times, we were running out of cash, and I was helpless to do anything but wait."

"I know how you felt," Shona said, looking up at him. "I felt like a trapped bear during the last four months of pregnancy. By the time Alex came, I wanted to rip him out with a hacksaw and forceps."

Gershom seemed surprised. "I would never have known it—you were so *happy*, we were wondering why men never get to be pregnant."

"You're welcome to have the next one," Shona offered. "They can do some incredible things with transplants."

"No, no," Gershom said, patting his flat belly, then turning his hand in the constricted space to tickle hers. "I like things the way they are." She squirmed, playfully batting at him, then captured his long hands in her small ones.

"You would. Gershom, I do so want another baby. As soon as this is behind us . . ." she trailed off hopefully.

"We can get out from under. Horne's inclined to be generous with his fees." Gershom was confident. "We're in the right place at the right time. He's throwing money at me like a drunken millionaire, but I won't take more than is fair. I won't cheat him. Your module comes down tomorrow, and you can get cracking with your side of the bargain. You find out what the age plague is, and I'll find out where it came from. I'll get the rest of the data you need."

"When will you leave?" Shona asked, feeling forlorn.

"No later than regional nightfall," Gershom said. "I'll be back in no time, sweetheart. You'll be too busy to know I'm gone." Shona doubted it, but wisely kept silent. "This . . . phenomenon is right in your special field of knowledge. You'll solve the problem and earn Horne's undying gratitude. Then, once we're on the way, more contracts, more deals, maybe a second ship, an exclusive contract for perfumes or pharmaceuticals—"

Shona giggled at the golden future he painted. "But seriously," she said, schooling her face, "it *could* happen to us. We've been exposed."

"Grow old along with me," Gershom said, reaching for her. "The best is yet to be."

Shona reached for the fastening of her shipsuit, then stopped. "But I don't have my birth control with me. It's my fertile cycle." She ducked her head apologetically. With a warm, indulgent smile, Gershom shook his head.

"Let's take our chances on the future. All of them." He took her hand and kissed the back of it, kissed the fingertips, upturned it, and kissed the palm. His free hand lingered on the closure of her suit, then started to undo it very slowly.

She looked into his warm, dark eyes, and smiled. She tilted her mouth up to his and felt his hands smooth their way up the muscles of her back. She wanted to tell him that he made her feel like purring, but she didn't want the long, sweet kiss to end.

Afterward, she lay on the smooth poplin of the bedroll, staring at the top of the tent, drifting in a sea of contentment. "Listen, it's still raining," she managed to say as sleep washed over her consciousness, pulling her under.

The warm mound next to her that was Gershom replied with a dreamy, "Hmmmm?" She let the next relaxing wave take her away.

The sound of an explosion yanked her out of a sound sleep shortly before dawn. Shona found herself sitting bolt upright in the tent. "What was that?" she demanded.

Gershom was sitting up next to her. "I don't know," he said, pulling on his shipsuit a leg at a time. He shouldered into the long garment and got to his knees to fasten the front. Cautiously, he extinguished the lamp and undid the flap and the rain fly. With Shona sitting nervously at the far end of the tent, he peered out into the silvery half-light. Droplets flew in on an errant breeze and sprayed her in the face. It took a moment before Gershom stopped squinting, then leaned back to report.

"It's a big branch. That last lightning strike must have downed it. I can smell burning. It fell right next to the tent." Another explosion of thunder, then a blinding show of lightning, made Shona jump twice. Gershom hastily closed the tent and crawled back to sit with her. "It's still pouring out there. Probably that old branch was ready to go. We were very lucky."

The sound of the falling branch had attracted the attention of the ottles. As soon as the rain stopped, they swarmed over and around it like curious kittens, marveling at its size.

"What fortune that it did not strike where you were," Chirwl said. He had come down out of his pouch at once, followed by Wla, to make certain his beloved humans were all right. Wla added her chirrup of concern.

"Such an occurrence is not to be looked for," she said. "Most often, we are throwing down such limbs before they become a danger."

"It was an accident," Gershom said. "It was an old branch, and lightning struck it." He kicked the trunk end, which was charred black.

"That was not the descent of dead wood," Chirwl said. He perched on the center of the limb where it had snapped, showing shards of wood like splinters of bone. He flicked chips of wood away with his sharp talons. "Sap springs yet."

"Cut with fire!" Wla said, after a quick sniff. "The sky flamed at the moment it fell." Gershom's brows drew together. He knelt beside her at the blackened end.

"It could have been lightning," Shona said, watching Gershom with alarm. She glanced upward when he did. The tree from which the heavy limb had fallen was otherwise untouched by the lightning stroke. Gershom straightened up and put his hands on his hips, his face set.

"Clean-cut. Looks more like a laser pistol. Someone doesn't want you looking into this epidemic."

"What? Why?" Shona asked, horrified. "Who could possibly benefit from having everyone on this planet age unnaturally and die?" As soon as the words were out of her mouth, a terrifying speculation formed in her mind. Her mouth dropped open, and she stared at Gershom.

"You don't think Verdadero . . . ?"

"No!" Gershom exclaimed. "He's in prison. He has no stake in this colony, and he has no way of knowing you were coming here. How could he?"

"Well, I had to notify Alien Relations, but I haven't told anyone else."

"There," said Gershom. "I doubt he has connections in such a small government office. So it's someone right here. I'm glad the kids are in the shuttle. You should be there, too."

"I have to stay," Shona said firmly. "These people need me. Chirwl and his co-mates need me. I'll be careful."

"This isn't an open attack," Gershom argued. He grasped her upper arms and lowered his face to plead with her. "This was done by someone who sneaks around and tries to make murder look like an accident, Shona. Your life is more important to me than all of theirs."

"I'll be in my module," Shona said, wanting to reassure him though she had to admit she'd been frightened, too. "It's made of space-grade ceramic. Nothing on this planet can get into it if the locks are set. I'll activate the alarm every night, and I'll have Saffie with me. We'll tell Horne what happened, so I can count on someone watching my back all the time."

"It could have been him," Gershom grumbled.

"You're not that bad a judge of character," Shona replied. "Well, as long as we're up, why don't we have breakfast?"

The returning shuttle glided carefully underneath the crowns of the trees until it came to the open field at the bottom of the village. Abruptly, it dropped power, and settled to the ground within a surprisingly short time. Shona, Gershom, Horne, Chirwl, and a few of the ottles were waiting for it.

Ivo, in the pilot's seat, signaled thumbs-up to them as he wheeled the stubby craft in a circle. One of Horne's men, carrying a blinking orange lantern as a beacon, walked the shuttle to a treeless spot at the edge of the settlement near the vegetable garden. Shona ran along behind to watch the rear doors open and the servos lower the white enamel dome of her lab module onto the forest floor. It settled with a thump.

Shona hurried to open it, knowing there would be protests going on inside. She entered her code on the external panel. The door slid aside, and a cacophony of animal noises all but knocked her backward. Saffie was jumping and barking in her crash cage. Harry had set up the angry wail that only a cat who hated descending through atmosphere could emit. Both of the rabbits had wedged themselves in the corner of their cage, and were kicking the walls. In their box, the mice were nowhere to be seen.

"All right! It's over!" Shona shouted. She closed the outside door and went around to each container in turn, making her way past a skid, hastily dumped in the middle of the examination room, that contained half a ton of four kinds of animal chow and containers of staple foods. Saffie galloped around and around the room as soon as she was free, stopping to bark at the door and whine at her mistress. Harry regarded Shona with suspicion, refusing to come out of his box. She left his door open and went on to the rabbits and mice. They were easily placated with some fresh greens from her hydroponic tanks. She stroked the rabbits' downy backs, feeling the sensitive animals' hearts pounding.

"It's okay, now," she said in a soothing voice. "It's all right. You just take it easy. We've got a job to do." Both the rabbits huddled with noses down, intent on munching every scrap of dandelion and rabe.

There was a rap on the door, the crew coming to help her stow her supplies. Almost as soon as she turned her back to answer it, Harry leaped from the door of his box up on top of the skid, trying to dig through the cargo net to tear at his food bags. He growled as Shona advanced upon him and dragged him away so the men could load the bags into the storage areas underneath the floor.

"Oh, shush." She kissed the top of his head. "You couldn't eat it all now anyway."

"You're hooked to a power point," Gershom said, walking over to the recessed switch box. He threw a lever. The lights browned for a split second, then shone steadily on the new energy source. "This is a good spot. There's a path to the ottle heart-tree if you just hug the right wall of the module and walk a third of the way around. The settlement is out the front door and up the hill."

"Good!"

"Here's a list of your food," Ivo said, handing her a datacube. He and Kai were dressed in white, disposable isolation suits made of a light, oxygen-permeable membrane. "I tried to give you a little of everything."

"Many thanks, Ivo." Shona put the cube into her clipboard reader. She read the list, feeling a little dismayed. Her real food consisted mainly of reconstitutables. She had dried protein supplies: meat, milk, and cheese; four kinds of beans; plenty of rice; potato granules; a small store of grain sealed in one-kilogram nitrogen-filled cans; dried and flash-frozen vegetables; and dried fruit from the shipment refused by a receiver six months ago. The only thing she had in abundance was nutri, cans upon cans of nutri. She shuddered.

"You didn't forget spices and extracts, did you, Ivo?" she asked anxiously as the men formed a bucket brigade to hand the bags down into the underfloor hold.

"Me? Never." He pointed to a box marked FRAGILE.

She patted his arm. "Thank you!" Shona regretted again that the circumstances made it impossible for her to enjoy the natural bounty of Poxt. The meals that were cooking in the human village, and even the stews bubbling over fires in the ottle center-place, made her rue the unlucky circumstance. And yet, if she ingested anything indigenous, she ran the risk of becoming one of her own patients. What the *Sibyl* was carrying in the way of foodstuffs was uninteresting, especially in light of Shona's hopes for fresh food and new recipes, but it was safe. The most serious concern she had with her supplies was boredom.

Gershom oversaw a final check of equipment, to make certain everything functioned, before the source of tools and the expertise to use them went away. He carefully checked off everything: life support, decontamination unit, microscopes, spectrograph, drug synthesizer, MRI and X-ray, refrigeration and freezer units, sterilization equipment, plus a microwave/convection unit and food processor for day-to-day living. Her sonic shower and bathtub unit seemed fine. Alex's high-sided bed had been moved into the room with her bed and communications console. She was about to ask what it was doing there, when she heard a disturbance outside the module.

"Mama!" Alex's siren voice was raised on high. Shona glanced at the crew. "Mama, where are you?"

"What's he doing down here?" she asked. "He and Lani should be with Eblich."

"Little one kicked up a fuss," Ivo said, looking everywhere but at her. "Lani wanted to come, too."

"Maybe to say goodbye," Kai said, but she didn't believe him.

"I see," Shona said, and marched outside.

Alex continued calling for her at the top of his lungs. As soon as he saw her, his face crumpled, and he began to cry hysterically. Lani, looking perturbed, carried him over to Shona. Both children were wearing isolation suits.

"He wasn't crying until he saw you," the girl said reproachfully through her plastic mask.

"Mama din't kiss night-night," Alex sobbed.

Shona gathered up her baby, rocking and patting him until the sobs died away. He pushed back his upper torso to look at her. His face shield was smeared with moisture. Lip quivering, he blinked, then snorted loudly.

"You'll have to wipe his nose, Lani," Shona said. "I'm not sterile."

The girl undid the child's mask and mopped his face with a cloth she took from a zipper pocket on the front of her own suit. "He's all right."

"Mama," Alex said unhappily, throwing his arms around her and burying his face in her neck again. Shona checked to make certain his hood was in place.

"Mama," Lani said, sounding equally forlorn, "we don't want to go away from here if you're staying."

"You know why I have to stay, honey," Shona said. She put her free arm around Lani. "And why you have to go. Daddy is going with you. Isn't that all right?"

"But I'm not a baby. I could stay," Lani protested. "I could help."

"Lani, you don't know what's involved here. I don't know yet, myself."

"We will find out," the girl said stubbornly. Her nose grew

as red as Alex's. "I don't want to leave Poxt. It's like Karela. And Chirwl is here."

"Honey, do you know what it means if you stay?" Shona asked gently. "Every time you make contact with anyone or anything, you'll have to go back and disinfect yourself before going into our living quarters. You'll have to make certain you haven't picked up any spores or mites in your clothes, so you'll probably have to wear an isolation suit all the time. You can't eat any of the native food. We've got dried stuff, but you'll get tired of that very quickly. I know that I will. I'll have to be testing samples of your blood and stool every day, maybe several times a day. And Chirwl's too, because he hasn't been exposed up until now."

Lani grimaced. "Poor Chirwl," she said.

"Poor Chirwl indeed," Shona agreed. "And poor us, too. If you go with Gershom now, I'll only have to make those tests once. Won't you save me the trouble?"

The girl's face contorted. Shona could tell she was wrestling with the desire to stay weighed against her foster mother's wishes and concerns.

"Oh, sweetheart, if it happened to you I'd hate myself forever. Come on. You *can* help me right now. I'll get you and Alex done, then we'll get those big babies out there one more time before you all lift off."

"All right," Lani said, relieved she didn't have to make the choice at once.

So far as Shona could tell, the tests on the crew showed nothing unusual. A rigorous cleaning was done on the shuttle interior. Gershom assured Shona he would void the atmosphere in the shuttle hold to space when they were in orbit, to freeze any parasites that might still cling to its wheels and body.

"Do you want to risk one beacon connection before I go?" Gershom asked.

Shona dithered between the security of not attracting attention to Poxt, and not getting her mail. At length she nodded.

"We'd better, in case there's news from the court on Mars. I don't want to be late in responding to any new queries. That would play straight into the hands of the meddlers." She led the way into the bedroom compartment of the module.

The first of the messages was a note of relief from Susan.

"Thank goodness you sent! I was beginning to wonder if you'd been swallowed up. Thanks for the videos of Alex. He's so big.

"You caught me in the middle of negotiations for the next project. I've actually got offers, twin! Nothing like success to give people confidence in you. I can't tell you much about them right now, because the walls have ears—" Susan gestured around her with mock furtive gestures, and Shona laughed. "Everyone wants to scoop me, hoping they'll get rights to the next big story before I can. I'll be surprised if you haven't heard from reporters galore. All of them want to ask you if it really happened, as if they couldn't check the court records. Dummies. Hoping this finds you as it leaves me. I want to hear from you again soon! Love to everybody. Bye!"

Shona punched the Reply button. "Believe it or not, I can't tell you where I am," she told the screen with regret. "We're all fine. I can say that I'm planetside in the middle of wonderful scenery, and I've met some new friends. Very *unusual* friends," she added, with a glance at Gershom. He quirked a grin. "I'll give you more details as soon as possible. I hope it's soon. Success in whatever it is you're doing. It sounds exciting. Love. Over and out!

"Whew!" she said, as she queued the reply for transmission. "She might understand what I mean from that. Susan could always guess my thoughts. I hope I do have good news for her next time."

"I do, too," Gershom said.

The next message punctured Shona's bubble of good humor. It was from Manfred Mitchell. The new CEO of the Corporation had not lost his good looks, and the gaze he fixed on the video pickup still had an ardent flavor that sent a quiver through Shona's fibers, but he looked more tired than she had ever seen him.

"It was good to hear from you, Shona," Mitchell said. "I wish I could help you. No one deserves aid from the Corp more than you, but we are still under heavy official scrutiny. We can't get involved with personal indebtedness. I am very sorry. I won't offer it to you as a gift, since you're not registered as a legal charity, and that would raise tax questions. Would a personal loan from me do? I'd be happy to send you whatever you need, to be paid off at whatever interval you specify." His warm hazel eyes twinkled. "My new job has a few perks, one of which is a greatly inflated salary. I can spare it. Please let me know. My best regards to your husband and family. Mitchell out."

Shona could feel her cheeks burning as she scrolled up to the next message. Her pride was hurt at having to accept charity. Mitchell was as kind as he could be, but it still hurt to ask. Following Mitchell's note was another rude message from the loan officer from MarsBank. Shona hit the Erase command, then recorded a humble missive to Mitchell, thanking him kindly for his offer.

"Please send the money directly to MarsBank One," she said. "Here's our account information. And bless you. I'll be in touch again soon. Your godson is growing big, and learning an amazing array of expressions in three languages, Standard, Karelan, and ottle, some of them very naughty, but then, he is two. Taylor out."

Beside her, Gershom looked worried. "I'd better send a personal message to Zeles. You ate crow the last time. It's my turn." He indicated she should scoot over to let him have the whole width of screen. Shona watched, feeling helpless and ashamed as Gershom recorded a note asking for understanding. "My business is just getting running again, and we have had to fulfill an obligation specified by the Galactic Government to my wife's guest ottle. I realize that the payment we sent only covers our main indebtedness but I have a lucrative commission now, at the conclusion of which I will receive a substantial fee, which I will remit to you. Thank you for your patience." He reached over to squeeze Shona's hand for confidence, then hit the Send button.

"I think that's all," Kai said, standing with hands on shipsuited hips. "We'd better go. I don't want to navigate out of here when it's dark. If I ram one of those big trees . . ."

Shona kissed Alex on top of his hood and handed him to Gershom. "You be a good boy for me. You do what Daddy tells you, and you mind Lani. All right?"

"Mama go?"

"No, darling. I have to stay here."

"No!" He leaned out of Gershom's arms and fastened onto her neck with his chubby arms. "Mama!"

His face turned red again, tears threatening. She tried to distract him. "But don't you want to go see a space station? Daddy is going to a big, interesting place. He needs you to help him navigate. Wouldn't that be fun?"

"No. No, Mama." His eyes brimmed over as he looked up at her. This wasn't the furious storm of a thwarted two-year-old, it was the helplessness of a very little boy who didn't want to be taken away from his mother. Shona weighed the dangers and difficulty of having him stay with her against the real possibility of psychological damage, and decided she couldn't make any other choice.

"All right," she said. "I'll keep him here, Gershom. He'll have to stay in the module unless I can supervise him, but I think it would be worse otherwise." Gershom nodded unhappily.

Lani, looking childlike and slim in the too-big isolation suit, was very solemn. "Can't I stay, too, Mama? I promise to help."

"Go to Daddy, Alex honey. Just for a minute, all right?" Shona handed the baby off to Gershom, and took Lani aside.

"I can't let you endanger yourself by staying with me," Shona said, enfolding the girl in loving arms. "You're brave and very kind for wanting to stay, but the situation is serious. No one has any idea what is causing this . . . this syndrome, and it's my job to find the answer. It's worse for Alex because he doesn't understand separation yet. You're old enough, and I don't want you affected by whatever this is. Every day—every minute—you remain here, you could come into contact with the vector."

"You said it wasn't that contagious," Lani said brokenly.

"Not too contagious and not contagious aren't at all the same thing," Shona explained kindly but firmly. "It will be difficult enough for me to try and safeguard one child. What you're doing is very important, too."

"What's that?"

Shona glanced over at her husband and met his eyes with her brows raised to tip him off as to what she was doing. He gave her the ghost of a nod, acknowledging.

"Keep Gershom safe. Watch his back. You know people are still looking for us. If you see anyone strange, or any kind of incident makes you suspicious, let him know right away. If I can't be there to protect him, then I want you to. That's almost the most important thing I can think of."

"You sent me away before," Lani managed to whisper, then burst into wrenching sobs on Shona's shoulder.

Shona's heart turned over as she remembered the forlorn little girl she'd been forced to give up once to foster care on Mars. She turned gently back and forth on her heel, rocking Lani against her and patting her back as if she were a baby.

"I'd do anything rather than send you away now, if only I could be sure you would be safe."

"I will!" The protest was muffled in the fabric of Shona's tunic.

"I—I don't know if even I'll be immune to whatever's going on here. I can't protect you from a bogey, sweetheart. Please. Go with Daddy." She peeked down. Tears were dripping from the black satin lashes, but the girl was nodding. Shona hugged her. "Thank you, sweetheart. I'll feel better knowing you're with him." Sadly, Lani mounted the steps to the shuttle and waved a goodbye with one floppy-gloved hand. Then she fled into the ship.

"It's time to go," Gershom said. They stood at the door of the shuttle. The other crew members had tactfully withdrawn to give them a last moment of privacy.

"I know." Shona's throat thickened, and she swallowed hard.

"This isn't the way I'd have chosen to say goodbye, but as Kai said we'd better lift while there's daylight."

"Safe going," Shona said solemnly. "All of you. I'll worry."

"*You'll* worry? You take care of your mother," he enjoined Alex, who was very solemn but not teary, sitting on Shona's hip. "You're a big boy, and I expect you to be very brave. You'll defend her, right?"

"Right!" Alex said. He bounced up and down once, making Shona stagger.

"He's getting too heavy to carry," Shona said, with a self-deprecating quirk of her mouth.

"Bye, baby," Gershom said. He leaned in to kiss his son, then turned his face toward his wife. "And goodbye to you. All my love, every day."

"Mine, too," Shona said, kissing him first fondly, then deeply. "I'll miss you. I can't send, not while . . ."

Gershom nodded, not needing to be reminded that Shona

would be vulnerable with no means of leaving Poxt. "I know. We'll be back as soon as we can. You watch yourself. I don't mind older women, but there's a limit."

"You be careful," she said. She stood, holding Alex with his legs wrapped around her waist, waving until the shuttle had lifted through the canopy of trees.

"She's here for good," Morganstern said unhappily. "She's snooping into the problem. Damn her, until she came along no one realized there was anything wrong!"

"I must contact LabCor for instructions," Volk said. She shivered. "I will assure them we have done nothing to attract attention. It was chance that brought her here, but we have to find out what to do. In the meantime do not cooperate. Do not talk about our research, and don't let her near the computers."

"We're not fools," Morganstern said coldly. Missa ignored him, thinking of how to address the rest of the staff. After Larch's near brush with death some of them were starting to think about mortality, too, and she couldn't have that. Frightened people talked. Even the threat of sharing the fate that had befallen Dennison wouldn't keep them silent forever. Even though, Missa thought peevishly, she no longer had the wherewithal to support that threat. At some point, the nanomites at large could reproduce, but those were out of her sphere of control. Would they affect others in contact with those who were already victims, or would a second dose only make things worse for the carrier? She thought of Dennison again, and decided for the first time in her life she would rather die quickly. Others in her encampment must be thinking that way, too. How many would sidle down to Dr. Taylor and tell her what they knew in hopes that the reputed wonder-worker could reverse the effects?

"She's all alone here. I wonder how free she is?" Hampton asked speculatively. Missa turned to stare at him.

"You can think about sex at a time like this?" Morganstern demanded, outraged. Hampton grinned.

"My dear friend, I'm thinking about eternity. I'd like to see if she's tied into a life-limiting single relationship. She's a very attractive woman, smooth-fleshed, bright, lively, probably fun in bed. Besides, if I explore a fragment of my psyche with her, I can keep an eye on her, and possibly drop another tree branch on her if she starts to get too close." He tilted his head casually. The eyes in his smooth, handsome face glittered reptilelike. "I won't miss the next time."

"Consider the morality of an approach like that," said Volk. "An ephemeral won't feel about relational freedom as we do."

"Morality?" Hampton pouted. "I'm not proposing to injure her. I want to provide her with pleasure. Over a few hundred years there is room for many encounters with many women and men. You know that. If you think about forever, there are no limits."

Volk and Morganstern exchanged thoughtful glances.

"We do have to keep an eye on what she's doing," Missa said at last. "I'll get onto LabCor. And for pity's sake, *don't* miss next time. Our grant's at stake."

There was no profit in recriminations, Ladovard thought as he increased impulse drive by a puff of power to match the rotation of the ZB-267-Sigma communications beacon. The *Sibyl* had eluded them near Venturi Station, but he had other means of finding out where they had gone. His two associates, Pogue and Emile, aimed curious glances at him from time to time as he prepared to dock the modified scout ship. He was aware of their scrutiny, but preferred to let them think he thought they were too unimportant to command his attention.

He could see his own reflection in the shining surface of the navigation tank before him. In a sliver-narrow face, deep-set eyes were no more than glittering suggestions underneath bony brow ridges. His hair was clipped short to show the broad, knobby brow that made it look as if the brain inside had shaped the skull outside. Long lines running straight down from beside his nose to his chin drew a letter H with his thin-lipped mouth. It was an uncompromising face. In a universe where things were so seldom what they seemed, Ladovard was pleased to be one of the things that was. He hunted. He killed. He enjoyed his job. He looked the part.

ZB-267 was one of the thousands of unmanned exchange points on the vast communication net that held the galactic community together. Since the Taylors had abandoned their original comm numbers, it had been a paper chase to find the next ones, then the next. There hadn't been time after the transmission of the *Sibyl*'s black-box number to find out the latest, but Ladovard didn't think then he'd need to concern himself with any future messages to be sent by the Taylors. It should have been an easy kill, so close that he could see the smooth, round shapes of the numerous zeros that followed the initial digit of the promised credit reward. Then, unexpectedly, the pilot of the *Sibyl* had repelled him far away, long enough to warp-jump. Incredible! They couldn't have had time to calculate it. Maybe they'd torn themselves apart, or slammed into a black hole. But Ladovard could not take a chance that they had. He couldn't claim those credits on a maybe; he'd heard about Jachin Verdadero, and how he punished people who tried to cheat him. A powerful man, even in prison.

The GBI's plan to keep the Taylors' comm number from betraying them had one serious flaw: the government agents had not changed, or did not think of changing, the numbers of the Taylors' correspondents, and the woman received a lot of personal mail. Ladovard had a tracedown going on a dozen messages from Susan MacRoy, all sent within the previous quarter. It stood to reason that Shona Taylor wasn't download-ing while the ship had been in Venturi; they'd been dry-docked. When those dozen messages were taken off the net, the beacon number at which they were received would lead Ladovard on the next step to finding the Taylors. He knew his prey: Shona Taylor wouldn't be able to resist checking into the net, and every time she did, he got closer and closer to earning the bounty on her head.

Instead of making a random jump in hopes of coming up on the fleeing quarry, Ladovard could triangulate from a distance; then, when he captured the most recent receiver number, he could ask for copies of all messages sent out from that address, letting the Taylors tell him where they were at the same time they informed their friends.

As the airlock of the assassin attached to the beacon's port, lights went on throughout the satellite, and the hum of awakening engines vibrated the scout's hull. Soon, Ladovard had green lights on his board to show that the small compart-ment beyond the airlock had been flushed with oxygen and warmed to approximately 18° Centigrade. Normally, the su-perconductive components worked quite happily in space's sub-zero temperatures, but facilities had been installed for the human installers who came by at intervals to check on the mechanisms. With a nod to Pogue telling him to stay on station in the scout, Ladovard and Emile slipped on protective suits and passed through to the beacon's interior.

The space allotted for technicians was no bigger than what was strictly necessary. Ladovard, tall and slim, and Emile, shorter and narrow as a whistle, moved around one another without difficulty. The station's designers had thoughtfully included two rollabout seats with gravity bearings so that they slid with barely a push-off from the person in the chair. In under three minutes they had broken past the security system and had hooked into the main memory banks. Emile produced a small rubber-gray box with three solenoid switches, two LED's, and a datacube niche set into its top surface. The lockdown was a complex and very expensive device guaranteed to break the scrambled signal on all messages transmitted through it. Ladovard had a list of keywords and names that the lockdown employed to pinpoint the user code he wanted. He inserted the datacube and activated it. The lockdown began to filter through the billions of message units waiting in the memory to be updated, released, or erased. It might take days, even weeks, until the station that had downloaded Taylor's mail reported, but Ladovard was patient. One could be patient for that much money.

It was nine days after they had docked with the beacon that the mole started beeping. Zedari sector beacon RE-388-Sigma reported a download and a match on fifteen of the hundred keywords Ladovard had listed as pertaining to his prey. Some of the messages had also contained the names Shona, *Sibyl*, ottle, Gershom, Mars, Elliott, and Taylor. Once viewed, they'd been erased, and replies had been transmitted to five addresses. The lockdown had recorded the numbers to which replies had been sent. The numbers matched ones Ladovard already had on file. Ladovard didn't have to worry about the one chance in 376 billion billion against such a match being incorrect, that those five people might have had a further contact in common beside Shona Taylor. The voiceprint he had for her that appeared in four of the five messages confirmed it further. Zedari was in fact the place his target had been. He snapped out a series of orders, and Pogue and Emile at once began preparations to leave the beacon for Zedari sector. They would find the next link in the chain there.

·7·

"My wife thinks I'm crazy," Tony Coglio confided as Shona listened to his heart and lungs in her examination room. "I was an athlete in school, you know."

"Um, no," Shona said absently, counting heartbeats. "Sorry. I just got here."

"Oh. I thought you were going through everybody's background."

"Purely for medical reasons," Shona said, tapping him on the back with her stethoscope. He sat up straighter to avoid the cold metal end. "Most of your secrets are still safe." Tony shrugged.

"Anyway, I can't run anymore. My blood pressure's up, and everything sends me panting. I'm only twenty-eight. I shouldn't be going like this. I look older than my dad. I shouldn't even have gray hair. My uncle's seventy, and hasn't got a white hair on his whole body. I grew up on Birnham, you know."

"Yes," Shona said, looking at Coglio's black curls which were shot with silver. His temples had turned entirely gray, and there were crow's-feet around his eyes and mouth. "That I do know. No one on Birnham has ever complained about anything like this?"

"No, and they would too." Tony shot a hand across, palm outward, for emphasis. "Everybody talks to everybody. I still get messages from my old schoolteachers. They're proud of me for being here. They say I'm an example for the human race. I like Poxt, I really do, you know."

"Do you have any idea what caused your accelerated aging?" Tony shook his head. "Tell me how it happened."

"I don't know. It's a great place, and the food's so healthy compared with where I grew up on Birnham. Big industrial planet, mines and factories, you know." Shona nodded. "My folks brought me here as a kid. I stayed here after they moved on, I liked it so much.

"One day, I suddenly felt so good, right out of the blue. I thought it was this planet's influence, you know, leaching the toxins out of me so I was pure. I could run a mile and not break a sweat, and I was so strong. Cartoon-hero stuff. I thought, *wooo-OO*! if they could bottle this, they could sell it for a million credits apiece. I had energy like I hadn't had since I was five, and my sex drive, well—" He had the grace to blush at Shona. "Well, say I impressed Kallua Martinez enough that she said she'd marry me, and she did. Now I can't do what I could six months ago, and she thinks I've lost interest. I haven't! Just look at me."

Shona did. She saw nothing wrong with him, except that he looked closer to sixty than thirty. His body had stopped entirely producing the hormone DHEA, and his testosterone levels were down, too. As he'd said, his blood pressure was high for his weight and calendar age. She sat down to look at his current charts, and compared them with his records since his arrival. They showed a dizzying drop in condition, all in the last several months.

"So what is it, Shona?"

She shook her head. "I have no idea yet. There's so much research to be done, and I'm starting up from zero. Lie down, please. I've got to get personal here for a moment." Briskly, she took tissue samples, including glands, and swabbed the cells into dishes filled with growth solution. While she wrote his name on the lids, she nodded to him to sit up.

"I'm going to start you on a course of hormone treatments in the meantime," she said. "You should also be taking antioxidant vitamins. I see that yolcho stems contain a wonderful concentration of vitamin A variants, and the colony has plenty of citrus trees. You can get vitamin C that way, or through supplements. It's up to you."

"I'm not that much of a vegetable eater," Tony admitted. "But I'd do anything to get back the way I was before. Well, not *before* before, but like six months ago." He grinned, showing gleaming white teeth in a wickedly attractive smile.

"We'll do what we can," Shona said, returning his grin. "Any help you can give me in tracking down the source of this syndrome would be wonderful. By the way, Governor Horne would greatly appreciate it if you wouldn't mention what's been going on to anyone off-planet. It might create . . . alarm."

"Could, couldn't it?" Tony said, nodding. "Sure. I'll keep it quiet."

"And *I* would greatly appreciate it if you wouldn't mention *my* name in any communications, either."

"Oh, yeah, the video." His brilliant flash-gun smile came and went again. "Sure. *Your* secret's safe, too. See you around."

Chirwl's parents came in with their offspring, Thio and Tsanan willingly, followed by Chlari, protesting all the way. In deference to his impatience, Shona took down his information first.

"There," she said, snapping the lid on the sample dishes she'd marked with his name. "That's all we need from you."

"That is good," Chlari said, but he stayed in a corner, watching his co-mates go through their examinations, as if he suspected Shona would commit some foul act on them if he turned his back.

"What ails that animal?" he asked, pointing at Harry, who paced back and forth behind the clear plastic curtain, crying out in protest.

"Oh, ignore him," Shona said, waving a hand. "He wants to go out. He can see the birds and little animals out there, and he wants to run around and tangle me up in his leash, the way he always does."

"Let him out without the leash," Thio said, sitting on the examination table as Shona listened to Tsanan's heart. The ova-donor twitched hir whiskers with amusement. "I will watch him. There is nowhere a cat can run that an ottle cannot follow."

"No, thank you. I'd rather keep him inside," Shona said. "He's just jealous because Saffie is allowed to go out and he isn't. She never catches anything that makes her ill for more than a few hours."

"I am told by our offspring that she dog is made, not born," Tsanan said in her soft chirrup.

"Not at all," Shona said, waiting to take a scraping from the inside of the nurturer's mouth. "Saffie was born, but her genes were altered so her metabolism can defeat any intrusive organism. Her breed is called a 'vaccine dog,' because I can inject her with a microbe or a biological sample, and her system will produce an organic chemical to knock it out. I have to be quick, though, or I'll miss that little reaction. It's amazing. She never even gets parasites, for which I am utterly grateful, because that thick fur is a chore to comb as it is. I don't want to take a chance on Harry getting sick, unless I have to use his talents. He can distinguish hundreds of chemical compounds. Sulfur is his un-favorite."

"Do you not worry then, when you use his talents?" Tsanan asked, laying a kindly paw on Shona's hand.

"Of course I do," Shona said, stopping her work with a sigh. "But that's his job, and mine. I have to care about other people's health more than my own."

"Then you are a good healer," Thio said. "We will persuade the others to come to such a one as you."

Varral, Chlari's enfeebled friend, showed up a few hours afterward.

"We are here for to be looked," Varral said, eying Shona sideways. "I bring escort two of my family who also so suffer: Parga, my mate, and Dlelal, our offspring the second."

"We are glad that such the is now public," squeaked the co-mate, a nurturer. "I am medical for our breed. What information will serve you best?"

"Where were you when you first noticed the change in your bodies?" Shona asked, making up a fresh dossier and noting down the ottles' names.

"There has been much conversation since you began to ask questions," Parga said, cocking her bewhiskered face to one side. "Our social is consumed by this matter, and all have much to say. Such as this is unprecedented. It is deemed that in time seven moon-revolutions since the feeling of high good, and not long thereafter the reaction to same." Shona nodded. It was the same time-frame as her human patients had reported. The human settlers operated on a Standard calendar, but ottle months were slightly shorter, with seventeen months in a Poxtian year.

"And what are your symptoms?"

"At first, activity, and hunger," the nurturer said. "Then gentle feeling of decline. Much stiff, weak. The skeleton does not knit as before."

"I see. Your bones are getting brittle, prematurely. I haven't got the hang of ottle physiology yet, but for a human in your condition I'd suggest hormone replacement therapy. Do you understand what I mean?"

"The substance of genderness," the nurturer said promptly. "I have attempted to chew roots that so stimulate, but nothing happens."

"Probably the system in your body that produces it has shut down, as would be normal if you aged. Do fe—I mean, nurturers become frail as they grow older?"

"Yes." The ottle nodded vigorously. "It is as if I am many years beyond which I am now."

"Fifteen of our number are eldered," the male added. "None so as Shnomri, but notice is made of them."

Shona chatted with the ottle healer about physiology, and made notes of the natural remedies that the small nurturer used for arthritis complexes and hypertension. When there was a moment, Shona planned to get the colony botanist to tell her if the humans had checked out these remedies to see if they could be used by either species. If so, then probably she could recommend, even dispense, growth-hormone treatments to stop the symptoms of aging, using synthesized material based on an analysis of Chirwl's secretions.

"Meanwhile," she told them, "I want you to eat a nutrient-rich diet, concentrating on calcium and magnesium supplements. Tell all the others what to do."

"Do you know ottle well?" The male laughed, a shrill chitter. "You do not *tell* ottles. You *discuss* with ottles. There will be arguments, but many will do as you suggest."

"Have investigations shown the source, other than humans?" the nurturer asked.

"No success there," Shona said. "It's beginning to look as if it fell out of the sky."

• • •

"Don't laugh," said Wyn Barri, with a nervous, sidelong glance as he boosted himself onto the examination table, "but what about biological material descending from the heavens in a fallen meteor?"

"At this point I'm willing to take any suggestions," Shona said. "The more I talk to humans and ottles, affected or not affected, the more I'm convinced there was a single circumstance that caused this syndrome back on, let's call it Day X. It isn't spreading, at least not so far. Those of you who have it, have it. Those who don't are entirely unaffected."

"Well, that's a comfort, I must say," Wyn said waspishly, and Shona remembered his grimace from the day she had first stated there was something wrong in the colony. "My companion is one of the unaffected, and while we promised to be devoted to one another through old age and death, I didn't think it was coming so soon."

Shona eyed him critically. "You're not as badly affected as some. I don't see signs of unusual calcification in your joints. Your vitals are good. What's the specific complaint?" Wyn opened his mouth a few times to talk, then pressed his lips together, looking embarrassed. To give him time, Shona busied herself with her instruments, and purposefully took a blood sample and a tissue scraping from the inside of his mouth. Wyn looked away from her.

"I'm getting fat," he burst out. "I've put on almost five kilos since the beginning of this year. I've never had a single extra *gram* since I shed the baby fat. It's very troubling for me. I'm a *nutritionist*. I know what my body needs to survive. I've put myself on a ten per cent fat diet, and it's *still* building on. I admit I ate a lot some months ago. I mean I was *starving* all the time. But that should have been gone, and it's not." He pinched his belly with both hands and showed her the fold. "Here it is."

"This is typical of the profile I'm building," Shona said. "But it's only a profile of a shadow. I have no idea as to the origin. Let me see you in five days. I'll do what I can to work out a regimen for you. In the meantime, keep exercising. It'll help with the weight problem, and I want you to keep up your muscle mass."

"I'll run every day," Wyn promised solemnly, tipping her a wink. "Come pain or come shine."

"What an incredible range of symptoms everyone has," Shona said, looking around for Chirwl. She glanced back toward the transparent barrier that separated the sleeping room from the examination room. Chirwl sat on her side of it, hunched up against Saffie's shaggy flank. The silence beyond meant Alex hadn't yet awakened from his nap. "Chirwl?"

"I am here."

"You're very quiet," Shona said. "You've been here almost all day, and you've hardly said a word. I was waiting for you to join in the conversation."

"I thought I would sit with my friend Saffie," Chirwl said in as subdued a tone as Shona had ever heard him use. "She is gloom, and so am I."

"Why? You're home again with your family."

"That is part of the sad. I am staying mornings and evenings with Wla and my generative ones, but Shnomri has gone back into the pouch and will not see me. I get answers from your questions when the ottle deigns to speak, but of personal and offspring matters there is no conversation. I am believe feel it is regretful that you came me brought back to Poxt."

"Now, that's not fair. People might have died if we hadn't come."

"But not with shame," Chirwl said. "They would have olded with no one to say speak otherwise. And there would have been only suspicious minds instead of anger and dismay."

"You can't be so cruel. Look at Marleen. Her son needs help. I don't blame Shnomri for not wanting to make a spectacle of hirself. I'm not sure I wouldn't be hiding out in a bag if it happened to me. But think of Bobby. He's only seven years old. Childhood is such a vulnerable time."

Chirwl ducked his head. "You are correct. I am selfish shameful. But what can be done for him? You cannot ungrow hair."

"True," Shona said. "There probably will be permanent alterations in his system. I'm waiting to take an MRI so I can see the ends of his bones. If this effect simulated puberty, he may never grow again, so if we get him back to normal, he'd still be only about four feet tall. The course of growth hormone injections can only do so much."

"But will the generative ones not be happy to have the offspring live?"

"Why aren't you spending much time with Shnomri?" Shona countered.

"Your argue is good," Chirwl said, with the long whistle that served him for a sigh. "I am satisfied to have Shnomri alive but that ottle misses hir lost youth, and I am only a reminder that there is wrong. No one thinks to blame us for your diagnose, but it is in their thought of the aging is with us all the time."

"You mean they associate us with finding out," Shona translated. "That can't be helped. You have to stop feeling sorry. I need you. Shnomri needs you. You're one of the most thorough and honest thinkers I know. We can analyze this problem, but you can't do it if you're moping."

The ottle perked up. "Is this a philosophical question?"

"It's logic," Shona said, taking her clipboard and going over to sit on the floor beside him. Saffie, with a contented sigh, picked up her great, shaggy head and settled it on Shona's knee. "Now, picture this. We have a certain number of victims, some with worse cases than others, in a single attack, dating from several months ago. What does this suggest to you?"

"If they were burning, some would be closer to the fire, and some farther away," Chirwl said.

"Ooh, that's a good suggestion," Shona said, making a note on her pad. "I hadn't considered radiation. Isotopes are used in certain surgeries to slow or stop the growth of cells. There was that old-time treatment of hyperthyroidism in which they injected radioactive iodine into the gland. Were the hormone-producing glands of these patients killed or slowed by a single blip of radiation?" She tapped the stylus against her teeth. "No. No, it couldn't be. Exposure to that much radiation is debilitating, but the first symptoms every single person has mentioned are euphoria and energy. Stepped-up sex drive. Super strength. Hunger. Radiation wouldn't stimulate hormone production, it would halt it. Yet their bodies had stopped producing hormones normal to their age levels. Hmmm."

"But an area effect is indicated," Chirwl said, perking up.

"Yes, it is. That's true," Shona said. "Marleen is coming later. Between the three of us, maybe we can start to figure out where it came from."

"Is anyone else here?" Marleen asked, poking her head through the door. Shona glanced up from her clipboard and punched the command to save her data, entering it into memory. The sunlight beyond the treetops had dimmed to a ruddy glow.

"No, it's safe," Shona said, standing up with her hand extended. "No one but Chirwl and me. Did you bring him?"

Marleen slipped around the door frame with Bobby in her arms. The child was enveloped in a big, dark-colored blanket with only his face showing.

"Hello, Bobby," Shona said, helping his mother put him on the examination table. Chirwl climbed up on one of the counters so he could see what Shona was doing. "Do you remember me? I met you about a week ago. My name is Shona."

"Ahhh."

The wrinkled mouth pursed in a distorted circle over gaping teeth. It was a smile. Shona felt her heart wrench for this poor child and his parents. She pointed to the ottle, and the boy's eyes briefly tracked the movement of her hand.

"And that's Chirwl. You know a lot of ottles. You're lucky. He's the only one I've known all my life. Aren't they nice?"

"Uh-huh."

"Say hello to Chirwl, Bobby," Marleen said in a husky voice.

"Hi."

"Hello, Bobby," Chirwl said. "How feeling are you?"

"Not good," Bobby replied haltingly; then slow tears dripped out of his eyes and down his furrowed cheeks. Shona reached behind her for a tissue and handed it to Marleen. She wiped his face and then moved back a step, her own eyes moist. Saffie, across the room, whined and tapped her tail on the floor.

"Well, let's look at you."

Bobby was passive throughout the examination, lifting his arms or opening his mouth when ordered to do so, but took no action on his own. Without coaxing, he held still during the magnetic image scanning. He didn't seem to understand why he was there, or that Shona was there to help him. His eyes fixed briefly on her face with a flash of intelligence now and again, as if the tenant in his mind looked out of a window, then turned away again. Marleen had tears in her eyes all of the time, but never cried. Occasionally she'd dab at her nose and the corners of her eyes.

"Marleen, why don't you sit down?" Shona said sympathetically, gesturing toward a chair as she lifted the child back onto the examination table. "I can take care of him. He doesn't weigh a thing. Now, tell me, Bobby, what happened to you?"

The child, staring into space, said nothing.

"Oh, sweetheart," Marleen said. "Talk to Dr. Shona. She's here to help you. Aren't you, Doctor?"

Shona's heart twisted with pity. "I sure am," she said, mustering a cheerful face for Bobby. "Let's have a look at you, all right? Do you know what this is? It's a stethoscope. I use this round end for painting circles on your body. Help me look for them. Oops, no, you have to breathe deeply. Good. Look, see the circle?" She pointed to the small, round indentation on the skin of his chest. Bobby glanced down and chuckled. "Let's make another one. Where shall we put it?" Bobby lifted his gnarled hand and pointed to his belly. Marleen gave Shona a look of deep gratitude.

Marleen had devoted herself to Shona from the day she arrived. No one before had suggested to Governor Horne that there was a real problem that needed investigating, leaving her torn whether or not to come forward about Bobby's condition. She had told Shona that if there had been a decision to do nothing, they'd have had to leave Poxt, to avoid making the boy a target of ridicule. Now Marleen was so grateful for any hope of returning her son to normal, she promised to do whatever she could to help.

Shona wished she could guarantee something, anything, but the mere sight of the child made her wish for a miracle. How his parents managed to function normally and not go mad with worry and despair she didn't know.

"He was a normal child," Marleen said, twisting her hands anxiously. "Then one day he became hyper. He'd zoom around like a loose comet, and then eat everything in sight. He came to me when he started to grow hair. I mean, *there*. He's just a little boy. That shouldn't have happened. That's when I thought of progeria."

"You were right: he hasn't got progeria," Shona said. "His symptoms are identical with those of everyone else I've talked to. Manic energy, followed by exhaustion, then signs of aging, more accelerated in some cases than others. With Bobby, it's easier to follow the whole progression, since all the other victims were already through puberty. He's showing signs of having produced adult-level testosterone; witness the beard and pattern hair loss, only to have the hormone activity cease again, leaving him prematurely aged. There is nothing at all wrong with any of these patients. They are each and every one of them absolutely normal, except for premature aging. I have twenty-five-year-old women in menopause, showing signs of osteoporosis. I have young men with advanced arthritis. Other reactions aren't as extreme. Governor Horne looks about ten years older than he ought to and he's having attacks of rheumatism, though he's pretending it isn't so bad. I've given him anti-inflammatories, which he's taking, he says, as a favor to me. Some people have a few extra gray hairs and a wrinkle or two, and that is all."

"But where did it come from?" Marleen looked woebegone. She had her hands clasped on her knees. The knuckles were white with pressure.

"That I don't know," Shona said. She paused. "Do you know, you can help me work that out to a certain extent, where the phenomenon began."

"I can?" Marleen exclaimed. "I'll do anything."

"Chirwl and I have been brainstorming an idea here. I have the records for everyone who was affected, human and ottle. I've been asking them to recall as best they can where they were six to eight months ago, when the symptoms started to appear." She showed Marleen the rough map she had drawn of the village and the surrounding area, including the ottle center-place, and little pieces of clear plastic on which she had written names. "Can you put everyone on the map where they live?"

"Why, certainly. How will this help?"

"If it forms a localized pattern, then it might lead me to where this phenomenon began. I can investigate a center point, and work outward. If it's not localized, I'll have to guess again." Shona coaxed Bobby into holding up his finger for a blood stick, while Marleen worked silently over the map.

"Um," Marleen said, looking at a handful of name counters. "Some families have swapped huts over the last few years. How far back should I go?"

"Sometime about eight months back. But let's ask Bobby," Shona said. "This is a game, Bobby," she told the child. It was very difficult to meet the innocent, frightened eyes in the wrinkled, foreshortened face. "You can help us. When you started feeling like you could run around forever, where were you?"

The boy's eyes were wide as he looked at the map and the piece with his name on it.

"School, maybe," he said, his voice quavering. "Mr. Allen said sit down. I couldn't! The other kids laughed."

"When was that, Bobby?" Shona coaxed. "Can you remember exactly when?" To her dismay, the child's eyes clouded and wandered away, and she couldn't regain his attention. Marleen looked stricken. "Wait, we're not out of options yet. Did you get a report from the teacher that Bobby was acting up?"

Marleen's brows went up. "You're right, I did. He e-mailed it to me because Bobby refused to take a notecube. I think I can find the date. Wait! I'll be back." Seeming grateful for any activity that could help, Marleen bundled up her son in his blanket and carried him out of the lab.

"Mama?" Alex appeared in the doorway, scrubbing his eyes with his fist. He looked so normal, so adorable with his cheeks and lips soft and pink from sleep, his light brown hair tousled, that she felt a desperate need to hold him at once.

Shona hurried to him and slid to her knees on the smooth floor. She reached for Alex, taking the flexible transparent curtain with her, and enveloped him in her arms. "Oh, my baby," she murmured, over and over again, rocking him against her. His warm weight reassured her. She cradled the back of his head in the palm of her hand, fingers playing with his hair. She was filled with compassion for the other mother whose child had been robbed of his childhood. "How was your nap?" she asked, letting him step back so her hands were on his upper arms.

"Good!" Alex said, wiping his nose on his sleeve. "C'n I have cookies? Pwease?"

"No cookies until dessert. Dinner first," Shona said, rising from her knees. "Let me suit up, and I'll be in in a minute."

Shona sat in her white isolation suit with Alex curled on her lap, rocking him quietly. He was listening to music from his Babytime Play Unit. The device was programmed with over ten thousand songs suitable for youngsters at each level of development, but seemingly to bedevil her, Alex had taken a fancy to one song with a monotonous beat and a simplistic melody that he wanted to hear over and over and over again. Not only was the tune boring, but so were the words. She had tried a hundred times to wean him off the "Love" song, attempting to entice him with perkier tunes and more interesting lyrics, but he always went back to "Love." Perhaps its very simplicity appealed to the infant mind, with its rhythm as uncomplicated and comforting as a mother's heartbeat. Nevertheless, she would have liked to kick the long-dead composer in the shins. She wondered if she'd driven her own parents mad with the "Love" song when she was a toddler. She couldn't remember.

"'Gain, Mama," Alex said, around his thumb.

"All right, sweetie," Shona said, sighing, and touched Replay. Gently, she eased his thumb out of his mouth and put a small stuffed toy in his hands instead. Tuning out the singer's thin tenor voice, she concentrated on her research. The screen on her communication unit stepped silently through the individual files as it collated factors in common.

She had examined each tissue scraping for the destruct:repair ratio of cells. Among other things, all her samples showed signs of oxidative stress. Such readings were perfectly normal for men and women ages sixty to ninety, but completely off the chart for her patients, especially a seven-year-old boy. The cells had seemingly been stimulated wildly for a short period of time, followed by prolonged physical decline that continued as she observed it.

Together she, Marleen, and Chirwl had mapped out the locations of the living quarters of each of the victims for the period beginning six months before. Marleen confirmed the date by showing her the note recorded by the primary schoolteacher. Frank Allen had also called to say that Bobby had had an unexcused absence a week earlier. That placed the boy in the radius of the unknown effect, and away from his untouched schoolmates.

"Would there have been an instant effect when the—er—energy ray hit?" Shona asked, lacking a name for her infective organism. "What I am trying to work out is, did it happen at night or during the day?"

"Well," Marleen said, rearranging the pieces more slowly. "Here's where everyone works. That hasn't changed in years.

But the kids should have been in school on a workday, so how was Bobby in the way of the energy ray?"

"He wasn't in school at the time, I'll bet the farm," Shona said, pulling the piece with Bobby's name on it into the middle. "Look. If you move him closer to the others, right in the heart of it near Shnomri, you get a perfect set of concentric rings. And Varral, who has advanced about half again on his physical age, is in the second ring, and Governor Horne is in the third, with most everyone else. What was in the heart of that circle?"

"And where was the circle?" Marleen asked, her brows drawn together around a deep furrow. "I mean, this only brushed the ottle village, and it didn't hit the scientists uphill, so it had to be closer to the center of town." She slid the counters down into the middle of the settlement. "There's more people there most of the time."

"This is very interesting," Shona said. "But it still doesn't tell us what the cause *was*. You don't have unshielded sources of radiation anywhere near here."

"Someone could have been transporting a power source," Marleen suggested hopefully. "And it opened up in transit."

"That would mean someone else was at ground-zero," Shona said, shaking her head. "No one is as badly effected as Bobby and Shnomri. It's a good suggestion, though. At this point I'd consider any cause. This aging virus just dropped into your midst, then vanished. It's the little germ that wasn't there."

But radiation left traces, and meteors left craters, or at least dust, and Shona had been able to find none in any of the potential center points to the target. She had placed some of her mice in protected cages at points here and there around the compound. Except for being teased by the tiny animals Horne called tails, the mice were unaffected by their surroundings. She rejected the idea of a food that Shnomri and Bobby had eaten, and had only been sampled by others, because ottles had eaten the same foods for millions of years, and all comestibles for humans had been tested by the settlement's chemists before mass consumption was allowed. And export. Now *there* was a chilling thought.

She started to explore the notion of an explosive fungus that had spread its spores, saturating certain victims, with the others caught in the overlap of an area effect. And why not? Everyone here was always out of doors, running here and there on

errands, or playing. Horne was right in saying they were a
healthy brood as a rule. Shona had read the monthly rosters of
teams on the outside wall of the community hall for baseball
and soccer games. One sport she couldn't figure out was
"steeplechasing," since there were no churches or steeples on
Poxt at all.

Because of the emotional ties she had to this assignment,
Shona felt more pressure to succeed than ever before. Poor
Chirwl. He had been looking forward to coming home after his
long travels. He would have been getting married by now, or
whatever the ottle equivalent was of affirming a permanent
relationship. Someday he'd be the father of little ottles; Shona
hoped she'd have a chance to see them, wondering if they
would grow up as quizzical and humorous as her friend.

Another pressure was cabin fever. Normally on any medical
assignment, particularly one involving environmental illness,
which this one seemed to be, she'd be all over the local area,
looking at scenery, meeting people, getting to know the planet.
But with Alex having to be sequestered, she had to stay with
him unless she sealed him into an isolation suit, and he was
beginning to chafe at having to suit up for any little foray
outside. He was cranky most of the time. Certainly he could see
the sunshine beyond the door, knew they weren't on the ship,
and wanted out. Saffie could go out, but Harry was stuck inside
with Alex, because he wasn't immune as the dog was.
Whatever side of the door the cat was on was the wrong side.
He spent at least part of every morning meowing. For the first
few days it distracted Shona, and worried Alex, who thought
the cat was in genuine distress. It took longer to reassure him
that the cat was just being contrary than to wait out the length
of Harry's tirade. At night when she closed up the module and
decontaminated the lab, the cat waited the bare minimum for
the air to clear and was into the other rooms like a shot. Shona
wondered whether his sensitive nose was necessary here. She
didn't know if she was looking for an organic threat, or a
chemical one. If it had been a chemical, it might have been a
volatile one, and be long, long gone, out of her reach to detect
it, since there'd been no new cases. But she didn't know. All of
her surmises needed to be checked, until one of them checked
out.

• • •

Dr. Oktari came the next morning for her examination.

"Oh, and there's your beautiful son," she said, smiling at Alex through the transparent curtain. "Hi, honey." The toddler was leaning against the curtain, bobbing back and forth on its elastic folds. He waved at the dark-skinned woman, then went back to his mindless activity, chanting quietly to himself and playing a finger game. Saffie lay nose to nose with Harry through the barrier.

"He's watching me," Shona said. "Dare I hope at this early age that one day he might want to be a doctor, too?"

"I don't see why not," the chemist said, throwing back her head and laughing. "I had twins, a boy and a girl, and both of them went into the field of science—I hope because they saw it was a good job to have, not just because I was doing it."

"You must be proud."

"Oh, I am." She glanced over Shona's shoulder at her file on the clipboard's miniature screen. "Oh, I'm bad. I haven't updated that in a tree's age. I'm up to date on inoculations, I don't have any chemical habits apart from an occasional drink, and I'm fifty-five years old."

"Permit me to say that you look it," Shona said. "And I'm so glad you do."

The chemist nodded, pursing her lips in a little smile. "I've seen what's been happening to my friends and neighbors. I'm happy you're here to help out. I don't think I've got an ache or a pain I didn't earn, so if there's anything I can do to help, just name it."

"May I impose on you, Doctor?" Shona asked, after just a brief hesitation.

"Of course; and it's Chele."

"Call me Shona. I want to walk the settlement. I've been working on a kind of theory, and I'd like to see the area for myself. Since I can't take Alex out with me, at least not for very long . . ."

"Say no more," Chele said with a broad smile. "I would be delighted to stay with him. Do you want me to wear a suit?"

"I'll show you where they are in case he needs a change," Shona said. "Otherwise, if you read to him, or play finger games, he should be all right through the curtain. I hope I won't be gone long. Shout out the door if you need me."

"Take all the time you need," Chele said. "I haven't played with a little one in *seasons*."

"Thank you so much. Saffie, want to go for a walk?"

The dog was at her feet before she'd finished the question.

Shona attached the dog's leash, packed a medical kit in her knapsack, and walked out into the sunshine. The day was warm, but there was a very pleasant breeze carrying the delicious scents of flowers and leaves, and the peaty aroma of damp bark. The wiry grass in the confines of the settlement was clipped to a few centimeters in length, providing springy footing. Shona enjoyed the lift in her step that it gave her. Saffie, thrilled to be out in the sunshine, romped to the end of her lead and back again, sniffing everything within reach. She yanked Shona uphill toward the center of the village.

·8·

In spite of the trouble Chlari had attempted to stir up over "humans' disease," it appeared that ottles preferred to think for themselves. Life in the mixed colony was running normally, or as normally as could be expected. Ottles and humans sat and walked and talked together. Shona recognized Varral and Thio lying on a low rock, chatting with Leon Brom, one of the settlement's nurses. The human had clusters of green herbs spread out, and seemed to be asking questions, which the ottles were answering animatedly. She waved to the little group. Others, going about their business, greeted her pleasantly.

Although in most places that Shona went within the settlement she was treated with friendliness, some of the settlers disagreed with Horne for having given her the assignment; in their opinion the aging syndrome was pure imagination. Others distrusted her because they'd seen Susan's video on tri-dee. Shona wished she could send Susan recordings of some of the incredible reactions her work had evoked in viewers. In the meantime, that distrust made cooperation harder for Shona to get, since some of the pooh-poohers were victims. In six months, they had aged the equivalent of ten to forty years, and yet they still ignored the signs. Two of her patients were developing hypertension, one was beginning to forget things, and several had developed brittle bones, putting them at risk for compression fractures.

The most tragic thing she observed was a perceptible drawing away from the sufferers by those who remained healthy. It wasn't deliberate, Shona knew. She held a couple of evening therapy sessions to discuss the psychological effect of being around patients with a chronic disease: avoidance, fear of contagion, breakdowns in communication. Some settlers actually came up to thank her later for addressing their concerns, and to admit shamefacedly that they had been guilty of isolating friends and relatives. The children had surprised Shona with their outpouring of compassion for Bobby. He still would not go out in public, but now he had one or two visitors every afternoon. The parents, naturally, were afraid their children would catch what he had, but the majority were sympathetic. Shona felt that if she accomplished nothing else, at least she was helping the community stay whole instead of fragmenting into the "normal" and "abnormal."

The ottle village was just the opposite. Instead of treating the victims as pariahs, the unaffected ottles interviewed their fellows, wringing from them every last detail of what it felt like to be aging, and discussing it among themselves. Shona sat through a few of those sessions and found them exhausting, but she learned a lot about ottle philosophy and resilience. It sounded cold-blooded at first, but she had had seven years of experience with the ottle need to *know*. And the academic aspect had no bearing on the loving care provided to the sufferers. As if Shona were one of them, the healers were eager to discuss with her what experimental steps had been taken to alleviate the aches and discomforts of their patients. She was included in all stages, from the wildly theoretical suggestions to the grimly practical treatments. Even though Chlari had condemned the other humans for hurting his people, he still welcomed Shona, as did the rest of his clan. He didn't blame her for what had befallen his ottle-in-law-to-be.

Her welcome very definitely did not extend to the LabCor compound. When she passed over the imaginary boundary that separated them from the colony at large, all conversation stopped, and cooperation was nonexistent. For a group of scientists, they were remarkably stubborn about acknowledging the evidence. She could document the decline of her patients, both human and ottle, and she still got amused glances or open scorn. And she was sure they were behind the hum of rumor suggesting that she had in some way been responsible for the misfortunes that had dogged her during her work for the Corporation.

She was grateful their opinion was not widespread. Elsewhere, she got considerably more cooperation. When she began her investigation in the community, she asked for cultures of every kind of foodstuff the two groups ate in common, plus soil and plants from common ground. One thing she could say for the colonists: they were good at chemical analysis. Everything that grew was fixed, labeled, and cross-referenced with original slides from the inception of the colony. Frustratingly, none of the current slides differed from the early ones, so her vector wasn't in the food.

Chele Oktari, the parfumier, had done a lot of the comparative work for her. She was a damned good chemist who claimed she'd gone into perfumes because she had an unusually good nose and there was better money in scent than in industrial chemistry. The better to keep them in luxuries, Shona told herself. A little joke, because everyone in the Poxt colony lived fairly simply, with no more elaborate paraphernalia than small entertainment/communication consoles, some with more speakers or screens than others, but scarcely the conspicuous consumption she'd seen in other prosperous settlements. They spent their time in more social pursuits.

Marleen had been keeping Shona up on the gossip in the main settlement, and Shona made sure Marleen took back full details of everything she was doing in her research. She didn't want the colonists to think she was holding anything back from them. In order to conduct any meaningful investigation she needed their confidence, and she'd just been too busy yet to socialize. It was a great pity. Most of the people here were expansive, intelligent individuals who were aware of the incredible privilege they enjoyed, above all others of their species in the galaxy.

How she envied the people who lived here! Colonies with breathable atmosphere were slightly in the minority, Earthlike planets were nearly unknown, and Poxt, with its intelligent extraterrestrial population, remained unique. The best things about this assignment was that Shona had had a chance to get to know more ottles, and that her separation from Chirwl was indefinitely postponed.

High summer had slowly shifted into early autumn since they had arrived. A couple of days ago she'd sat with Alex, wearing his iso-suit, at the edge of the crop field while the colonists had harvested rows of potatoes and thousands of gourds and tomatoes. The soil was a volcanic loam, rich but fine, and everything grew well in it.

The air smelled good. Avians and small animals gathered seeds and crumbs in the compound, and retired to safety in the thick bushes to chatter over their booty. Shona grinned as a tail scooped up a nut as big as its whole minute body, and scurried in a flurry of fur to a safe perch on a tree branch above her head to eat it. Such a beautiful, pastoral place. She wished Gershom could be there to share it with her. With fierce fingers she reached forward to scrub Saffie's back, and was rewarded with a whine of pleasure. At least she had someone with her to enjoy Poxt.

It had been only fourteen days since Gershom left, and she missed him dreadfully. In the last three years they hadn't been separated for longer than a few hours. She'd found it difficult to sleep without him beside her. Again and again, she turned to tell him about something interesting, and he wasn't there. *Was this what widowhood would be like?* she wondered, then hastily put down such a horrid thought. Gershom was all right. The *Sibyl* was on her way to Zedari, and he was fine. Shona just wished she could open up the comm board and send him a message. She was lonely. Her eyes filled, blurring the sunshine.

"You look so glum, Shona," a voice said. She glanced up.

"Hello, Doln," she said, smiling. "I was just thinking."

"Oh. With tears? Are we all doomed?" he asked with a mocking grin.

"No. Oh, no! It was personal, nothing to do with my assignment."

"That's a nice way to put it, *assignment*," Doln Hampton said. "Much less alarming than 'epidemic,' or 'plague.' May I walk with you? Can I carry your bag?"

"No, thank you," Shona said. "I'm just making my rounds."

"Isn't it a beautiful day?"

"Oh, yes. I was just thinking so," Shona said, tossing her head back to get a faceful of sunshine. The perfumed breeze felt good. "I do like it here, present 'assignment' excepted. Where are you going?"

"I'm free for a while. I'll tag along with you. Hello, Saffie. How's the girl, eh? Come on, girl!"

He clapped his hands and beckoned to the dog. Saffie greeted him exuberantly, rearing onto her hind legs to lick at his face. He laughed, reaching for her furry ears with both hands to give them a good scratching. She ran around him, threatening to tie up his legs in the leash. He leaped over it and grabbed her around the neck, pretending to wrestle. Saffie let out a mock growl and mouthed his arm. Delightedly Shona watched the man and dog play. Doln had been a regular visitor to the module. Unlike the rest of the LabCor people, he was friendly. Although forbidden to talk about his work, he was knowledgeable and forthcoming on any other subject. Shona found him a witty, charming companion. Gershom would like him, too, when he came back.

"Well, *some* of us have to work," Shona said at last, shouldering her medical bag. Hearing the tone of mock exasperation in her mistress's voice Saffie heeled at once. Doln, his cheeks flushed from playing, came to walk on Shona's other side.

"Sorry," he said, sharing a grin with her. "We were just having fun."

Shona turned in at Governor Horne's door. With a surprised glance at Shona's companion, the administrator rose to greet them.

"Afternoon, Shoshana. Hello, Hampshire. I'm feeling fine," Horne said, before Shona could ask. "I don't need any of your potions or shots, so go see some sick people and let me be."

"I need to practice on healthy ones like you first," Shona said blithely. "This way, if you don't mind."

Leaving Saffie with Doln, she took Horne into his sleeping room and shut the door. She ignored the governor's protests, and tested the joints of his right hand and arm with a miniature ultrasound. The arthritic condition had worsened slightly. Over the course of two weeks, since Shona had started checking, there'd been a buildup of calcification consistent with a normal advance of approximately six months, but less than half of it had accrued in the second week since she'd started him on palliative therapy. In time she hoped to see actual reversal.

"Are you in pain? How much of the arthritis medicine have you got left?" Shona asked, entering the results on her clipboard to download later.

"No, and plenty," Horne said, rolling his sleeve down again. "What's that?" he asked, pointing to the pressure hypo Shona had taken from her bag.

"Another dose of human growth hormone," Shona said, adjusting the dosage.

"I've stopped growing," Horne said mulishly, but he held still for the injection. "Confound it, Sarah, I'm just an old man."

"Shona," Shona corrected him automatically, meeting his eyes. "This is slowing your symptoms, the same as it's doing for everyone else. I still haven't figured out what's causing the phenomenon, and I won't have everyone galloping forward into their hundreds while I'm limping along behind in my research." She matched his glare with one of her own, and packed up her instruments.

"Well, I'm still glad you're here," Horne said. "It's good for morale, anyhow, even if you're wasting my time."

"Thanks," Shona said. "Now I'll go look for some really sick people."

With Hampton in tow, she dropped in on several other patients, taking readings from them, and dispensing treatment where necessary. Because she was not alone, she bypassed Marleen's home. She thought she spotted a shadow move behind the window curtain. She tossed a small wave to Bobby, wondering if he'd recognize her. He, too, had responded favorably to a course of hormone therapy. A light fuzz of hair was growing in his bald patches, and his skin was starting to tighten up, although so slowly the change was only perceptible to her computerized micrometers.

"Was that your last patient?" Hampton asked as they left Wyn Barri's office. "Would you care to come up to my hut for a drink?"

"One more stop, and then I have to go back to my module," Shona said with regret. "I've got a volunteer baby-sitter, and I don't want to impose longer than I need to."

"Well, if I may continue to enjoy your company for that small interval," Doln said, "I'd certainly like to." He followed her to the center of the village.

She handed him Saffie's leash and sighted up and down the long oval of the compound. There was the governor's hut, and up that way was Tony Coglio's craft workshop. The Oktaris were out of it, so the radius of the circle couldn't reach as far downhill as their home.

"May I ask what you're doing?" Hampton said.

"I'd rather not say at this moment," Shona replied, a little distractedly. "Because it may turn out to be a silly guess."

"Ah." Doln threw himself down into the short grass under the shaggy-barked tree in the middle of the common and hooked Saffie's lead over the toe of his shoe. The dog walked back and forth, sniffing at his and Shona's feet, hands, and pant legs in between investigating interesting smells around the tree.

Not wanting to air her theory to Hampton, Shona left the plastic map in her bag. Instead, she sighted on her landmarks, and paced the distance between them to figure out the center of where the "bio-bomb" or "energy ray" might have gone off. By using Bobby's absence from school as the date, Shona had been able to guide the memories of her patients back to where they had been most of Day X. Bobby and Shnomri could not remember specifically where they had been, nor if they had been together at any time on that day. She got more information from her second-tier group, but still there was no single obvious place she could pinpoint as ground zero for the bio-bomb.

A couple of ottles stopped under the tree to speak to Hampton, and stayed to watch her. Shona finally decided on her best choices, and reached into her bag for a handful of sterile sample dishes. After all this time, because of rain, wind, and erosion, there was probably nothing left to find, but she needed to check out every possibility. If these samples all proved negative, she'd just have to keep searching.

"It must look as if I've gone crazy," Shona said, a wry twist to her mouth, when she returned to claim Saffie.

"Not at all," Hampton said, rising and brushing leaves off his clothes. "It's good scientific procedure. You forget, I'm in your line of business, too." Saffie rushed over to lean heavily against her mistress's leg. Shona staggered.

"I did forget," she said, catching the big dog's head and fluffing its ears. "I know what you're working on is classified, but is it too nosy to ask what your specialty is?"

"Oh, no," Doln said, with a laugh. "I'm a biologist. Purely laboratory-bound. I'm no good at all with people. I couldn't do what you do. People always want something from you: your attention, a cure for this or that imaginary ailment, ego-stroking. I don't have time for that."

She interrupted him. "You don't think this is imaginary, do you? Because I've got some very sick people who would tell you otherwise, and plenty of empirical observation. Just because I don't have a *cause* . . ."

Doln held up his hands in surrender. "Oh, no. This isn't a reference to what you're doing. Just why I'm not in medical practice. I'm just a lonely ascetic." He grinned down at her, a roguish twinkle in his eyes.

"Uh-huh," Shona said, with a sly smile that matched his. "I doubt both those claims, sir. I must get back now. It was nice of you to walk around with me."

"Wait," Doln said, reaching out for her bag. He swung it onto his shoulder. "I wanted to show you something special. Well, special to me." He looked wistful for a moment. "Would you like to see it?"

"How very mysterious of you," Shona said. She glanced down the hill toward her module, estimating how close Alex was to wanting a bottle or a nap. "Well, all right. But I can't be too long."

Making way on the narrow bank for Saffie, Hampton braced his legs apart. As soon as the dog was safely down with him among the reeds on the river's edge, the scientist held up his hands for Shona. Gingerly, she took a step off the high bank. He caught her under the arms and guided her down until her footing was steady.

"How could you have found this by accident?" Shona asked, elbowing thick brush away. She looked around and cocked her head, listening. They were only a few hundred yards from the extreme edge of the settlement, and yet there wasn't a sound to show they were on the same planet with any other humans. The surprise of shrill birdcall right next to her ear made her jump. Hampton grinned down at her.

"This isn't the best part yet," he said. "Follow me."

Shona had to step smartly to keep up with Doln, whose long-legged pace threatened to take him out of sight among the leafy overhang. It wouldn't do to get lost down here. Hampton was the one who knew the safe places where the bank wouldn't give way. She reached down nervously for Saffie, who paced at her hip.

On her left, the broad river collected in little swirls and

eddies, exotic lace made of a thousand irregularities in the sandy shore. Insects, twigs, leaves, and feathers decorated the patterns. It looked unimaginably delicate. All the same, Shona respected the power of the river, which only a few yards farther out was sweeping whole branches away. She could see sleek-backed ottles swimming against the swift current, coming up on the other side of the river. On the right, the bank rose, veiled in pliant vines and withies. Something small and black shot across her path almost underneath her feet. She jumped. Saffie barked at the creature, and leaped to follow it into its secret burrow under the boughs of a willowlike tree. Shona grabbed the big dog's leash and pulled her backward. Her heels dug into the silt underfoot.

"Whoa, Saffie! It might bite you."

The dog retreated, whining. Shona glanced up the bank.

"Doln?" He was gone. Drat the man, abandoning her in muddy wilderness. Well, she could follow his footprints. She glanced down at the path. His trail was gone. Suddenly, a hand shot out of the greenery to her right and seized her arm. Shona screamed.

"It's all right!" Doln said. His handsome face, grinning, followed the hand. Shona gaped at him, then felt her heartbeat slow down to normal. "Here we are. Come on in. You'll find there's plenty of room for all of us."

He held up the swath of osier branches. Shona ducked to come in under his arm. Saffie followed. Behind Doln, the bank opened up into a dark hole.

"It's a cave," Shona said. She squinted, but couldn't see the back of the narrow chamber. A tangle of skinny roots hung down from the ceiling and caught the light. She sniffed. The dense smell of clay was sweet and earthy.

"Uh-huh," Doln said. "I often come down here when I absolutely have to get away from people. For a hole in the ground, it's rather homey." He sat down on a long stone and patted the place next to him. "Join me."

Shona did. Saffie remained beside the cave's entrance, sniffing, probably hoping that the small black creature would make another appearance. Shona started to ask a question, but Doln held up an imperious hand, and she remained silent. In a moment she became aware of the rushing of the river, filling her ears with white sound. It was very soothing. She relaxed her neck and let her head fall back. The sound seemed to carry away all her worries about the ottles, her shaky finances, and Verdadero's hired killers trailing her around the galaxy. All that was here was peace.

"Like it?"

She nodded. "It's so tranquil, I can see why you want to come here to be alone."

"I only share it with very special people," he said. "Like you." He stopped, smiled, and then Shona felt his hand gather in her hair at the back of her head. He leaned down and kissed her.

She was so surprised, she drove both hands into his chest and shoved him off the rock. He sprawled onto the mossy floor, and sat goggling up at her.

"What do you think you're doing?" she demanded, standing over him with her fists clenched at her sides. Saffie, on guard for her mistress, was between the humans in a moment, growling down at Hampton.

"Was it that bad?" Doln asked, looking hurt.

"Well," Shona said, pausing for half a second. It had not been unpleasant, far from it, but her outrage bubbled over at his pure gall. "Well, what's that got to do with it? What made you think you *could*? I'm married. Happily married."

"Your lips are very inviting."

"I don't recall that they invited you."

Doln sighed, rubbing his chest with his fingertips. "Monogamous. You would be. You're delightfully old-fashioned."

Just the way he said that made Shona's face burn. Resisting the urge to give him another shove, she replied coldly, "Old-fashioned enough to want to go back right away. Thank you for showing me your special place." Blind with fury, she stumbled out into the sunshine with Saffie behind her.

·9·

That afternoon, Shona threw herself into her work. She decided she might as well channel her anger at Doln into something constructive instead of sitting and steaming. How dare he kiss her like that? Had she given him one microgram's reason to think she might welcome advances? No! What nerve! Just because Gershom wasn't there, did she look like an easy mark?

She slammed a test slide into a carrier, and jostled it until all of the slides jingled. It was bad enough that Doln's co-workers ignored her or talked behind her back, but to have the only friendly one among them become too friendly was positively infuriating.

She stopped for a moment to take control of herself. No sense in breaking the equipment just because she felt a little guilty. Doln had kissed her, and it felt nice, and she'd enjoyed it, to her embarrassment. The real truth was that she missed Gershom. Not only would his presence have prevented this awkward situation, but he might have been able to use his famous tact to deal with Doln's stony-faced comrades.

Considering that they were scientists, she was getting remarkably little cooperation from them. Since what little attention they paid her was forced by Horne, they would neither submit to physical examinations nor lend her any of their own expertise. She understood their not extending her the use of any of their equipment or supplies. They were engaged in contract work, whatever it was, and every pH strip had to be accounted for, but the breath to give answers cost nothing. She couldn't get so much as a timetable from them as to where they were on Day X, even though it was as much for the benefit of

137

their people as for the rest of the colony. They could be in danger, too, should the phenomenon recur.

"I suppose one of the reasons they aren't taking me seriously is because I'm not quarantining myself," Shona said to Chirwl, who had appeared in her module with Wla to keep her company.

"Then why are you not?" Chirwl asked reasonably.

Stona sighed. "Because it makes it easier to talk to other people. They don't like having to share intimate information with someone in a plastic mask. Besides, I've already *been* exposed. It wasn't an easy decision, I can tell you that, but some whisper of instinct deep inside keeps telling me there's nothing for me to worry about. Yet the *other* part, the one that worked for the government, is nagging that I'm not doing my job properly, risking falling victim to the same environmental illness as the others."

"But when they confide, do they not breathe on you as well?" the ottle asked.

"Well, yes, they do," Shona admitted. Suddenly concerned, she got up from her stool and went to a mirror on the wall to examine her face for wrinkles. Her reflection's cheeks reddened, and she couldn't face her own eyes.

"This is ridiculous," she said, turning away. "I see no difference between the way I look now and any other woman my age. I've shown none of the symptoms. Neither have you. I've tested us every day."

"It would be well to be wise, and wise to be well," Chirwl said.

Shona shook her head. "I know that. I simply cannot make myself believe it. It's highly unscientific and unprofessional of me. I'm concerned enough to keep Alex in isolation, but this morning, when I thought of suiting up and staying that way, I balked."

"What is here is not the fault of ottles and humans be together, is it?" Wla asked with concern.

"Not at all," Shona reassured her. "Chlari must have been talking to you again."

"It is so," Chirwl admitted, ducking his head.

"That ottle does not give up a theory with ease," Wla said, tittering.

"Each night the harangue begins anew," Chirwl said. "I must

defend, as I believe, but he has many on his side who are angry and frightened. He is not letting ottles from other center-places come here, because the humans might infect all heart-trees on the world."

"Well, you tell him that I had Governor Horne message to Alien Relations for the addresses of all the other ottle hosts. You'll see. When he asks them, they'll send back that they've never had any problems except for having their ears talked off."

"Yours remain attached," Chirwl said. "Yet Chlari will argue then that it is these humans here who are a danger."

Shona sighed. "That's what Gershom is supposed to be finding out for me. I'd like to make peace with Chlari. The GG is so sensitive to your people's concerns that if a sniff of this got out, I wouldn't have a chance to finish my investigation."

"You cannot convince him except to make Shnomri and the others young again and stop the threat," Chirwl said reasonably. "I will make a theory that all can be made well, based upon your wise for determining health faults before, and he must mull that over. It will give you some time. Not all ottles agree with him. Many are listening to me and to Wla. Thio also likes you greatly."

"Thank you, Chirwl," Shona said. "Then the best thing for me to do is to find a way to make Shnomri young again, if it's possible."

The soil samples had come up negative. None contained anything out of the ordinary: no bio-organisms, no heavy minerals, no traces of radiation. Shona had already been trying the rabbits on local food. So far the colonists' instincts and research had been sound: Moonbeam and Marigold munched their way contentedly through offerings of vegetables, fruit, grain, and particularly the nuts, without ill effect. She'd almost been tempted to supplement her own dull diet with some of the things they indicated were safe, but caution stepped in to prevent her. She hated to give up such a good theory as the bio-bomb, but she was frustrated. There was a pattern of increasing symptoms pointing toward an imaginary, temporary center. All she lacked was proof.

"Aargh," Shona said, pounding her hands on the table. Saffie looked up at her mistress and whined. Alex, behind the curtain, laughed. Shona made faces at him, which he mimicked

gleefully. "I need to do a more widespread search," she told
Chirwl while playing peek-a-boo with her son. "Maybe my
Level Ones and Level Twos wandered through something in
between the two settlements."

"How will you check that?" Chirwl asked.

"I'll call out another member of my animal team." She
looked speculatively at Harry, who was lying in the doorway of
the bedchamber. "I've been considering whether it might have
been exposure to a toxic chemical. Harry can sniff around, and
I'll sample whatever he pinpoints. My tests haven't been
all-inclusive; they can't be in an unlimited environment. He's a
better indicator than running one chemical analysis after
another on the same blob of dirt."

The cat played dead the moment Shona buckled him into his
walking harness, and lay passive until Shona turned her back.
The moment she took her hands off him to put Alex into his
isolation suit, Harry took off like a fox-colored rocket, zipping
up and down counters, chairs, tables, trailing his leash through
the racks of glass tubes and delicate machinery. Fearing broken
glass and the loss of all her samples, Shona was afraid to grab
him, lest the leash catch in the equipment. Chirwl and Wla
sprang after Harry, calling softly. With admirably quick reflexes the nurturing ottle headed the cat off on top of the
examination table and clasped the back of his harness with her
small paws. Harry folded his ears down against his head and let
out a mournful howl. Chirwl, right behind Wla, gathered up the
leash before it pulled the microscope over.

Shona got Alex into his suit and put him in her backpack
carrier. "Take Harry outside," she instructed the ottles. "You'd
think he hasn't been nagging me to let him out for weeks.
Cats!"

Alex was delighted to be outside, even to the point of
forgetting to protest his plastic mask and suit. He crowed and
kicked at his mother's back. Shona reached around with one
hand to catch his foot before it impacted with her kidneys
again. As Shona had feared, Harry showed no interest in any of
her putative ground-zeroes, so she led him on a general tour of
the compound, and up and through the pathways leading in
between the two species' settlements. Saffie, already accustomed to a certain degree of freedom, loped behind Shona

alongside the two ottles. Chirwl introduced the dog all around as if she were a veritable person. Smaller ottles, children, rode the dog around the center-place until she sat down or shook them off.

"I feel like a walking zoo," she said to Chirwl. "I want to check my mice. Will you take Harry down to the garden walk toward the governor's house? That's one of the areas both species make use of the most."

"I shall do," Chirwl said, reaching up for the leash. "You ought should let him run. He will sniff out clues his own self for you."

"I don't want him loose," Shona said, wriggling the loop off her wrist. "He might go any—"

Harry, seeing his opportunity, wriggled loose from his harness, and shot across the green. Saffie broke away in pursuit, followed by the ottles. Shona ran after them, shouting. Alex shrieked with glee.

Harry scampered into the colony compound, streaked across the grass, and bolted up a tree. The dog stood at the bottom, barking, while Chirwl clambered up after the cat. Both of them appeared a moment later on a low limb. Harry jumped down, looking very pleased with himself. He had a mouthful of fur.

"What's that?" she said. "Drop it!" The cat paid no attention. Chirwl headed him off and pried open the cat's jaw. He handed Harry's booty up to Shona.

"Why, it's nothing but *fur*," she said, turning it over and over.

"Chasing his tail, eh? That's a tail's tail," Mr. Oktari said, coming up. "Afternoon, Shona. Hi, son." Alex gurgled at him through the iso-suit mask. The old man bent down to pet Harry. "Nice cat. We don't have too many pets here. Too many predators. If we want furry companions, there's always ottles. Much more intelligent than cats."

"So we are," Chirwl agreed blithely.

"I'm wondering if Harry's not more trouble than he's worth," Shona said, gathering him up. With her hands full, she couldn't put his harness back on. He squirmed, threatening to kick loose. Because of Alex's weight on her back, she knelt with difficulty to stuff the cat between the straps Chirwl offered. The ottles let Harry play out his leash, then followed him on an exploration of the nearby bushes. Saffie trailed behind, sniffing and whining happily.

"Well, can I help you?" Mr. Oktari asked.

Shona glanced up, then noticed Doln Hampton stumping down the hill toward them. There was no way to beat a hasty retreat, so she appealed to the nutritionist.

"Yes. Stay here just a moment with me, will you?" Mr. Oktari turned his head and saw Hampton approaching.

"Sure I will, honey," he said, kindly, and deliberately turned his back toward Hampton. "You already have as much as you can handle. Tell me, did you put those little mice in a box on our eaves? They've been rustling up a storm, and I get a shower of shredded paper on me whenever I go outside."

"I'm sorry about that," Shona said. "I put them in what I hoped were strategic locations around the settlement. If they're a bother . . ."

"Not a bit. What do you mean them to do? Catch the germs in their teeth?"

"Oh, something like that. Have you ever heard of Harvard cancer mice? They were specifically bred in the twentieth century to be susceptible to cancer. Ordinary mice are over thirty times more prone to cancer than humans. The new breed was twice as likely to become ill. Since most cancers were cured in the last century, the vulnerability of this strain has been expanded to include other contagious illnesses. They catch almost anything that's going around, providing me with an easily studied subject. If there's anything catching, they'll catch it. Privately, I hope the vector isn't airborne. My mice don't have much personality, but I'm as fond of them as of the rest of my pets."

"That's nice of you," Mr. Oktari said. "How about the kitty?"

Shona grinned. "He hates being called 'kitty.' He thinks it's beneath his dignity. He ignores the mice, mostly."

"How are you today, Shona?" Doln Hampton had come up beside her, smiling politely.

"Oh, hello," Shona said coolly, standing up. She wished for once that she was very tall, so she could look down from a height onto his supercilious face. He must have caught her thoughts in her expression, for he dropped his gaze to her feet.

"Shona, I came down to apologize. I am so sorry. You're a beautiful woman, and . . . the moment just took me." Oktari looked interested, but he remained silent, for which Shona blessed him.

"The moment? Aren't you a trifle too civilized to fall back on pre-cephalic techniques?" Shona asked acidly.

"I abase myself." Doln dropped to his knee in the center of the common and held out beseeching hands. Oktari stared. "I plead stress, stupidity, cupidity, or whatever of a thousand offenses will get you to forgive me. I'll do anything to make it up. Will you forgive me?" He clasped his hands and shook them. She ignored it. He shook them again, his face innocent and hopeful. Shona felt her jaw threaten to drop. She wouldn't have guessed that someone as outwardly dignified as Hampton had so much clown in him. "Please?"

He looked so ridiculous, Shona laughed in spite of herself. "Oh, all right. No harm done. Please get up."

"Is it all right?" Oktari asked.

"Yes," she said, squeezing the older man's fingers gratefully. "Thank you so much for staying with me." He grinned at her and went back to his hut.

"Friends again?" Doln asked, when Oktari had gone.

"Certainly," Shona said. She put out her hand and he shook it. "In fact, you *can* do something for me."

"Name it."

"Explain steeplechasing. I saw the lists on the side of the community hall, but there are no steeples, let alone churches, anywhere in this settlement."

"Oh, that!" He broke into laughter. "Yes, it sounds odd, doesn't it? It's a sport, all our own invention. Pure immigrant-Poxtian. Watching the ottles getting around suggested it to us."

"But what is it?"

He guided Shona to the edge of the settlement and pointed up. "Do you see how the branches of the heart-trees almost touch at the tips?"

"Hi!" Alex announced, gazing up at the tree limbs.

From below, the branches looked like black lace, but Shona nodded. She could see ottles the size of her fingertip moving around on them.

"Well, they're almost exactly at the same level planetwide. This species of tree has a terminal height of five hundred feet, so the branches begin to intersect at about two hundred fifty and go up to four. The ottles use them as a network. They can get almost anywhere without coming down, which is why their system of direction is expressed in how many trees, figured from a given gap in the canopy. We climb up and run from tree to tree to cover a certain distance. You can go in any direction you like to reach the goal, usually a flag or a ring. There are some favored routes, more or less dangerous than others. You can climb easily between some of the trees, but in others you have to jump. It's a long way down if you miss."

"You're all mad!" Shona said, picturing him dashing from branch to branch like a squirrel. "You don't want to live forever, do you?"

"Who says I don't?" He grinned. "It *is* a sport for younger folk, that is to say, the more stupid of us, especially if you have long legs and a good grip. I love it. You get an adrenalin rush like nothing else. Maybe you'll see a match while you're here."

"You'll need me to set the broken bones!" Shona exclaimed.

"Ah, no, it's safer than it seems. Those branches are much thicker than they look. Isn't it true, friend?" he asked Chirwl, who loped up with Harry on his leash.

"From a distance all looks thinner," Chirwl said. "I have not seen steeplechasing, for it must have developed while I am away. I recall humans following ottles through the treetops, but very slowly."

"That's more my speed," Shona said feelingly.

"You'd be surprised." Hampton grinned.

"I sure would. I'm not wild about heights."

He cocked his head at her. "I was going to ask you to be on my team. Oh, well. How is your research going?"

"I still have nothing. I've spun down samples for viruses, and found nothing out of the ordinary. I haven't detected any significant amounts of key proteins. There are no really unusual bacteria anywhere, nor parasitical organisms, especially not ones that pick on some people and not on others. I'm still looking, but I have no idea where to look next. I've really got to *think*. It would seem as if Poxt really is the paradise the original discoverers thought it to be. Humans can live here as naturally as they once could on Earth, with only low-to-average risk."

"That's exactly what we thought," Hampton said with a smile.

"Have you got any suggestions where to go next?" Shona asked.

"I'm sorry. My brains are not for hire."

"I am not trying to hire you. I'm trying to help this colony, the one in which you live," Shona said with some asperity.

"I know," Hampton said apologetically. "But you see, I've already pledged my expertise to LabCor. My contract says I can't free-lance."

"Oh. Oh, well. I do have another favor to ask you," Shona said.

"Anything. What?"

"Escort me into your compound. I want to see how Larch is doing. I'm so thoroughly snooted whenever I go in there by myself, I have to go home and check the mirror to make certain I still exist."

Hampton smiled. "Of course. That I'd be happy to do."

Shona couldn't suppress a swagger as she walked into the circle of huts beside Hampton. She had the satisfaction of seeing the usually remote expressions of the LabCor scientists change to dismay when they noticed her companion. Hampton hailed a tall dark man he called Lionel.

"Where's Larch?"

"Up there," Lionel said, pointing into the thick bushes above the compound. He shot a suspicious glance at Shona. Hampton patted her on the hand.

"I'll let you see your patient by yourself. I've got some work to do for that onerous contract I mentioned."

"Thank you, Doln," Shona said. With the medical bag banging on her backside, she climbed the steep path.

In a small clearing, the elderly woman sat all by herself on a low canvas seat before a patch of tall weeds. By her complexion, Shona guessed that Larch had recovered entirely from her bee-sting and was back to the simple work of picking herbs. She was glad to see that the LabCor people allowed their subjects to have the dignity of work, no matter how feeble or disassociated they were.

As Shona watched, she could tell that the old woman was having trouble concentrating on what she was doing. Larch went back again and again to examine sprigs of herbs in her basket, comparing them with the live specimens growing in her patch to make certain she hadn't picked the wrong ones. It was heartbreaking to see.

"How are you?" Shona asked cheerfully, coming up to kneel beside Larch.

"Go 'way," the old woman said, after one glance at her.

"It's a beautiful day. How long have you been here on Poxt, Ms. Larch? Do you like it? How did Dr. Volk find you?"

"Find me?" Larch asked incredulously. "I'm a botanist. Damned good. Love plants. Hate insects. They hate me. *Find me?*" she spat.

"Who hates you?"

"Insects! Bugs! You damned stupid?"

"Well, I can see why you think insects hate you. Stings are cumulative to those allergic to insect toxins."

"Don't haveta tell me that, you snip," Larch said offensively. "Damn kid, with your kid." Suddenly her face contorted, and she put a hand to her upper arm. Shona sprang up.

"What's wrong? What hurts you?" Shona reached out a hand for her wrist, and Larch slapped it away.

"Go 'way," Larch said again, her lips tight. "Go. You give me a headache."

"What's wrong? Can I help?"

"No. Go 'way."

Very reluctantly, Shona backed away, then dashed down the hill. She stuck her head into one hut after another until she found Hampton.

"Larch seems to be in some distress. She doesn't want me, but someone should go to her right now. She might be having a heart attack."

Hampton sprang up from his bench. "I'll go. Thank you, Shona. I'll see to her. You go home now, all right?"

"Are you sure I can't help?"

Hampton was gathering up an emergency kit. "No, thank you. We've got everything she needs right here. Better take your son home."

"It's true what I told Doln," Shona said to Chirwl that evening after she had put Alex to bed. "I still have absolutely nothing. That leads me to take a step I would have done anything to avoid."

"What step?"

"Saffie." Hearing her name, the big black dog tapped across the white floor and laid her head on her mistress's knee. Shona ruffled the dog's fur. "For the first time in my career I'm not certain what will happen if I inject her with a biological specimen. Normally she would throw off any ill effects in a matter of minutes or hours, no matter what it is. She's immune to every disease known to humankind, nearly every type of chemical poisoning, but old age? *Everything* is subject to old age. I . . . " She felt tears starting at the back of her throat, and swallowed. "I'll have a hard time handling it if Saffie becomes old like everyone else, and—and dies, and I can't help her."

Chirwl jumped up on the chair beside her and put his bewhiskered muzzle very close to her face.

"You have said it is your job to do what is necessary to help. I know my friend Saffie feels as helpful as you. Trust her to do what is right also. I am sure the unusual metabolism of hers will manage."

"I know. At least, I hope I know."

Very reluctantly, Shona prepared the sample. As if she knew what was coming, Saffie leaned her big body against her mistress's leg. With a look of infinite trust, she waited for Shona to apply the pressure hypo to her back.

"Now," Shona said, with a deep sigh, "we wait and see." She hugged the dog, who tapped her great plume of a tail on the floor.

Hampton appeared in the doorway. His handsome face contained deep lines she hadn't noticed before, and his cheeks were hollow.

"I wonder if you have a drink somewhere?" he said, his voice very hoarse. "Alcohol would be preferred."

"I'm sorry," Shona said. "Not a drop. We traded the last case for a tune-up. Can I help?"

"No. Not really. Larch died. She had a devastating heart attack. You were right. The coronary came on not long after I went to her. I can't believe it. She was . . . so old." He sat down at Shona's table and put his head between his hands.

Shona watched him for a while. He didn't cry, but occasionally would fetch a sigh from deep in his belly. Shona knew it was hard to lose a patient. As a scientist without a medical practice, it must be harder for Hampton to encompass the reality of life and death of actual human beings. Chirwl loped over to the grieving man and sat up to speak. Shona mouthed

"No," and shook her head. After a few moments she went to her pantry cabinet and made Hampton a cup of herb tea. She returned and set the cup down smartly before him.

"Drink this." Obediently he took a mouthful, and sputtered.

"What's in it?" he gasped, but he took another sip.

"Peppermint and ginger. Good for what ails you."

"You don't mess around, do you? Or do you?" He smiled at her with a speculative gleam in his eyes.

"Let's not start that again," Shona said patiently. Hampton nodded apologetically.

"No. We won't. You're a very comforting person, Shona Taylor. You care." Hampton emptied his cup and rose. "Thank you."

"I nearly broke down back there," Hampton said, setling wearily into a chair in Missa Volk's hut. "To think of one of us being the first to die. Of *old age*! At least the ephemerals expect death."

"Do I hear you losing your grip, Doln?" Lionel Morganstern asked silkily. "Or does associating with the short-lifers rub off after a while? How you could think of bedding that female! It would be like kissing a corpse."

"Shut up, Lionel. Unless you're planning to give me advice from your own experience of necrophilia?"

"Are you pretending you're not afraid you'll be next? Aren't you wondering where you were when thc nanomites' lid blew off?" Morganstern asked. His expression dangerous, Hampton pressed in to within a handspan of the other man's chest, until Volk feared he would push him to the wall.

"No and no," Hampton said, his voice low, like the growl of a tiger. "I'm not pretending or wondering. And I'm not playing games with you, either. Shut up, or I'll end your worries about what it'll be like to die." He snapped his fingers under Morganstern's nose. Morganstern flinched away, and Hampton's eyes narrowed in satisfaction.

"That's enough," Volk said, raising a hand. Her fingers trembled. She lowered her arm hastily and gripped the chair arm to hide the trembling. She no longer knew whether it was from stress or from the progression of her condition. "Everyone is under pressure. I've been forced to allow sedatives and mood-enhancers to supplement daily meditation, and I do not like dispensing drugs. We can't risk a breakdown in our own camp. There'd be a flood of confession to the authorities, and I for one don't want the humiliation. Lionel, don't indulge your agitation. It will only build on itself and do harm to your circulatory system. Doln, you had intended to monitor Taylor so we could keep up with her research. What is she doing now?" Hampton backed away from Morganstern and visibly composed himself.

"So far, she's made chemical analyses of soil, food, air, and living tissue, and found nothing at all, of course. She's investigating every avenue that occurs to her. She hasn't made a visual survey of genes, which is all that's saving us so far. And she has a good brain, so I don't think it will be long before she eventually stumbles onto the truth. Are we close to counteracting the nanomites' effect, or even turning them off?"

"No," Morganstern admitted. "We programmed them too well. They slow down for a time, but they keep going. Clegg has made a computer model that responds to within ninety-eight percent of the original. Any technique that is assured of killing the nanomites would also kill the host, and time alone will do that."

Volk's eyes slid to Hampton. He shook his head.

"Taylor will have figured out where her 'bio-bomb' came from—that's what she calls it—by then," Hampton said. "She's too smart, too tenacious a researcher, and she cares about the people who have been affected by our little accident. It's only a matter of time before she gets onto the right track. My money's on her rather than Lionel and his bug-extermination squad. She's a hazard to our security."

"Admitting your attraction to a mayfly?" Morganstern sneered.

"I admire her," Hampton said frankly. "She'd have made a good colleague in Forever—if only she wasn't fixated on that life-shortening monogamy. What can we do about her? What should we do?"

"Let LabCor make the decision," Morganstern said. "It isn't our fault if we're being spied upon, only if we allow information to slip out of our hands."

"I'm sure they won't see it that way, Lionel," Volk said, wondering if he was as naive as he sounded, or simply wishing out loud. "I received a message today from LabCor asking if the project has been compromised. You two are my closest advisers, and I trust your judgment. Has it?"

"No!" Morganstern said emphatically.

"No," Hampton agreed. "Not yet. But I don't think it'll be long before it will be. Tell them that. If Shona Taylor doesn't figure out what we've done, pretty soon we'll be unable to conceal our own symptoms, and then even Governor Horne will guess we're to blame. What happens when someone else dies? And Dennison is still trying to get out. He slipped loose again last night. Faraoud only just caught him before he rolled down the hill. We need to get in first with the solution, which means speeding up our own research."

"It can't be done, dammit. We're at a standstill. What did LabCor say?" Morganstern asked.

"They've asked if steps should be taken to stop Taylor," Volk replied, watching the men's faces for reactions. "They might be . . . extreme."

"Only extreme if necessary," Hampton said, turning his deep-set eyes fully upon Volk. The intensity of his stare made her uneasy. "It's possible LabCor might choose to pick Taylor's brains for our research. She might have some innovative ideas. You could suggest it."

Volk hesitated. "All right. Although I don't want to lead them to the conclusion that she's within range of the truth."

"Besides, how could she necessarily trace the nanomites back to us?" Morganstern asked. "They're not monogrammed, Doln."

"She'd have to be stupid not to trace them back to us," Hampton said. "And believe me, she's not stupid. Occam's Razor, Lionel: the simplest solution is almost always the correct one. Item: a genetically engineered molecule-sized organism. Item: a nearby scientific community reputedly working on something having to do with geronotology. Item: a rash of aged freaks dyeing their hair and using glycolic acid on their skins. Even you could work it out, Lionel." He dismissed the glowering scientist and turned back to Volk. "Give LabCor the suggestion. Say it came from me, if you like. Perhaps they'll pay her off, make her sign a confidentiality agreement. That would make sense. But this is their project, and they're paying the bills. Let them decide what to do about her."

"It's as simple as that, is it?" Morganstern asked.

"It is that simple," Volk said, after a long moment to consider. "I will send LabCor our suggestions. Keep me informed."

"This is Communications Beacon RE-388-Sigma," the woman's voice said. "Scout ship, please identify yourself."

Emile opened up the channel and smiled pleasantly at the technician's image. "Greetings. We are agents of the Galactic Bureau of Investigation from Government Post Sixteen. This is a security spot inspection. I am transmitting our identification code for your records."

The female tech groaned. "We just had an inspection four months ago," she said.

"I'm sorry. I will inform Post Sixteen that you may be on more than one list. Prepare to be boarded."

The Sigma Zedari beacon, a main transfer point for redirection of data, was far larger and better defended than the repeater station in the Venturi sector. Ladovard took note of the laser arrays in the structural arc that surrounded the core. Such things were of no use, of course, if the human beings operating the beacon were easily gulled.

The two technicians inside were pleasant but harried. The tall woman with cropped red hair, who had answered the call, and the short, stout, blond woman who rose from her seat at the console as the three entered immediately broke out into protests.

"I just got back on for this monthlong shift three days ago, so don't blame me . . ."

"We've got a lot of work . . ."

Ladovard cut through their protests with a gesture. "This will go much more quickly if you cooperate. I'd like to inspect the main data banks, please. Privacy leaks have been reported in this sector. I have orders to confirm which beacon they're coming from."

"Security leaks?" The red-haired technician looked shocked. "We've just replaced the buffers and scramblers. There are no red lights on any of the components."

"We have to check all complaints," Pogue said, getting between the two women and his employer. He gestured to the two seats underneath a bank of video screens. "Please just go sit down, and we'll get through this as quickly as we can."

Ladovard moved swiftly to the memory decks and flipped the lockdown from his pocket. He attached it over one of the input drives and turned it on.

The blond woman tried to shoulder past Pogue, who stiff-armed her easily.

"Just a minute," she squawked, over his back. "You shouldn't be touching those, sir. The scramblers are in the other bank."

"We need to take a random check of uploaded files," Ladovard said crisply. Messages that were sent along the electronic network were officially erased, but usually traces of them remained in memory until those particular tracks were overwritten. A major beacon like this one contained enough memory to hold a thousand messages for every citizen of the galaxy, so it was likely that at least some of what he was looking for had not been dumped.

He watched the readout on the top of the small device and smiled coldly. It had already made a match on seven of his keywords. One of them was "Shona." His previous search was confirmed. This was the beacon from which the Taylors had downlinked those weeks ago after escaping from him. He let the lockdown run, and gestured to Emile, who removed de-encryption equipment from the pouches on her suit arms and legs. Now to find out the comm number from which the five messages to Shona's connections were sent.

The two technicians had retreated under Pogue's guard to the far end of the room, where they conferred in low voices. Neither of them looked like a specialist in unarmed combat, but it was well to be ready to repel an attempted attack. Pogue saw the slight narrowing of his employer's eyes and nodded his chin about half a centimeter.

"Sir, I am reading four different addresses for those five messages, but they all contain code words. Could there be an error?" Emile asked from her station.

"No error," Ladovard said.

"But which is the real one?"

"All of them. It is an attempt to conceal the actual comm number of our subject. They conjoined at a remote beacon to another number, where they were held until claimed by this number." He showed her the readout on the top of the lockdown. "A very clever ploy, but traceable. Now there is no doubt that this single number is the correct one. Such a difficult and complicated protocol would not be used by accident."

Ladovard heard sounds of a struggle behind his back. "Wait a minute, you're not from the GBI," the stout blonde burst out. "Leave those alone! People have privacy rights guaranteed in the Galactic Declaration of Citizenship. You're committing illegal tresspass." She was trying to go through Pogue to get to him. Ladovard turned to stare her down.

Thinking she had a chance while Pogue was engaged with her companion, the redhead lunged. Tripping the shorter woman to the ground, Pogue drew his side arm and put three slugs into a neat pattern at the base of the redhead's neck. She collapsed. There was no blood because of the self-sealing cartridges, but she was unmistakably dead. The blonde started to tremble, then screamed. Pogue put the barrel to the side of her head and fired. She collapsed.

"You fool!" Ladovard snarled. Pogue retreated until his back was against the data bank.

"Sir, I . . ."

"You killed them for nothing! *Never* kill for free." Ladovard couldn't believe he had trained such an impulsive fool. The younger man cowered, his mouth opening and shutting like a data gate.

"I'm sorry. I'll never do it again."

"Never! Once you lose the reason for which you're killing, you become a mindless beast! Next thing you know you will be committing random acts of violence. We are not barbarians."

Pogue lowered his head, his cheeks blazing.

"Now, clean up this mess," Ladovard said, kicking one of the corpses. "We have work to do."

·10·

"Is that you, *Sibyl*?" the voice of the station operator came over the audio pickup. The *Sibyl* had arrived within visual contact range of Zedari Station almost thirty minutes after hearing the hailing signal from the perimeter beacons. The six-limbed wheel, spiraling closer and closer to their viewscreens, turned slow cartwheels amid a busy cloud of ships that looked like glowing gnats. The host sun, a white star with one huge, uninhabitable gas giant orbiting it, hung in the distance, its diffused light rippling through the spokes and occasionally picking glints of color from them. "Commander, Captain Gershom Taylor?" the deep female voice repeated.

"Yes," Gershom said, leaning forward in his seat. "I'm Captain Taylor." There was a slight pause before the operator's reply, attributable to the distance between the ship and the station.

"Ah, Captain, we've reviewed your request for docking. Unfortunately, the credit number you transmitted to cover landing fees and taxes . . ."

Gershom glanced at the screen showing the readout of his message. "Did it garble? I'll be happy to retransmit."

"It's not that, citizen. The number, if correct, belongs to a credit file that suffers from an insufficiency of funds," the operator said delicately. "Perhaps you were unfamiliar with our current charges, or had not checked your balance lately? Under the circumstances we cannot permit you to dock. I'm sorry. Do you have another credit account we can use?" The data on the screen was interrupted by a fare sheet from the station. Gershom, who knew to the minim how much was in the account, calculated the discrepancy, and reddened. He was glad the operator couldn't see his face. He twisted to glance at Eblich, seated behind the pilots' couches. The small man mouthed "letter of credit." Gershom nodded.

"Operator, I am sending you the text of a letter of marque I am carrying on behalf of DeWitt Horne, human governor of the Poxt colony. The *Sibyl* is on assignment from him. I think you'll find that the letter represents enough credits for a great deal more than just the landing fees." He brought up the text of Horne's document, and punched Send. There was a pause while the operator reviewed the details.

"Well," the voice said, with evident relief. "Yes, indeed. Here are your landing instructions: please synchronize your rotation with the station and drop velocity to approach speed under one point two. You are assigned to Docking Bay Sixteen, that's one-six, halfway up the blue vane, that's *B* for boy *blue*. Refueling depots are situated between every two bays. El-Jay, FrangipaniCo, and Sennex serve this facility. There is a handling fee of two credits per ton for shipments transferred on or off your ship while in the dock. Meals in all facilities can be charged to your ship account. Welcome to Zedari, citizens."

Gershom let out the breath he'd been holding. "Thank you. *Sibyl* out."

"The remainder will pay for refueling and a few supplies. Nothing like what we need," Eblich noted in his quiet voice as Gershom and Ivo negotiated the length of the dock and set the ship into rotation with the space station. Running chase lights on the station's skin, visible from a thousand kilometers away, led them to their mark, spiraling in on the huge hexagonal door marked "16." A drone tug zipped alongside them, then held back as the *Sibyl* eased forward on inertia and touched the hull plates. Outside the airlock they heard the clamp and whine as Zedari's atmospheric system engaged in the airtight bay.

"So what?" Ivo said bluffly, standing up and slapping himself on the belly. "Zedari's a major trade outpost. Big time. We can find a short-hop contract here, or we aren't as good as I think we are."

"I've got some connections here," Kai said blandly, ignoring the sour expression on Gershom's face. "It's like the old days, when we didn't have enough fuel to make liftoff if we didn't hustle. We sink or swim together, Gershom. You know that."

"Maybe I'm getting complacent," Gershom said, twisting his mouth wryly to avoid unnecessary protests. His crew was right. They could be arrogant and starve, but it made more sense to reawaken the old skills. "I hate to go back to those old days, when we were hungry in more ways than one. Do you want to live on nutri again?"

"Hell, no."

"Then, hustle we will."

"Papa," Lani spoke up hopefully. She had been standing toward the rear of the bridge, braced between straps for the docking. "If you ordered plenty of supplies, I could lend you the difference until Mama gets paid by Mr. Horne."

Gershom looked at her open face turned up to his, and smiled at her. She only wanted to help, but the final hearing date on the adoption was so close, he could not risk accepting even a loan from her. He knew how much it cost her to offer again, and it pained him. Lani couldn't understand why he and Shona turned down gifts; to refuse to borrow needed capital even with the full and expressed intention of paying it back must have seemed insane to her, but he couldn't explain that anything involving her money might set off the rabid busybodies back on Mars who could take her away from them. That, he would not risk. He didn't want to lose Lani. Nobody would love this child as they did, no one could give her a better family, but all it would take was a single mistake. This was precisely the kind of thing the vultures were hoping to spot. Better to appear foolishly proud than to set off another bureaucratic chain reaction.

"Thank you, little one, but no thanks," he said, in the gentlest possible voice. "We'll make it. We always do. We'll turn up a job, you wait and see. Don't you trust Kai and his connections? Or Ivo's charm?" Ivo knelt down beside her and gave her a melting grin, wiggling his eyebrows at her. At his coaxing, Lani managed a small smile, but Gershom could see her pride was hurt. "Come on, little one, let's get out of here. You've been on Mars, and Venturi, but you've never seen anything like Zedari in your life."

"What's here?"

"Shopping!" Ivo said, sweeping his hand out before her as if to call attention to a beautiful vision. He bounced up. "C'mon, pretty girl. You shouldn't pout. We're the ones who have to work." He took Lani's hand. At her nervous glance backward, Eblich moved up beside her and tucked her other hand through his arm. Thus protected, Lani stepped out onto the scout's ramp.

Outside the ship, a small man wearing coveralls spotted them and strode purposefully in their direction, brandishing a clipboard.

"Uh-oh," said Gershom. "Paperwork."

"Geershum Taller?"

"That's me," Gershom acknowledged, with a sheepish grin at his fellows. The small man scratched his head with the stylus.

"Hey, you got sam' nam' as toother goy. Yoo know." He gestured toward the ceiling with his pen. "Yoo famous on tree-dee or sompin'?"

"Sompin'," Gershom said, foreseeing a long conversation over the cargo manifests.

"I'll take it," Eblich said, stepping into Gershom's place. "You go."

"I'll go talk up our refit in the bar," Kai said. "I've got the possible short-hops between here and Poxt outlined. If anyone's got a cargo going that way, I'll let them know we're looking."

"I'm coming, too. My friends might be hanging around there," Ivo said. "Eb, how 'bout you?"

The small man smiled. "While there's time, I'm messaging my wife. The station booths are private."

"Meet you back here at 1800," Gershom said, tipping a grateful wave to his bookkeeper.

The group split in different directions when the group reached the exit. Kai pulled Ivo toward a short hallway from which the sounds of voices, canned music, and loud laughter could be heard. Gershom and Lani followed the signs that said "Shopping Center."

"I want," Chaffinch L'Saye said in a tone that brooked no disagreement, "*one* decent meal before we blow this arena."

His camerawoman and producer, Lettitia Nalbandian, lowered her camera case to the floor of the Galactic Video Network runabout and shoved it into its lockdown with a foot. They'd spent fifteen days gathering footage for a half-hour miniseries feature on Zedari Station, and in that period had had neither time nor room for good food. During the first few days, L'Saye, who was a well-known face on tri-dee, ended up glad-handing and posing for video opportunities with administrators who claimed the holos and autographs were for their spouses, kids, relatives, anybody but themselves, leaving few waking hours for anything but doggedly taking video and wild sound on memory. Food had to be snatched on the run. During the last days, L'Saye had to eat at every single one of the fast-food emporia because most of them were sponsors of GVN broadcasts. Unless he had wanted to resort to purging, he couldn't have found room for the fare of the gourmet establishments on the uppermost level of the entertainment center. Lettitia herself found the thought of anything fried or prefabbed more than a little sickening. With the whole show in the can and nothing to do between systems except edit the piece together, she felt they could celebrate a little.

"Why not?" she said. "All we've got is time. They're not expecting us at our next assignment for over three weeks. I'll treat."

"You've got a deal, boss." But before going out the airlock, L'Saye turned to the mirror at the door of the runabout and examined his hair and teeth. Vanity, for a tri-dee personality, was a necessary adjunct, Lettitia thought. If you got videoed looking like a *zhlub* your ratings went down. GVN wouldn't fire you, but you ended up on night-shift documentaries, and never got another raise. Chaffinch L'Saye was too hot a property to waste on flower shows, so it was just as well he took care of his image. She'd nag him if he didn't. Her career was tied to his. He gave a twist to his tunic collar to make it stand up properly, and shot her a smile in the mirror as if he'd read her thoughts.

Chaffinch had the gift sometimes called charisma, that indefinable charm that made people like him even though they had never met him. He was superbly handsome. Countless fans had fallen for the killing alabaster smile in the dark-walnut complexion. His black hair had unusual red highlights that the camera loved. Gossip columnists speculated that they were added by a colorist, but Lettitia knew the effect was natural. Just like his voice, smooth and sexy as chocolate. He even had a handsome nose, broad and well-formed; you could *trust* a nose like that; millions did. But his good looks weren't his only asset. Behind that perfect face was a clever brain with a retentive memory and the vocabulary of a college professor.

People frequently failed to notice Lettitia beside him. Her hair and lashes were almost colorless, and only a sculptor would be interested in her face, which though well-formed was sallow and blotchy unless she put on makeup, which she despised. She didn't mind anonymity. It gave her the latitude to control situations without interference, to provide Chaffinch with the support he needed to get his story on tape. It was he who was supposed to attract attention, and attract it he did. Her job was to find him stories to report. Zedari was supposed to have been a reward for covering a minor war on a Corporation colony world. Too bad the schedule had forced them to eat so much grease. Well, gustatory paradise awaited them, three levels up.

As they came out of Bay 17, a skinny man in a jumpsuit holding a clipboard ran toward them, elbows and knees threshing the air. "Mr. Chaffinch! Yoo dint leave yet. Yoo got to sign here, sir. Pleeze, Mr. Chaffinch."

He pulled a soiled, creased time card out of his pocket and fastened it in the top of the clipboard. Beaming, he offered the journalist the stylus that he took from behind his ear.

L'Saye glanced at the unnamable grime smeared on it and waved it away. "I've got my own scriber," he said grandly, taking out the rutilated prism pen he'd been given by a planetary president. It flashed in the overhead lights of the corridor. He inscribed his name "with best wishes" and an elaborate flourish. Leaving the little man babbling his thanks, he strode away, Lettitia trotting along behind him.

"What's worth doing . . ." Lettitia said, with a playful glance behind her. L'Saye's fan was staring bug-eyed at his treasure.

"If it means that much to him," Chaffinch said lightly, "he deserved the whole show. He must be the only person on the whole station I haven't shaken hands with."

He surveyed the landing bays as he passed by them. In Bay 15, mechanics had taken apart the engines of a luxury cruiser, the *Miranda*. A woman in a very plain but expensively tailored tunic, an executive secretary of some kind, watched them with her arms folded.

"Huh. Someone is in trouble," Chaffinch snickered. "Wonder who gets to sleep in the airlock tonight?" Lettitia snorted.

The bay across from that one contained a small scout ship. The ramp lowered, and Lettitia watched four men and a teenaged girl emerge. She was a little beauty, with long legs and lashes. On one side of her was a burly man with big arms, golden-brown skin, and wavy blue-black hair. On the other, a very short, slim man with short-clipped light brown hair and scroll-like ears flat against the sides of his head. The two men behind were both tall. The bigger of the two was loose-jointed, with hollow-cheeks in a light-pink face, big staring eyes like an Earth owl, and fluffy hair the color of raw cane sugar. The other, Lettitia thought, would make very good video. He was slender, with very long legs and broad shoulders. Longish, black-brown hair made a frame for his narrow, high-cheekboned face, and he had dark eyes and a falcon's beak of a nose. Chaffinch's fan, alerted by the humming whine of servos, scurried past them with his clipboard. The handsome one took the board from him and perused its miniature screen.

"*Sibyl*," Chaffinch mused as they passed. "That sounds familiar. Why? Why would I remember it?"

Lettitia cast her mind back. The name set off alarms in her memory, too. It wasn't a news broadcast, or not a recent one. Something exciting, all the same. No, it was a video . . . a documentary drama . . . "*The Angel of Death*," she said triumphantly.

"Rii-iight," Chaffinch said, tapping the air with a forefinger. "But the producers wouldn't have used a real ship's name, would they?"

"Who knows?" Lettitia said, swinging over to a public terminal. She slid her credit chit down to pay for access to a library memory. She entered the look-up keyword, *Sibyl*. Skipping over references to a mid-twentieth-century Terran multiple personality and to a Cumaean oracle of ancient civilization, she found a handful of other entries. "They would, and they did use a real name," she announced to Chaffinch. "This ship is registered to one Gershom Taylor. That was the name of the woman in the show: Taylor."

Chaffinch was watching the crew. "They're going somewhere in a hurry," he observed. "I smell a story, Letty."

"But our dinner?"

"Space the dinner, baby. I sense news." Chaffinch spun on his heel and sauntered back toward his jumpsuited fan. The little man had gotten his clipboard signed, and was on the trail of his next prey. "Hey, friend, can you stop a moment?"

"Yoo want me, Mr. Chaffinch?" The dockworker couldn't believe his luck. He waded toward them, limbs working. "C'n I doo anythn' for yoo?"

"It so happens, you might be able to help us. This is my producer, Letty." She rated a swift nod from the little man, who swiftly turned his eyes back to his hero. "We're trying to remember if we know the man who owns that ship in Bay Sixteen. Can you tell me his name?" The worker's face fell.

"Aww, Mr. Chaffinch, I c'n't doo thet. Security, I han't tell anybuddy 'bout *yoo*."

"I know, but it might be important to him, if that's our friend. In fact, you might have provided the link for us. That would mean we'd need to video you for the story, too. How about that?"

The little man's jaw dropped open. "Mee, in yer stoory? I . . . well, shuure. Cap'n's nam' is Geershum Taller. That t'oon yer looking for?"

Chaffinch and Lettitia exchanged triumphant glances. "You are a big help, sir," Letty said, moving in swiftly. "Now, you're not going to spoil it for Mr. L'Saye by telling anyone you mentioned Captain Taylor's name to us, will you?" She tucked a credit chit into the breast pocket of his tunic.

"Naaah." The little man was still bug-eyed.

"Say, friend, where did the *Sibyl* just come from? Her point of origin?" Chaffinch asked. He flashed the famous smile and leaned a little closer to the small man, whose eyes filled with alarm.

"No! Can't tell yer that. Can't doo't." His voice suddenly became shrill. Letty looked around quickly to see if a dock supervisor was on the prowl. No, she decided, they'd just used up all the initiative their source had.

"Thanks, anyhow," she said, linking her arm through Chaffinch's and pulling him away. "We'll be back later to take some video of you—C'mon," she urged Chaffinch under her breath. "I can try to get the point of origin out of the computer. He might have a total breakdown if we keep at him."

"Let's go after the crew," Chaffinch agreed.

• • •

The bright lights of the main thoroughfare caught their eyes as soon as they came out of the lift. Lani's face shone with excitement as she craned forward, trotting faster so that Gershom had to open his long stride to keep up. Having spent all her early life on a plantation planet, then traveling on the scout, then sequestered on Mars, then back on the scout with only short stops on other worlds and stations, mostly outposts, Lani had had no experience with the heart of society, specifically commercial centers dedicated to the pursuit of enjoyment. The electronic advertising beamed to the *Sibyl* had boasted of over five hundred shops, plus an arcade filled with individual carts of craftworkers and artisans, three banks, a twelve-screen tri-dee emporium, a casino, an amusement park, a speaker's corner, live theater, wandering entertainers, and acres upon acres of food concessions. Thousands of men, woman, and children wandered from shop to shop, some eating snacks while they walked, all laden with packages, most shouting to each other over the din.

"It echoes," Lani said, shielding her ears with her hands. Gradually, she let them drop. Gershom was tickled to see her eyes grow so big with wonder.

"There," he said, as they reached the edge of the avenue. "If this doesn't keep you busy for a while, nothing will."

"It's wonderful," Lani exclaimed. She ran from one place to the next, excited as a small child. Each window display, each artist, each street performer she stared at with huge-eyed intensity. At the end of the first street, she turned a shining face up to Gershom. He smiled.

"So you'll have fun while I'm working. You can go anywhere you want here, do anything you like. You're nearly fourteen, so you'll be fine on your own. Check in at the ship by 1800, just like I told the others," Gershom said. "See all the security guards?" He pointed to the uniformed men and women walking casually through the crowd, sending idle-seeming glances after passersby, and occasionally talking into lapel-mounted transceivers. Lani nodded solemnly. "You'll be safe here. Have a great time." He gave her a pat on the shoulder and turned to go.

He'd started to glance around for directions to the administrative offices, when a hand clamped his upper arm like a vise.

He looked down. Lani's eyes, wide open with mixed awe and fear, fixed on him.

"Don't go," she pleaded in a whisper almost inaudible under the roar of the crowd.

He patted her hand. To one accustomed to small groups and simplicity, such an extravaganza must be overwhelming. He should have guessed. "All right. I'll stay with you for a while."

Together they toured the fun fair and the concessions. With a loose credit chit, Gershom bought them both fizzy drinks. He finished his in a few gulps and put the container in a reclamation bin near the door of one of the banks, then noticed the logo. It was a branch of MarsBank One.

"Look, Lani," he said, "you can get credits here, if you want chits in your pocket. Otherwise just use your credit account number at each store. Buy yourself something nice. You can go back to the *Sibyl* when you're tired. I'm not sure when I'll be finished."

"Can't I help?" Lani asked, starting to follow after him.

"I'm not sure how long it'll take me to find what I need in the library services," Gershom said. "I'm anticipating a fight with the administration to get access at all. You shouldn't have to sit through that. I'm sorry *I'll* have to. Meet you later. If I'm through, we'll come back here after supper, and maybe we'll see the live show. How about that? Will you be all right now?"

Tentatively, she nodded. He smiled sweetly at her. "Good girl. I'll see you later." He waved and loped off toward the lifts.

Lani took another step after him, then checked herself. He was sure she'd be able to get along by herself, Lani realized, so whether or not she felt ready inside, she would try. She wished he had stayed with her to shield her from contact with too many strangers, but she knew when they came here he had his job to do. If she was too nervous, she could always retreat to the *Sibyl*. Just the knowledge that she had a haven in this big, frightening place took the rubber out of her legs.

Having a protected place was important. It wasn't the place so much as the people in it. They never forced her to do anything she wasn't ready to do. They were all very kind, thoughtful people, who coaxed her out of her shell. When her family died, they were there. When she cried, she had five sets of shoulders on which to weep—six if you counted Chirwl. Lani thought miserably that she would miss Chirwl once they lifted off Poxt. It was too bad, since his homeworld was so like Karela, with its big trees and weepy vines all over, and fruit on every bush. She might like to live in a place like that someday, but that would mean leaving the *Sibyl*. The thought formed such a lump of ice in her belly that she wanted to go back to the ship that moment. No, don't be silly, she chided herself. It's still there; it will always be there.

Not if the bank took it away from the Taylors, she realized suddenly. She might not have joined in the discussions about the mortgage, but Shona and Gershom never hid anything from her. There was very little money since before the refit. The nasty loan man made veiled threats about foreclosure. That worried Shona, though she tried not to let it show to Lani.

Gershom had a more immediate concern. The lack of money almost kept them from landing here when he needed to in order to do his job, and although all he had to do was ask, he still acted as if her inheritance did not exist. Why? If he lost the ship, he lost his livelihood. Dr. Shona could practice anywhere, but traders had to have ships. Why did Gershom's pride stand in the way of help, freely offered? It must be because he said no once, and now he felt that he couldn't go back on what he'd said originally. She remembered once, in her village, the son of the woman next door had sworn he would not sleep under her roof again after a very loud argument. His mother begged him. He said no several times, and made his bed between two trees. Of course, it rained a torrent that night. His mother stood on the threshold and pleaded with him to come in, but his pride wouldn't let him. He sat out all night, and got a chill. But surely that kind of silly pride wasn't natural to Gershom's character? She'd heard him admit to being wrong in many other situations. He had even been humble to her, and she was only a child.

"Ms.?" a voice broke into her thoughts with an intensity that suggested the man had addressed her several times without her being aware of it. "*Ms.*"

"What do you want?" she asked. The man was clad in a seedy uniform without insignia. He held out a clutch of roughly wrapped packets.

"Buy some holocards from a man down on his luck? Eh, pretty lady?"

"No, thank you," she said. He was blocking her path, so she

dodged away from him down a narrow avenue. The shops on this road were smaller, and there were fewer well-dressed people walking about. A woman with several small children leaned out of a doorway toward her, a hand extended palm up.

"My children and I are stranded," she wailed. "Please help us, miz."

"I . . ." Lani gaped. An unshaven man appeared next to her.

"Spacer down on his luck. Can you spare a credit?" He was joined by four more beggars with desperate faces.

"I haven't got . . ." Lani began.

"Sick and can't work, citizen. Just a credit. Half a credit."

"Got laid off. We're starving."

"Of *course*, but . . ."

"I need medicine." More beggars appeared from around corners and out of doorways, pleading faces fixed on hers. Some of them were children, their faces smudged with dirt. One little girl with big dark eyes looked much like Lani did at six, but thin, so thin.

"Help, please, Ms."

"I don't have any money. I'll . . . I'll get some," Lani said, backing away. "The bank's back there. I have to go." She edged away, glancing around for the sign Gershom had pointed out to her. The beggars pressed forward, each bleating his or her demand in woeful, insistent voices. She felt terrified, stifled in their midst. "I'll help you, but you have to let me go!"

A hand grasped her upper arm, and dragged her into the middle of the busy fairway. Lani stifled a scream as she saw a woman's face close to hers. The woman had a strong chin, and her mouth was set, but her eyes wore a kindly expression. She shook Lani's arm firmly.

"Don't do it, honey," she said. "Some of them are fakes. Think you know enough to pick out the real hard-luck cases?"

"N-no," Lani gasped, staring. The mob of beggars melted away among the hurrying passersby.

The woman tossed her head toward the now-deserted wall. "None of them are starving, no matter what they say. There's a Traveler's Aid program here, and shelters and meals for anyone who needs them; not swill, either. They shouldn't be asking *you*. Pay no attention. Just keep your head up and keep walking. Bless you for wanting to help, though. You've got a good heart."

Lani was still shaken as the woman disengaged herself and disappeared with a smile into the crowd. Blindly, the girl felt her way forward to a cluster of benches surrounding a play yard in the wide intersection of two avenues. They were plenty of respectable-looking people all around. Children of all ages shouted at each other from swings and jungle gyms. Banging and laughter rose from the miniature fun house in the center of the yard. Parents and caretakers, packages piled around their feet, chatted together while their children played. Lani swayed uneasily toward an empty bench and sat down to think. The pounding of her heart slowed to a normal pace.

It was true she probably didn't understand the weight of her inheritance yet. Eblich had told her that over and over; but even if she did understand its value, she would offer it freely to Shona and Gershom. She wished she could speak volumes to them of her gratitude for giving her love and support, but when she opened her mouth, no matter how she tried, just a few words came out. It was easier to show her affection. The wrong gift is worst than none at all, one of the grandmothers of her village used to say. She knew money was the right gift, but why wouldn't they take it—why? They wouldn't tell her. They never lied to her, but in this case she didn't think they were telling her the whole truth. Who would tell her the truth? *Someone* must.

A little girl on the swings cried out with delight, and ran to meet two women. They knelt down to embrace her and one of them handed her a package. Eyes wide with anticipation, the child tore off the wrappings to uncover a doll dressed in a floaty sari of sparkling green gauze. She chattered her thanks and kissed both women, who exchanged a pleased squeeze of the hand. Wistfully, Lani wished she'd had a beautiful doll like that when she was little. Her cherished Tallah, made for her by her late mother and father, was sewn of scrap cloth and painted with homemade dyes. Not that she scorned her handmade treasure, then or now, but this doll with its tea-colored skin and curly, brown- and blond-streaked hair was so exotic and otherworldly that she longed to touch it. The thought struck her: why should she not have such a doll now? She could afford it. But no, she still balked at buying anything extravagant for herself. Would Mama Shona like something pretty?

Suddenly Lani felt ashamed of herself, wasting time sitting, when she could be exploring this huge, wonderful place. Opportunities simply to wander like this were scarce in the schedule of a busy trading ship. Shona would have loved to be there with her. Was she growing old, just like those other, unfortunate people? Shona had asked her to take care of Gershom. She wouldn't be much good at that if she was afraid to take care of herself. Resolutely, she propelled herself off the bench and went to look at the holographic store directory near the wall.

·11·

Gershom uncrossed his legs, then recrossed them with the left leg over the right knee. The three clerks behind the glass wall passed back and forth, stopping occasionally to tap in a few keystrokes beneath a screen. No one paid any attention to the four men and women waiting in the reception area. Gershom was tempted to climb up onto the counter and hammer out a fusillade with fists and feet against the window to see if any of the clerks would even break stride. Occasionally, very occasionally, a lucky customer would be summoned to the glass, where he or she would carry on a conversation with roughly the same amount of privacy given to sufferers of private itches in tri-dee commercials. Gershom had tried to explain the urgency of his business in a low voice to the clerk who took his name, but was told he would just have to wait his turn. No such thing as a life-or-death situation existed behind the glass.

At last his turn came. A balding man whose thin-bridged nose sported flaring nostrils appeared on the other side of the window and beckoned to Gershom. He slid into the chair before the window.

"What is your business, citizen?" the man asked. His face was arranged in the bland set of every government employee, but the flared nose made him look arrogant. He shuffled a few of the hundreds of plas-sheets stacked on both sides of him.

Gershom bent down to get his mouth closer to the opening at the bottom of the glass divider. "I'm here to request—"

"Louder, please," the man said peevishly, peering shortsightedly at him. Gershom thought he looked like a lesser bird of prey with a name tag. Withers. He sat up and cleared his throat.

"I'm here to request the personal health records for a number of people. On behalf of Governor Horne of Poxt." He pushed the datacube containing Horne's letter under the glass. Withers took it and poked it into a reader.

"This is very vague," he complained. "Unnecessarily so. I take it you are prepared to be more specific?"

Gershom hesitated. He peered over his shoulder. The one woman still waiting checked her wristwatch against the chronometer on the wall, and went back to her personal reader without looking at him.

"I've been asked to provide details only to the person who is in the position of granting access to the records," Gershom said. "Governor Horne would prefer they weren't widely known at present. I need to speak specifically to that person."

The man tented his fingers and squirmed slightly more upright in his seat. "I am that person, Captain."

"Very well. Both major parties of settlers bound for Poxt stopped here on the final leg of their journey. Were you here at either of those times, either fifteen or two years ago?" The man nodded. "I need specifics from the decontamination phase. Was anything saved?"

"No. We rarely keep those records."

"Did any anomalies strike you? Anything curious about their itineraries or personal histories that stuck in your mind, from either group?"

The man stared pointedly at Gershom's hand, then to a place just in front of his own clasped hands. Gershom, embarrassed, felt in his tunic pocket. He could ill-afford a large bribe, but since this bureaucrat was obviously not going to cooperate without one, he had to offer something. He hoped the man wasn't too greedy. Taking his time, Gershom slid a ten-credit chit under the glass partition and nudged it into a pile of plas-sheets, where it wasn't obviously visible to anyone around them. Glancing around to make certain his supervisors weren't paying any attention, the bureaucrat crept his hand forward, and under the cover of straightening out the pile, palmed the chit into his lap.

"Wee-e-ell," the bureaucrat said, tapping his cheek with a forefinger. He stared over Gershom's head, eyes narrowing. "I don't remember anything odd at all, really. I *was* here when the group was being checked out for the colony, naturally. It was important in retrospect because it was the first colony on an inhabited planet, you know. I'd have remembered if there was anything really strange about the colonists, I'm sure. But that's all in public archives. You're welcome to rummage through those, Captain. Is that all?"

"Not quite. I need copies of the settlers' health records, and those of the LabCor research group that arrived between two and three years ago. The safety of the colony might depend on my bringing those records back in a timely manner," Gershom said.

Withers looked bored. "If they are urgently required, then why didn't the governor simply message us to send them?"

"Electronic mail is too open," Gershom said tightly. "Sir, there may be an epidemic brewing on Poxt. It's very serious."

Withers shrugged. "People get sick all the time. That's not good enough to get me to open confidential records."

"The ailment in question seems to be affecting the *ottles* as well as the human population," Gershom said. The man's eyes widened.

"Shh!" he said, hunching over and looking around to make certain he wasn't being overheard. "The ottles are sick, too? This is terrible! What's wrong?"

"I'm not a diagnostician," Gershom said. "I've been instructed to bring back the complete records of each person on that list"—he pointed to the datacube—"for comparison with their, er, present condition." As concisely as he could, he outlined the discovery of the aging syndrome, and how the history of the settlers might be tied to its origin.

The bureaucrat looked horrified. The color drained out of his face, leaving it gray. "This sounds most serious. I hope word of this hasn't leaked out."

"So far as I know, no one but the settlers, my crew, and now you, have any inkling that anything is wrong."

"You must keep it that way, you must! Tell no one else! Poxt is our hope for the future! If anything happened to decimate the native population, there would be an outcry! It would be the end of cooperative ventures—that is, when we encounter more sentient life forms," the man corrected himself automatically. He swallowed. "The press would make a meal out of this, Captain."

"I am prepared to keep this entirely confidential," Gershom

said solemnly, amused at the reversal of the man's attitude. "Providing you can cooperate with the governor's request."

"Absolutely! Now, if you'll just give me your security clearance, I can copy these records for you right away."

"Clearance? What do I need that for? This is a public information service center. I could bring up my grades from day school on those terminals in the reading room."

Withers gestured impatiently. "Yes, you could access *your* personal dossiers, or those of your immediate family and dependents, but I can't give you the personal records of a hundred and ten other people without a security code." He tapped his fingertips on the desktop. Gershom glared.

"What about my wife?" he asked suddenly. "She's been hired to investigate this epi—" At the bureaucrat's hasty gesture, he lowered his voice. "—situation."

"Shona Taylor." The man nodded, glancing at the screen to his left. "Yes, she has a level-six clearance. From her years of government service, I see. More than adequate, sir. I will have to seal the records for her eyes only, you understand." He narrowed his eyes waspishly, looking to Gershom for a reaction. "Since your clearance is inadequate."

Gershom refused to rise to the bait. He turned up a hand. "I'm only the delivery pilot in this case, citizen. I'm trying to help save a valued government installation from *certain ruin*." He raised his voice slightly, to attract the attention of the clerks in the rear of the office.

"Shhh!" Withers gave him another impatient frown, then went to a cabinet for a box of datacubes. Some of the employees glanced curiously at Gershom, looking as if they wished they knew what could make Withers jump like that. He smiled pleasantly at them.

Withers, still frowning, scanned through Horne's list, and hit a few keys. The screen began to scroll rapidly up through pages of data. As soon as the first image flashed by, a printout of a magnetic scan of someone's skull, Withers tapped another key so that a private graphic came up instead.

"Do you need lifelong itineraries?" he asked over his shoulder while the program ran. "Activities? Full contacts?"

"Er, I don't think so. If you can list locale and date for anywhere each of these people stopped or stayed for a while, that should help," Gershom said, watching the man's quick fingers type in more commands. "I'm sure Shona and those helping her can contact you for more data, should it become necessary."

"Yes, of course," Withers said, and turned to face him. "Please make certain they message me personally. In fact, please tell them to provide me with monthly reports. I shall have to inform my supervisors, and they will wish me to monitor the situation closely. You understand the necessity."

"I certainly do," Gershom agreed with feeling.

"The fact that there's been an incident will be enough to twist a lot of people's underdrawers in an ugly knot. You know," Withers added wistfully, as he pushed the cubes under the glass divider, "this is the first time there's ever been a real use for these dusty files. We collect them, we store them, we catalogue them, but no one ever wants to see them. In a way, the disaster justifies my job. Good luck, Captain."

Gershom rose, stuffed the cubes into his pockets, and departed, wondering at the workings of a mind that could find a silver lining in such a dark cloud.

"So which one are they taking?" Chaffinch asked as he barged back through the crowd toward Lettitia. She had tried to make herself invisible next to the servers' station at the bar, but it hadn't stopped three spacers from hitting on her or one feebly drunken female spacer from mistaking her for a barmaid and ordering a drink.

"Can't say." Lettitia cocked her head toward one wall, then the other. "The big guy got a tentative contract hauling fresh fruit to Viner's Planet. The tall guy is arguing over the finer points of a deal for a mail courier run of datacubes. The shipper wants to pay for weight, and the spacer wants him to pay for value." Lettitia shrugged. "I did hear the destinations, so it's a fifty-fifty chance we'll guess right if we can't get confirmation on the dock. Besides, the stuff will be in different kinds of crates," she reasoned. "How'd you do in Library Services?"

"Gershom Taylor was there, all right," Chaffinch said. He looked perturbed. "I couldn't get a single thing out of the man he talked to. Caa-*gee*! And worried. There's something big going on, Letty, something cosmic, but I couldn't tell you what. We'll just have to follow them to where they're going and find out."

"Fine. We'll stake out the dock to see what gets loaded on the *Sibyl* so we know where she's bound from here." She glanced at the clusters of spacers and pushed away from the wall. "We better get out of here before they see us and start to add up the coincidences. You want to get something to eat first and spell me?"

Chaffinch wrinkled his nose. "More fast food. The things I do for my art!"

The clerk in the toy store had very kindly offered to have the presents for Alex sent directly to Bay 16. Lani surrendered the boxes, plus the bag containing two cartons of Crunchynut bars for Shona and Chirwl. She couldn't wait to see Alex's reaction to the model spaceship and the soft toy animals with talk-chip mechanisms inside. How was she ever going to endure the weeks of travel time before she got back to Poxt and gave them to him?

She had gotten past being overwhelmed by the magnificence of the entertainment center and the weight of her other cares. It was difficult not to enjoy oneself in a place like this; the whole center was geared toward having a good time. There were so many stores, and every one of them was different. Lani felt as if her catalogue mail dump had come to life. Beautiful women and handsome men offered her miniature flasks of cologne, sips of exotic coffee, bites of pastry, plastic and metal trinkets. Not expecting giveaways, she'd had nothing in which to carry them. A store owner beckoned her over, and in exchange for Lani's tour of her shop, she presented her with a woven carrier bag imprinted with the shop's fish-on-a-bicycle logo. Lani liked the logo so much she bought a casual shirt with the same design on the front, her first-ever purchase on her own, for herself, and with her own money.

Clothes were the biggest attraction for Lani. Shona, who had very good taste, had taught her how to dress in a flattering fashion using the few garments she had. Lani surveyed the clothes of women passing by, trying to judge if what they had on would look good on her. Some new fads had come along since her last mail drop of catalogues. Girls and boys her age were wearing weird black belts studded with long spikes that kept them at arm's length from one another as they walked. Combat tutus, Lani giggled to herself. Another style revealed parts of the body under clear plastic while the rest of the clothing was thickly opaque. In some cases the effect was becoming, but the placement of the "windows" seemed random. She found herself behind one woman whose entire derrière was on view. Lani was clearly more embarrassed than she was, and hastily turned into the very next store.

"Welcome to Arias Boutique," the doorjamb recited as she passed over the threshold.

"Thank you," Lani murmured. In response to the musical chimes triggered by her entrance, a young man emerged from the rear of the store. Lani looked at him, then glanced away, blushing. He was very handsome, with big, dark blue eyes and long lashes.

"Hello, pretty lady," he said with a smile. "Can I help you?" He gestured toward racks and shelves of garments with the air of a magician revealing wonders.

He may have been close to a wizard. Instead of the strange fads of the moment, most of the clothes on display in Arias were cut along lines that caressed the figure, inviting one's eye to linger instead of being repelled. She was drawn at once to a shimmering blouse of rich red, but stopped short of touching it.

"Can I—?" she began, then lost her nerve.

"Of course," the young man said, with a gentle bowing of his lips. "You may try on whatever you like. Our booths are very private."

That reassurance answered a question she didn't realize she would have liked to ask. She tried on half a dozen blouses of various fabrics, all in jewel colors. A dark blue one of crisp lace attracted her on the hanger but showed too much skin through the fine netting. She handed it out the door without a word.

"You're supposed to wear a bodysuit under it," the clerk said, looking at her hot cheeks. His eyes twinkled as he turned away to get her another outfit.

None of the blouses or wraps quite suited. Back in her shipsuit, she wandered around the shop, idly fingering an item on a rack here, a display there. The young man smiled at her from a distance, keeping an eye on her but not crowding. She thought he was very good at his job.

She glanced at business suits and tunics, dinner clothes, formal trousers, nightwear that ranged from warm and com-

fortable to virtually absent, never intended for mere sleeping.
Then she saw the dress.

Like a beacon in the form of a woman, it flamed gold
underneath the spotlight. Lani moved toward it like a sleep-
walker. The young man was at her elbow in an instant.

"Do you like it?" he asked, holding out the gold-lamé sleeve
for her to touch.

She nodded, lips parted, gazing at the lovely, smooth lines.
She couldn't figure out how it had been put together. There
were no seams, but the fabric . . .

"It's wrinkled," she said, cocking her head at the clerk with
a worried frown.

"No, that's the style of the fabric. It gives it texture. Try it
on."

Lani hurried back to the booth while the clerk removed the
dress from the mannequin. She slipped the skirts over her head,
feeling the crumpled fabric give just enough to pass over her
shoulders and breasts, then compress snugly around her waist.
She stepped out of the booth and into a circle of mirrors to look
at herself, feeling the crisp skirts sweeping gently against her
bare legs. The hem came down to the middle of her calf,
swirling like a shining cloud.

"That's exactly where it's supposed to fall," the young man
said admirably. "You're built like a model, Ms. You look lovely
in that."

He knelt to help her into matching shoes. Lani touched her
thick hair, wishing it was tidy enough for the dress. She had to
admit she did look lovely. She'd never seen anything like this
beautiful, gleaming gown that seemed as if it had been made
just for her.

"I'll buy it," she said impulsively, feeling proud of her
boldness. She'd managed to get the words out without stopping. Oh, Mama would be pleased! Shona was always encouraging her to indulge herself, though Lani never did. And it was
such a *good* dress, something she wouldn't be ashamed to wear
in public. But where would she wear it?

"Oh, you couldn't afford that, Ms.," the clerk said, half-
teasingly. "It's five hundred sixty credits!"

"I . . . I can," she said. "Really. Please."

The young man smirked a little as he entered her account
number on his screen. His amused expression was abruptly

replaced by open shock. Numerals marched across the screen in a straight line punctuated only by commas. He erased it, then reentered the account number, more carefully. The same line of numbers filled the screen from one side to the other. Lani knew what he was seeing. The value of deeds for just one small continent on Karela was worth hundreds of millions of credits. His mouth fell open.

"Does your daddy own the whole planet?" he asked, looking incredulous.

"No," Lani said, suddenly finding his discomfiture funny. She giggled. "I do."

He was positively respectful as he made out the receipt and wrapped up her package in gauzy paper and placed it gently into a box.

"I would be happy to bring your package to your ship, Ms.," he said.

"Thank you, no," Lani said, watching him slip the dress box into a carrier bag. She was disappointed. He had been so nice before, when he thought she was just a dazzled girl of modest means browsing in the fancy shop. Once he'd known she was rich, he backed away from being warm and personal. So that's what Eblich meant; in a small way she was seeing what respect for wealth could do. And it was too bad, because she'd liked the young man the way he was before. Maybe other people would behave like that. Could she help Shona and Gershom by forcing respect for her fortune?

She glanced at his wrist chrono, and realized it was nearly 1800.

"I have to go," she said. "Thank you. You were very helpful."

The ardent looked reappeared for just a moment, and his long lashes dipped seductively. Lani felt her heart flutter and her cheeks redden. He smiled very politely, but it wasn't the same.

"Come again, anytime, Ms. It was a pleasure to help you."

Lettitia came out of the lift, scanning the crowd for Chaffinch. She saw him a moment later, his arms full of fast-food containers, nodding and smiling at a couple of young men who were enthralled to meet the great Chaffinch L'Saye.

One of them held his parcels while he signed an autograph, then posed for pictures with them.

"I'm so sorry," Lettitia said, hurrying up. She relieved the one man of the containers and swept her free arm through Chaffinch's. "Mr. L'Saye has to get to his next assignment. The news can't wait! See him on GVN, tonight!"

"We will," the two chorused.

"Nice save," Chaffinch said. "What have you got?"

"It's Polidice," she said. "They're going to Polidice. Tons of refrigerated crates on the dock, and the burly fellow arguing over dock fees with your little fan."

"What's so important about Polidice?" Chaffinch wondered.

"I don't think our story's there," Letty said impatiently. "It's where they're going afterward I want to know, but no one's talking. Look!"

"What?"

Letty pointed. "That's Taylor. Where's he going now?"

Chaffinch squirmed. "That girl, she's coming out of Arias with a couple of bags. He must be meeting her."

"I don't remember her from the docudrama. Who is she?"

As soon as Taylor and the girl were clear of the door, Letty hurried into the boutique with Chaffinch on her heels.

"That girl," she said, pointing. "What's her name?"

The young man turned large, surprised eyes on her, then blushed. "I can't give you the name of our customers."

"Do you know who this is?" Letty said, gesturing behind her. "This is Chaffinch L'Saye of GVN. It's very important."

"Mr. L'Saye, it's a pleasure!" the young man said, extending his hand. Chaffinch clasped the hand, then moved closer to the desk to cover Letty's movements behind him. One of the oldest tricks in the book, she thought as she entered commands to scroll up the computer screen to the last purchase. Taxes, hmmm. Destination, none, purchase taken with customer, hmmm . . .

"You know we've been here for a few days," Chaffinch was saying. "We've been interviewing a lot of the area merchants, trying to get a handle on how things are in what used to be a remote corner of space. Now, this is a very exclusive shop. Arias is known for being pricey. Do you think you're doing well in this location?"

The young man's face was flushed with pleasure. "Yes, sir.

This is our busy time, the last few weeks of every season. There are more spacers here at quarter-ending than at—"

"Leilani Taylor! Got it!" Letty exclaimed, hitting the Escape key. "Come on, Chaffinch." Realizing he'd been tricked, the clerk looked stricken, and L'Saye pumped his hand.

"You've been very helpful, young man. I promise you, you've helped the cause of investigative journalism more than you can ever know. Thank you."

Once they had broken the encryption on the data banks, there was no difficulty in calling up each message, viewing it, and then discarding it. Ladovard sifted patiently through the files, confirming each transmission to one of the dummy numbers used by the Taylors, and each reply sent on from the actual number, decoded right in this single beacon. Why the GBI used a system that was so easily penetrated he couldn't guess. Surely someone in their ranks had more imagination—but no, not necessarily. In forty years they had never caught a sniff or a glimpse of him, and he had carried out some of his assignments right under their noses. The GBI didn't so much as know what he looked like. He had long ago wiped his records from the Central Records Office memory, from just such a beacon as this one. Another indignity modern technology had thrust upon humanity: with the advent of computer communication networks there was no privacy, no security, and above all, no secrets, except those which never were entered on the net.

"No idea where they went, sir," Pogue said. He had been reticent since his blunder, and was assiduously trying to make up for it. "Sixty transmissions checked, and no reference to a destination."

Ladovard nodded. "Start checking landing and docking records. Ships can pass unnoticed while they're flying, but as soon as they wish to land somewhere, they must create a record. Find it."

"Yes, sir."

It took a cash bribe to get their takeoff moved up to the next slot after the *Sibyl*'s, plus all of Chaffinch's charm. "The news can't wait," he reminded the operator, a girl with golden skin. She reddened slightly to bronze as he leaned in toward the video pickup. Out of sight of the camera, Lettitia rolled her eyes. It worked; it always did. She punched out of the landing bay as quickly as she could once they got the go-ahead.

"Did you get anything more out of the research library?" she asked.

"Not a thing," L'Saye said, checking his shock belts with the tips of his fingers. He was paranoid about the webbing coming loose and propelling him either forward or backward into the metal bulkheads. "They were scared, really scared. I couldn't get a sniff of what Taylor was there for. Soon's we're clear, I'm going on beam all the same. Where that ship is, and where it goes, is news. He's working on something big."

"You can *hint* at something big," Lettitia said. "Well, even if it turns out to be a bust, maybe we can get an interview with Taylor at his next stop. I got in touch with the producer of that video about them, but she wouldn't give me an address or a comm number for them. Wants to keep the whole thing exclusive."

"You can't stop the people," Chaffinch said. "They have a right to know. And we are the people. I'm going to go get made up."

"Great," Lettitia said. "We can bounce this off the beacon right here. It'll feed Zedari immediately, and every repeater in the galaxy will pick it up next. I'll message GVN on a squirt and tell them we're onto something."

"Good day, ladies and gentlemen." The famous image smiled into the tri-dee camera. "I'm Chaffinch L'Saye, on assignment for GVN in the Zedari sector.

"You may recall Shona and Gershom Taylor, the brave spacers who three years ago uncovered the heinous plot to kill off thousands of Corporation colonists using germ warfare. You see me now just departing Zedari Station, on the trail of their ship, the *Sibyl*." Lettitia edited in a stock shot of a scout ship detaching from a docking ring, then a captioned picture of the Taylors, taken from the GG archives. Chaffinch's voice continued over the images. "We believe the doughty crew may be on another mission of mercy. Captain Taylor called in at Zedari Station just last shift to glean information from the public information database, which will most likely be used to prevent a disaster." The camera returned to Chaffinch, and he favored it with a sincere, concerned gaze. "Will he be able to reach his destination in time? For security reasons we are withholding the subject of Taylor's inquiry . . ."

Behind the camera, Lettitia pulled at her nose, pretending that it was growing a foot long. Chaffinch's eyelids lowered slightly, but he made no other sign he could see her. He concentrated on the lens.

". . . but you may be sure that we are looking further into this matter. Chaffinch L'Saye, for GVN."

Ladovard's two assistants spoke almost at once.

"Sir, I have the *Sibyl*!" Emile said, her narrow face alight. "She's recorded as docking at Zedari Station!"

"Sir, listen to this!" Pogue said, at a console across the room. Since the murdered technicians had no further use for their equipment, it seemed only sensible to Ladovard for his team to make use of it. "Open broadcast, five keywords. It's them." Pogue pushed a button, and the large screen over his head displayed the head of a handsome, dark-skinned man with brilliant white teeth.

". . . For security reasons, we are withholding the subject of Taylor's inquiry. A spokesman for the Central Records Office refused to comment . . ."

"Very good!" Ladovard said. "Good timing as well as good fortune. The *Sibyl* is only a single beacon away."

"Should we find their vector and follow them, sir?" Pogue asked.

"No. Not yet. We don't know where they're going. What transmissions have you located?" Ladovard asked Emile.

"Following sixty per cent of all keywords and on-file comm numbers, I have seven outgoing transmissions to four known accommodation codes plus one I hadn't seen before, all datamarked two to three weeks ago, two different beacons. The recipients are mostly public numbers: two shipping companies, MarsBank One, Child Welfare Bureau of Mars, and I am still waiting to identify the others, sir. The stranger is likely to be the news reporter, sir."

"Save that one. It may be useful to audit their transmissions about the *Sibyl*. And that is all? None of the personal correspondents?"

"No, sir. Not for several weeks." Emile slid away from the console to show him.

"Most uncharacteristic. That worries me," Ladovard said, pinching his thin lower lip between thumb and forefinger. He whirled and pointed at Pogue. "No. We don't follow them. Find out where the *Sibyl* came *from*."

"Sir," Pogue said, and went back to his screen, though he looked confused. He began entering code.

Within hours the Zedari Station docking computer downloaded their active files into the beacon's memory. The alarm sounded, waking Ladovard from a light sleep. Emile was asleep in the corner, thin limbs folded up close to her body like a discarded marionette. Pogue was out of it, leaning backward in his chair with his heels on the console. The bounty hunter slapped the soles of his employee's feet to wake him.

"Report," he snapped.

Pogue was awake in an instant, feet down, fingers running over the keyboard. The screen flashed from one data file to another. He scanned them until he saw the one he wanted, then froze it. "She came from Poxt, sir. Isn't that the extraterrestrial homeland? She's going to Polidice."

"Yes," Ladovard said, pleased. In her corner, Emile rose as if on invisible strings and stalked over to see what they were doing. He turned to her and barked orders. "Back onto the ship. We're bound for Poxt."

"Sir!" Emile said, her face expressionless.

"Poxt?" Pogue asked. "Shona Taylor is going to Polidice."

"She's not on that ship," Ladovard said.

"Sir?"

"The *Sibyl*, out in space for several weeks' transit, but not a single personal message in that whole time? This does not fit the behavioral profile we've built up for over a year now, and I refuse to countenance a personality change of that magnitude. Either that woman is on that ship and she's dead or unconscious, or she is not on that ship."

"But it's going to Polidice. A mission of mercy, that reporter said."

"A ploy. They've been canny enough to mislead us before, but Taylor can't change the facts. She has an ottle. Poxt is the ottle homeworld. The *Sibyl* is not transmitting constant streams of friendly babble as it always does when she's aboard. There may be some errand on Polidice, but it has nothing to do with her. They left her on Poxt. *We* go to Poxt. Any argument?"

Pogue stared, then scrambled up and headed for the airlock. Emile was already there waiting for them. "No, sir."

"It is our opinion, therefore," Missa Volk's image reiterated from the video screen, "that there is no security breach at this time. However, we ask for your advice regarding how to handle Shona Taylor. It is possible that she may come to an independent conclusion regarding the source of the 'aging plague,' and may even make her own determination how to halt it. Although she was not an original part of the project, her experience and intelligence could be of use to us. Therefore, I would appreciate hearing from you as to whether you would approve an expenditure that would serve as a fee to buy her cooperation and confidentiality."

LabCor president Amir Eleniak settled back into his black leather armchair and tented his fingers together. The shining hide was a nice match for his glossy black hair.

"It is very difficult to admit to having made a mistake," he said to the vice-president in charge of procurement. "I wouldn't have thought that Dr. Volk would cry uncle."

"Nor would I, Amir," said the vice-president, who was his brother Sajjid, and strongly resembled him. "She is very proud. If she thinks that this Dr. Taylor would be a boon to the project, I would say go ahead and hire her. It sounds as if she may be doing part of Volk's work for her already. Particularly we should do it before she accidentally exposes the research. It is our great good luck that such an error occurred in a place where the local government is so eager to avoid GG interferences that they are letting an independent take a hand."

"That's my thought, too," Amir said. He stretched out a hand across the onyx desktop toward a textured panel of studs, and pressed one.

"Franz," he said to the young blond man who entered the office. "I want a datacube with secrecy clauses made up. Thumbprint platen, please."

"Sir." The corner of the secretary's mouth twitched with supressed agitation. "Sir, I think you should put on the beacon news video."

Amir raised an eyebrow, but leaned forward for another button.

A sheet of paneling slid discreetly behind another, and the

screen behind it moved forward slightly. A dark-skinned man with red highlights in his hair was speaking. His image was replaced first by that of a ship, then of a man and a woman. The text at the bottom of the third scene read "Shona and Gershom Taylor."

". . . We believe the doughty crew may be on another mission of mercy. Captain Taylor called in at Zedari Station just last shift to glean information from the public information database, which will most likely be used to prevent a disaster. Will . . ."

Sajjid's fist slammed down on the desktop.

"Is this a repeat?" Amir asked Franz. "Did the reporter mention LabCor, or the research station?"

"No, sir."

"Then he doesn't know about it," Sajjid said definitely. "Our juvenology process will be big news when it breaks."

"I don't want word of the nanovirus to be made public," Amir said, his eyes flashing. "And I do not want this woman to make the connection between her 'aging plague' and the experiments. She cannot be trusted to maintain security. Volk is wrong."

"A known snoop," Sajjid said smoothly, as if he had never urged his brother to hire the woman in the first place. Amir glanced at him. "If her involvement is made public, it will erode confidence in our product when it is finally available on the open market."

"And now all eyes will be on Poxt," Amir said, narrowing his eyes. His fingertips drew together again as if magnetized. "She must be stopped." He turned to Sajjid. "Go yourself. Prevent this from becoming an embarrassment. I will notify Volk."

"Puffery," sneered Verdadero, watching the GVN news report in the prison common room. "Mission of mercy, indeed." He eyed the comm console underneath the main screen. It was operated by a trusty, one whom Verdadero had approached and found incorruptible. Consequently, he'd have to employ a more subtle method to communicate his next move.

"Will we dine in our room, Your Majesty?" asked Duncan, his broad face split in an insufferable grin.

"I don't wish to put you to any trouble, Mr. Duncan,"

Verdadero said, favoring him with a pleasant smile. "If I could stay here for a while, I would appreciate it."

Duncan glanced at the trusty, who was changing the video input from GVN to a two-dee movie from Old Earth. "Forget it. You won't get any change out of him, Jaci."

"I assure you, Mr. Duncan," Verdadero said, "you won't see or hear me exchange a single word with him." He looked down at his ill-fitting prison garb. How unpleasant it was, he thought, to wear such a costume, intended to deprecate. Though clad in the same fabrics as the prisoners, the guards were deliberately dressed in tailored, better-cut uniforms that defined them as the masters. After a while, most of the prisoners began to act in a submissive fashion; and even timid men dressed in guards' attire eventually took on the characteristics of the dominators and were accepted as such. Even if neither prisoner nor jailor believed in the charade, each of them played his part effectively. Duncan, satisfied that he had cowed his charge once again, retired to the far side of the room to speak to another guard. The moment his back was turned, Verdadero caught Domitio's eye.

The other inmate nodded his round head. His black hair was a mere quarter centimeter long, and his facial hair covered his jaw and upper lip, so that the small dark eyes peered out of a horizontal patch like a white domino mask. Domitio was at home here. He knew the system and worked well within it. Helpful, because he was sentenced to life imprisonment. Useful, because Verdadero needed his expertise. Whatever small favors he'd been able to do for Domitio, he had done. Now it was time for the payoff.

"You, you high-nosed pansy, what are you looking at?" Domitio came over from the wall and poked a hand at Verdadero's chest.

"One must look at something," Verdadero said, without raising his voice. "You were in the sweep of my vision."

"How'd you like to have your vision swept across the floor?"

"Now, now, man, is this necessary?" Verdadero asked, with the combination of steel and silk he'd used to terrify his employees. As he'd calculated, it enraged the lifer, who picked him up bodily by the front of his tunic.

"I'll say what's necessary and what's not," Domitio growled in a low tone.

"I have done you no harm," Verdadero said, in a similarly low tone.

"I'm in charge here."

"Call today, tell Schauer to accelerate the program," Verdadero said in the same reasonable voice, but low enough so no one else could hear. "The *Sibyl* must be seized as soon as it lands anywhere."

"Gotcha. You dusty coward," Domitio said, throwing him back onto the bench. By now the guards had noticed the fracas in the middle of the room and were coming to break it up. Three of them grabbed Domitio around the arms and the neck and pulled him away from Verdadero. "Don't get in my face again!" he warned the former executive, shaking a thick finger at him. He was removed, struggling, amidst the shuffling guards.

"Well, Jaci, you sure do rub people the wrong way," Duncan said, appearing at his elbow. "C'mon, I'll bring your lunch to your cell. Table for one?"

"I think now that would be very nice," Verdadero said, rising and falling in beside his so-called rescuer. Shona Taylor was on her way to an assignment. He was grateful to the GVN reporter for keeping a running tab on her whereabouts. Domitio would pass the word to Schauer, a vice-president of MarsBank, who still owned Verdadero many favors from times past. When he foreclosed on the ship's mortgage, the Taylors would be trapped wherever they were, without means of escape. It would make it so much easier for the anonymous bounty hunter who had answered his latest advertisement to find them and eliminate them.

He sat down to his lunch with a good appetite.

·12·

The *Sibyl* cleared Zedari effortlessly and made her way out through the mass of spacecraft into clear space. Traffic was heavy, so Gershom had to monitor the autopilot program, often going to manual to keep from colliding with other ships. The proximity alarm went off twice. First, a huge freighter came out of warp too fast and too close to the space station. There wasn't time to be frightened before the behemoth veered away in a parabola, missing the station and all the smaller craft. By then Gershom and every other pilot in the vicinity whose alarms had gone off had fled around the perimeter of the great wheel, out of harm's way.

Lani had barely relaxed when another ship rode up too closely on their tail departing Zedari's restricted space. Gershom turned on the rear external pickups to see a handsome new scout ship visibly dumping velocity, its side retros firing out into space.

"Hot-dogs," Eblich complained sourly, slapping off the alarm. "What else did you get for your birthday, eh?" Gershom shook his head.

"Maybe it's his shakedown cruise," he said generously.

"I don't care. He's a hot-dog."

"We're intact," Gershom said. "And we're on our way."

As soon as the navigation tank began to calculate the first warp jump, Gershom twisted his head around in his seat to smile at Lani.

"The fruit for Polidice is a premium load," he said happily. "We get a speed bonus for every day under ten that we can beat. I think I can get us there in six days flat. And it won't take us

186

a day longer to get back to Poxt, because by going this way we're missing anomalies that we'd otherwise have to jump around."

"Good!" Lani said, smiling at him. It was good to see him feeling optimistic. He grinned back, and patted her on the arm as he stood up.

"Kai, let's go over the manifests, all right? Eblich, the conn is yours. We'll be aft. Let me know if there's any problems. We jump in about four hours."

"Right," said the co-pilot, punching buttons so that the main controls lit up under his hands. Lani waited until the other two men were well out of hearing before she crept forward and sat in the pilot's seat beside him.

"Eblich?"

"Yes, little one?" The navigator turned his head to smile shyly at her.

"I was thinking. I'm worried about Mama and Papa."

"Uh-huh. What?"

"Well, this run. We should go right back to Mama Shona, and we can't because of the money Papa needs to get from this cargo, right?"

Eblich settled in his crash couch and tilted his head back to look at the ceiling. "That's about right."

"But why? When I can pay for fuel or anything with no trouble."

"Gershom and us, we're used to doing for ourselves, dear," he said.

"But just now it's harder," Lani said, trying to frame her question. "Until things are better, why would it be bad to take money from me? I want to. I love them. I love you." The bald statement escaped her lips before she could stop it, and she blushed.

Eblich turned his head to look at her fondly. "I know, little one. I can't go against my captain's wishes, but since you ask, I'd say to get in touch with Harry Elliott at MarsBank."

"Uncle Harry?"

"Um-hm"

"Why? My credit is open. I can pay for things *now*."

"Nope. Gershom and Dr. Shona can't take your money direct no matter when. Nohow."

Lani gawked at him. "Why not?"

Eblich made a decision. He sat up and took her hands between his. The palms were dry and scratchy, but warm. "Because that's what people think they want to adopt you for."

"But it's not true."

"Of course it's not, but people think that way. I'm not supposed to talk about it, so you're not hearing it." He shot a glance down the corridor, and Lani leaned close so he wouldn't have to talk loud. "The Child Welfare Bureau keeps getting nosy-business briefs to keep Gershom and Dr. Shona from adopting you final, because they think you're a piggy bank the Taylors can shake any time they're broke. Too convenient. One of 'em's offered to take you himself so we won't have you." He let her go and sat back, gasping a little at having delivered such a long speech.

Lani was speechless with outrage. "But couldn't those people want me for the same reason?"

Eblich, silently, wearing a knowing expression, tapped the side of his nose with a forefinger.

"So that's it," Lani said, planting her chin in the palm of her hand. "And they couldn't tell me."

"No."

"So what can I do?"

"Your money's got power you can use. If the captain won't take the money from you direct, and he can't, then you buy the mortgage from the bank, and you don't foreclose when the payments are late. You're not giving them a thing, but then no one's taking anything from them. That's what Harry Elliott can do for you."

"Why," Lani stammered, feeling delight dawning at the simplicity of it all, "that's wonderful! It's ideal. Yes!"

"Glad you like it. We're still near the beacon. You can send a squirt to him to do it right away."

"That's expensive!" Lani explained.

"That's the power of money, lass. You mean business. The bankers'll respect that. Send to him and tell him what you want. I'll go aft and keep Gershom out of your way while you do it."

"But I don't know what to say," Lani said anxiously. She felt very small in the captain's chair, and drew her hands and knees together.

"I'll tell you," Eblich said, running a fingertip over the board to bring up the communications program. "But you're going to have to do the talking."

Lani stared at her reflection in the screen for half an hour before she was finally able to bring herself to record her message. Eblich's carefully written speech rolled in large, clear print across the bottom of the screen for her to read aloud. She let it run through once more before she pushed the button.

"To Mr. Harry Elliott, from Leilani Taylor. I wish to purchase the mortgage obligation for the trading ship *Sibyl*, contract number 3342801 stroke A 9845 dash four from MarsBank. I offer full payment for the current outstanding balance plus any reasonable fees for the immediate transfer of the title to me. This message gives you permission to make this purchase on my behalf. I trust you will treat the matter as entirely confidential. My credit account number is in your files." She read the technical description of the purchase proposal straight off the teleprompter without understanding a word. Mercifully, she didn't stumble over a single syllable, and her voice kept going strong throughout. Her throat only threatened to squeak very close to the end of the message.

"I would appreciate an immediate reply by return squirt. I authorize you to use my communication account for the expenditure," Lani finished, then blurted, "Leilani out." She leaned forward and punched the button to Send, then sat back breathing quickly. She'd never done anything so bold in her life. She wished desperately she could go and tell Gershom about it, but she'd done it for him, and for Shona, so he mustn't know. She clutched the secret to her like a teddy bear, and crept back to her little cabin to think about what she'd say to them when she got the good news.

The light on the top of the lockdown on Ladovard's control console flared red. He removed the datacube from its niche, and popped it into the reader at his right side.

"How convenient," he said, peering at the readout. "They're leaving us a trail of messages." His blunt-tipped fingers tapped out a command on his keypad, transferring the data to Emile's console.

"MarsBank," Emile confirmed, glancing up from her reader. "Still no personal number."

"Then we continue on to Poxt as planned," Ladovard said.

Lani waited impatiently by her small personal communications unit for the ship to emerge from warp. As soon as they had reentered normal space, Gershom signaled an All Clear. Immediately Lina booted up the comm program and entered her number. They weren't as close to a beacon as they had been at the space station, so it was a long time until the line-of-sight connection was made.

There was no news. Uncle Harry had all the coordinates for the jump stops from Zedari to Polidice. Lani checked her copy of the message she'd sent him again and again to make sure. Either he hadn't gotten her urgent note yet, or he didn't have a reply. It was going to be hard to wait. Perhaps in the next one.

Six times the *Sibyl* bounded in and out of warp. Each time, Lani checked in on the net, and each time she was disappointed.

"We're in warp for so long, and out of it such a short time, my mail might be missing me," she fretted to Eblich when they were alone.

"It'll be at Polidice," he assured her. "Why would Elliott take a chance on missing you in between?"

"If I got good news we wouldn't have to go to Polidice," Lani complained.

"Now, you have to leave a man his pride," Eblich said. "Gershom's contracted to deliver the shipment, so he will. I wouldn't tell him all at once, now. Keep it."

Lani had no choice but to agree.

Six days out of Zedari Station, the *Sibyl* broke warp outside the heliopause of a star system with a small yellow star at its hub. Gershom and the others burst out into cheers as the computer confirmed that the sun and its planets were indeed the Polidice system.

"We did it, folks," Gershom said smugly. "Four days' worth of speed bonus!"

"Nearly shook the ship apart," Ivo complained. "I'm gonna have to use part of the bonus for repairs."

"Live it up," Gershom said happily. "Whatever it takes. All

I need is enough to make this month's payment to the bank, and we can whoop it up with the rest. There'll be the other half of our fee from Governor Horne when we get to Poxt. At this rate, we'll be earlier than expected!"

"Bravo!" said Kai, applauding.

A Klaxon blared from the panel. Eblich looked down.

"Proximity alarm," he said.

"Where?" Gershom asked, switching the controls to enhanced manual.

"Thirty-five degrees off starboard," Eblich said. He punched up the command to put on the exterior video pickup. Gershom nudged the ship to port and down through the plane of the ecliptic, but the alarm continued to sound.

"It's that ship," Kai said, studying the screen. "The one that nearly rammed us off Zedari."

"Impossible," Gershom said. "It can't be the same one."

"It sure is," Ivo said definitely. "That new scout, white with a colored seal on each flank. That's it."

"It is," Eblich confirmed, his mouth small and tight. "Not the same one as Venturi, though."

"Two different assassins," Gershom said. Lani behind him, let out a small gasp. He could see her big eyes reflected in the navigation tank. "Don't worry, sweetheart. They can't catch us."

"I'm reading a big power source on board," Ivo said, checking the telemetry station. He reached over one big arm, and unbuckled his harness with the other hand. "I'm heating up the asteroid probe."

"Do it," Gershom said. His senses sharpened so that he was aware of every sound in the ship. He found he was watching three things at once: the navigation tank, the intruder on screen, and his own crew as they prepared to fight.

The other craft was a sleek job. No ports or ungainly hatches broke the lines to show where its weapons were hidden, leaving Ivo without obvious targets. This pilot was as good as the other had been. Gershom hoped that his luck would hold out again. He put the *Sibyl* on full manual and started evasive maneuvers, but the enemy stayed right with him all the way through a difficult loop and thrust. Kai cursed colorfully over the shrieking of the *Sibyl*'s engines. Her increased mass was interfering with Gershom's long-honed techniques of maneuvering. One day, Gershom vowed, if they survived this, he was going to have to take the ship somewhere and practice hard turns until he got used to her increased weight and size.

Inertia pressed them all back in their seats as he increased acceleration. Ivo was flat against the bulkhead, holding on by main strength to the bars at the third pilot station. Lani was almost invisible behind him, clutching her shock webbing with frightened fingers. Gershom felt his teeth rattling as he cut in the port engines and spun to starboard 180 degrees almost on his fins. To his dismay the white ship followed close behind, missing turning in Gershom's wake by only a few hundred kilometers.

"What is this, sky ballet?" Kai demanded.

"Power source on board building," Ivo said, peering at the scopes. "Are they waiting to get in close for the kill?"

"Wants to see our faces," Kai said. Gershom vowed the intruder wouldn't get a chance to do that.

He scanned the tank for hiding places. The nearest planet of the system was not far away. They were lucky the wanderer was in this point of its two-hundred-year orbit, ready to provide cover for the *Sibyl*. No, wait, there was an asteroid belt only a few million miles farther in toward the sun. Gershom increased acceleration, keeping his path erratic to prevent an easy shot up their rockets from behind.

The intruder seemed to become aware that the *Sibyl* was heading for the safety of the asteroid belt, and was pouring on speed to overtake her. Gershom had too good a head start. He was going to get among the giant's dance of space debris first.

"Power getting higher," Ivo said. "I'm picking up high-frequency tones on board her. Higher, higher . . ."

The laser! Forcing his ship to go faster almost by his very will, Gershom laid on the last erg of speed the *Sibyl* had in her, and swooped into the asteroid field. Once past the first shard of broken rock, he made a sharp downward curve to port. The white ship couldn't have touched them with a laser beam, not unless they'd taught one to go around multiple corners. He prayed she didn't have missiles.

Now the *Sibyl* was in as much danger from spinning rocks as she was from the ship behind her. What little light had been coming from the distant star was cut off almost completely by the network of asteroids. The *Sibyl* was surrounded by faint, shifting shadows in the dark; ominous, and silent. Gershom set the navigation controls on enhanced manual, letting the computer help him guide the scout through the obstacles. Each asteroid had its own velocity and path, set in motion a billion years ago. Gershom could only hope the computer-modeling program would be able to pick up the gravity wells of each large body, and figure out where it bent space to guide the passage of smaller objects, and so on down to particles smaller than sand, so he could maneuver between them.

Tiny pieces of stone tapped on the video pickups and the portholes. Occasionally a thump warned them that a larger fragment, maybe fist-sized, had rammed them. Gershom glanced over his shoulder to Ivo, who had settled himself in with the probe controls, shivering advancing asteroids into harmless pieces, or diverting them off to one side. Smithereens ricocheted dangerously off the huge turning boulders to either side, and pocked the soft protective coating on the *Sibyl*'s hull. Gershom felt sweat rolling down the center of his back.

"She's coming in," Eblich warned, pointing at a red light behind them on the field scanner.

There could be no mistake. No other power source existed for billions of miles in any other direction. Gershom refused to believe in a chance-met miner, or a wealthy hermit occupying a hollowed-out meteor. The white ship had followed their energy traces. It couldn't catch them in this, but by the same token, neither could Gershom put on a burst of speed and get away.

Abruptly, they spilled out into a long, irregular hollow, created while asteroids that normally occupied those spaces were momentarily elsewhere. Gershom negotiated the gap as swiftly as possible, monitoring the red blip behind them. Suddenly, it too was loose in the free space, closing the gap. Recklessly, the pilot swerved upward along the y-axis of his navigation tank, slipping between two jagged rocks each the size of a moon. The white ship hesitated, giving Gershom a good lead. He wound his way through the maze heedless of the dangers to either side of him, seeing only the gaps that opened and closed ahead of him, timing his passage so that the rocks slid by just behind his tail. They saw flashes of white getting smaller and smaller in the rear-pointing viewscreen.

"Start calculating," he said to Eblich. "We don't need a long jump, just something that'll get us out of here."

"From what point?" the co-pilot asked, hands flying over the keyboard.

Gershom glanced at the telemetry computer. "A thousand klicks ahead," he said. "If we're not completely clear yet, too bad. I'd rather be blown apart jumping than boiled in my skin by a laser."

"Lousy choice," Ivo grumbled.

A shard of planetoid five hundred meters across suddenly cartwheeled into their path. Lani let out a tiny shriek. Gershom had to burn rockets hard on the port side and under to avoid it. They veered starboard into the crater of a toroid moonlet. He fancied he could see the wreckage of another ship scattered across its surface. Ivo fired the mining probe and a gray asteroid burst into silver sparks. They flew through the shower. Gershom shook his head to clear his vision.

"Coming up fast," Ivo snapped. The red blip was back on the near scope, and closing in on them.

"What?" Kai said. "They must be drilling straight through the asteroids, not ducking them. Jump!"

"Not yet," Eblich said, watching the small screen. "Not ready. A hundred klicks to go. Eighty. Sixty. Forty. Twenty." Clear space appeared ahead, the tiny points of stars glowing steadily. Suddenly, they were surrounded by the myriad lights. The darkness dropped behind them.

"We're out of the belt!" Gershom yelled.

"Mark!" Their heads were flung back against the shock padding as the ship accelerated into warp. Gershom gritted his teeth against the juddering of his ship.

"Stay with him," Chaffinch said, arcing his body to the right as *Sibyl*, ahead of them, veered around another asteroid. He jerked to the left and flung himself forward until his nose was nearly up against the forward port. "Steady. Ooh! Look out!" Lettitia dodged splinters of stone that were as large as their ship. The camera beside him hummed, taking video of the whole chase through hidden external pickups. "Stay with him . . . easy . . . Down! Around! Damn! You *lost* him." He smacked his hand on the console.

"He warped out," Letty said irritably, as the GVN shuttle

shot out into clear space. The *Sibyl* was as gone as if it had never existed. "You try figuring out where he went." Chaffinch scowled and thrust out a hand.

"Well, I have no idea. There must be a thousand colonies straight out in that vector. And he's a wily enough fox to change direction on his next jump. I'll bet he doesn't come back to Polidice. What do you think?"

"He's got to deliver that load," Letty said thoughtfully. She tapped her fingers on her lower lip. "But why take a side trip if he's got an emergency big enough to worry the bureaucrats?"

"Because it's on the way there?" Chaffinch suggested.

"Yeah," said Lettitia, the light dawning. She began to poke away with her forefingers at the computer keyboard on the right edge of the console, the beginnings of an idea forming. "Yeah."

"What are you doing?"

"I'm checking the data I got off the docking computer."

"You hacked the docking computer?" Chaffinch asked, his eyes wide. She raised her eyebrows at him.

"Isn't that what you pay me cuantos credits for?—Here it is. The *Sibyl* came from Poxt. Is this on the way there?" She entered the coordinates for the Polidice and Poxt systems into the navicomputer. "Yes. It. *Is!*" she crowed, her voice rising in triumph.

"Zow!" Chaffinch said, shooting a fist forward in a victory salute. "*Nice* work, boss. *That's* where he's bound." Lettitia leaned back, preening. She felt she deserved the praise, and more.

"I'll send to GVN that we're following Taylor to Poxt. You start writing copy," she said. "We've got to justify the fuel for this silly side-trip, since it didn't result in the interview we wanted."

"You've got to pay if you want to play," Chaffinch said imperturbably.

"This is Chaffinch L'Saye. Today, we witnessed the heroic travails of the medical rescue ship *Sibyl* as she fought her way through the dangers of an asteroid belt to make an emergency delivery to the Polidice system."

"They're carrying fruit!" Letty said crossly as Chaffinch smiled with aplomb at the lens.

"Can I help that?" he asked, grinning.

Letty groaned, and rolled the video memory back to where he had broken off from his script.

"Try it again."

"An emergency which required their immediate attention."

Over Chaffinch's narration, Lettitia made the most of the video of their pursuit of the *Sibyl*, adding exciting sound effects and a few musical phrases to heighten the tension. She cut back to the journalist's face.

"Now the Taylors are off on another mission of mercy, at an unknown destination." Letty made a comical grimace, but Chaffinch continued. "We are accompanying the *Sibyl* there, where we will file the next report in this exciting series. This is Chaffinch L'Saye for GVN."

"Wrap it and send it," Letty said. "We'd better make our calculations good if we want to beat them there."

The *Sibyl* broke out of warp after half an hour's transit. As soon as the normal sensors were functioning again, the shrill cry of the hull breach alarm sounded.

Gershom turned anxious eyes to Ivo at the telemetry station. "Where is it?" he demanded.

"In the holds."

"The fruit!" Kai snapped off his restrictive harness and flung himself to his feet, heading aft all in one movement. "I'll get a pressure suit."

"Can we make port?"

"It's not that bad, Gershom," Ivo said. "It's already sealing up, so it had to be less than a couple of centimeters across."

"Thank the Blue Star. Are we alone?"

"Yep," Eblich said. "We've lost them now, but they might still be waiting around there for us. I've got a scan going for them. They didn't follow us."

"You're sure?"

"Yep. How could they?" Eblich turned his palms upward. Gershom nodded sharply, throwing his long hair forward. It was as wild as he felt.

"All right, then. Check everything else for damage. We'll risk heading back toward Polidice in a little while. I'll have calculations ready in case we have to jump again right away. Dammit, how did they know where we were going?" he asked.

"Bribed the port officials?" suggested Ivo.

"But those spacers would have to know we were going to Zedari in the first place. No one knew that except Shona and Governor Horne and the other folks on Poxt. None of them would have risked the repercussions."

"Opportunity," Ivo said simply. "Somebody who read Verdadero's cash offer for our heads just happened to see us in port, thought he'd collect."

"Then why wait until we were in space again? There are plenty of secluded places to shoot us right there in the station."

"Yes," Lani said, remembering getting lost in the lanes of the shopping precinct.

"Didn't want to risk being picked up for murder in a closed environment's my guess. I'm going to search us for a transmitter," Ivo said. "It may lay us up for a few hours or a day, but at least no one will follow us to Poxt."

"All right," Gershom said. "Good idea."

"Is there time for me to get my messages?" Lani asked in a small voice.

"If you like," Gershom said, managing a smile for the girl. She must have been terrified by the chase and subsequent alarm, but was showing him a determined little chin. "You're getting to be as dogged a correspondent as Shona, sweetheart. Go right ahead."

The intercom went on, and Kai's voice squawked. "Gershom, we've been pinholed! A rock the size of your fingertip went straight through us. The fruit's freeze-dried. I've been checking box after box, and it's ruined!"

"Oh, no," Gershom groaned. He slumped back in his chair and put his head between his hands.

"There goes our speed bonus," Ivo said.

"There goes the mortgage," Gershom said miserably, without looking up.

"Papa, please let me help," Lani's voice came, very softly. "This time?"

"No," Gershom said automatically. He raised his head to meet her eyes. She was frightened. He covered her hand with his own, and realized they were both trembling. "It'll be all right. I promise. Why don't you go listen to your messages? I've got to think."

Lani fled up the corridor. Gershom plodded his way more slowly to the cabin he shared with Shona. He only half-heard

Eblich say he and Ivo would do a full diagnostic while Kai assessed the damages.

He flung himself into the built-in chair beside the low double bunk without feeling the pad under his seat or the hard arms under his elbows. He stared past his booted feet at the floor, and felt an everlasting headache starting between his brows. His precious ship was imperiled. That flight through the asteroid belt was nothing. He could fight enemies he could see. Bad luck, bad timing, and debt, he could do nothing about. Nothing, except possibly humble himself again, and hope for the best.

He'd lost the value of the cargo. Eventually insurance might make up the value of it, but the delivery and speed bonuses were gone for good. The crew had counted on those to pay the next influx of bills. There wasn't enough left from Horne's letter of marque to cover the next mortgage payment, and he couldn't possibly get back to Poxt to collect the other half in time to transmit those funds to Mars. His only chance was to send to MarsBank and ask for clemency.

If he didn't pay, he was in danger of losing his ship, his beautiful, lovely *Sibyl*, refitted just right. She was neat and tidy, with a place for everything, and she ran like a dream, no matter what he put her through. Look at the gantlet they'd just run! And yet she was still a trader, with three, *three* cargo hulls. He was so proud of her that he strutted when other spacers praised her. He couldn't bear the thought of someone taking her, someone else captaining her.

There *was* one alternative. All he had to do was go to Lani and ask for the money. That way, he'd keep his ship, but the Child Welfare Bureau would swoop in and take the girl away. It was still months before the final adoption hearing was scheduled. Any peccadillo would mean they could scoop her out of his custody without the hope of an appeal.

But was it wise to keep her, knowing that life was so uncertain here on board? Was it fair to her, never knowing from month to month if they'd be living on caviar or nutri? She'd be terrified, even furious, if Gershom let the authorities take her, but wouldn't things be better for her? She'd . . . she'd be brought up on a planet with atmosphere. She'd have friends her own age. She'd no longer have to worry about leaking hulls, or have to live in a room that'd make a good-sized closet on Alpha. She was wealthy; why shouldn't she live as though she was? Until the Taylors could put an end to the constant threat from Verdadero's hired killers, they were always going to be pursued wherever they went. Was that any life for a child?

Gershom felt his cheeks burn, and realized he was rationalizing. He flung out his long legs and crossed his ankles. It came down to a simple choice—not simple to make, but to define: Take the money, lose Lani. Keep the child, lose his ship.

He felt a hole in the pit of is stomach at the thought of being deprived of either. Running his own trading ship had been his dream since he was a child. To give it up, to risk losing everything when financial salvation was only steps down the corridor, twisted his insides in a knot. It was a great temptation to let his morals lapse for just one moment. All he had to do was walk down there to her room, and say "Lani, I've decided to take you up on your offer of a loan. Help me save my ship." He tried to form the words, but they wouldn't come out, not even in jest. The moment he opened his mouth, he could picture the government ships warping out of nowhere to take her away.

He remembered Lani the way she was when he and Shona first found her. She was skinny, feverish, frightened, and all alone. Their first child had recently been stillborn, so he and Shona were vulnerable to an emotional appeal, but it would have taken a heart of stone to ignore the needs of this little girl, orphaned in such a monumental tragedy. So helpless, so afraid, her big dark eyes watching every move, afraid to let her rescuers out of her sight for days on end. It was heartbreaking. Since then she had blossomed into quite an amazing, delightful girl. He had to admit he was tickled by her crush on him. She trusted and admired him, and she adored Shona. Well, so did he. He couldn't think of how he'd tell Shona he'd given in. So, he just wouldn't give in. He would have to appeal to the mercy of Chang-an Zeles at MarsBank One, a man who so far had shown little signs he knew what that concept meant.

He raised his head, and with an effort, straightened his back. When he picked up his feet, the chair swung of its own weight in toward the screen set into the wall of the cabin. He pulled down the keyboard and called for the comm program. Better to record it now, and put it on Auto-send, so he couldn't change his mind.

Resolutely, Gershom cleared his throat and faced the screen.

"Mr. Zeles, Gershom Taylor here. I know you and MarsBank have been more than patient with us over the years. I am asking you for one more favor. You can see exactly how much is left in our credit account. At the moment, that is all I can pay toward the loan this month. I have just run into space junk that holed my hull, and destroyed the cargo with which I intended to get up to date with our loan. I am asking for your understanding. It's only a matter of weeks until I will have more, which I shall forward at once to MarsBank, but I simply don't have it now. I hope you will accept a partial payment. I understand that you will have to add late charges, and possibly penalties. Sir, this ship is not only my home but my livelihood. My family, my crew, and I depend upon it. Without it, we have nowhere to go. I am asking you to take that into consideration, please. I humbly await your reply. Sincerely yours."

He punched the button to queue up the message as soon as there was a connect. Suddenly restless, he got up to find himself a cup of coffee, wishing there was something stronger to drink on board. There was no hope that the bank would say yes to another extension. He wanted to take the shortest way back to Poxt, to be with Shona when the axe fell. At least he could have his family back together again. Maybe Horne could give him a job while he saved up to buy another ship. The thought depressed him so much, he broke into a run toward the galley.

Lani appeared at the rear of the bridge and fixed her eyes silently on Eblich's back. The co-pilot had a lapful of equipment that he was putting together with a spanner and a soldering iron. She didn't dare tell him why she was there, because Ivo was sitting close by, and she couldn't trust her voice. At last, the shuttle pilot got up from his position underneath the control panel and saw her standing there. She nudged Eblich's knee and gestured toward the back of the cabin. Eblich smiled at her and put his work aside at once.

"Back in a moment," he told Ivo.

Ivo, who understood the laconic bookkeeper's office as unofficial father-confessor to the orphaned girl, just grunted.

"It was there on the beacon," Lani said in a whisper as she led Eblich down the corridor to her cubicle. "You have to see it. I don't know what to do! I've never been so *angry*. In my *life*."

"Bad news?" Eblich asked, puzzled.

"They didn't respect me," Lani said.

She was too upset to sit down. She hit the command to replay the recorded transmission for Eblich and paced around the small room while he viewed it. Three steps took her to the wall. She kicked it. It would have been more satisfying to kick her way *through* it. She wheeled on the ball of her foot and counted three steps back to the other side. She didn't want to listen to the hateful voice on the speakers. She already knew every word by heart. Never in her whole life had she felt like this. How . . . how *dare* they?

The message wasn't from Uncle Harry at all. He must have passed her request on up the ranks as she had asked, and someone was so upset by it that she replied to it herself instead of just saying no to Uncle Harry and letting him tell her.

"Ms. Leilani Taylor. I am Marca Katt, vice-president of MarsBank One. I have been informed of your request to purchase an outstanding mortgage from the bank, and I wish to inform you that that request is denied. In the inexperience of your youth, you apparently do not understand how business is transacted. It would not be in the interests of MarsBank's shareholders to relinquish assets at random. This is not a music store where you can buy the recordings of one of your 'faves.' We maintain each contract in a stable manner so as to give confidence to those who borrow from us. MarsBank, like all other reputable financial institutions, runs its business in a dignified and time-honored fashion. To sell off an obligation is not in keeping with our practices. We appreciate your contact, and hope to continue to do business with you in the future. We would be glad to offer our experience to help educate you in these matters so that you can manage your own assets well. I am sincerely yours, Marca Katt."

"Wondered if they mightn't go for it," Eblich said quietly, after a moment's thought. He rubbed the side of his nose with his thumb. "Didn't have to be so nasty, though. That came from the belly. That woman doesn't understand *in her head* you're worth billions. No talent for public relations, either. So if we can't work exactly within the system, we'll have to work from the outside." He patted the seat of Lani's desk chair. "Sit down.

Here's what we'll do next. We're going to send another message to your uncle Harry."

"But they've said no!"

"Calm down, little one. You aren't beaten yet. You'll get your day."

Lani stared at him for a moment, panting. Then she focused, really *focused* on the narrow, neat-featured face and what he was saying. Eblich was her friend. He was trying to help her, and Shona and Gershom. She wasn't mad at him. The enemy was out there, at MarsBank. She sat down and leaned in to listen.

·13·

"Confound it, Scarlet, leave me alone!" Governor Horne protested, pushing away the hypo Shona was brandishing.

She sighed. It had been only a few weeks since she'd arrived on Poxt, and Horne was looking seventy instead of fifty-five. He had become more cantankerous every day. She glared up at him.

"Governor, I am not doing this for the amusement value. I have a dozen other patients to see, and then I have to go look at the ottles."

Horne frowned. "What's in *this* one?"

"Vitamins, calcium and magnesium, boron, and zinc."

"Sounds like you're making me into the Tin Man, one snootful at a time," Horne grumbled, but he let her take his arm. He continued with his meeting, paying no more attention to her. She rolled up his tunic sleeve, pressed the nose of the hypo to his skin, and pulled the sleeve down again, as if she were working on the arm of a mannequin. The others in the room regarded her with a kind of horror. They appreciated why she was there, but to have the reality brought home to them in the middle of business was upsetting. Shona regretted it, but there was no other way to get an audience with Horne. He kept himself busy all the time, and deliberately missed appointments with her at the lab. This was the only way to make sure he didn't miss his shots.

"All done," she said, putting the hypo away. She smiled at her audience. As one, they all looked down at their notes and burst out talking.

"Hey, hey, hey!" Horne bellowed, raising his big hands. "One at a time." He pointed at her. "Say, Sharon . . ."

"Shona," she said patiently, turning to leave.

"Got that message for you. Datacube's on my desk."

"Thank you!" Shona said.

She detoured around the group and squeezed into the small private office. The governor was one of the tidiest people she knew. Everything in his personal domicile was squared away, or arranged for easiest reach, except one thing. A single cube, marked ST in blue ink, sat a little apart from the others. Shona grabbed it up. She was tempted to listen to it right there, but in case it contained bad news, she didn't want to worry the people in the next room any more.

"Bye, everyone," she called as she left. "See you all tomorrow morning on the jogging course!" There was a chorus of groans. For the last week, Shona had led anyone who would show up at seven A.M. on a run around the common. She had aimed the exercise chiefly at her patients, to make sure they had some kind of aerobic exercise to keep up bone and muscle mass, but no one liked to be singled out, or left out. The therapeutic run had turned into a daily community event. As long as Shona appeared, in running shorts and a floppy shirt, sometimes carrying Alex in her backpack, she got a good turnout, rain or shine. The one day she tried to let the event manage itself, Wyn Barri reported that the few who showed up straggled off back home or went to work early.

Her patients had continued to become more feeble, more forgetful, and, most worrisome, more fragile. Her experiments with hormones helped to a certain extent, but couldn't keep up with the progressive decay. Coupled with this was her concern for Saffie. The black dog was showing the first signs of the aging syndrome. Within days of receiving the injection of biological material, Saffie had started to behave like a lively puppy.

The dog wasn't waiting for her just outside the hut where Shona had left her. Instead, Shona heard a bark, and Saffie barreled down on her from the top of the hill. She arrived at her mistress's feet, panting with her pink tongue out a foot.

"How are you, girl?" Shona asked, scratching the dog's bony head. "Come on to the next patient. We're going to see Bobby, all right?"

Saffie barked once, shrilly, and galloped downhill toward Marleen's hut. Having so much energy confused the dog. At night, when she finally wound down, she apologized with a small whine before going to sleep as close to Shona as she could manage. Alex was worried about his friend's behavior at first, but then he decided he liked it because it meant that the usually sedate dog was always up for a game.

Shona tried to be optimistic. Saffie was eating well. In fact, she was eating *everything*, which infuriated the cat, who got one chance at his food before it disappeared. When Saffie showed signs of distress and hunger, three days after the injection, Shona increased her meals, worrying that the dog was going to get fat, but she burned it all off and more over the course of a day. Her muscle tone was splendid. Her fur was growing faster than normal. Shona was impressed, wishing that the condition could stop right there, after it had done so much good. The symptoms, if one could call them that, were precisely what her human patients had described. She wondered how long it would be before Saffie started to gray. She prayed it wouldn't happen, but science dictated that a process that worked the same way over and over again should yield the same results.

Bobby's aging had definitely slowed, but not enough to make Shona feel optimistic. Fingering the cube in her pocket, she went back to her module for her personal reader and Alex before going on to the ottle center-place.

Tsanan greeted her and Alex with alacrity as they appeared. "Hello from up!" she called, spiraling down the deep-rutted bark of the heart-tree. "See who comes," she chirruped, poking a pouch on the next branch down. "Friend of Chirwl Shona, and her little one." Chlari stuck his head out irritably.

"To make more noise instead of less," he said, but he waddled down the trunk after his co-mate. Thio was already at eye level, making child-talk with Alex, who reached for hir with both arms.

"See, he is my little friend," Thio said happily. Other ottles left their discussions and clambered out of the swimming pool to come greet the guests. Shona immediately hunkered down and freed Alex from his carrier. The young ottles, who were fascinated by a baby human, gathered around to play with him.

"Do we have an honor of your visit, or mere pleasant?" Thio asked, rubbing up against Shona's leg like a cat.

Shona displayed her reader. "I know you distrust machinery, but it's all we humans have to rely on to communicate from one far-off place to another, so please understand that I will believe what is on the cube I have just received. This is a message from Alien Relations. You know I asked for information from all the other ottle hosts, asking if any of them had experienced irregularities. I didn't name the symptoms of the aging plague, because I didn't want to describe it to *them*, I wanted them to describe it to *me*."

"Sense," said Chlari grudgingly.

"I have not previewed this, so you're seeing it at the same time I am." She set up the reader on a rock against a tree bole, and sat back as far from it as she could and still distinguish what was on the screen. Dozens of ottles, both declared for and against humans, huddled together to watch.

All the reports from the ottle hosts were similar. None of them reported difficulties or illnesses of any kind.

"Except for indigestion," one young man said in his recorded message. He had made his call from a public booth with his ottle friend crammed in on the seat beside him. "Errlilit likes goodies too much."

"It is so," the ottle, a nurturer, admitted, with a soprano giggle. "He, too."

"Say, give her regards to her family, will you? I can't remember how long it's been since we reported in—Wait, that's our trainbus. Gotta go." The sound of an air horn blared in the background. The young man grabbed up the ottle under one arm, while reaching for the video controls with the other. The screen went blank. The group in the glade stared at the blinking reader for a moment before anyone spoke.

"This is possible to be a lullaby tell," Chlari said, breaking the silence.

"It is possible," Shona acknowledged. "But I think it's true. Do you want me to hold my hand over fire to swear that these are actual transmissions, not made up?"

"Is not necessary," Varral said, coming up to rub flanks with his friend. "Chlari has a good inside feel for those he loves. Most protective."

"If it is not false, what does stay left for the cause of the aging?" asked Wla.

"I'm waiting for Gershom to get back with the life histories of the colonists," Shona said. "My guess is that somebody brought in some kind of invasive organism from somewhere they traveled to. I think it likely that it was opportunistic, attaching itself to ottles as well as humans because your circulatory and nervous systems are very similar to ours."

"How to stop it?" asked Thio.

"I don't know that yet," Shona said. "I'm still trying to work that out. I do know that it can be transferred from being to being by injection. I gave Saffie a sample of tissue from the little boy, Bobby. You can see, she's got some of the symptoms you reported on the early stages." The ottles turned to watch the dog, who was energetically stalking a tail, and chasing it back and forth in the clearing, preventing it from running up a tree to escape. "Saffie!"

The dog turned to look at her mistress, and the slip of fur streaked up the nearest bark channel.

"I hope to learn a lot from observing her."

"You have our cooperate," Thio said. All the other ottles, including Chlari, added their assent.

"I'd better get back," Shona said. "Saffie, heel!" The dog galloped up, and frolicked at her side while she attached the lead. She walked Saffie to the place where Alex was playing with the younger ottles. "Alex, it's time to go."

"No," Alex said very distinctly, without looking up from his game.

"Is this normal facet of his growing?" Tsanan asked, as Shona ignored her son's protest and bundled him into his carrier.

"Oh, yes," Shona said. "It's called the 'terrible twos.' I hope you didn't have this with your offspring."

"But yes." Tsanan chuckled warmly, and Shona was reminded how much she liked this kindly, quiet ottle. She settled down on her paws to watch the little ottles in the pond. "In fact, Chirwl was muchly the same as a young one. In truth, he will tell you so."

"At least now we know it's a physical vector," Shona said to Chirwl as she helped Saffie onto the examination room table.

"But what? I've been unable to see anything unusual in anything, her tissues, blood and fluid samples, blood gases." Harry appeared from the sleeping room and arched his back luxuriously against the door frame. Saffie whined and pawed at the tabletop, eager to be down on the floor with the cat, who was openly flaunting his freedom. Shona stroked Saffie's back and made her sit down. The dog complied, obedient but unhappy. Harry turned with tail high, and stalked provocatively out again.

"Drat that cat, he's insufferable," Shona said.

She took a scraping of skin from the dog's mouth, and very swiftly drew a blood sample from a paw pad. "There, that didn't hurt, did it, sweetie?" She took two glass slides and smeared them with fixative. "That'll take a moment to set. I might as well start lunch."

None of her swiftly dwindling supplies looked particularly appetizing, Shona thought, as she went through the storage cupboard. Wait, there was a can of chicken flavoring. "What about a nice bowl of soup for lunch?" she asked Chirwl.

"I say yes," Chirwl agreed. "I wish you would find out what is the cause of the age plague so soon. It is difficult to visit the heart-tree when there is cooking, because so much smells good, I am tempted."

"I know just what you mean," Shona said. She opened a can of nutri, poured three servings into a flask with the flavoring, and put it on to heat.

"Maaa-ma!" Alex said, coming up to tug on Shona's pant leg.

"Ooh, I can smell *you* from here, right through that suit," Shona said, picking up her son. "When are you going to be toilet trained, eh?" She carried him into the bathroom and slipped into her own environment suit. After swabbing the changing table with disinfectant, she undid Alex's fastenings and looked down at him with dismay. "You've made a real mess of this one. Congratulations. I've never seen so much . . . effort in one diaper." Alex crowed at his mother's mock dismay.

"My friend Saffie is so much more energetic than is usual," Chirwl noted from his perch on the countertop. Shona glanced out at them. The dog was lying down with her head on her paws, but her limbs and tail kept twitching. Chirwl was watching the manic activity with concern. "She is not yet like the ones who have become used up."

"Used up?" Shona looked up from buttoning Alex into a clean playsuit. "Used up? What an interesting expression."

"Well, it is seems so to me," Chirwl said. "First all have said they have much power of life, and then it is all gone after a time, leaving them husklike."

"Empty . . . and dry . . . Yes, I guess that's a good description of the effect of the bio-bomb." Shona set Alex down in the sleeping room and closed the curtain. Absently, she turned on the Babytime Play Unit, and handed him a few favorite toys. Alex took them and went into a corner to play. "I only hope Saffie can throw it off. She's showing high levels of certain hormones, glandular secretions like thyroid and adrenal. Remove them, and . . . you know, all those things in combination would give the impression of premature aging, and what would logically have created the sensation of being superhuman, or super-ottle, in the beginning."

"What makes glandular secretions?"

"Well, glands," Shona said. She sat down at her computer and started to bring up file after file. "So something in those glands is probably what's being affected. But everything looks normal. I've taken cells of the adrenal gland, and a few others, too, and there's nothing there."

"Nothing big small, perhaps," Chirwl said. "Is there such a thing as the cell that makes up a cell? What makes glands?"

"Well, molecules, of course," Shona said. "But the genes on the chromosomes at the nucleus of a cell are what program its activity. Like wheels within wheels within wheels." She looked at Chirwl, whose whiskers were standing out the way they did when he didn't understand her. She ought to have known better than to use a technological metaphor. "Like a nut with one shell inside another, and another inside that, until you get to the kernel, which is very small."

"Ah."

"Hello?" Doln Hampton stepped in, carrying a covered tray.

"What's this?" Shona said, looking up at the delicious smell coming from underneath the cloth.

"Lunch," Doln said, whisking the cover away to reveal two glass-domed dishes. Shona smiled at him. Hampton had been a lot nicer since the day she stalked out of his cave. He hadn't made another pass, but was trying to form a real friendship with her, for which she was grateful. He frequently stopped by her lab in the evenings to chat, or escorted her on her rounds. Alex liked him, and Saffie, especially in her current manic-puppy state, was pleased to have someone to frolic with.

"That is so kind of you, Doln, but you know we can't have any local food. Mmm, that looks delightful." Under each dome there was a filet of some kind of white meat covered with a pale green sauce and flecks of light brown, surrounded by a veritable garden of very handsome miniature vegetables. "Oh, those are adorable."

"*Mange tout*," Doln said flippantly. He looked a little hurt at her refusal, but continued to offer the tray to her.

"What's that mean?"

"That's what these dainties are called. It means 'eat them all,' in Earth French."

Shona shook her head, with genuine regret. "Well, I can't eat them *at* all. But thank you again. If you don't mind, I'll take a few of the vegetables for the rabbits. They'll appreciate them very much."

"Are you sure you won't have some yourself?" Doln said. "Smell. Tempting, no?" Shona inhaled, and scented nutmeg, chives, rosemary, and a few subtler odors she didn't know.

"Tempting, *yes*." She sighed. She picked up a miniature steamed cabbage and a couple of finger-sized carrots from one plate. They looked so moist and tender, but no. The rabbits scrambled to the back of their cages as she opened them to put the treat inside. Moonbeam and Marigold both came up, sniffed the offerings, then ignored them. "How strange," Shona said. "Maybe those smell bad to them because they've been cooked." She pulled the vegetables out to sniff them.

"Mama, want it!" Alex called from behind the curtain. He reached for the little vegetables, about the size of his plastic toys.

"No, sweetie. We already have our lunch. See?" She held up a bowl of soup.

"Don't want it."

"No, Alex," Shona said, just a shade more firmly, but with love. She turned apologetically to Doln. "You can't tell a two-year-old anything." Doln looked disappointed, but she smiled at him. "Perhaps I can offer you some of *my* home cooking."

"Smells . . . interesting," he said carefully.

Shona laughed. "You're very kind. It's chicken-flavored nutri soup. It's not so bad," she said, looking at her bowl, and poking the surface speculatively with her spoon. The white substance had been colored with saffron food dye and flecks of parsley. "I crave the stuff every time I'm pregnant. And afterward, I can't figure out how I could stand to swallow another mouthful." She suddenly stared into space. "You know, I didn't feel very well this morning." She reached for a clipboard and made a note: pregnancy test. "At least I hope it's that, and not the bio-bomb."

"Mm," Doln murmured. "Er, what was that I heard you saying as I was coming in?"

Shona was bewildered for a moment at the change of subject, then remembered her thoughts of a few moments back. "I said I might have to consider gene splicing as a therapy for my patients," she explained. "Hormones are holding some patients at the level I found them four weeks ago, but others are declining rapidly. The levels of protein degradation and turnover, and oxidative stress, all controlled at the genetic level, are consistent with the behavior of two genes first described in the twentieth century, called 'Age-one' and 'Age-two.'" She caught Hampton nodding. "Oh, but of course you're working on gerontology. How silly of me to forget."

"No problem," he said, looking over her shoulder with interest. "Ah, well, if you can't have lunch with me, I'll take myself away."

"Oh, don't go," Shona said.

"I—I can't stand the smell of nutri. But I'll see you later," he promised. "Goodbye."

"Funny," Shona said, after he had left. "Nutri *has* no smell."

"It is all in the psychology," Chirwl said. He accepted a small cup of soup, and helped himself to cat food out of the bag on the side. Harry came by to sniff around for offerings.

Shona drank her soup, then fed Alex, who ate with good appetite and a lot of energy. As much of his meal went down his front as into his mouth. Shona had to change his romper again.

"Do you know," she said, coming out of the bedroom after

putting Alex down for his nap, "they *are* working on some kind of gerontology project. That poor, strange old man accosted me again, and a couple of white-tunics took him away, kindly but very firmly, telling him it was time for his treatment. So I guessed right. There's no reason why I shouldn't ask for their help. Maybe if they accomplished anything, it could be used to benefit their patients, too."

"It is a good idea," Chirwl agreed.

Volk looked up in surprise as Hampton exploded into her office.

"She's starting to investigate genetic treatments," he said, pacing back and forth, thrusting his hair back with an impatient hand. "She's getting very close to discovering the truth."

Missa stared at him. Her stomach twisted into a knot at the thought that the secret might be exposed. Such incredibly bad timing, as it turned out. "I've just downloaded a message from LabCor, Doln. Mr. Eleniak is very unhappy. He's sending his brother to look into this mess himself."

"They might even pull funding, depending on what they see when they get here," Morganstern said, looking more funereal than usual.

"What they see? What can we conceal?" Hampton asked. "Did they say whether they would consider hiring her to keep her from blabbing her discovery to the general public?"

"No," said Volk. "I have no idea. Perhaps Mr. Eleniak will make her an offer in person. In the meantime, we keep working."

"Excuse me," came a voice from outside.

"It's Taylor," Hampton whispered. He flattened himself against the inner wall while Morganstern confronted the petite woman at the door.

"Well?"

"I want to speak with Dr. Volk," Taylor said.

"She's busy."

"Never mind, Lionel." Giving up, Missa pushed her way past her assistant, who hulked behind her, prohibiting Shona from seeing farther into the room. "What can I do for you, Dr. Taylor."

Shona was pink-cheeked, and her clothes were disheveled from running. "I need your help. I've ruled out native bacteria, and pretty much all other native organisms as being to blame for the bio-bomb. I have another line of inquiry to pursue, a genetic examination. It could take some time. I respectfully request that you and your people help me investigate it. You have the expertise, and the equipment. Time is running out. The sooner we get this problem solved, the better."

"Dr. Taylor, that was very nicely put, but to use a phrase of popular slang: What's in it for us?" Volk peered down at her. Taylor straightened up defiantly, and her big brown eyes blazed.

"If you absolutely must have personal gain, once it's solved you can be known as miracle workers," Shona snapped. "For all I care, you can take all the credit for the cure yourselves. I don't need to appear publicly at all. I just want you to turn your brains on." Volk admired her tenacity as much as she was appalled by her presumptuousness.

"Absolutely not," she said, and Shona's jaw dropped.

"Why not?" she demanded. "If this unknown organism destroys the colony, you know the Galactic Government would rather see every human being displaced and quarantined on a barren rock than have a single ottle harmed. Wouldn't you go to some trouble to avoid losing your facility? Look here, Dr. Volk, what if it's a genetic condition someone has brought here and passed on, either from blood transfusions, skin grafts, or other invasive bodily contact? Do the gene names Age-one and Age-two mean anything to you? There are others. I have a list—" Volk, feeling rising alarm, cut her off before she could finish.

"This is a pathetic ploy, Doctor. We are very busy, engaged in classified research for a major pharmaceutical firm. Can you pay for our help? Of course not. I heard your discussions with Horne. You're struggling just for basic expenses. Well, use your wits, woman. They're free. Mine are under contract. That is my final word on the subject."

Scarlet, Taylor clamped her jaw shut and marched away from the door without another word. Volk drew in, feeling exhausted.

"That's done it," Lionel said, shutting the door and following her back inside. "Now we'll have another visit from Horne, bellowing like a hungry bull."

"I don't think so," Hampton said thoughtfully. "You hit her

where she's vulnerable, Missa. Well played. She won't be back."

"I hope not. She's getting close, too close." Missa sank into her chair.

Shona stormed into her lab, furious. Her pride was stung, but most humiliating of all, she knew she'd brought it on herself.

"What is wrong?" Chirwl asked. He and Alex were rolling around on the floor, doing ottle-style gymnastics. Shona scooped up the baby to make certain his suit was fastened properly, and gave him a fierce hug before letting him down again.

"MA-ma!" Alex squeaked. "Look at me!" He braced himself on all fours, then tucked in his head to do a fairly creditable somersault. Shona applauded.

"Wonderful, honey." Alex, delighted with the praise, did somersaults all over the lab, with Saffie following him, sniffing curiously. "I just saw that horrible woman!" Shona made an effort to control herself, then wondered what was the point. She balled up her fists, and shook them. "Do you know," she demanded, "if she wasn't just there up the hill, I'd never be tempted to ask for help, but I keep going, and getting my nose swatted! I *should* pretend that they aren't there at all. But I can't! They should be helping me!"

"What has she done?" Chirwl asked.

Shona sighed, and settled down on the floor among her pets and her son. Harry came over to sit on her lap. "Just put me in my place. I don't know why I assumed everyone would come running and help in case of an emergency. It's my job, not theirs. Still—it affects them, too, or it could."

"If they will not help," Chirwl said reasonably, "then you must progress on your own."

"You're absolutely right," Shona said resolutely. "And I will."

Long past midnight three nights later, Shona pulled away from the eyepiece of her electron microscope and rubbed her eyes. Chirwl, hearing the wheels of her chair squeak, woke up from his drowse on the counter and waddled around the shelves until he was next to her. She lifted him into her lap and gave him a hug.

"I'm getting too tired," she said to him. "My eyes are going.

These genes are fuzzy. They shouldn't be. I ought to be able to see them with perfect clarity."

"That machine will not squint closer?" Chirwl disliked and distrusted all technology, and treated machines as if they were unfriendly organisms.

"I can't focus it any farther than I have," Shona said, pushing at the two-meter microscope's base with a toe. "But the images ought to be clear, even at this magnification."

"So the genes have hair? Or they have parts other genes do not have?"

"I mean they look like they're out of focus, not that they have hair. They don't," Shona said. "Well, not exactly hairs, but there seems to be something unusual attached to them." She leaned forward over Chirwl. Removing the slide she was looking at from the holder, she put in the sample from Saffie. It took only a glance to confirm her suspicion. "This one has it, too. What *is* that? They're so tiny, I can't bring them into clear focus at my highest magnification. They'd add up to less than a gram's weight per person. No wonder I kept missing them when I did protein counts." She examined another slide, and another, frowning in thought. "There's a particular concentration of these in the glands. Only one or two on other kinds of tissue, but thick clusters of them on the pituitary, which produces human growth hormone."

"Ah! What you have been giving to Bobby and the rest. What do these too small things do?" Chirwl asked. He stood up on her lap to take a look through the eyepiece, then sat down again, shaking his head.

Shona transferred the image of the genes to her computer screen, and instructed the computer to keep expanding the image to the maximum. The genes appeared as tiny interlocking pieces in the long strands of the chromosome double-spiral. Here and there were attached indistinguishable blobs that seemed to vibrate as she watched them. Even at the highest magnification, the bits of fuzz refused to come into clearer relief. "They're very specific mechanisms," she explained to Chirwl. "The glands that produce that hormone to keep the body young slow down, then stop functioning entirely as we age. These tiny particles must stimulate them at the molecular level." She blinked. "That means it isn't a natural phenomenon. It's deliberate. They are probably supposed to go in and reconstruct the tissue at the molecular level, so they start working again. These particles must be *manufactured*."

"What happens if it the pituitary gland starts to work again?" Chirwl asked.

Shona felt her heart beat faster. "Increased energy, tightening of skin, regrowth of hair, formation of bone tissue, and maybe even rebudding of teeth, depending on what else was twiddled at the genetic level."

"Ah! That is what ottles and humans describe."

"Right. No wonder everyone felt wonderful for a while. You'd have high comprehension, superior memory, a youthful appearance, super-high sex drive—Where it went wrong was that whoever did this misjudged the stimulation factor these were capable of, so once they got the glands going, the mini-machines forced them into overdrive. The new tissues started producing more and more hormones until the glands were worn out all over again from speeding like that. What do you think would happen?"

"The fur goes gray, and the mind wanders."

"Right. The effect was devastating in relatively young people, as you can see, but it would *kill* anyone in poor condition, or over a certain age. Like Larch. She must have been too old to, well, *rejuvenate*. Yes," Shona said, almost to herself. "But she must have been a victim, then, not a scientific subject."

"So this process was to make one young again?"

"Or to keep young indefinitely," Shona said. "But it made them old instead. If these things were working properly, as long as they remained operative, reproduced themselves or could be replenished, a body would always maintain youthful functions. You could live forever."

"That is not such a good thing," Chirwl said severely. "Life has its period, and then all should be over."

"I guess they don't think so. Ah! So that's it." Shona shook her head. "Volk and her people must be from Forever. Doln Hampton was dropping hints of a sort. Now I know what he meant. I saw magazine cubes in their quarters, like *Eterna*, and *Magnivite*. LabCor must have hired people from Forever. *They're* responsible for this."

"How can one be from forever?" Chirwl asked.

"It's a society of people who believe that with the proper diet and lifestyle one can extend one's life span indefinitely. They're fanatics on nutrition, exercise, meditation, and so on. It looks as if Volk and her people are close to a practical scientific breakthrough that might fulfill their dreams."

"But yet all has gone backward," Chirwl pointed out. "Since all who would be younging are olding instead."

Shona nodded slowly. "They're responsible for what happened. These things aren't natural, they're engineered. They should be able to reverse it, somehow, or at least help me turn the process off. It must be devastating to them, to be subject to wrinkles and gray hair just like the rest of us." She picked Chirwl up and set him down on the lab table.

"It isn't making them old," Chirwl said, watching Shona sort through her datacubes until she found the ones she wanted. It was marked with the date they arrived on Poxt.

"It might be. They've been claiming all along that nothing has happened to them, but that's a lie, I'd stake my life on it." She took a scraping of her own skin, to compare it with her original sample. "I may be doing just that. No," she said, after a look through the eyepiece. "No acceleration, and no fuzziness. All this time I've been treating it like an epidemic that could recur, but it hasn't. It might be capable of doing so, but it hasn't. It *was* confined to a certain group, but I bet the Foreverites are at the center of it, both literally and figuratively. I am *certain* that their compound is my missing ground zero. Oh, that would explain so much! Look at these things." Shona hit the desk with her fist. Saffie woke up and whined softly. She came over to join them.

"Then they should help you," Chirwl said practically. "They must want to cease olding."

Shona remembered Volk's insistence on the confidentiality of their research. "They won't. They can't, or they'll lose their jobs."

"Even at the possible of dying? Do you know how to make Shnomri become young the second time? And all the others who as well so suffer?"

"Well, Shnomri's basically healthy, except for the aging bug," Shona said. "I may know how it happened, but I still don't know how to reverse it. Whatever I might try, I'd be guessing, just as I was in treating patients with growth hormone and antioxidants. Volk's not about to give me her database. I'm tempted just to march in and demand it. If I have to blackmail them with public exposure to get it, I will. Somebody's got to straighten out this mess, and I'm the one Governor Horne hired to do it." Shona laughed bitterly. "To think that all this time I've been slogging away here, picking up empirical evidence, while that woman was laughing at me from the top of the hill!"

"I do not think she laughs easily," Chirwl said, his furry face screwed up in thought. "I recall her, and she wears lines of pain."

"I don't mean literally laughing," Shona said. "I can't do anything more without the real data. Every time I treat the symptoms, they slow down, then suddenly speed up again, making things worse. It's as if these bugs eat the adrenalin I feed them, then get excited and ask for more."

"Like Saffie. So hungry."

"That's it," Shona said. "I will not sacrifice my dog for their pride, or their rotten classified contract. I will march right up there and get the original files. I may have to walk right over Volk to do it, but I'm going. They'll have to pull a gun to stop me."

She stood up and looked out the window, feeling confident for the first time in days. The sun had crept up over the horizon while she was making her great discovery. It was daylight. Late enough to roust everyone out of bed. Saffie sprang to her feet beside her mistress, stretching and yawning. Shona patted her.

"Chirwl, this is going to be a confrontation. It may take some time. Can I leave Alex with you?"

"As a matter of course," he said, "but I am coming with you, and so is my friend Saffie. It is honor which matters here. My family shall look after the small one. They would feel delight at his presence."

"Good," Shona said. She suited up and went into the isolated bedroom. She picked Alex up from his little bed.

"No!" he howled, waking suddenly and seeing her masked face. Shona rocked him to soothe him.

"Honey, Mama has to go and drag information out of some people. You're going to visit Chirwl's family. Would you like that?"

"No!" Using all his small strength, he kicked and struggled, tears of rage beading his eyelashes. "No-oh-oh-oh." Shona felt

like bursting into tears herself, she was so tired, but she just
held him and moved her head around to catch his eye.

"Alex, that's enough," she said gently. "Are you saying you
don't want to see the ottles?"

"No. I don't wanta go."

"You like ottles. There will be dozens and dozens of them
to play with. Chirwl's parents will give you breakfast.
You've never eaten ottle food, you know." In spite of himself,
the toddler began to look interested. Shona set him down on the
bed and started changing his diaper so the ottle baby-sitters
wouldn't have to cope with it—at least not right away. She
kept talking in a soothing voice. "Chirwl says all of his parents
and his friends want to see you, just like the first day. Would
you like that?"

Alex put his thumb in his mouth and nodded, his eyes still
heavy. He slept all the way to the ottle center-place, where
Chirwl's nurturing parent took charge of him.

"I appreciate this, Tsanan," Shona said.

"You are welcome, as is he," the nurturer said, tucking a
floppy pouch around the boy's shoulders for warmth. The
morning was still cool.

"She is doing it for the sake of Shnomri," Chirwl informed
his parent.

Tsanan peered up shortsightedly at Shona. "Then she is
doubly welcome. I shall care for the little one. Go well, and
come back happy."

Shona started to explain, but her voice was drowned out by
the roar of engines. The colony was waking up for the morning,
starting business as usual. But it wasn't going to be a usual
morning. Shona would see to that. With thanks to Tsanan and
the others, Shona marched out of the glade with Saffie and
Chirwl beside her.

·14·

"What's going on here?" Shona said to herself, looking at the LabCor compound.

They had hiked from the heart-tree, through the jungle, to the edge of the scientists' camp. Volk and the others, dressed hastily after being rousted out of bed, stood talking to three humans in uniform. Behind them, an official-looking shuttle stood flattening the bushes and young trees above the encampment. Halfway down the slope, Horne came barreling out of his hut straight up toward the crowd on the crest. He was flinging on his bathrobe with furious energy that had to hurt, considering his arthritis, but he looked too mad to care.

"What in the ding-dong *heck* is going on here?" Horne demanded. "Dr. Volk, there is a place for shuttles to land, and it is *not* on top of our plum grove. Have the pilot remove that craft at once!"

"I suddenly have a bad feeling about this," Shona said to Chirwl. She withdrew from the edge of the compound and made her way up along the outer lip of the hedge, through the artichoke field. The ottle plowed along behind her, and raced up a nearby tree bole to see what she saw.

A very tall man with an austere, tight-fleshed face stepped down toward the governor. Horne, usually unstoppable in a temper, slowed to a cautious walk. The stranger came the rest of the way to meet him. His uniform was of subdued gray with an electric blue stripe. The fabric had a shiny surface that Shona guessed was the laserproof cloth she'd heard about on the news programs. It was very expensive, and used chiefly in law enforcement, for the lucky groups who could afford it. At his side was a formidable laser pistol, and a small, square device that Shona couldn't identify. Behind him were two more people, each with an expressionless face and clad in a familiar, nondescript all-climate tunic. She froze, clutching Saffie's leash close to the collar. Chirwl started to ask a question, and she shushed him. He climbed up higher on the tree bole to see better. The thin man was speaking.

"Citizens, I am Special Agent Fromart, GBI." With a single, lightning-fast flick, he produced a badge case, opened it, and returned it to his pocket. The afterimage of a multicolored holo shimmered on the air. I require your assistance. I am in pursuit of a dangerous character named Shona Taylor. Passes herself off as a doctor of medicine. Can you help us?" He extended his other hand, and in it was a miniature projector. He flicked it on with his thumb, producing a ten-centimeter-high image of Shona.

"I'm not a fraud. He's lying! Who is that?" Shona whispered, sinking to her knees in the wiry grass.

"No idea comes to my mind," Chirwl hissed down at her. "But he means you harm." By now a crowd was gathering around the newly arrived ship and her crew. The colonists, alerted by the roar of engines, were scrambling up the hill to find out what was going on.

Across the green, Missa was stunned. She had been expecting a ship, yes, but one that contained a delegation from LabCor, not the GBI. And yet, perhaps this apparent lawman was the solution to her problems. She stepped forward.

"Yes," Volk said, examining the hand-sized pocket holo with care. "We do know her. She's staying in the ottle enclave, about two kilometers to planetary east of here. She misled all of us, Agent, er . . ."

"Fromart."

"Yes, Fromart . . . into believing that she was a legitimate scientist. We'd be happy to help you find her."

"What are you doing?" Marleen Orthon demanded, pushing her way between Missa and the uniformed man. "You know Shona is a real doctor."

"I don't know anything of the kind, Ms. Orthon," Missa said sternly. "She appeared here one day, that's all I know."

"Stand aside, please, Ms.," the agent said. "Where can I find this ottle enclave?"

"Hold it a minute. I'm in charge here," Horne said, his bald head turning ruddy with fury. "No one pursues anybody here without my say-so."

Agent Fromart turned a fishy eye toward him. "Would you interfere with the function of a government official."

"You're damned tooting I would. I am DeWitt Horne, governor of this settlement."

"And you are in violation of Galactic law if you stand there one more moment," Fromart said without force, but the threat was sheathed there as surely as the gun was at his hip. "Where is the ottle enclave?"

Missa pointed across the green toward the path. "It lies in that direction. But her laboratory is at the bottom of the village, that way." She shifted to point down the hill.

The humming of another shuttle engine distracted her. A second craft, this one bearing the LabCor logo, landed next to the first one, crushing more trees. Over an outcry from the settlers, a dark-haired, bronze-skinned man clambered out, followed by a handful of other men in scarlet and black uniforms, armed with needleguns.

"Missa Volk?"

"I am Dr. Volk," Missa said, stepping forward. She recognized the bronze-skinned man from her employment interview. He shared with his brother the beaklike nose, the fierce black eyes, and the sensuous, cruel mouth.

"Sajjid Eleniak. I am glad to see you again, Dr. Volk. I wish to . . . *speak* to the woman Shona Taylor." He stopped abruptly as the GBI agent snapped off his holo projector. "Wait just a minute," he said. "What is *he* doing with an image of Taylor? Who is he? What's he doing here?"

"He's from the Galactic Bureau of Investigation," Volk said, tossing her head back defiantly. "He wishes to solve all our problems with that woman. He says she is a fraud, and is here to arrest her."

"We can't let him take her away," Eleniak said in a patient voice, as if Volk were a stupid child. "She has vital data about the project going on here. We need to speak to her urgently."

"I have a warrant to take her into custody," the austere man said, pressing forward. Volk felt as if she were a sheep, caught

in a ravine between a wolf and an eagle. "And I intend to do so.
I advise you not to attempt to stop us. Where is she?"

"I don't know," Volk said. "Until five minutes ago we were
all asleep."

Eleniak turned to Volk. "We'd better find her ourselves, and
you'd better pray we do, too."

Volk suddenly felt a thousand years old. "Yes, sir."

Shona waited to hear no more. She turned and ran. Saffie and
Chirwl fled after her.

"What was that?" demanded Eleniak, hearing a rustling in
the bushes.

"I have no idea," Volk said, peering in that direction. "An
animal, perhaps. This is a natural site."

The vice-president dismissed all sites, natural and unnatural,
with a wave of his hand. "We must speak to the woman at once.
Where are her quarters?"

"I'll lead you to them."

"I want to talk to you, Dr. Volk," Horne said, getting in front
of them.

"Later, Governor," Volk said, sidestepping him as Eleniak
dragged her away.

Her breath loud in her own ears Shona ran across the field
and into the arcade of trees. She went hunched over, keeping
her knees up so she didn't have to slacken her pace. Who were
those security forces, and what did they want with her? The
LabCor insignia on one group was easy to pick out. Shona had
seen it again and again on Volk's people's possessions.

The others were dressed like GBI agents. Shona had reason
to remember their uniforms, since some of them had protected
her and her family through Verdadero's trial. Had they come to
warn her about another attack? Were they here to prevent one?
But why announce to everyone she was a criminal? Something
was terribly wrong. She didn't want to stay there to find out
what it was. They had guns!

"We will hide you," Chirwl promised, loping along at her
side. Bent over, she was going slow enough for him to keep up.
The dog had easily outdistanced them, and had disappeared up
the narrow tunnel. "If you but return safely to the heart-tree,
there will be ones who know good places of concealment."

"I have to get my baby," Shona cried. "If only Gershom was here!"

She dashed into the clearing. Sunning himself next to the pool was Chlari, who flipped himself onto all fours as she hailed him. "Where's Alex? I have to, I have to *hide*," she said breathlessly. "There are people after me."

Chirwl interrupted her. "I will explain more quickly," and he broke into a trill of whistles and chirps. Chlari's whiskers stiffened, and dozens of ottles within hearing range swarmed down to them from the trees. They clustered around her, all talking in shrill voices.

"We know where you must go," Chlari said, briskly, with a piercing whistle that cut through all the others'. "Behind you we will hide your tracks."

"Thank you," Shona panted. "My son?"

A couple of the larger ottles took hold of the loose fabric of her trouser legs and hurried her toward the place where Alex was playing.

"Mama!" he crowed. She snatched him up, away from the simple toys, and he protested. Shona held him and put her face very close to his.

"He is well and clean and has eaten," Tsanan assured her. "He is ready."

"Oh, thank you, thank you!" Shona put her face close to his and spoke in a very clear, low voice. "Honey, we have to go and hide now. It's very important. The most important thing is for you to be quiet all the time while we hide. Can you do that for Mama?"

Alex's round eyes were fixed on her face as he nodded.

"Good baby," she said. With well-practiced movements, she hastily tucked him into his carrier and strapped him onto her back. His arms came out and folded around her neck. She patted his fat little hands and turned to Chlari. "Doln Hampton showed me a cave on the river bank. It's close by. Can you help me find it?"

"I will lead you," Wla said. "I know the paths in that direction."

"We will protect behind," Thio said, closing ranks with hir co-mates. Shona nodded her thanks, and followed Wla across the center-place. "Where's Saffie?" she called.

"We will keep her safe, and your other friends," Thio assured her.

"But the door's locked in my module."

"Chirwl will tell us how to enter. Now, go!"

The young nurturer shot out through the green arcade toward the human settlement. Burdened with Alex, Shona stumbled along behind, trying to catch up.

"Why are we going this way?" Shona asked in a loud whisper. "They might see us."

"Best way," the ottle whispered. "Come with me, come!" When the ceiling opened up to the sky, instead of following the path that led through Horne's garden, Wla turned a sharp left around the rear of the bole of a heart-tree, and scuttled down toward the river. They were just cutting through a dense thicket, when they heard the sound of angry voices, Horne's loud baritone above all.

"You just wait a minute. I want to see your identification again, and I want to see your mission documents. This is a lawful colony. You can't just come zooming in here and harass my people."

Shona flattened herself backward on the river path with Alex protected under her body, watching over her head, listening. The boy let out a murmur of protest at going backward, but he didn't cry out. As soon as the threshing footsteps passed, Wla nudged them with her nose, and led on. Shona rolled to all fours, rose to her feet as quietly as she could, and followed.

She recognized the hanging withies that marked the cave entrance just as Wla shot underneath them. The nurturer waited just outside the low arch while Shona got to all fours and crawled in.

"I am get many more ottles. Chlari and Chirwl will have discussed with them what to do," Wla said. "Be calm. Wait here." She scampered back along the river bank, her broad body flattened out as much as possible, shuffling her feet to cover the human footprints.

Trembling, Shona let herself down on the stone seat and sat forward so that Alex's weight wouldn't overbalance her. The small cave smelled comfortingly of clay, and its coolness soothed her. She realized she was sodden with sweat.

"Mama, where we going?" Alex asked, in the closest he could come to a whisper.

"I don't know yet, Alex," Shona murmured back. "It's an adventure, just like on the screentank. The ottles will show us where to go, all right?"

"Okay," Alex said. "Sing for me? Pwease."

"Oh, not here, sweetie. They might hear."

She heard a subdued sniff, and realized that all the excitement was more than he could be expected to cope with. He was only a baby, and things were happening so fast.

"All right, darling, but you have to help me with the words." She turned her head, and sang in the lowest voice she could manage, the much-despised "Love" song. Alex rocked in tune with the melody, his thumb in his mouth. When she was done, he put his head down on her shoulder.

"I love you, Mama."

"Oh, my baby, I love you. You're so *good*." Shona bent her arms back and gave him an awkward hug. She rocked him back and forth, trying to ease the strain on her lower back muscles as much as to soothe the baby. There was no telling how long she'd have to stay in that position.

Volk's eagerness to give her up to the authorities, however spurious their claim, didn't surprise her, but what *had* she said to her superiors at LabCor to make them come in looking for her with guns? Was this secret research of theirs worth killing for? Certainly not, since the process didn't work properly. Shona wondered if that was it, if her reputation was a convenient out for the Foreverites, to blame the "Angel of Death" for the failure of their project. It had been so obliging of Shona to arrive just when she did.

Horne would make them see reason fairly soon, she thought sleepily, and then she could come back and have a civilized discussion with them all.

A crowd, protesting the intrusion into the colony, followed the two groups of uniforms through the settlement, although at a respectable distance. They shouted and muttered, but without open fury, or much direction. Missa stared down the insufferable Wyn Barri, who was talking loudly about messaging the Government Guard to come in and protect innocent citizens who were being threatened by uncontrolled agencies. Eleniak and his men were conducting a house-to-house search on one side of the green, and the strangers were doing the same across the way. Marleen Orthon threw herself across the door of her home, but was thrust aside and held by Sajjid Eleniak while two of his thugs went through the hut.

The LabCor men came out a moment later, looking sick but shaking their heads. They must have seen Bobby. Their expressions enraged the settlers, who resented anyone taking an attitude like that to one of their own. They advanced in a mob on the uniformed men. Eleniak's guards drew their needleguns and stood ready, eyes darting back and forth, choosing targets. Gasps rose from the crowd. Missa thought with horror for a moment that the men might start shooting. The settlers, wisely, retreated to their original distance, their protests quieter than before. Governor Horne pushed through the crowd, and caught Missa's arm.

"Okay, Volk, you've had your little adventure," he said. "Call them off."

"I can't," Missa said, favoring him with as blank an expression as she had in her repertoire. "I work for Mr. Eleniak."

"You admit you're responsible for them being here."

"I . . . don't admit anything, Governor. I've been sending in my reports to my employers, as usual. They just arrived."

Horne leveled a finger at her nose. "You knew and you didn't tell me. We're going to talk about this later." He addressed the leaders of both groups, Eleniak and Fromart, who had converged on the last house in the irregular ring.

"Look here, neither of you informed me you were landing, so legally, neither one of you is welcome on this planet. If you think you can somehow justify your presence here, talk!" Horne bellowed.

The narrow-faced man in GBI uniform turned sharply from supervising his people to face Horne.

"We need to remove Taylor to headquarters for interrogation about crimes committed against humanity on no fewer than four colony planets."

"Well, that's very interesting," Eleniak said, spinning on his heel and taking a step closer so that he was chest to chest with his opposition, "but my colleagues require *interviews* with Dr.

Taylor for the *data* she has on this project before you, uh, lock her up. Once you have her, we'll never get her back."

The narrow-faced man looked amused. "That's true. And vice versa, as well. Government interests must be served first, Mr. . . ." He raised the small device from his belt.

The LabCor man pushed closer until he was actually pressing the other man backward. "Eleniak. Spell it right."

"Now, now, Shona's not guilty of any crimes on any planets," Horne interrupted. "And she's no danger to LabCor either. Get the hell off my planet." The two teams, having searched the last house, started purposefully for the garden path toward the ottle center-place. "Do you hear me?"

The narrow-faced man nodded to the woman behind him, who detached herself from the group. She glided to the last house remaining open, and stepped inside. Its owner, a plump-faced man, followed her in, yelling. There were sounds of a scuffle. She emerged carrying a communications console, which she dumped on the ground and lased into four pieces with the pistol from her holster. The plump man staggered out behind her, clutching his jaw. Volk didn't know who these others were, but she was certain of two things: they were not GBI, and they were very, very dangerous.

"Dr. Volk," bellowed Horne, closing in on her like a thundercloud. "I want to talk to you!"

Wla ran back to join Chirwl and the others under the heart-tree, just as two sets of angry humans, one group in gray uniforms, the other in scarlet, entered the glade. She reported in a swift whistle to her clan and the Clan-One-Tree-Nearer-the-River.

"Friend Shona and offspring Alex-ss are under the bank. They must move soon. It is cold there, and no food."

"She has not eaten all day," Chirwl added, concerned.

"We will attend to it," Varral promised her. "My offspring and hir co-mates are gathering supplies for them."

"We will bring it to them," said one of Shnomri's cousins, a thick-pelted father of the cell.

"Attention, please." A tall male human with a dead-looking, long, thin face looked from one to another of the clustered ottles, then grabbed up the nearest, Tsanan, with a lightning-fast thrust of his hand. Chirwl wanted to race at the human and dig into him with his claws until he dropped the nurturer, but evidently he didn't mean Tsanan any immediate harm. "I want to find Shona Taylor. Where is she?"

The ottles regarded the gray-clad stranger blankly. Though obviously enraged, the man responded by tucking his emotions still further inside himself. He held Tsanan face to face with him until her whiskers were almost touching his skin. "Where is she? She's dangerous. We need to take her away."

"Which is the she you seek?" asked Chlari in the Standard tongue, staying close to help his co-mate. The man turned to glare at him, and one of the other flat-faced ones in gray uniforms stepped forward and put a hand on the weapon at his side.

"I'm asking him, not you," the cold voice said. He shook his prisoner.

"It is not a *him*," said Chlari obstinately.

"Where is Taylor?" the man demanded, shaking Tsanan again. The old nurturer declined to emit anything but a squeak of pain. He shook her harder, making her legs flail limply in every direction. Chirwl, hoping to distract the man, leaped onto a tree trunk just a little above the heads of the intruders and spoke hastily.

"That one does not speak your language. Neither do I, if I now think of it."

"It sounds like you do," a pugnacious male in a scarlet and black uniform said, pushing forward, followed by two other males in similar dress. He produced a small holopicture and held it up to Chirwl at the same time Tsanan's captor removed a similar device from his pocket.

"We're looking for *her*," they said almost in unison. The two men glared at each other. "*We* are." Chirwl gazed at them innocently.

"You seek two human beings?"

"No, just one," said the man with black hair in scarlet.

"She looks alike?" Chirwl asked, looking from one holo to the other.

"Yes, dammit!" the man in scarlet said irritably. "What about her?"

"All human beings look alike to all ottles," said Chlari, joining the argument with gusto. "If we have seen her, it is . . . difficult to say."

"But she's been here!"

"Where is here?" Thio asked, sounding puzzled. "There is no human but yourself that has been in this spot where you stand. I think not ever in the time from the Great Cooling."

Hissing, the thin man in gray flung the nurturer away from him. With acrobatic reflexes, the ottle twisted in midair, grabbed the nearest tree bole with her needle-sharp claws, and scurried up it to safety. The two parties of uniformed humans eyed one another, then departed in different directions from the clearing. Each group looked over their shoulders suspiciously at the other until they were out of sight.

"We regret not to help you," Chirwl called after them.

Shona drowsed on the flat stone. She had been up nearly all night at her microscope for days on end; now she was on the run from unidentified pursuers. All she wanted to do was curl up and sleep. Alex, who didn't let such things as threats of arrest or death interrupt his schedule, was napping contentedly in the backpack. Shona turned her head to breathe in the scent of his soft skin, and let herself be overwhelmed by her love for her sweet child.

It was only a moment's peace. She was surprised out of her reverie by the sound of voices from some distance away. They carried well, probably because of the river's surface only meters from Shona's hiding place.

"Well?" Volk called peevishly. "Did you find her?"

"She's not in the ottle camp," said the smooth voice of the LabCor man.

"She wouldn't stay there," said the rumbling voice Shona recalled as Morganstern's. "It's too open. Nowhere to hide."

"Her module is locked," said a male voice Shona couldn't identify. "We'll have to get override codes to get in."

"Never mind. She's not there. I know where she is," said Hampton's pleasant tenor, as lightly as if he were telling them it was a nice morning. "She's in a cave I showed her. Just below here on the bank. Follow me." Multiple sets of footsteps threshed away from her, with voices calling a sort of view-halloo as they followed the master of the hunt.

At that moment, Shona had never hated anyone so much in her life as Doln Hampton. If he'd been alone, she would have crawled up the bank through the brambles and told him exactly what she thought of him. As it was, she had to move quickly before they discovered her. She ducked out of the cave, and blinked at the bright sunlight. It must be nearly noon. She wished she had some lunch. She wished she'd eaten breakfast.

Alex was quiet as Shona carried him along the river bank through the weeds. She tried to step only on the springy grass to avoid leaving footprints, but it was too slippery. She didn't want to fall into the river, as she hadn't a chance of surviving with the heavy child on her back.

"Sss-shona!" a whisper came from above her head. She looked up, startled.

"Oh, Chirwl, you nearly scared the life out of me," she panted, her heart pounding.

"I will not do that," he said, clinging so closely to a tree he looked like a growth on the bark. "I can take you the next step. Others are following."

"Who are they, Chirwl?" Shona asked, crawling with difficulty on hands and knees up the low slope and under a curtain of vines. Chirwl hung over her head and braced himself so that the greens under which she was passing wouldn't smack Alex in the face.

"One group says LabCor, one says GBI, as they did when we listened, but the loud Horne doubts the latter," Chirwl hissed. "Each of us is to take you from place to place so no ottle is missing for very long. The LabCor ones are not very observant, but the dead-faced man comes back to look at us. I think he is the spirit of Verdadero who comes where the man cannot."

Shona was grim. "I was afraid of that. I *wish* Gershom were here."

"I do also, but he would be in danger, too. So far, those humans who know me from the rest are not cooperating with either group, so they cannot ask me about you."

"Thank heavens for that," Shona said.

"Horne does not like them. He follows them, yelling, but they are not listen. The dead-face's assistants spent time tearing out machines from each person's home place."

"Damn them. Probably damaging communications so no one can call for help." Shona had envisioned sending such a message herself.

"Then we must rely upon whom is here," Chirwl said. "Come. We must move. You cannot go back."

They guessed the bridge was being watched, so it was fruitless to make an attempt to cross the river from there. Chirwl led her on a circuitous path that led kilometers to the north of the human settlement, where he was relieved by one of the young ottles, a grandchild of Varral's. This small one carried a parcel strapped around its middle that contained fruit and dried meat, and a round skin of water. Shona, discarding caution in favor of survival, ate eagerly.

"There is also this from Tsanan," the small ottle said, handing her a lightweight pouch. Shona opened it, and found it full of gray fluff.

"What is it?" she asked.

"Vegetable fiber," Chirwl explained. "It is put in the pouch where the very young sleep."

Shona grinned. "Ottle diapers. Thank you. Thank Tsanan."

"You should change your scent, too," the little one said, presenting Shona with a tightly wrapped package sealed with resin. He had evidently been instructed thoroughly. She opened it and was nearly floored by the intense citrus-spice perfume of the leaves inside. With Chirwl's help, they washed out Alex's messy diaper cover, and gave him a bath in a small pool nearby. He splashed happily, tearing up weeds and flinging them at his three caretakers, but miraculously kept his voice down. Shona kept looking over her shoulder the whole time, wondering how far ahead of the assassins they were. She packed the diaper cover with the gray fluff, and buttoned Alex into it. He wiggled.

"Tickles," he complained.

"But it's what ottle babies wear," she said chidingly. Alex, fascinated, decided it must be a good thing after all, and submitted to being daubed with scented leaves and packed up again in the carrier. Chirwl disappeared into the crown of the nearest tree, and Shona and her new guide set off in the opposite direction, heading westward toward the river. Another ottle paced them far overhead, keeping an eye on a network of its fellows, to make sure none of the malign humans were following them.

Ladovard was perturbed. He knew it wouldn't be easy to take custody of the woman, but someone must have tipped her off that he was coming. She had vanished too easily. None of the buffoons in the human camp seemed to know how or where to look; they ignored the fact that the jungles were well known by the intelligent indigenous species. The ottles obviously saw Shona Taylor as a friend, and they were hiding her in places no human knew. Threatening them seemed to do no good. He would have to trick her into revealing herself.

He was even more annoyed by the incredible hindrance of the team from LabCor. Whatever they were determined to keep Taylor from revealing must be hot. If he had a sideline in industrial espionage, it might have been worthwhile investigating it once his present job was done. The LabCor man had nerve and intelligence. He had called Ladovard's bluff when faced with a threat to report his name. The device at the assassin's side wasn't a communicator anyhow. It was a very powerful tracking device, miniaturized like all of his other favorite tools. It could sniff out a difference in temperature down to a hundredth of a degree over an area of more than three square kilometers. Ottles had a body temperature slightly higher than that of human adults, but lower than human children, so he had to judge his target by mass. He swung the detector from side to side, reading the screen. Too many traces here, and they were clustered. He was looking for one single tree, isolated from the rest.

The terrain just ahead showed an irregular cold spot of four square meters. There was no other in the immediate vicinity. The LabCor woman had said that Taylor's baby boy was missing from the encampment. Carrying a child with her was bound to slow Taylor down, and make her stop more frequently for refreshment and rest. She would need water most of all.

The freshwater pond seemed to be well-used by the local wildlife. Several narrow paths had been worn in the thick bushes around it. He worked himself into the undergrowth near the most likely route Shona Taylor would take, considering the way she had been traveling the last time he saw her. With hand signals, he directed Pogue and Emile to conceal themselves in the brush around the small pool. Emile hid herself with silence and grace, Pogue with more muscle and less finesse. They waited.

In a short time, his infrared sensor told him a body was approaching, of the correct temperature and mass to be the small woman and her child. He let out a low hiss through his teeth to warn his assistants. Steady. His hand sneaked sound-lessly to his holster. Steady. The woman was shuffling along the path now, her tread heavy under her burden and hesitant with caution. She paused.

"Now!"

Ladovard sprang out, his slugthrower drawn. To his aston-ishment, instead of Shona Taylor, he was face to face with a dark-haired man carrying a metal foot-trap. Eleniak of Lab-Cor's face turned purple with fury.

"Will you get *out* of here?" Eleniak shouted. "I thought you were *her*."

"You are interfering in our arrest," Ladovard said.

"Nonsense," spat Eleniak. "Who gets her first wins this one, friend."

Ladovard narrowed his eyes at the LabCor man. Only his long-held credo about not free-lancing kept him from putting a laser slice right through the arrogant dark-skinned face. He retreated. The woman was not here, and that was all that mattered to him. He was furious. While he'd been stalking the other group, the women had gotten farther away.

No matter where he turned, the rest of that day, Eleniak and his fools were underfoot, setting off his traps, or setting ones which he and his people sprang by accident. Taylor could have passed them again and again, and he would never know it with the LabCor hindrance. His temper was fraying. If it wasn't for the sweet thought of reward, he would throw the whole project up and go on a different assignment.

Around the oval table in the MarsBank presidential confer-ence room, a dozen men and women, wearing suits that were so expensive they were subtle, sat listening to the man who was at the foot of the table. He was wearing the least costly suit in the room, and bore the most unprepossessing figure, but they were paying close attention to everything he had to say. There was an elegant woman seated next to the pudgy little man. She gazed back at the others with a cool expression on her well-arranged face.

". . . So you see," Harry Elliott said, keeping his head down so he didn't have to look into those many pairs of surprised and angry eyes, "my client accepts the bank's contention that it can't sell her the mortgage. That's all right.

Instead, she has another proposition. But before I spell it out for
you, may I introduce Ms. Raki Seymour, from the Securities
and Exchange Commission?"

Shona's last ottle guide brought her around in a great circle
to an ancient grove far to the south of the center-place. There
they found a huge hollow log with enough clearance underneath for her to sit upright. The ottle departed, promising to
send others in the morning.

Shona crept in and undid the fastenings of the backpack,
sliding it gently to the mossy, chip-strewn ground. Alex
crawled out and lay flat for a moment. Shona let him alone.
He'd had quite a traumatic day for a two-year-old. He had
insisted on getting out to run for a while. In no time, he'd tired
himself out, and wanted to lie down for a nap. He wasn't
pleased to have to get back in the pouch, but Shona was
adamant. That had started a tantrum, during which he'd kicked
her kidneys for half an hour. She wasn't comfortable, and he
got no rest.

"Mama?" Alex asked. He was still facedown on the ground.

"Yes, sweetheart? We're okay now. We're safe until morning." She patted him gently on the back. Instead of drifting off
to sleep, he started to cry.

"What's the matter, lovey?" she asked, looking down at him
with concern. "Can you tell me?"

"Wanna go home." He sniffed loudly.

"Me, too, baby. Me, too." Shona wiped his tears with her
handkerchief, and made him blow his nose. She checked the
store of food. There was enough for only one of them. She was
the adult; she'd be able to get along without food until
morning. "Do you want some fruit?"

"No," Alex said, without moving his head.

"You sure?"

Alex paused and looked up hopefully. Bits of decayed wood
and moss clung to his fresh, pink cheeks. "Yes."

Shona smiled, and wiped his face. "Good. You eat up, and
I'll tell you the story about the brave young prince who had to
travel to strange and dangerous lands."

"Like me?"

"Just like you," Shona said. She sat cross-legged, with

Alex's head on her lap. "In a land far away, on a planet a lot like this one, lived a little prince and his trusty camel . . ."

As soon as Alex's breathing slowed and became regular, she let herself relax. She was tired, too. She had walked at least twenty kilometers, wading through ponds, climbing hills, and all with a baby strapped to her back. It had been years since she had had to exert herself that much. That was the trouble with living in space, she told herself, trying to find a little humor in her situation: you got so far out of shape. She wondered if anyone would get inside her module to feed the cat. Harry was going to be so mad at her. The inside of the rotted log was as soft as a cushion, and she drifted to sleep.

·15·

Around dawn, Shona thought she heard a rustling in the bush. Alex woke and nestled in her lap, and she wrapped her arms around him to protect him.

"Whozit?" he whispered.

"I don't know, sweetie," Shona whispered back, gathering him closer. She braced herself on the ground with one hand to push up and run. The crashing came from all around them, getting louder and nearer. She bent her knees, wondering which way to run, when something wet touched her hand.

"Aaaaggghh!" Shona yelled, then clamped a hand over her mouth.

"Saffie!" Alex crowed, throwing himself out of his mother's arms to hug his friend. The big dog licked both humans and sat on her haunches with her pink tongue hanging out, panting. "Oh, *Saffie.*"

"Shh, honey," Shona said, and put an arm around the animal's shoulders. "Saffie, you're wonderful. Is Chirwl with you?" She glanced past the dog into the underbrush. No ottles. The birds that had been disturbed by the dog's noisy passage started singing again. "I am *so* glad to see you."

The dog tilted her head to one side and whined softly, not comprehending her mistress's words, but perhaps getting the sense of them. She flattened down, panting, and rested her big head on Shona's legs. Alex, bubbling to himself in two-year-oldese, patted the dog's back and played with her long fur, distracted now from dangerous boredom. Shona was grateful.

There were burrs and twigs caught in Saffie's thick coat, and silty mud in the fur between the pads of her paws. She must have tracked them along the river bank and right through the jungle. It was a wonder that she had found them, considering how many times Shona and Alex had taken to the trees or crossed small streams to elude their human pursuers. Maybe Chirwl or one of the other ottles had set the dog on their true trail.

"I wish you could talk," she murmured to the dog, who had lowered her eyelids halfway with pleasure at Alex's attentions. "And I wish you'd brought something to eat."

It had been nearly twenty-four hours since she'd eaten. Since she'd been so busy with her research from the time of her arrival she didn't know what food was safe, and she didn't dare crawl out to go foraging now.

At no time during her life had she ever had to go so long without food. No matter how dangerous or removed an assignment was from normal sources of nutrition, there was always the hated nutri.

She felt an urge for some now. It would certainly fill up the gaps in her shrinking middle, and assuage her fears that Alex wasn't getting enough to eat. The meat and fruit given her by the ottles was good, but the baby was growing bored with the simple diet.

Like it or not, she was going to have to move them to another spot soon, risking discovery and having the ottles lose track of her, but the risk was better than sitting with a crying baby, waiting for the inevitable.

The more she tried not to think about food, the more it haunted her. She imagined the flesh was shrinking beneath her cheekbones. Her jaws hurt, not from actual malnutrition, but probably because the muscles hadn't been given much exercise over the past twenty-four hours. Her head was beginning to ache, partly from hunger, partly from strain, and partly from the sun and the humidity. She exercised her jaw and neck, rolling her head back and forth. The worst discomfort was the knotting of her empty stomach. Every time she breathed, it twisted inside her. It seemed to have roots that reached out to every extremity, reminding her that there was no action without a price, and she hadn't paid it, couldn't pay it. What would happen to her if she had to hide out here for a week? She shook the water skin. There was only a little left, which she needed to save for Alex.

Saffie's head lifted suddenly, swiveling to follow her erect ears. Shona turned to look under the edge of the log in the same direction, but saw nothing. Saffie growled, low in her throat. Shona understood. Trouble. Very carefully, she eased her legs under her, gathering Alex to her hip. The faint echo of a man's voice reached her, then the rustling of boots marching through the wire grass. Saffie's growl got louder, and the dog stood up. Shona was on her feet in a moment, hunched over to run in the opposite direction.

"Come on, girl," Shona urged her. The dog ignored her, holding her ground. Shona realized she couldn't persuade her, and if she didn't get moving soon, the men would discover her. She ducked under the far edge of the log, and ran. As soon as they were out of sight of the dog, Saffie started barking.

Shona thought of turning around to help her, then picked up her pace again as she heard the rate of footfalls increase and grow louder. Voices started shouting. Saffie was deliberately trying to attract attention away from them! Not wanting to waste the dog's initiative, Shona huddled over Alex, cradling his head in her hand, and scurried off into the brush.

She heard the crackle-crash of laser pistols shearing through branches and the rush of boots behind her. There was an explosive crack as the dry, dead log under which she had sheltered exploded and burst into flame. The barking gave way to fierce growls as the pursuers burst into the tiny clearing. A surprised yell erupted as Saffie must have thrown herself at one of the men, followed by more yelling and crashing of broken brush.

"After it!" a deep male voice shouted. Slugthrowers boomed, and bullets pinged off rocks. Keeping her head down to avoid being whipped in the face by small branches, Shona fled. To her relief, she heard distant barking: Saffie mocking her pursuers.

It wasn't until Saffie was out of sight that Shona realized the dog was behaving like her calm, old self again. Miraculously, Saffie's incredible immune system had thrown off the aging bug. That was something she'd have to think about, but for now, she had to keep running.

Ladovard ran through the jungle, signaling to Pogue and Emile to fan out. The woman had sent her dog to distract them, which meant she was close by. He read his sensor. There was a heavy heat-trace only fifty meters ahead, moving approximately one meter per second. The woman must have concealed herself nearly underneath his feet. He ran with weapon in one hand and the tracer in the other, leaping over the remains of a burning log. They were within twenty meters now.

He had made sure of the LabCor men. They were over sixty kilometers away, and going in the wrong direction. They always moved in formation now, making it easier for Ladovard to distinguish them from his target. *His.* He would get her first.

The target turned south. Ladovard waved his gun to have his assistants wheel to the right. He ran after them, watching the trace. The jungle was too thick, full of too many obstacles. He wouldn't see the woman until they were nearly on top of her. According to his sensor, she was now coming straight toward them. All he had to do was keep on in this vector, and he would have his prize.

"Here, Sss-shona!" came a hissing from above.

Winded, Shona stopped running and looked up. A clutch of ottles were huddled almost invisibly against the dark bark of a thick tree, like furry fruit.

"Ones are ahead of you!" another one whispered.

"Where can we go?" she whispered back frantically. "They're behind me, too."

"Where they will not look," said one. He raised his head, and Shona recognized Varral. "Up!"

"How?" Shona asked. In answer, dozens of ottles poured down the channels of bark. Several of them helped anchor a narrow length of hide that disappeared into the far-off treetops. Just looking up made Shona feel dizzy.

"Oh, no," she said.

"But yes," Varral said. He helped Shona stick her legs into a double loop at the end of the hide rope. She held on tight to the rope between them. At Varral's signal, the ottles drew on the length that was thrown over a branch hundreds of feet up. Shona was lifted in swaying jerks toward the crown. Alex stared huge-eyed over the edge of her backpack, and whimpered.

"It's okay, love," Shona said. "Hang on. Don't look down. It's okay—Ooops!" she gargled, as her ride came to an abrupt halt. She was helped out of the loops, and followed the ottles on hands and knees along the great limb. It was wider than an urban walkway, so she could easily have gone upright, but her acrophobia refused to allow her to let go with her hands. She went along as swiftly as she dared, and found she was actually making good time.

"I'm steeplechasing," she said, breathlessly, as two ottles passed her and helped her up onto another branch.

"Do not speak!" Varral said. "The dead-faces have long ears in their hands, and they notice when humans make sounds."

"Microphones?" Shona gasped. "All right."

A living line of the little aliens held onto the smaller branches with their sharp-clawed paws and held onto her clothing and Alex's backpack with their feet, passing her from one to the next. Shona felt sick as she came to a meter-wide gap between the branches of one heart-tree and another. Alex was taken off her back and passed over the gap by pairs of ottles, since he was too heavy for a single one to take. At last it was time for her to make the jump.

"I can't," she whispered desperately. She felt sick and closed her eyes.

"Hold to me," Varral's voice said. "Touch my back. Open your legs, yes! Foot forward to your next step. Bring forth your other foot. Good! Open your eyes."

"I made it," Shona said, panting. She lay facedown on the rough red bark and wound her arms around the limb.

"Come quickly," Varral said. "You are easily seen here." She raised her head, caught sight of the ground far below, and buried her face again.

"I can't go down," Shona whispered helplessly. "I can't go down."

"You do not need to," said the calming voice of Tsanan. "A pouch has been prepared for you. Come." Shona crept forward slowly on her belly toward the trunk of the tree.

Ladovard stood and glared at his device. The trace seemed to have gone straight through his position and vanished.

"Impossible!" he growled. "She was on her way here. She couldn't pass us like a ghost. The woman can't fly." And then he realized his mistake. He looked up. The network of tree branches over is head was as obvious a road as the one under

his feet. She had run straight overhead, and he was too intent
on his scope to realize it. With a gesture to his assistants, he
spun on his heel, and started back the way he came.

It was too late. The body-temperature trace had split into a
hundred. Ninety-nine of them were undoubtedly groups of
ottles, nestled in the treetops. No single mass was distinguishable as a human female and child. He'd lost them.

Shona ate and drank gratefully everything the ottles offered
her with the exception of a handful of dry cat food, which even
her shrunken stomach quailed at. She spent the night nestled in
a dark green leather bag. It smelled faintly of fish, but was
warm and secure. It must have been like returning to the womb,
for she slept very soundly, Alex in the pouch next to hers. He
was glad to be back among the ottles, petting them and
prattling his few words of their language over and over again.
Once fed, he'd settled in for the night without a murmur.
Between the sounds of night-avians and the chittering of
tree-insects, she occasionally heard little snorts of breath. If he
woke in the night, someone else soothed him back to sleep.

Shona, her legs crouched against her chest in the fetal
position, fell into a dream in which her glands had been set on
ultra-overproduction by the engineered particles she'd seen
under the microscope. All her body processes were sped up
unnaturally, making the baby in her belly grow to maturity in
a month instead of nine like that Old Earth Norse godling in the
legends. She would have to give this child the same name.
Then her dream self laughed at her and chided, "You can't call
a girl Heimdall."

"And why not?" Shona woke up with a certainty that she was
pregnant again, and the child was a girl. The thought delighted
her so much, she forgot for a moment to be frightened about the
people who were trying to kill her.

She was still in a good mood the next morning when Tsanan
appeared, bringing fruit and cooked meat.

"Take it the pouch," Tsanan said. "You can carry Alex
offspring in it much easier than your heavy bag."

It was certainly more comfortable to strap on. Alex didn't
object to staying in the green leather case as the ottles helped
lower them to the floor of the jungle. Squeezing her eyes shut,
Shona clutched creepers, tree branches, and finally the inches-

thick bark itself to help her get down. She wanted to drop to her
knees and kiss the ground.

"Where am I?" she asked.

"You are having slept exactly north of the ottle center-
place," said a large ottle whose name she hadn't heard. It
pointed down a narrow path with low-hanging trees, which she
would have to negotiate hunched over again. "Go that way. We
will find you and give you more food later. We will help you
cross the bridge today. It ought will be safe."

"Thank you," Shona said. She humped the leather pouch up
higher on her back, and started walking. "Come on, honey.
Here we go again."

Gershom knew something was wrong when they came into
orbit and he tried to radio his position to Poxt. There was
nothing on the appropriate frequency but static. He tried the
surrounding frequencies until he could hear shiptalk from two
systems away. All his instincts were humming with fear. He
had to get down to the planet. Lani begged to come with him
on the shuttle, but he insisted she stay on the ship. He gave
orders to Kai and Eblich to keep the communicators open to his
channel, and to fly out at all speed if he gave the word.

He fidgeted in his seat in the shuttle, scarcely seeing the
great green canopy part and show the blue landing lights. Ivo
made record time setting down in the remote glade on the far
side of the river.

He didn't wait for Ivo to follow him, but took off running,
his long legs eating up the distance to the bridge. As soon as he
was on the other side, ottles began to pop up from the long
grass, all babbling at him in their shrill voices.

"Where's Shona?" he asked them. He saw one he thought he
recognized, one of the older ones. "What's going on here?
Where is Shona?"

"She is gone," Chlari said. "She is hiding from the dead-
faced ones."

The ottles followed him en masse across the field and into
the colony common, where a crowd of humans joined them.
Ignoring them all, Gershom stormed into the governor's hut.

"What in hell has been happening here?"

Horne looked a good twenty years older than when Gershom
had left. He raised his white eyebrows at the sight of the trader.

"Gerald, thank goodness you're back. I need a working radio. Those damned assassins have broken every communication unit in this entire colony!"

"Assassins? What assassins?"

"It's a long story, son, but . . ."

"And where's my wife?"

"She's gone into hiding, and there's not a thing I could do about it, Jeremy. God knows I've tried. Now sit down and let me tell you all about it."

Gershom sank into a chair. Not wasting any words, Horne told him everything that had happened, up until two days before, when the shuttles appeared out of nowhere. He described Volk's complicity with the LabCor group.

"I put the whole boiling mess of scientists under house arrest," Horne said wearily. "I've been trying to get information out of them, but not one of them's talking sense."

"Let me see Dr. Volk," Gershom said. "I want to ask her what's going on."

"You can ask her, but all she keeps saying is 'I don't want to die.' That's all, for two days now."

"She must know where Shona's gone."

"If you'd seen the men who came here after her," Horne said, "you wouldn't say that. She'd have told them if she knew."

Gershom kicked his chair back and stood up. "I have to find my wife and son."

His belt radio went on in a burst of static. "Gershom, that white ship's just made orbit!"

"*Three* assassins!" Gershom cried. He tossed his radio to Horne and ran out of the hut.

"Gershom!" Chirwl said, loping up to him through the crowd. "You are back! Come hastily!"

In the bushes near the river bank just under the east end of the bridge, Ladovard watched his pocket infrared device with hooded eyes.

"She is coming," he said. "Remember. One shot, the adult only. We do not kill children."

"Yes sir," Pogue said.

"Yes, sir," Emile said.

•   •   •

"We finally have them," Sajjid Eleniak said, monitoring the audio tracking device he held in his left hand as he marched north along the east river bank. "Three days! She's ahead of us. She's trying for the bridge. We can catch her there, before she gets over it. Double-time march!" He broke into a jogging trot.

Shona shifted the straps holding Alex's carrier. The skin on her shoulders had been rubbed raw. There were probably blisters in an X-pattern starting from her hips up. Her feet were blistered, too, right through her socks, which were nothing more than rags ringing her ankles and rubbing the backs of her heels. She was so tired she would just have lain down on the path and let both squads of hit men fight over her if it wasn't for Alex.

He had fallen into a sniveling fit early that afternoon, and was chanting a tuneless, "Uh-uh-uh-uh-uh," in time with her pace. The sound had taken her about to the end of her patience, not to mention worrying her sick when she thought about the microphones Varral said were hidden throughout the jungle. She didn't dare scold the child, guessing that he was close to hysteria, something she wanted to avoid if possible. She'd run out of moss, and had to substitute dry glass, which chafed and made him angry. If only she'd had him toilet trained—but only a clairvoyant would have known she'd have to take him cross-country camping to save his life.

But where was Horne? Surely the colonists hadn't just given her up to the two bully squads. No, that wasn't fair. She couldn't ask anyone else to face guns on her behalf. Not for her. She would beg the assassins to spare her child. Saving Alex was the only thing she could think of. The obsession filled her mind as she hiked laboriously through the wilderness. Should she hide him, and try to get a message to the ottles where she'd concealed him? When would Gershom get back? Was he there in the settlement already?

At least the bridge was not far away. Her last ottle escort had disappeared into the trees, promising to send the next relay. He, she, or it hadn't appeared yet, but Shona could tell by the clear sky ahead that the river was close. She marched on steadily. The rhythm was all that was keeping her on her feet.

•   •   •

"Are you sure the village is this way?" Chaffinch asked, following Letty through the heavy wire grass. Poxt certainly was a natural paradise, but some kind of concession should have been made for tenderfeet coming in to visit, particularly itinerant journalists on deadline.

"Yes it is," his producer said, shouldering her heavy video pack. "I got the planetary map from the navigational computer."

"We ought to have waited for Air Traffic Control to come back on the line."

"We couldn't wait; the *Sibyl* is up there. The action will probably be all over with by the time we get to the village," Lettitia said patiently. "So hurry up."

Black flies rose in clouds as they neared the river bank. Chaffinch produced a spray from his shoulder pack and coated both of them in choking vapor. Letty coughed and pawed the air to clear her eyes. She blinked, staring across the river.

"Look!" She pointed. Chaffinch peered over her shoulder through the reeds. A small woman with brown hair, whom he recognized immediately from the holos as Shona Taylor, was trudging wearily toward the other end of the bridge.

"Whoopee," Chaffinch crowed. "Exclusive interview, here we come."

"Wait, look at that." Letty pointed again. Invisible to Taylor, and to one another, on each side of the bridge was a group of uniformed men, one group in gray, the other in scarlet. As if in answer to a signal, both squads leaped out of the reeds and surrounded Dr. Taylor.

"Chaffinch, they're going to kill her!"

"That will utterly ruin my story," Chaffinch said firmly. "Dammit, we won't let them. Stay with me, girl." He picked up his feet and dashed across the bridge.

Shona could have cried for joy. She had nearly reached the first plank of the suspension bridge. Only a few hundred yards to go. Soon she could sit down and comfort Alex, who surely needed it as much as she. Safety was within meters, when out of the reeds to either side leaped men and women in scarlet or gray uniforms. They were all heavily armed and grim-faced.

"Not you again!" the black-haired man in scarlet snarled. Not at her, but at the narrow-faced man in gray.

"Stand back," the man in gray warned, voice cold as a corpse. "This woman is my prisoner." He felt for his pocket.

"Keep your phony ID's," Eleniak barked. "We'll settle this right now. Men, arm! Ready?"

Disbelievingly, Shona saw six guns rise and point straight at her head.

"Oh, please, not my son! Please!" she shrieked. She threw up her hands to protect Alex's face and dropped to her knees. Frightened, the baby started screaming. Suddenly, the assassins' guns wavered and dipped. The killers were no longer looking at her. She spun on her knee to look.

Shona saw only a tall, dark figure advancing on them, then white and red glints lit up like LED's. A familiar ebony-skinned face with black, red-streaked hair stuck a short rodlike device under the nose of the nearest LabCor man, and flashed brilliant white teeth toward an unknown third party.

"Tell me, sir, were you sent by Mr. Jachin Verdadero, or are you working entirely on your own? Would you describe your mission here as private security, or public mayhem? Good afternoon. I'm Chaffinch L'Saye, on assignment for GVN, the Galactic Video Network."

The gunman tried unsuccessfully to secrete his needlegun in the side pocket of his tunic before the female handcam operator was on her knees, taking a close-up.

"Er, no comment. No comment!" Eleniak babbled, trying to shove a hand in the lens. The camerawoman moved off the plank bridge, out of his reach, maneuvering to get a good group shot of all six of Shona Taylor's pursuers.

As soon as they saw the camera, the three in gray tunics melted away again into the undergrowth without a sound.

"Sir, she's right there," Pogue hissed, from the reeds. "We can collect on the contract. Shoot!"

"With a news camera in my face?" Ladovard growled. "We can't risk exposure. If she fell, they'd know where the slug came from. One frame of us, and a hundred law enforcement agencies will be on our trail! Abandon the mission."

"After we've made so many attempts, spent so much time?"

Ladovard hissed through his teeth. "To hell with Verdadero and his bulletin board contracts. A smart businessman knows when to cut his losses. Back to the ship, before they follow us." He slipped swiftly away, keeping one eye on the video camera.

Pogue exchanged a puzzled glance with Emile. They scurried after their employer.

"Uh, we're here to *oversee security*," Sajjid Eleniak was saying into the microphone. "LabCor has invested *billions of credits* in this project, and we want to make certain everything is under control. Er, everything *is* under control." He looked up at the camera lens and tried to smile.

"As you can see," Chaffinch continued in a chatty voice as if he was discussing the weather, "that was a Helmet Mark IV needler, a powerful weapon, in Mr. Eleniak's holster. As with all needlethrowers, it is swift, silent, and deadly. A dangerous weapon, but with industrial espionage more of a reality than ever in today's marketplace, possibly not a surprising choice. In the jungles of Poxt, the Ottle planet, I am Chaffinch L'Saye for Galactic Video Network."

Shona knelt down on the ground behind L'Saye, clutching Alex, feeling how precious he was, and how near she'd come to losing her life. She couldn't believe they'd been saved. Her whole world was right there in her arms, small and beautiful and alive.

She heard wild barking coming from the forest, and looked up. Saffie bounded toward them, leading a whole crowd of humans and ottles, all talking and shouting questions. One head, higher than all the others, was familiar to her. She smiled, holding up her arms to him.

"Where's my wife?" demanded Gershom. He pushed past the LabCor men and the reporter. Shona looked up at him with her dirty, woebegone face, and let him gather her up. He lifted her straight off her feet and kissed her. The reporter closed in on the family, and the camerawoman focused her lens on them, but Shona was too relieved at seeing Gershom to care that she was being broadcast to billions of viewers or on view to half a hundred Poxtian settlers. Saffie danced around them all, barking jubilantly.

"Oh, I am *so* glad you're back," she said, with tears in her eyes.

"Hello, love," Gershom murmured.

Now that he was completely safe and his family was back in one place, Alex took advantage of the opportunity to perform for a larger audience than he normally got.

"Daaaad-dee!" he wailed, suddenly bursting into tears. "You wenaway and bad mans chased us and I slep inna tree, and Saffie and Chirwl came, but you were gone!"

"Aw, poor love," Gershom said, bending down to kiss his son. "But you were a big boy for your mother, weren't you?"

"Uh-huh. Daddy, I'm hungry."

Shona looked at him and laughed. She matched her son's wistful expression and looked up at Gershom. "Me, too."

"Great video!" Lettitia exulted, joining finger and thumb in a triumphant ring for Chaffinch.

Shona entered the village as a returning heroine, limping between Gershom and the GVN news team. Chirwl loped to join them. Saffie slurped him over the head, and ran around him and her mistress and master, barking as Governor Horne came to offer his best wishes.

"If there was a key to the city, you'd have it, Doctor," he said. "Good to see you in one piece."

Marleen ran up to Shona and threw her arms about her. "You're all right!" she cried. "We thought, when that other shuttle took off, that . . ."

"That he'd gotten me," Shona finished. "Almost. I don't know why he left when he did. I'm just glad he's gone."

Chele Oktari bumped her way past the reporter and put an arm around Shona's waist. "I fed your cat and rabbits," she said, low in Shona's ear. "Chirwl gave me the code. I put all the mice in my house in case *those men* went on a rampage."

Shona squeezed her back. "Oh, *bless* you. I was so worried. Where's Dr. Volk? I have to see her."

"Governor Horne put her under house arrest," Marleen said. "Is she responsible for what happened to my Bobby? Did she do it?"

"Yes," Shona said. "But it was an accident."

"Accident, shmaccident," Tony Coglio snarled. "I'll strangle her if I can get my hands on her. Look what she's done to the rest of us."

He followed Shona toward the scientists' enclave. Wyn Barri and a large man with huge, broad hands, joined the march. Others fell in beside them.

"You can't see her," the man from LabCor said, maneuvering

to get in the way of the advancing mob. "I'm the patent-holder on her research, and I insist on total confidentiality."

"Oh, save it for your deposition," Horne said, laying a heavy hand on him. "GBI agents, *real* ones, are on their way here now. You're under arrest, too." Shona stepped up to Eleniak.

"I think I can help minimize the damage if you let me speak to her *now*."

"Before I say anything," Shona said, standing in the director's hut, "I want to know what your research is for." She looked at all of them. "What is it supposed to accomplish?"

"We can't tell you that," Morganstern said. "We signed an agreement."

"So has she," Eleniak barked, tilting his head toward Shona. "Tell her."

"Tell me something first," Volk said to Shona. She was sitting upright in the canvas chair behind her table, exactly as she had when Shona had first seen her, except she looked tired, and about twenty years older—no, thirty. So did Morganstern and Hampton, who was standing with his shoulder propped against the wall. That confirmed another guess Shona had made. "Tell me," Volk continued. "Why would you help? You're not a saint or a bodhisattva."

"I'm a thinking, feeling being," Shona said. "Isn't that enough? I didn't come into this for gain. Or for anything at all. All I want is to put things back the way they were before you started meddling. That's all. And I want to leave here in one piece."

"You can go right now," Morganstern said obnoxiously.

"Shut up, Lionel. You're affected, too." Volk turned away from her subordinate and paused, as if getting used to the idea that Shona was now authorized to hear what she had to say.

"This project is intended to extend youth or rejuvenate warm-blooded creatures. Theoretically it works on any mammal on Earth or Poxt. Indefinitely."

"Make them young forever?" Shona asked, stunned. "That's a loaded subject. Is that *right*?"

"Yes," Eleniak admitted grudgingly. "It is."

"No. You say it as if you mean *correct*. I mean, it is *moral*?" Shona asked. She paused, shaking her head. "I sound like Chirwl. But is that really a good thing?"

"It's our dream," Missa said simply. "It's my dream, anyhow. But look at me!" She held out her hands, which were no more than sticks bound in wrinkled leather. "I'm dying of old age faster than any ephemeral."

Shona faced the LabCor man. "Mr. Eleniak, I disapprove of your project on ethical grounds, but I have to tell you that Dr. Volk and her people came amazingly close to success. I don't know how to correct what went wrong, but I do know how to shut the aging bugs down."

Volk had so far held onto her dignity, but now her jaw dropped open. "How? How can you turn off the nanomites?"

"Well, what exactly are they supposed to do?" Shona asked. "They're machines, engineered to do something. They have a purpose. What is it?"

Morganstern recited in a singsong voice. "To raise the body's hormone levels to normal by rebuilding, then stimulating the glands that produce them."

"And then they're supposed to shut off, right?" Shona collected nods from all the researchers. "But they don't shut off, not when a normal human being reaches normal, youthful levels of hormones. But that's how my vaccine dog threw them off. She's back to normal, but possibly a year younger in body condition. Everyone else's glands fulfilled the demands as much as they could, but were inadequate to fulfill the standards built into the aging bugs, I mean nanomites. The dog's glands are engineered to meet challenges like that, so her system revved up to meet levels to defeat intruders. Precisely because the demands for the hormone by the nanomites were so high, every time a human's or ottle's glands tried, they were 'used up' right away, in Chirwl's parlance. They suffered all the symptoms of lack of those hormones: brittle bones, wrinkled skin, loss of muscle and bone tissue. The key is what the 'normal' level is that the nanos seek."

Volk was dumbfounded. "As simple as that."

"Is she right?" Eleniak asked, turning his glare from one scientist to another. Volk nodded.

"She should be. Yes, I'm positive. We never thought of completing their program. We've been concentrating on just stopping them or ridding the body of them. But it would take a tremendous level of hormones and brain chemicals to turn them off. We may lose some people by high-loading like that. It could be very dangerous."

"We will try to be careful, but I don't think there's a choice," Shona said. "It's either this way, or a slower but fairly sure death from advanced old age, maintained by artificial means, injections, and so on until the body systems just break down entirely."

"Like Larch," Volk whispered. Shona nodded.

"I'll volunteer to be first," Hampton said, pushing off from the wall and coming forward. Shona still hated him for attempting to betray her, but at that moment she admired him.

Covered by only a sheet, Hampton lay sweating on the hospital bed. "How long's it been?" he asked in a whisper.

"Forty-eight hours since the first injection," Shona said, smiling down at him.

"It worked?"

"It worked."

Hampton gave her a debonair smile, and for a moment Shona wished she'd be on Poxt long enough to see him restored to the way he was before the nanomites started work on him. He was one handsome man, treacherous though he might be.

"I'm sorry," he said, so low she had to stoop to hear him. "I'm sorry three times. For making a pass at you, for dropping that tree limb on your tent, and for trying to feed you nanomites the day before you disappeared."

Shona was shocked by the last two revelations. She'd thought the one was accidental, and the other ignorance of quarantine practice. In a moment, she found her tongue. "Four," she said. "I heard you leading those gunmen to the cave."

Doln turned his head weakly from side to side. "Ah, no. I knew you were there. I knew you could hear me. I wanted to buy you time to get out." He smiled. "Friends again?"

Shona swallowed hard. "Perhaps one day," she said. Doln looked sad, but nodded understanding. Shona looked up at Volk, who stood across from her on the other side of the bed. "You wouldn't answer before. How many of your people were affected?"

"All of them," Volk admitted, after a pause, and her eyes dropped. "You were right about that, too."

"Thank you," Shona said quietly. "Who is next?"

Volk led her over to the bed of the old, old man who had come up to Shona on the first day she had been on Poxt.

"His name's Dennison," Volk explained. "Do your best for him, will you?"

Shona came out of the hospital hut, stripping off her gloves. Gershom was waiting outside for her. He was sitting on a rock with his legs crossed in front of him. She thought he looked preoccupied. He glanced up at her and smiled, his expression as warm as ever.

"How is it going?"

"Everything is looking good," she said, sitting down alongside him. "Bobby is already recovering nicely. He's even awake. Call it the resilience of the very young. Once the nanomites are out of his system, I'll start him on controlled levels of growth hormone. He *may* get taller, but he will certainly be the only boy in his grade ever to have had five o'clock shadow."

Gershom laughed. "What about the adults?"

Shona flexed her hands, which were stiff from effort. "All of the LabCor employees came in for their treatments. Some of them had very bad reactions, but in most cases their conditions were worse than any of the settlers except Bobby. And Shnomri.

"It was trickier to use the technique on the ottles, since we have such limited data on their brain chemistry, but with all the resources of LabCor, we were able to whip up three kinds of experimental soup in no time. One for each of the genders. Shnomri was the most delicate case, since hir condition was the worst, but she insisted on being the first. I considered the case touch and go, but it was probably because I'm personally interested in seeing a recovery there. But Shnomri came out of hir coma sleep as cranky as ever. Chirwl and Wla were delighted. They started at once to make their plans for the future."

Gershom frowned. "I should be upset because you didn't need the data I went all the way to Zedari to get."

"But I do, if only to satisfy my own curiosity," Shona said, taking the cubes from her pocket. She popped one into the niche on her clipboard. "I have to know how old Larch was when she died of old age two weeks ago. Morbid curiosity, I suppose." She scrolled through the biographical extracts, in alphabetical order. She looked up at Gershom with a shocked expression on her face.

"She was thirty-five," Shona said, holding out the screen for Gershom to see.

"That's possible, from what you told me about the nanomites," Gershom said. "So why the open mouth?"

Shona scrolled upward and showed him another file. "Hampton is *sixty-seven*. I could have sworn it was the other way around. Perhaps there's something to Forever's theories of longevity?"

"Maybe." Gershom didn't seem enthusiastic.

"What's the matter?" Shona asked.

For answer he pushed his personal reader toward her. Shona took the battered board from him, wondering why he had brought it down from the ship.

"First message," Gershom said tersely.

"Dr. and Captain Taylor," said the female caseworker, looking radiant. It was the first change of expression Shona had ever seen in her. "I am happy to inform you that the Child Welfare Bureau has approved your petition to adopt Leilani. The notarized paperwork will follow this message. Please send a signed acknowledgment to your attorney to forward to us when you get it. That's all for now. Congratulations!"

"Oh!" Shona cried, throwing up her hands for joy. "Wait until we find Lani. Oh, it's marvelous! Come on, we have to go tell her." She stood up.

Gershom shook his head, and pulled her down again. "Wait. See the second message."

Shona knew as soon as she saw Zeles's face what the import of the message was, but she listened to it anyway.

". . . cannot reasonably expect to have a record of late payments as you have and ask for further clemency. We are foreclosing on the contract. We will notify you as to where to deliver the ship."

Shona was aghast. She stared at Gershom. "But didn't the governor pay us?"

"You know he did," Gershom said dully. "But it was too late." He emitted a mirthless laugh. "The crew asked me if we should go pirate, but with our luck, we'd be intercepted the first time we tried to make port. Our dream is over. The Taylor Traveling Medicine Show and Trading Company is grounded."

Shona found it hard to talk through her tight throat. She hugged Gershom's arm and leaned in to put her head on his chest.

"It isn't grounded. It's just been delayed a while. We'll wait to find out where to deliver the ship. Wherever that is, I'm sure we can find jobs and start over. We'll rent a little dome. I can go into practice. You could work in the industry, you know so many people already." At that moment she didn't want to tell him her other news. Gershom wasn't placated. She wasn't content, herself.

"Sss-shona!" Chirwl came lolloping up the hill with Wla close behind. They joined the Taylors on their rock. Wla nestled between Chirwl and Shona, and blinked her black-lashed eyes affectionately at the human doctor.

"We have seen Shnomri. That ottle is improving, with thanks to you, although hir temper is not of the best."

"Glad to hear it," Shona said. "I mean, all but the temper."

Chirwl shook his whiskers. "I have decided since I must wait for my co-mate to age backward again it is of no point for me in remaining. In fact, I would be wise to stay away. Shnomri is contentious, resulting in a good deal of refutation of otherwise sound argument. Especially is espousing one I do not like of making legitimately older ottles young with the new treatment. I would come away with you my friends again until hir mind as well as body is healed."

Gershom looked away. Shona gathered up Chirwl and kissed the top of his head. "Oh, we can't," she said, suddenly feeling like crying. "We're not going anywhere. The bank has taken our ship. I should ask if we can stay here with you instead."

"Whhee-eet!" he whistled. "You may! You must. All my clan and Shnomri's clan, too, like you. You can live with us. Or I am certain that DeWitt-Horne will keep you. You would be of value to our world."

The governor seconded it. After a week of treatments, he was already more robust, which only meant to Shona that he had more energy to be cantankerous.

"You bet you can stay here," Horne said firmly when the question was put to him. "We'll build your people some houses, and you can take charge of our trading from the ground for a while, Gerald—I mean, Gershom. No one knows more about it than a trader. What do you say?"

Gershom, as much as he disliked it, was beginning to get used to the idea of being a groundbounder for a while, and Shona knew that of all the places they had visited in many years this was the most attractive and unspoiled. There were the further incentives of being with the ottles, and letting her stay long enough to oversee her patients, who, like Horne, were recovering well. It wouldn't be so bad. Gershom stood up to shake hands with the governor.

"I'd say yes, sir. And thank you."

"It's nothing to me," Horne said, standing up, too. "I'd like to give more than just a job to the lady who saved my life and my colony. You would have seen us on the corner with our suitcases, waiting for the bus, if she hadn't done such good work. We've got a government overseer coming down in a couple weeks to make sure nothing else nasty sneaks out of that lab. It'll be good to know Shona's here, to tell him where the bodies are buried."

"You called me Shona!" she exclaimed, clapping her hands. Horne looked at her curiously. "That's your name, isn't it?"

"We'll tell the others," Gershom said as they traversed the garden walk and passed under the limbs of the great heart-tree. "Let them decide if they want to stay here or ship out with someone else. Eblich will probably want to go home. He could take the *Sibyl* with him so I don't have to buy a return ticket here."

"Look," Shona said, squeezing his arm. "There's Lani, talking to Tsanan. All our news wasn't bad, remember?" She called out to the girl. "Lani, we've got something important to tell you. Wonderful news! The adoption's been approved. You're ours forever." The girl's face lit up, and she flung herself into their arms. Shona hugged and kissed her and passed her on to Gershom, who swung her around in a circle and gave her a smacking kiss on the top of the head.

"I have something to tell you also," Lani said, pushing free, her cheeks glowing.

"Well, we've got some more news you have to hear first," Shona said sadly. "It's not as good as your adoption—well, it's not good at all." She put her hands on the girl's shoulders and took a deep breath to get the awful news out all at once. "We lost the ship. We couldn't pay the last payment, and MarsBank stopped our loan. But we can stay here on Poxt. You'll like that, I know."

"You *must* hear my news," Lani said. "At once. You *have* to." She had a cube in her hand which she thrust at them. It was rare for the shy girl to insist, so Shona took it.

"It's our day for messages," Shona observed. "Your reader or mine?" Gershom put the datacube into his battered clipboard. "Who's it from? Susan? Aunt Lal? Uncle Harry?"

Lani took a deep breath to explain everything, then let it out in a rush. "Sort of."

The speaker on the holoscreen was a solemn man in a very plain but expensive-looking tunic. "Ms. Leilani Taylor, as per your instructions your nominees have been added to the Board of Directors of MarsBank. With your eighteen per cent of the voting shares, coupled with those of several other major shareholders, your motions were all carried."

"Eighteen percent? Of MarsBank?" Shona asked. "When did that happen?"

"When they told me No," Lani said stubbornly, her cheeks red. "There's another message."

Uncle Harry, his plump face glowing, appeared in the next transmission. "Hello, kids," he said, punching in a formal caption beneath his image. It read "Harold Elliott, Vice-President." "I want you to see the letterhead. Your aunt can't believe it—me on the senior executive staff, after all these years. After I got finished voting Lani's positions, there was a vacancy for a vice-president, and look at me, I'm it! She's such a smart girl. Oh, she asked me to let her know where Ms. Katt ended up. Um, there's a remote dome station out near Neptune. She's been reassigned there, as Lani suggested."

"I suppose she's the one who told you No," Gershom said, raising his eyebrows.

"Yes." Lani held her chin high.

Harry Elliott's voice continued. "So here's my instructions to Gershom. The bank repossessed your ship. That's final. But you're on the Board of Directors now, too, you and Shona—I voted your positions in absentia. I hope you don't mind— Anyway: you are to deliver the *Sibyl* to *yourself*, son. You have a ninety-nine year lease at one credit per year, as a goodwill

and public-relations gesture for bringing medical aid to Galactic Government colonies. We'll take the credit out of your
salaries as directors. My instructions to Shona: send more
messages! Don't be a stranger. Love to all of you. Send soon.
Oh, yes: the lease is renewable.''

"I should live so long," Gershom said, but his eyes were
dancing. Shona turned off the reader. She handed it back to
him, shaking her head.

"That's quite an amazing thing. Lani actually bought part of
the *bank* so she could save our ship, then give it back to us."
They turned to look at the girl, who was watching them
anxiously. Gershom bent down so that his eyes were level with
hers.

"You know we didn't want you to give us any big gifts.
Especially not one so large as our whole ship."

"But I wanted to," Lani said helplessly. "You wouldn't let
me."

"And suppose we tell you No. You got someone sent to the
outer reaches of the planet Dismal. What happens to us?"

"Nothing! I . . . I will be hurt, that's all," Lani said in a
very small voice. "The ship is the only real home I have, and
you are my *family*. If it was gone, where would we go? All I
have done is to make sure we can be together where we are
happy. I don't want to upset you, but, but that's how I feel." She
looked at them both hopefully, and waited.

Shona studied the girl. She'd certainly grown up in a very
short time. What a lot of trouble she'd gone to, to think of an
acceptable way to save the ship without violating any of the
rules they'd imposed on her. Shona was impressed, not only by
her magnanimous heart, but by her intelligent grasp of prin-
ciple. Suppressing a smile with some difficulty, she looked up
at Gershom.

"I hope we have more sense than to let everyone we care for
suffer because we're too selfishly proud to accept a present
from someone who loves us as much as we love her."

Gershom, who hated being beholden to anyone, was scowl-
ing. "I suppose," he said slowly and thoughtfully, "that we can
always go back into debt on our own if we want to." He raised
his eyebrows at his wife, who burst out laughing.

"If you insist," she said, counting on her fingers. "After all,
there's cargo, and repairs, and fuel, and long runs without

cargo. Why, in no time at all we can be back where we started."
She seized Lani's hand and squeezed it. "The things people will
do just to keep their families together . . . Thank you,
honey."

Lani's golden face was beautiful with relief. "Thank you,
Mama."

"Dr. Taylor?" An ancient man walked toward them, taking
great care where he planted his feet. He was tall, and when in
his prime must have been big and muscular. With time and
care, he would be so once again. Not all miracle cures were
quackery.

He shook hands first with Gershom, then took Shona's hand
between both of his, gazing down at her with open admiration.
"My name is Edrad Dennison, and I wanted to thank you
personally for what you've done."

Shona beamed up at him. "I'm delighted to have been able
to help."

·16·

The interview conducted by Chaffinch L'Saye had aired only that afternoon, but Jachin Verdadero had already replayed it in his cell five times. It was like a sore tooth: he couldn't help wiggling it just to feel how much it hurt.

In the screentank, the popinjay reporter leaned in again to ask his subject another penetrating question. "Dr. Taylor, you still refuse to disclose the reason you were called to Poxt for such a dramatic rescue."

"I'm sorry," Shona smiled. She wore a worn and mended shipsuit, and there were scratches on her cheek. Over her shoulder in the background, a pair of ottles clinging to the tree behind where she was sitting chittered something, then dashed upward into the treetop, but their voices could still be heard on the soundtrack. "I'm now engaged in confidential work on behalf of LabCor. You'll hear from them when they're ready to announce it."

L'Saye pursed his lips in a playful pout, then parted them in the brilliant, gleaming smile. "You realize you'll have all of us up for nights guessing. I hear also, Doctor, that we have to congratulate you and your husband on an impending happy event?"

"That's right," Shona said. The camera pulled back enough to show her with her arms around a tall girl with shy eyes, and a rambunctious toddler running a toy across his lap. A red-brown cat on Shona's lap batted at the ears of a black dog who sat panting its tongue at the camera. "We expect our third child in seven months."

"Our best wishes to you all," the interviewer said. "And my

260

last question. Is it true, Dr. Taylor, that you have made an agreement with producer Susan MacRoy for yet another docudrama based on your exploits?"

"That's correct," Shona said. "Although I wouldn't say exploits. None of this was deliberate. It all just happened."

"Well, we'll look forward to seeing it, whatever you'd like to call it," Chaffinch said with a wink at the camera. "I hope I get to play myself. This is Chaffinch L'Saye reporting for GVN."

Verdadero shook his head. It was incredible. Not only was the woman still alive and well, she was an acclaimed heroine yet again. And his anonymous hired assassin had written Taylor off as an impossible job. Fate seemed to conspire against him.

The door behind him slid open with a hiss, and Duncan appeared at Verdadero's side. The guard reached over and turned off the console over the credits.

"Lights out time. Huh. You look like you're gonna shout 'off with their heads' in a minute, there. Forget it. Jaci, you ain't gonna be more than just a minor annoyance to nobody for a long time to come."

Verdadero turned away from the screentank, and away from the grinning face of his guard, keeping his emotions to himself. "I think, Mr. Duncan, you may be right."

He sat in the dark for a long time before he could fall asleep.

"Redwall is both a credible and ingratiating place, one to which readers will doubtless cheerfully return."
—<u>New York Times Book Review</u>

BRIAN JACQUES

SALAMANDASTRON
———— A Novel of Redwall ————

"The Assassin waved his claws in the air. In a trice the rocks were bristling with armed vermin behind him. They flooded onto the sands of the shore and stood like a pestilence of evil weeds sprung there by magic: line upon line of ferrets, stoats, weasels, rats and foxes. Banners of blood red and standards decorated their skins, hanks of beast hair and skulls swayed in the light breeze.

The battle for Salamandastron was under way...."
—excerpted from <u>Salamandastron</u>

___ 0-441-00031-2/$4.99

Payable in U.S. funds. No cash orders accepted. Postage & handling: $1.75 for one book, 75¢ for each additional. Maximum postage $5.50. Prices, postage and handling charges may change without notice. Visa, Amex, MasterCard call 1-800-788-6262, ext. 1, refer to ad # 484

Or, check above books and send this order form to:	Bill my: ☐ Visa ☐ MasterCard ☐ Amex	
The Berkley Publishing Group	Card#	(expires)
390 Murray Hill Pkwy., Dept. B		($15 minimum)
East Rutherford, NJ 07073	Signature	
Please allow 6 weeks for delivery.	Or enclosed is my: ☐ check ☐ money order	
Name	Book Total	$
Address	Postage & Handling	$
City	Applicable Sales Tax (NY, NJ, PA, CA, GST Can.)	$
State/ZIP	Total Amount Due	$

New York Times **bestselling author**

R.A. SALVATORE

__THE WOODS OUT BACK 0-441-90872-1/$4.99
"Fantasy...with literacy, intelligence, and a good deal of wry wit."–<u>Booklist</u>
A world of elves and dwarves, witches and dragons exists–all in the woods behind Gary Leger's house. There, Gary discovers he is the only one who can wear the armor of the land's lost hero and wield a magical spear. And if he doesn't, he can never go home again...

__DRAGON'S DAGGER   0-441-00078-9/$4.99
"Looking for a pot of gold? Read this book!"
–Margaret Weis, <u>New York Times</u> bestselling author
Gary Leger longs to return to the land of Faerie...but things have changed since his last visit. The sacred armor and magical spear that made Gary the land's greatest hero are missing. An evil king threatens to wage war, while a banished witch plots her revenge. And a dragon recklessly wields his power to engulf the countryside in flames. Now Gary must traverse the enchanted world to battle the forces of darkness.

Payable in U.S. funds. No cash orders accepted. Postage & handling: $1.75 for one book, 75¢ for each additional. Maximum postage $5.50. Prices, postage and handling charges may change without notice. Visa, Amex, MasterCard call 1-800-788-6262, ext. 1, refer to ad # 496

Or, check above books   Bill my: ☐ Visa   ☐ MasterCard   ☐ Amex
and send this order form to: (expires)
The Berkley Publishing Group   Card#_____
390 Murray Hill Pkwy., Dept. B   ($15 minimum)
East Rutherford, NJ 07073   Signature_____
Please allow 6 weeks for delivery.   Or enclosed is my: ☐ check   ☐ money order

Name_____   Book Total $_____
Address_____   Postage & Handling $___ -
City_____   Applicable Sales Tax $_____
                                (NY, NJ, PA, CA, GST Can.)
State/ZIP_____   Total Amount Due $_____

Somewhere beyond the stars, the age of dinosaurs never ended...

ROBERT J. SAWYER

"He's already being compared to Heinlein, Clarke, and Pohl."—Quill and Quire

"Thoughtful and compelling!"—Library Journal

__FAR-SEER   0-441-22551-9/$4.99

Young Afsan the saurian is privileged, called to the distant Capital City to apprentice with Saleed the court astrologer. But Afsan's knowledge of his dinosaur nation's heavens will test his faith...and also may save his world from disaster.

__FOSSIL HUNTER
0-441-24884-5/$4.99

Toroca, son of Afsan the Far-Seer, is a geologist searching for the rare metals needed to take his species to the stars. But what he's discovered instead is an artifact that may reveal at last the true origin of a world of dinosaurs.

__FOREIGNER   0-441-00017-7/$4.99

A new age of discovery is being ushered into the saurian world. Novato, mate of Afsan, is mastering the technology of space travel, while Afsan, to overcome his blindness, is seeking the help of a new kind of doctor–one whose treatment does not center on the body...but the mind.

Payable in U.S. funds. No cash orders accepted. Postage & handling: $1.75 for one book, 75¢ for each additional. Maximum postage $5.50. Prices, postage and handling charges may change without notice. Visa, Amex, MasterCard call 1-800-788-6262, ext. 1, refer to ad # 483

Or, check above books and send this order form to: The Berkley Publishing Group 390 Murray Hill Pkwy., Dept. B East Rutherford, NJ 07073	Bill my: ☐ Visa ☐ MasterCard ☐ Amex (expires) Card#_____ ($15 minimum) Signature_____
Please allow 6 weeks for delivery.	Or enclosed is my: ☐ check ☐ money order
Name_____	Book Total $_____
Address_____	Postage & Handling $_____
City_____	Applicable Sales Tax $_____ (NY, NJ, PA, CA, GST Can.)
State/ZIP_____	Total Amount Due $_____

Shadow Novels from
ANNE LOGSTON

Shadow is a master thief as elusive as her name. Only her
dagger is as sharp as her eyes and wits. Where there's a
rich merchant to rob, good food and wine to be had, or
a lusty fellow to kiss...there's Shadow.

"Spiced with magic and intrigue..."–Simon R. Green
"A highly entertaining fantasy."–_Locus_

___SHADOW   0-441-75989-0/$3.99
___SHADOW HUNT   0-441-76007-4/$4.50
___DAGGER'S EDGE   0-441-00036-3/$4.99

And don't miss other Anne Logston adventures...

___GREENDAUGHTER   0-441-30273-4/$4.50
Deep within the Mother Forest, Chyrie, an elf with the
gift of animal-speaking, must embrace the human world
to fend off barbarian invaders...and save both worlds.

Payable in U.S. funds. No cash orders accepted. Postage & handling: $1.75 for one book, 75¢
for each additional. Maximum postage $5.50. Prices, postage and handling charges may
change without notice. Visa, Amex, MasterCard call 1-800-788-6262, ext. 1, refer to ad # 493

Or, check above books   Bill my: ☐ Visa ☐ MasterCard ☐ Amex _____
and send this order form to: (expires)
The Berkley Publishing Group   Card#_____
390 Murray Hill Pkwy., Dept. B   ($15 minimum)
East Rutherford, NJ 07073   Signature_____
Please allow 6 weeks for delivery.   Or enclosed is my: ☐ check ☐ money order

Name_____   Book Total $_____

Address_____   Postage & Handling $_____

City_____   Applicable Sales Tax $_____
                                       (NY, NJ, PA, CA, GST Can.)
State/ZIP_____   Total Amount Due $_____